She left WCF and stepped into the still, chilly air. She loved walking and didn't even mind the cold that much—though she still missed sunny, temperate So-Cal. She pulled her scarf up to cover her ears and neck and walked briskly toward the Metro.

A chill brought goose-bumps to her arms, like fingernails on a chalkboard. She told herself it was the cold, but she knew better—the feeling of being watched was far too familiar. She faked a cough and stepped to the side so she could discreetly observe the people walking around her, the traffic on the street, the dinner crowd eating in the restaurant on the other side. A man passed her, nodded a greeting, and kept walking.

She sighed, frustrated with herself for being paranoid. For six years she'd never been able to shake the sensation that people were looking at her, that they knew what had happened and somehow blamed her for her fate. The sensations had faded over time, but Lucy doubted they would ever disappear completely.

Her past would always be chasing her, no matter what she did.

"Suck it up," she whispered to herself.

You're about to put a ro_____ _____ _____son. You have a lot to celebrate.

With that thought _____ _____ _____ Metro station, hyperaw_____ _____ _____her.

LOVE ME TO DEATH

A Novel of Suspense

Allison BRENNAN

BALLANTINE BOOKS • NEW YORK

A Ballantine Books Mass Market Original

Copyright © 2010 by Allison Brennan
Excerpt from *Kiss Me, Kill Me* copyright © 2010 by Allison Brennan

Published in the United States by Ballantine Books, an imprint of The Random House Publishing Group, a division of Random House, Inc., New York.

BALLANTINE and colophon are trademarks of Random House, Inc.

This book contains an excerpt from the forthcoming book *Kiss Me, Kill Me* by Allison Brennan. This excerpt has been set for this edition only and may not reflect the final content of the forthcoming edition.

ISBN 978-0-345-52039-5
eBook ISBN 978-0-345-52040-1

Cover design: Scott Biel
Cover photograph: Roy McMahon/Stock Images/Getty Images

Printed in the United States of America

www.ballantinebooks.com

987654321

For Charlotte Herscher and Dana Isaacson, my amazing and insightful editors.

Your high expectations, sage advice, steadfast guidance—and Dana's ruthless pencil— are always needed, and very much appreciated

ACKNOWLEDGMENTS

I would not have been able to write this book without the kindness of experts who were willing to answer numerous questions—some common, some definitely unusual. I've probably taken some liberties with the facts, but I tried hard to keep the spirit and truth intact.

Authors Terry Spear and Kathy Crouch for information about the United States Air Force; the two soldiers from Travis Air Force Base who let me pick their brains about the USAF and the Ravens between SWAT training exercises at McClellan AFB (you know who you are!); SaVern Fripp with the D.C. Office of the Chief Medical Examiner, who graciously responded to my emails with terrific imagination; and my longtime friend Dora Kingsley, a California transplant to Georgetown.

A special thank-you to the Sacramento FBI Citizens Academy and fellow alumni for indulging my questions—and detours—during our trip to Quantico, FBI headquarters, and Georgetown; and especially the dedicated SAC Drew Parenti, and FBI SA and media rep Steve Dupre who joined us and made it all happen. I appreciate your time and answers to even my oddest questions.

I especially want to thank the volunteers and staff at the National Center for Missing and Exploited

Children who took the time to give our group an extensive and informative tour.

Stories may be written in solitude, but they are produced by many. The Ballantine team is truly exceptional in the industry. From editing to copyediting to production to cover design to marketing to publicity and the entire sales force, I'm lucky to have such a great group of people backing up my books. I particularly want to thank Scott Shannon, Kate Collins, and Gina Wachtel for their support and enthusiasm. And I would be remiss if I didn't thank my agent, Dan Conaway at Writer's House, who has taken over the reins with both vision and class.

Where would any of us be without the unconditional love and support of our friends and family? Toni, Rocki, and Karin—you guys stuck with me in good times and bad and I don't know what to say because thank-you seems so inadequate. How about I'm buying the next round when we all meet again?

My husband, Dan, who picks up the slack when deadlines loom, thank you for understanding my long hours and wandering mind. My kids—thank you for being you, keeping me focused on what's important, and occasionally making me stop everything just to play games. And of course my mom—wouldn't be here without her!

Finally, my readers—who love the Kincaids as much as I do. Thank you for the letters and emails and enthusiasm for Lucy's series. I hope you enjoy her stories as much as I enjoy writing them.

What lies behind you and what lies in front of you,
pales in comparison to what lies inside of you.

—Ralph Waldo Emerson

PROLOGUE

One Week Ago

This was Roger Morton's big chance—his *only* chance—to get out of the country and re-create the life he used to have. All because of a box of cheap jewelry.

The marina was closed this late at night, but Roger still kept to the shadows as he walked toward the docks. He'd picked this place because it was mostly open and flat; he could see who approached. Tonight, the marina was empty of people, covered boats monuments to warmer days. The security lights over the docks provided the only illumination; it was too foggy to see D.C. on the other side of the Potomac.

He stuffed his hands in the pockets of his leather jacket, wishing he had a warmer coat. It was friggin' cold. He couldn't wait to grab his money and get out of this miserable town. He already had a place lined up in South America. Even after six years in prison, Roger had contacts. Once he had the money in hand, he'd be sitting pretty.

Six long years behind bars. His attorney had said he was lucky to get away with only that after the attempted murder of a federal agent and felony rape. *Six years in the federal pen was lucky?* He'd spilled his guts, given the cops everything they wanted, admitted to everything—well, he *had* left out the crucial detail that he'd killed one of their own people. That fact he'd most certainly kept to himself, thanks very much. Anyway, the Feds didn't have anything implicating him—no gun, no witnesses, nothing. It had been easy enough to lay blame for that escapade on someone else.

Six years of his life gone. For *cooperating*.

Everything had changed while he was in the pen, and he was damned if he was going to sit around working as a car mechanic making chump change. Not when he knew how to make real money. The kind of serious dough that would set him up in his previous lifestyle, the kind that bought freedom. In prison, his life had been on hold. Now he had the chance to start over.

Adam had spouted off that Roger was the dumb one. Well, Adam was *dead*—how smart did that make *him*?

Roger cautiously approached the meeting spot on the far side of the dry docks. The air coming off the Potomac was so damn cold he wished they could have found a bar to make the exchange. Except Roger couldn't be seen in his old stomping grounds. He had to keep a low profile. Make the exchange on neutral ground. Of course, he'd left his half of the bargain back at his motel. No fucking way was he going to have his new partner double-cross him. First, he'd get the money, then he'd tell him where to find the jewelry. He wasn't an idiot; cops were bastards and Roger wouldn't put it past any of them to set him up. But he'd vetted this guy, demanding to see some of the action he planned on sharing with Roger's new venture. No way he was a cop.

Roger had enjoyed the digital files of young women

getting screwed every which way. Some were experienced actresses; others were junkies desperate for a quick buck to pay for their next fix. Some of the recordings—the best, in his opinion—were those where the chicks didn't even know they were being filmed. Amateur whores—Roger saw the marketing potential for that campaign, practically salivating over the dollars he'd rake in. Straight porn wasn't illegal, but the money was in edgier areas—hidden cameras, underage teens, fantasy rape that wasn't necessarily consensual.

When there was this kind of money involved, he knew not to bring the merchandise without cash up front. *All* of it. They'd tried to pull a fast one on him yesterday; they'd learned real quick they weren't dealing with a novice. Adam had been a prick, but he'd taught Roger the tricks of the trade. Only now, with Adam six feet under, Roger wouldn't have to take orders or get a small percentage of the take. He'd run the website, handle the back end, and his new partner would provide the sex tapes. Fifty-fifty split. Roger was confident the cash would stream in fast, and he'd learned from Adam how to manage the credit cards of their customers and funnel money to offshore accounts. Best of all, without Adam around, Roger wouldn't have to worry anymore about the snuff films that had brought the Feds down on them in the first place. If Adam hadn't gotten his ya-yas off strangling the women he screwed, they'd never have been busted. Rape was a crime, but murder was a whole other story.

All Roger needed was some up-front cash to set up the offshore operation. It didn't matter that he was on parole; he'd skip out and never again step on American soil. That took more money than he could make working fifty-hour weeks at his cousin's car dealership changing oil. Originally, he'd demanded twenty thousand for startup costs, but when they expressed interest in Adam's old jewelry box, Roger doubled the buy-in.

Roger's contacts had given him the thumbs-up on the players involved, but he still hadn't liked any of the meeting places they suggested—too great a chance of being caught on a damn security camera. He'd told them the marina. Secluded, but close to everything and best of all, no surveillance cameras, few hiding places, and no witnesses. He was taking a risk, but the potential rewards were well worth it. Besides, using his old contacts, Roger had tracked these guys down. It wasn't as though they'd been looking for him. He'd kept a low profile since getting out six months ago.

He'd rather be dead than go back.

He spotted his new partner approaching the rendezvous point. The man was wearing jeans, a dark windbreaker, and a Yankees baseball cap—just like he'd said. Roger glanced around, saw no one else, and waited for the man to reach him.

"Hey," Roger said casually, sizing up the other man.

"The box?" The man's voice was raspy, as if he'd been a two-pack-a-day smoker for decades, though he didn't smell of cigarettes now.

"You got my advance?" Roger was waiting for entrapment clues—such as him explicitly saying that he was using the money to set up an illegal porn website—but the guy didn't go into details. An agreement could mean anything in court. Sure, he was in the marina after dark—a misdemeanor, and he could technically be thrown back in prison for even the smallest slip-up—but they still couldn't get him on anything big.

"I want the jewelry box and everything inside."

"I want to see the money first." Did this guy think he was an idiot?

Tensing as the man reached into his pocket, Roger's hand moved to the gun in his waistband, but he didn't need to use it. His new partner handed him an envelope.

Roger frowned. "A little thin for forty g's. This isn't what we agreed to."

"You were supposed to bring the box."

"You were supposed to give me half the cash yesterday. What kind of partnership is this if you can't live up to your end of the deal?"

"Open it. You'll understand."

Cautious, but curious, Roger opened the unsealed envelope and removed a folded piece of paper. It was blank, with a faded photo tucked between the folds. A beautiful teenage girl with long black hair and large, sultry brown eyes stared at him in the faint light.

His instincts had him reacting almost before he recognized the dead girl, but not fast enough. Roger dropped the photo and paper and went for his gun, but the man moved faster, karate-kicking his wrist. In the faint glow from the dim lights over the dry dock, for the first time Roger saw the man's face dead-on.

Another ghost from his past.

"I wish I could be the one to put the bullet in your head," the man said before slamming Roger face first into the hard-packed dirt. A burst of pain told him his nose might be broken. He swallowed a thick wad of blood.

Coughing, Roger tried to rise, but the traitor kicked him between the legs three times with steel-toed boots. Excruciating pain froze him. It was worse than when he'd been raped in prison. And then, he'd had his revenge. This time he wouldn't get the chance. Panic and self-preservation rose with the pain as he tried to stand, only to be knocked back down.

"Mr. Morton." The quiet, cultured voice didn't belong to his attacker. Roger hadn't heard another man approach, and the idea that two—or more—men stood over him made him tremble even as he tried to get up one last time.

A boot in his balls had him seeing nothing. He almost didn't hear the slide of the nine-millimeter.

"I wish this hurt you more, but in this case expediency is more important than my personal satisfaction at seeing you suffer. Rot in Hell, bastard."

Roger Morton was dead before he registered the sound of the gunshot.

ONE

Present Day

Brad Prenter thought he had a get-out-of-jail-free card, but Lucy Kincaid would set him straight.

She glanced at the clock on her computer and frowned. It was nearly six, and she'd promised her brother Patrick she wouldn't be late after canceling their dinner plans twice last week.

"Come on, come on," she muttered as she split the large screen into six open chat windows that she could monitor simultaneously. "You've been here every day this week at five. Why are you late tonight?"

Out of the corner of her eye, Lucy saw *Women and Children First!* director Frances Buckley walking toward her desk. Fran had retired from the FBI nine years ago after putting in twenty-five years, and though she was sixty, she looked and acted a decade younger. After Lucy had started volunteering for WCF three years ago, Fran quickly became her mentor. She'd written a glowing recommendation letter for Lucy's FBI job application and had helped her prepare for both the written and verbal tests. And for the last three months, Fran had helped Lucy cope with the anxiety of waiting to hear whether she'd made it to the next stage in the hiring process.

Lucy didn't allow herself to think that she could be rejected. Still, she knew the process could take months, and not knowing either way was frustrating. For the last six years, all she'd wanted was to be an FBI agent. Everything she'd done—her double major in psychology and computer science; her internships with the U.S. Senate, the Arlington County Sheriff's Department, and now the D.C. Medical Examiner's Office; her volunteer work at high schools and here at WCF—was calculated to help her get into the FBI. She hoped the hiring panel could see that what she'd learned would make her a strong addition to the Bureau.

Fran put a hand on the back of Lucy's chair. "Tick-tock. It's six o'clock, Lucy."

"Five more minutes. Prenter isn't online yet, and he always logs on in the late afternoon."

"Life happens. You can't sit here all night waiting for him. You have a life, too. Don't you have dinner plans with your brother tonight?"

"Yes, but—"

"Lucy, Prenter will be here tomorrow."

She said, "I have some time—twenty minutes and I'll make it to Clyde's by seven."

"If you sprint to the Metro."

"I'm a fast runner." She smiled at Fran, mentally crossing her fingers.

The older woman shook her head but returned the smile. "I'll pull the plug if you're still here at six-fifteen."

That wasn't an idle threat—Fran had literally cut the power before. Lucy crossed her heart with her right index finger and blew Fran a kiss before she turned back to the fast-moving chat rooms.

WCF had a secure bank of computers, as secure and untraceable as any in the FBI, where they investigated the illegal sexual exploitation of women and children. When they collected enough evidence to identify a victim or perpetrator, they turned over the files to the FBI or local police for further investigation.

Aside from their primary charter, WCF tracked paroled sex offenders. By law, felony sex offenders had to register with local law enforcement after release from prison and with every subsequent change of residency.

Yet, depending on the state, on average half of all sex offenders required to register either never did or moved and didn't re-register. These parolees were the most likely to commit another sex-related crime, and therefore were the target of WCF's tracking project. Creatures of habit, these guys often made small changes to their online profiles but still targeted the same types of children or women; they thought because they'd moved to another town or state, they wouldn't be discovered. And if it were solely up to law enforcement, the predators would be right: they'd get away with it. There wasn't enough time or manpower to track down every sex offender who skipped registration.

For her master's thesis, Lucy had deduced that while most sexual predators may modify their behavior after serving time in prison, usually these changes were superficial. They could still be identified by vigilant trackers by scientifically breaking down the creeps' past activities: how they were caught, coupled with their victim preference—which rarely changed after incarceration. Lucy's research told her that predators could still be spotted even if they changed their location or online identities. Since graduating, she had continued to develop her database to incorporate all known data as well as a psychological scale that factored in minor behavioral changes. The more information she added, the more powerful—and effective—the system became.

Groups like WCF could use their private resources and volunteers to identify predators online and, if a parolee, it was much easier to put a predator back in prison if he violated parole. Lucy's database, though still technically in beta testing, had been instrumental in finding and tracking parolees most likely to reoffend, resulting in more than a dozen arrests to date.

For the past two weeks, Lucy had been working on one specific parolee, Brad Prenter, a convicted rapist who'd been paroled after serving only half his time. Normally, WCF targeted predators who hunted children and skipped town after parole, but Prenter was a special case. He used homemade GHB—Liquid X—on his dates. Mixed with alcohol, GHB was especially dangerous. The victim who'd sent him to jail—a Virginia college freshman he'd met because he was the teaching assistant in her chemistry class—had had the wherewithal to text her roommate when she started feeling strange. Otherwise Prenter would most likely have gotten away with his crime.

During the investigation leading up to his trial, authorities learned that Prenter had been suspected of raping another girl in his hometown of Providence, Rhode Island, but there had not been enough evidence to go to trial. He'd given that victim such a high dose of GHB that it had left her in a coma. Due to a delayed investigation—the police weren't immediately called, because the hospital didn't find signs of forced sex and didn't initially test for date-rape drugs—Prenter had time to dispose of his home chemistry lab.

There had been circumstantial evidence that Prenter targeted other victims online. He'd hook up, drug and rape them, then drop them at their house. Waking up, the women remembered very little. The only reason Prenter's name came up in another investigation was because a friend of the victim had seen him with her the night she was raped.

But even in that case, there had been no physical evidence, and the victim didn't remember anything. Prenter's house and car were searched, but the investigators found no GHB.

Two weeks ago, the research arm of WCF identified Prenter's new online persona, and based on his profile he was living in northern Virginia. He had registered as a sex offender and received permission to attend college at American University. He trolled a particular dating website to hook up in the flesh, so Lucy created a fictional character that met Prenter's personal criteria: a petite, blond college girl who liked running, rock music, and live bands. It didn't matter that Lucy was tall with black hair, her job was to draw him to a public location where he'd have the opportunity to violate his parole in full view of law enforcement. It had worked many times during her three years volunteering for WCF, and Prenter was already hooked. Lucy just had to reel him in.

And when she did? One of WCF's volunteer off-duty cops would be there to cuff him and haul him back to prison.

Justice would be *fully* served. All three to five years.

For too long she'd felt helpless. Even with all the self-defense training, her education, and her dreams, Lucy had felt she needed to be doing *more*. Interning with Senator Jonathon Paxton on the Judiciary Committee had been interesting, but when he introduced her to Fran at WCF, it had changed Lucy's life. She was a far stronger, better person today because of the work she did for WCF. She could almost believe she was a normal, average woman.

Even her brother Patrick had admitted the last time they'd talked that Lucy was back to her old self.

Perhaps not her *old* self. She was no longer the naïve teenager she'd been six years ago when she trusted too easily and thought she was invincible. But she'd finally let go of most of the pain and anger. Some righteous anger, the outrage for injustices in the world, kept her focused on what was important. Saving the innocent. Stopping criminals. Her inner drive was so strong that if she didn't get into the FBI, she'd find something else in criminal justice. She could go to law school and become a prosecutor. Or join a local police force. Or even go to medical school and become a psychiatrist specializing in crime victims.

But instead she wanted to be on the cutting edge of federal law enforcement in cybercrime.

Talking to predators like Prenter, even in the anonymity of a secure chat room, made her physically ill, but it was for a greater good and taught her more about cybercrime than years in the classroom.

Lucy had done her part to entice Prenter—playing coy and sexy, never suggesting they meet but always giving him the opportunity. He'd asked once, early on in their online chatting, about "hooking up" somewhere, but she'd declined. If she made it too easy for him, he'd smell a cop. And if the case ever came to trial—highly unlikely because he was a registered sex offender on parole—WCF would need to testify that Prenter had plenty of opportunities to walk away, that he actively pursued his intended victim.

The second time he asked, she again declined, but hinted that she was interested, just busy. She'd never suggest a meeting, because WCF played by the same rules as law enforcement—don't give them a chance to cry entrapment. Be as passive as possible while still giving the pervert the hints he needed to convince himself that he could have sex with the person behind the computer.

At 6:10, Lucy's computer softly beeped. *aka_tanya* received a private message from *bradman703*.

bradman703: u there?
aka_tanya: yep. studying. sorta. lol.
bradman703: u free tonight?

Lucy's pulse quickened.

aka_tanya: i have a big test
bradman703: 2mrrw?
aka_tanya: where?
bradman703: ur choice

Even though Prenter was on parole and Lucy wasn't a cop—so this wasn't technically entrapment—the conversation was moving into the gray area. Lucy would much prefer to have Prenter pick the place.

> aka_tanya: i dunno. someplace fun. close to fx.
> bradman703: Firehouse?

Lucy rolled her eyes. She didn't hang out at bars, but everyone under the age of thirty knew of the Fairfax-area meat market that catered to a rowdy college crowd. Lots of drinking, music played too loud, and crowded. Not a place for quiet conversation; definitely a place to hook up. It was perfect for men like Prenter, and perfect for the WCF operation.

> aka_tanya: fab. time?
> bradman703: 8?
> aka_tanya: ☺

Lucy smiled herself as she typed the online happy face.

Fran called from the doorway: "Ten, nine, eight—"

"I got him!" she called out as she quickly typed a message to Prenter that she was logging off to study.

Then she sent the transcripts of all her conversations from the afternoon to her personal email, shut down each of the chat rooms she was monitoring, and logged off. She sent Officer Cody Lorenzo a text message.

Prenter will be waiting for "aka_tanya" at the Firehouse, eight tomorrow.

"You got Prenter?" Fran looked over Lucy's shoulder. "Good."

"Hope so. Cody has twenty-four hours to set it up, Prenter picked the time and place." She spontaneously gave Fran a hug. "Finally, I feel like I've accomplished something!"

"It's been a while since we had a victory, but don't count your chickens before—"

"They squawk. Right." But nothing was going to diminish Lucy's good mood. Now she had something to celebrate with her brother. She glanced at her watch. She was definitely going to have to run. "I wish I could be there when Cody arrests him."

"Lucy, you know the rules." Fran forbade any of them from getting involved in the field, even on the periphery.

"I know, I know." Lucy shut down her monitor and grabbed her raincoat and scarf from under her desk. "I'll be satisfied with Cody's report." Not as satisfied as seeing Brad Prenter's expression when he realized his date was a setup, but it would have to be enough.

Movement in the lobby caught Lucy's eye. Fran glanced over to the doorway at the same time Lucy did.

"Jonathon." Fran smiled. "You're early.

"You work too hard, Fran." Senator Jonathon Paxton kissed her cheek lightly. "Hello, Lucy."

Lucy hid her grin. No wonder Fran wanted her out on time! She had a date, though Fran would never categorize her occasional evenings out with Senator Paxton as "dates." She said it was all business, but Lucy had hopes that two of her favorite people would get together.

Lucy stood and gave the senator a hug. "I didn't know you were coming by."

"Fran and I have a lot to discuss before Saturday night. You will be at the fund-raiser, correct?"

"Of course," she said automatically, though she didn't want to go. She would do anything to support Fran and WCF, but she never liked the large public events. Her brother Patrick had promised to attend with her, but then he got an assignment out of state. He wouldn't be back in time, which meant Lucy had to go alone.

"See you both later," she said and pulled on her coat. She draped her purse over her shoulder.

"Need a ride?" Fran asked.

"The Metro is only three blocks away," Lucy said. "But thanks."

She left WCF and stepped into the chilly air. She loved walking and didn't even mind the cold that much—though she still missed sunny, temperate So-Cal. She pulled her scarf up to cover her ears and neck and walked briskly toward the Metro.

The cold brought goose-bumps to her arms, like fingernails on a chalkboard. She told herself it was the frigid weather, but she knew better—the feeling of being watched was far too familiar. She faked a cough and stepped to the side so she could discreetly observe the people walking around her, the traffic on the street, the dinner crowd eating in the restaurant on the other side. A man passed her, nodded a greeting, and kept walking.

She sighed, frustrated with herself for being paranoid. For six years she'd never been able to shake the sensation that people were looking at her, that they knew what had happened, and somehow blamed her for her fate. The sensations had faded over time, but Lucy doubted they would ever disappear completely.

Her past would always be chasing her, no matter what she did.

"Suck it up," she whispered to herself.

You're about to put a rapist back in prison. You have a lot to celebrate.

With that thought, she continued toward the Metro station, hyperaware of the people around her.

TWO

After ten years as an officer in the U.S. Air Force, Special Agent Noah Armstrong gave and took orders in stride, but even so, he found it unusual to be called into FBI Headquarters for a seven o'clock evening meeting with Assistant Director Rick Stockton. In addition to the time, it was odd that Stockton's secretary didn't give Noah a reason for the meeting. He was curious but unconcerned. He could think of no past or current case he'd worked to merit the attention of the higher-ups, and Noah didn't care much for speculation.

Noah passed his shield and ID through the slot at the main desk on the ground floor of the Hoover Building. Reception was closed, but the night guard was on duty to check credentials. The building was a virtual fortress, protected by bulletproof glass and multiple levels of security just to get upstairs. Once he was cleared, it was smooth sailing to the top floor since it was after business hours.

When Noah stepped out of the elevator, he recognized Dr. Hans Vigo, a behavioral science instructor and assistant director at Quantico, the FBI training institution.

Dr. Vigo extended his hand. "Agent Armstrong, thank

you for coming after hours. Rick was delayed in a meeting, so I'll brief you."

He shook Vigo's hand. "Not a problem, sir. I understand."

"It's good to see you again. You were in the class—seven-thirteen or fourteen, correct?"

Noah nodded. "Seven-fourteen, sir."

"I've heard extensive praise of your work in the Bureau, most recently the Annapolis murders."

Noah raised his eyebrow, surprised that someone of Dr. Vigo's stature would concern himself with a typical mass murder. Under normal circumstances, the FBI wouldn't have involved themselves with murders by a disgruntled employee, except that it had taken place in a federal building and the shooter and victims were all federal employees.

While he acknowledged that his military experience helped him rise above being merely a competent agent, Noah didn't see why his record would have been brought to the assistant director's attention.

"Thank you, sir."

"Please call me Hans. I'm not one for formalities."

Noah followed Hans down the quiet hall. Every office door was open, lights off. There were two people meeting in a small conference room, visible through the partly open blinds. But the normally bustling headquarters was nearly empty.

Hans asked, "Coffee? Water?"

"No, thank you, sir."

Hans turned at the end of the hall and opened the door to Stockton's office. He closed it behind them, then motioned for Noah to sit at the long table on the far side of the large, organized room.

Hans took a seat across from him, "We have an extremely sensitive investigation we would like you to head up, Noah."

"Yes, sir."

"Early Saturday morning, a park service employee found a body at the Washington Sailing Marina, on the Virginia side of the Potomac. The victim was shot once in the back of the head. He had no identification on his person, but his prints confirmed that he was Roger Morton. I got the call early this morning."

The FBI didn't handle routine homicides. Noah's curiosity was piqued.

Hans said, "Morton was released from federal prison in Oregon six months ago, on July first." Hans opened his file and slid over a prison mug shot. Morton had the hardened expression shared by many violent criminals, the half-snarl curling his lips telling Noah this guy felt remorse only over getting caught.

Hans continued. "This case is sensitive for two reasons. First, the nature of Morton's crimes. He was the right-hand man for a vicious killer who ran both a legal and illegal pornography business, specializing in online sex videos. Most of Morton's crimes were committed at the direction of his boss, Adam Scott, who was killed during a confrontation with federal agents."

The case sounded familiar, but Noah couldn't remember why. "How long ago?"

"Six years last June. Are you familiar with it?"

"I was still in the Air Force." He hadn't even been stationed in the States at the time.

"Scott charged online viewers to watch him rape and kill his victims live on the Internet."

Now Noah remembered. "The case was discussed in my cybercrimes class at Quantico."

"The agent who tracked Scott to his hideout made incredible strides in tracing masked Internet feeds. Many of her protocols have been integrated into our e-crimes unit.

"The reason this case is so sensitive," Hans continued, "is because Morton was killed here, just outside D.C. We've taken the case from the local police; all evidence is being sent to the FBI lab. Traditionally, jurisdiction is ours anyway because the murder was on federal land, though we usually let the locals handle routine homicides."

Apparently, this situation was not routine.

"As part of Morton's probation," Hans said, "he wasn't allowed within ten miles of anyone involved in his case, including his victims and their families. His last victim lives in Georgetown, as well as one of the agents involved in his capture."

"Victim?"

"He was a repeat rapist."

"And he only got six years?" Noah frowned. "Sentencing guidelines require—"

Hans cut him off. "There was no trial. It was a plea agreement." He slid over the file in front of him. "It's sealed, not public. I made you a copy, but I don't have to tell you how sensitive the information is. Morton was apprehended while Scott was still at-large. In exchange for leniency, Morton gave us information that helped lead us to Scott, which resulted in saving lives. In addition, he turned over all bank accounts and financial documentation from Scott's money-laundering operation.

The legal sex industry brings in a small fortune, but that doesn't even touch the amount of money in the illegal sex trade."

Noah opened the file on Morton, slipped the mug shot back in, and skimmed the summary page while Hans continued to bring him up to speed on the case. A name in the files jumped out at him.

"Kate Donovan." He looked up from the papers. "It says here she wasn't an agent, but she's the e-crimes instructor, correct?"

"Donovan was suspended at the time of Morton's arrest," Hans said. "I have another agent flying in from her current assignment to help—she can fill you in on the details not in that file because she was part of the original investigation."

"Pardon me for asking, but why would you bring in an agent when Donovan—who was also involved in the investigation—is local?" When Hans didn't immediately say anything, Noah added, "Do you think Donovan is involved in Morton's murder?"

"No," Hans said quickly, "but I'm personal friends with Kate and her family. That's why you are investigating the murder, not me. Morton could have been killed for a hundred different reasons. But—"

Noah finished his thought. "A bullet to the back of the head suggests execution. Punishment."

"Exactly."

Noah skimmed the M.E. report. "Was he tortured prior to death?"

"Broken nose, bruising on his right wrist. The medical examiner believes his nose was broken when the killer pushed his head into the ground. However, someone kicked him repeatedly in the groin area while he was prone. So violently that had he not been killed, he would have lost at least one of his testicles."

Noah shifted in his seat and said, "Morton was a rapist; that sounds like revenge."

"On the surface."

More than on the surface, Noah thought, but he continued reading the file. "His last known address is in Denver. Do you know when he moved to D.C.?"

"We just got the case this morning," Hans said. "We don't know anything more than you do at this point, and what's in Morton's records. Rick Stockton wanted to speak with you directly, to explain the extreme sensitivity. He expects discreet due diligence. You will report directly to me, and I'll keep Rick informed. Any clearances, anything you need from the U.S. Attorney—warrants, interviews, access—it's yours. If you need to go to Denver to follow up, it's approved. Anything you need, consider it approved. Just shoot me an email to CYA."

"I understand what you need." They had to believe someone in the Bureau was involved to go to such extreme lengths to avoid traditional channels. "Anything else?"

"You should know that one of Morton's victims was Kate Donovan's sister-in-law, Lucy Kincaid. She lives with Donovan and Donovan's husband, Dr. Dillon Kincaid. Lucy wasn't told of the plea agreement and as far as I know, she didn't know Morton was out of prison."

"Kincaid?" Noah stared pointedly at the assistant director. "The same Kincaid with the private security company Rogan-Caruso-Kincaid?"

"That would be Jack and Patrick, brothers of the victim. Kate is married to Dillon, a forensic psychiatrist and civilian consultant for the FBI."

Hans leaned forward and eyed Noah. "You have a relationship with the Kincaids?"

Not the Kincaids. Face impassive, he said, "No, but I've followed the interesting career of the firm." RCK was known to skirt the law and had access to information Noah suspected was in the darker gray shades of what a private security company should be able to access, which made him wonder just how many people inside federal law enforcement fed them intelligence.

While his initial assignment of the Morton investigation was sticky, RCK's potential involvement made this muck as thick and foul-smelling as molasses. Specifically the *Rogan* part of RCK.

"Do you have any questions?" Hans asked.

"I need the investigator's files, forensics, everything you have on Morton. Where he served his sentence, terms of his plea agreement and probation." Noah paused. "And Kate Donovan's personal contact information. I think it would be better if I went to her house. For the sake of discretion." He glanced at Hans. "And it would be best if you avoid speaking with anyone involved until I have a chance to interview them."

Hans agreed. "But don't delay. While we took over the case, the Kincaids and RCK have a lot of friends in a lot of places. I'm sure no one knows yet—I would have gotten a call—but I'm waiting for the phone to ring."

Lucy sat on the Metro train pretending to read a book. It wasn't the writer's fault that she wasn't engaged in the story. Any other ride and Lucy would have been absolutely riveted by the action-packed plot, but tonight all she could think about was a rapist going back to prison. When the subway train slowed as it approached her stop at Foggy Bottom, she shoved her unread paperback in her satchel and snapped the buckle without thought—a habit from self-defense training.

Muggers go for the easy mark. Don't be an easy mark.

She stood and maneuvered toward the doors, eager to meet her brother. Patrick was leaving tomorrow morning for two weeks at Stanford University, where he was working on a security system for their new laboratory. He'd been living in D.C. only a month, she was just getting used to his comforting presence in her life, and already he was going away again.

As soon as the doors slid open, Lucy exited amid the throng of commuters. Starting up the stairs, the back of her neck crawled with the all-too-familiar sensation of being watched. She unconsciously stiffened and stumbled, bumping into the businesswoman in front of her. "Excuse me," she said automatically, but the woman never looked back. Painful tension started at the base of her skull, spreading rapidly, her heart racing as if she were running a marathon. By the time she reached the top of the stairs, she was fighting a full-fledged panic attack.

You're in the damn Metro station! Of course people will see you.

But it was more than a casual perusal of her looks; someone's eyes were focused on her. Dammit, hadn't she just gone through this thirty minutes ago? When was it going to stop?

Hand shaking, she reached for her pepper spray while simultaneously thinking she was being ridiculous. Her vision was fading and she willed herself to breathe deeply. *In and out. Keep moving forward, no one's watching, you're fine, just fine.* She focused on the exit and calmly strode toward the stairs. Away from the eyes she couldn't see.

"Lucy—"

She spun to face the voice and backed up at the same time, stumbling over a briefcase resting next to a businessman talking on his cell phone.

Cody Lorenzo reached out and grabbed her before she fell on her ass. "What's wrong?" he asked, his face all cop, his eyes glancing left and right.

She pushed him back. "Were you following me?"

"I saw you get off the train. I was waiting for you because—"

"It was you." She breathed deeply and closed her eyes, rubbing her temples until the tension retreated into a tight ball in the back of her head. At least now she could think. "Don't do that."

"What?"

"Watch me!"

"I didn't mean to."

She shook her head. It wasn't fair to Cody, but she couldn't shake the fear. She'd never be normal!

"I thought someone was following me. My fault," she muttered.

He rubbed her arm. "I should have called. I just got off duty and saw your message, thought I'd take you to dinner to celebrate."

She discreetly moved out of his reach and said, "I'm sorry, I'm meeting Patrick for dinner. Rain check?"

"Of course. Can I walk with you?"

"Isn't it out of your way?"

"Not far."

She relented, though didn't feel wholly comfortable. She'd met Cody through WCF and they dated for nearly two years before she broke it off. Working with her ex-boyfriend on WCF projects was one thing; socializing with him was completely different.

He took her elbow to steer her through the Metro station and into the chill January mist. She pulled her raincoat tighter around her and tilted the collar up to shield her ears, shivering. Born and raised in San Diego, Lucy still wasn't used to East Coast winters.

"It'll snow tonight," Cody said.

"And you know this because the weatherman is always right?"

"Because I was born and raised in Maryland. The first snowflake will fall before midnight."

"You sound happy about this."

He grinned as they crossed the street and turned left on Pennsylvania Avenue toward Georgetown. Cody looked and acted like a cop: broad-shouldered and physically fit, he moved with a swagger and arrogance that came as much from fear as from confidence. He had the Cuban good looks and manners that had Lucy's mother singing his praises, with just enough wildness on the side that had Lucy enjoying his company. She had thought she'd loved him at one time, but she hadn't known what love was. She only knew what love wasn't.

It wasn't Cody Lorenzo.

When she'd broken up with him, her family took it harder than Cody. They'd parted amicably, as friends, but Lucy knew Cody wanted to get back together. Lucy didn't.

"Good work getting Prenter," Cody said as they walked.

"We haven't put him back in prison yet," she said. "Do you think the judge will do it? They seem to be big on second, third, tenth chances these days."

Cody grinned humorlessly. "Fifty-fifty. Though lately we've been having more success."

Her stomach sank. Fifty-fifty. "If he has GHB or another drug on him, that increases our chances."

"I'm hoping he will. If he's truly going back to his old ways, he'll keep doing what worked for him in the past. Possession of a date-rape drug would be hard even for some loony, feel-good judge to overlook. At the very least, Prenter will be spending one night in jail."

"Small consolation."

Cody stopped walking, and Lucy turned to look at him. He seemed angry. "I'll do everything I can to make sure he finishes the full five years, Lucy. I promise."

"I know—" She frowned, worried about her friend. "Are you okay?"

"I'm fine. Frustrated. I had a domestic violence case earlier that really got to me." He looked over her shoulder, off in his world, more pain than frustration in his eyes.

"Cody?"

He shook his head, not wanting to talk about it.

She said, "Remember what you told me when I couldn't stop that teenager from meeting with her online boyfriend?" Lucy had befriended a thirteen-year-old in cyberspace, though WCF strongly discouraged it. Lucy did everything she could to stop the girl from making the same mistakes Lucy had made six years ago. She had failed.

Cody turned to her, gazing deep into her eyes as she spoke.

"You said, 'We can't save everyone, so we have to do what we can when we can.' That changed my life, gave me something to have faith in again. We're doing what we can. At WCF and on the job."

His intense stare began to make Lucy feel uncomfortable. Maybe she should have let Cody be angry and frustrated, not tried to talk to him about it. She didn't want to lead him on, give him any ideas that she wanted to restart their relationship. She smiled, squeezed his hand, then dropped it and started walking. "I'm going to be late meeting Patrick," she said.

"I'm going to cut through Rock Creek Park to get home."

She stopped walking and looked back at him. "You sure?"

"It's only a couple more blocks to Clyde's. I wanted to make sure you were okay with this Prenter thing, and of course you are. You're an amazing woman, Lucy." He stepped forward and kissed her cheek. "See you Saturday at the WCF fund-raiser."

Cody turned down the pathway through Rock Creek Park and raised his hand in farewell before disappearing from view. She walked briskly toward Clyde's, already late.

Lucy still had that creepy feeling someone was staring at her. She glanced over her shoulder, but no one even remotely suspicious was there. She stopped, looking in every direction, the street lamps providing ample illumination. The only people not walking stood on the corner waiting for the light to change. No one seemed to be watching *her* specifically.

She breathed in deeply, the icy air clearing her lungs and her mind. She willed the feeling away, as she'd learned to do six years ago when the sense of being watched by unseen eyes never left her, day or night, in public or locked in her bedroom.

It worked. She smiled to herself and continued toward the restaurant, where her brother was most likely irritated that she'd made him wait.

THREE

Noah Armstrong had been assigned Roger Morton's homicide less than twenty-four hours ago, and every answer he received led to twice as many questions.

True to his word, Hans Vigo had provided Noah with all of Morton's files. Morton pled on two counts of felony rape and one count attempted murder of a federal agent, but mandatory sentencing guidelines had been tossed out the window. Scott had been killed while evading authorities, and all they'd had was Morton's word that he'd turned over everything. And while Noah understood the necessity of plea arrangements, this one seemed grossly circumspect. Six years? Hardly enough time for what he'd copped to doing—and there were dozens of other charges that had been dismissed. Lives had been on the line, but it seemed that the investigators had been desperate. And desperation breeds mistakes.

Morton had been released from federal custody and put on probation, the federal system's concept of parole. The terms of his probation were rigid: he could not leave the state of Colorado, where he had secured a job with a cousin who owned an auto body shop outside Denver. He could not possess a firearm, enter any adult businesses such as strip clubs or sex shops, engage in any of his previous activities in legal or illegal pornography, and could not communicate with any of his former associates or attempt to contact any of his victims. Any violation would have sent him straight back to prison.

Noah's new partner on the case was Special Agent Abigail Resnick, a ten-year veteran of the Bureau who'd started in Washington but transferred to Atlanta five years ago. Abigail was in her mid-thirties, efficient, and moved into the cubicle next to Noah's with authority. She seemed pleased to be back in D.C. She had a slight accent, but Noah didn't think it was Southern—it had more of a hint of Boston.

Abigail hung up the phone at her temporary desk, where she'd already spread out, and spun around in her chair before leaning back with a wide grin. "So Morton flew from Denver International on the last flight out on January fifth, arriving at Dulles at five-forty a.m. the next day. According to his probation officer, Morton was required to meet every first and third Wednesday of the month and submit to inspections. The last time probation saw him was on the fifth at four-thirty in the afternoon." She glanced up from her notes, her eyes sparkling. "My guess is he left the meeting and headed straight to the airport. He bought the ticket online same day using his cousin's ID and credit card. The cousin swears he didn't give Morton permission to do it."

Noah shook his head. "Hard to prove he did, but we should send a pair of agents to shake the cousin and see what else falls out of his pockets."

Abigail made a note. "Monica Guardino heads the white-collar crimes squad in Denver. She's familiar with Morton's probation and is headed now to his apartment."

"Did Morton have a return flight?"

"*Nada.* One-way ticket, Denver to Dulles. No other reservations under his name or his cousin's name. He could have picked up a fake ID here or in Denver."

Had Morton planned on returning to Denver? Or was he planning to go underground? Why was he in D.C. in the first place? A temporary stop before leaving the country? Though he'd ostensibly turned over all his off-shore accounts to the government, they'd have no sure-fire way of knowing. But why now and not when he was first released? Why wait six months?

"Hello?" Abigail said, knocking on her desktop. "You there, Armstrong?"

"Sorry, thinking."

"Think out loud, buddy. We're partners, right?" Her eyes widened as if in warning.

He was used to working alone, but Abigail had a point. "I was just wondering what he had planned in D.C., and whether this stop was permanent or a layover before fleeing the country."

"He'd need a fake passport. His cousin doesn't have a passport issued to him."

"Not impossible," Noah said. "Check the State Department and see if there is a pending application under the cousin's name and social."

"Got it." Abigail made a note. "I read over the autopsy report again. Morton's body was found at seven a.m. The coroner puts his time of death at eleven p.m. Friday night."

"Security cameras?"

"Nope. I was going to go check it out, just to get a feel of the layout and where the vic was found, but the local police did a thorough job when they were first called in.

I read through all the interviews of the marina employees. The last staff left at five-thirty p.m. on Friday. After the murder, they checked boats and supplies and told police that nothing was taken or disturbed."

"Footprints? Evidence?"

"No prints—the ground is hard as concrete. It's friggin' thirty-one degrees right now, did you know that?" She shook her head in disgust. "Morton's clothing was sent to the FBI lab for trace evidence. There was nothing found on his body—no identification, no hotel card key, no keys at all. It is possible he brought nothing, or the killer robbed him."

"What would he have to steal? The crime appears to be motivated by revenge based on the attack to Morton's genitals."

"But it's still an execution. No rage in a single bullet to the back of the head."

Noah considered that point. "Morton must have been taken by surprise."

"That would have been hard to do—did you look at the crime scene photos? It's open, right there on the river, near the dry docks."

Noah had looked at the photos. "The killer could have been waiting among the boats. They're stored close together."

"But Morton's body was found in the open."

"Suggesting a meeting."

Abigail nodded. "But no car was found. We're checking rental agencies and motels."

"He could have come with someone. There're no drag or scuffle marks to indicate a fight or body dump."

"Why the marina?"

"Convenience. But it wasn't a body dump—the evidence proves that the victim was shot where he was found."

"I have an analyst contacting motels starting with those closest to Dulles and working out toward D.C. If we find where Morton was holed up, we might get a much better idea what he was up to."

Noah looked down at his notes. "What if he threatened his last known victim? Or Kate Donovan, the agent who took him down? Maybe she killed him in self-defense."

Abigail shook her head. "If Morton threatened either Kate or Lucy Kincaid and was killed as a result, they had cause."

"Maybe. Though if it was a justified shooting, she should have come forward."

"You don't know Kate Donovan."

"Well, I will now. We're going to her house this afternoon."

Abigail sighed. "This is a conversation I'm not looking forward to."

"Why? If she's innocent in Morton's murder, then we need to know."

"She's very protective of her sister-in-law. Do you know what happened to Lucy Kincaid?"

"I read the file." It had been rather slim. Lucy Kincaid had been kidnapped and held hostage on an island off the coast of Washington State. For nearly two days she'd been repeatedly raped by Morton and two men unidentified in the records, before being rescued by Agent Donovan and others. What made the crime even more heinous was that her assault was shown live on the Internet and several thousand people had paid to watch. Worse, they'd voted on how she was supposed to die.

Noah had seen a lot of tragedy in his career, both in the Air Force and in the FBI, but he'd never known anything as sick as people paying big money to watch a teenage girl being raped and murdered.

"I worked the case, saw some of the footage," Abigail said. "Adam Scott and Roger Morton nearly destroyed the entire family. While Kate was tracking the web-feed, Scott set a trap. We sent an agent to check it out. One of Lucy's brothers went with them, a San Diego cop, and he was nearly killed. Had brain surgery and ended up in a coma for two years. Then after they rescued Lucy, Scott held another brother hostage and tortured him while she was forced to listen. Rigged his house to explode."

Only vague references to those events had been mentioned in the report. Noah said, "The report said Lucy Kincaid killed Adam Scott."

"Lucy was under incredible pressure. She was only eighteen."

"She shot him six times. Enough pressure that she snapped? Maybe she never recovered."

"You weren't there; neither was I. It was a fucked situation. One brother in a coma, the other held hostage, and the bastard told her he'd kill everyone in her family if she didn't come to him. And," Abigail added, "from what I've heard she's done very well since. She's set on becoming an FBI agent."

Noah stared at Abigail, stunned by the information. "There's no way they'd allow a victim like Lucy Kincaid into the Bureau."

"Why not?"

"She's obviously been traumatized beyond comprehension. Psychologically, she'd—"

Abigail held up her hand to silence him, and said, "Hold it. You haven't even met her." She pulled a file from her drawer. "I can't access all her files—they are being reviewed by the hiring committee—but she passed her written test with flying colors. She has two degrees—one in computer science, the other in psychology, with a master's in criminal psychology, all from Georgetown. She worked for a year at the Arlington Sheriff's Department and has certifications up the ass—self-defense training, volunteer search and rescue with diving creds—she was on the swim team in high school and college, could have qualified for the Olympics but she opted out."

"You admire her."

Abigail blinked. "You bet I do. After what she went through, she's made a good life for herself. Just because a woman is raped doesn't mean she should carry around that stigma her entire life, that it should limit her options."

"I wasn't suggesting anything like that, merely that being an FBI agent takes a certain detachment. I would question whether anyone who'd survived such emotional and physical trauma would be able to handle some of the cases we're assigned."

"Really. What about soldiers?"

He stiffened. "What about them?"

"Well, you were career military, right? Ten years in the Air Force? You were in combat. You probably killed the enemy. You lost friends, didn't you? Men and women you considered brethren."

"That's completely different. We're well-trained to serve in the armed forces and to face loss of life."

"And all I'm saying is that some soldiers probably don't handle active duty well at all. And some do. Some rape victims never get past their attack, but most find a way to deal with it and lead relatively normal, successful lives in a variety of professions, including the FBI."

"I'm sorry, I didn't mean anything—"

"I'm just pointing out that there is still a stigma attached to rape that is hard to shake, and not just for the victims. When we meet with Lucy, treat her as you would any other interviewee."

"Or suspect?"

Abigail took a deep breath. "Or suspect."

FOUR

On Thursdays Lucy didn't work at WCF, so she went straight home that afternoon when her shift ended at the Medical Examiner's Office. She walked up the stairs of the Foggy Bottom Metro Station, a cold wind whipping around her. She was thankful it wasn't snowing but wished it would warm up a few degrees. By the time she'd walked the mile to the house she shared with Dillon and Kate, she was damp from the moist air and a few snow flurries had blown past her.

She let herself in through the front door and heard Kate talking in the dining room. She almost called out, but stopped herself when she heard an unfamiliar male voice.

Lucy walked quietly down the hall, not knowing what to expect. She didn't like surprises or unexpected visitors. Through the open double doors she saw Kate sitting rigid at one end of the long, formal table, and a man and woman in business attire sitting across from each other, the woman's back to Lucy. By their clothes and demeanor, Lucy pegged them as federal cops. She eyed the female agent's holstered gun on her waist and the files on the table in front of her partner.

Lucy caught Kate's eye as soon as she stepped through the doorway. Her face fell. Kate was a master of the straight face, but something had upset her enough to let her emotions show.

The two agents looked at Lucy, and she straightened her spine. Something was up—this wasn't a friendly chat. Was it Dillon? Her bottom lip quivered before she could bite it, and she feared something had happened to her brother while he was at the Petersburg Federal Penitentiary, where he was interviewing a death-row inmate. But she couldn't ask.

Kate said, "Lucy—," then she was at a loss for words. Kate was never at a loss. But she wasn't crying; it wasn't Dillon. It couldn't be. Someone else she cared about? Or maybe it had nothing to do with her. It was an FBI meeting. Nothing to do with her or her family.

"I'll let you finish your work," Lucy said. "I'll be upstairs."

The male agent rose to his feet and nodded a greeting. He was about six feet tall, with conservative-cut light brown hair and a square jaw. "I'm Special Agent Noah Armstrong. My partner, Special Agent Abigail Resnick. Lucy Kincaid?"

"Yes." She glanced from Agent Armstrong to Agent Resnick. Her blond hair, a shade or two darker than Kate's, was long and pulled into a tight ponytail, making her fine features sharp and edgy. "Is this about my application?"

Noah Armstrong looked surprised. "No, it's not."

"Oh—then do you need me for something?" She glanced at Kate, keeping her face impassive though her gut instincts told her that something was very wrong.

Please not Dillon. Not Jack. Not Carina. Not anyone I love! Her family meant more to her than anything, but they all worked dangerous jobs. Cops. Mercenaries. Private investigators.

"Please sit down," Armstrong said.

Lucy didn't want to sit, she wanted to know why these two agents were in her house, why Kate was so worried that she kept tucking her hair behind her ear, and what it all had to do with her.

She shrugged off her coat, draped it over a chair, and sat at the opposite end of the table from Kate. She pulled off her gloves and tried to make her face a blank. She took heart that Kate's eyes weren't red, that maybe no one they cared about was hurt.

Agent Armstrong said, "Roger Morton was shot and killed last Friday."

Lucy blinked several times, completely confused and caught by surprise. Roger Morton was dead—she let that sink in. The base of her skull tingled as shame filled her, not in remembrance of what Morton had done, but in her quiet rejoicing over his death.

"Why does the FBI need to deliver the news in person?"

"We're investigating his murder, Ms. Kincaid."

Lucy glanced at Kate, who had her mouth firmly shut. It was obvious Kate wanted to say something but felt she couldn't.

Apprehension grew along with Lucy's confusion. "I don't see how I can help in your investigation, Agent Armstrong. I can assure you I never visited that man in prison. Is it customary to interview a convict's victims?"

"In these circumstances, it is."

"I must be missing something, because I haven't been in Oregon in years—in fact, the only time I was ever there was on a family trip when I was about nine."

"Mr. Morton was killed at the Washington Sailing Marina."

She knew she hadn't misheard him. Her voice was hardly more than a whisper, as if the wind had been knocked out of her. "In Alexandria?"

Agent Armstrong nodded. "He's been on probation since July first."

Lucy stared at the agent, who was observing her closely. Too closely. Her skin heated as the truth hit her.

"Probation?" Her voice cracked.

Roger Morton had been cut loose? That couldn't be right. And he'd come to D.C? Had he been looking for her? To hurt her again? Rape her?

No! You wouldn't let him get that close to you. You're smarter now. You can defend yourself. He cannot hurt you. He's dead.

"You didn't know?"

"Know?" Her mind was running full speed in multiple directions: Morton on probation, Morton in D.C., Morton dead. Her body quivered, but she didn't feel it, almost as if she were detached and watching the conversation from the sidelines. She saw the tremble in her hand but barely comprehended it was hers.

She looked at Kate. Her sister-in-law couldn't keep the pain and the guilt from her eyes. She realized Kate had already known about Morton's early release.

"You didn't tell me?" she asked, letting the anger in because anger conquered pain. The pain would come—of betrayal and fear and regrets—but she wanted to be alone for that. Needed to be alone to protect herself.

"I'm so sorry," Kate said. "I wanted to, Lucy, but at the time, six years ago when he made his deal, you were—" She let the sentence drop.

Lucy knew exactly what she was six years ago. Disconnected from everything and everyone as she ever so slowly came to terms with what had happened during the unspeakably heinous twenty-four hours when she'd been held captive by Adam Scott and Roger Morton. She'd told her brother Patrick everything, because then Patrick was in a coma and he didn't look at her with pity and fear and worry. He didn't tell her she had to eat, that she should sleep, that she needed to talk to a professional. It was the only way she could cope. Some days she hadn't left his room, preferring his even breathing to the concerned whispers filling every corner of her home, friends and family all worried about Lucy. That Lucy had been raped. That Lucy had been humiliated online. That Lucy had killed a man and showed no remorse.

"And later? When he was released?" She paused. "Six years ago—how did you know he'd be paroled six years ago?"

"Probation," Agent Armstrong corrected. "The terms of Morton's plea agreement were that after six years in prison he'd be released on lifelong probation with severe restrictions, including no contact with his victims and, in fact, he wasn't allowed to leave Colorado without permission from—"

Lucy slapped her palm hard on the table, startling both the agents and herself. She didn't care one iota about the restrictions placed on Morton; he'd been freed. The truth turned her stomach into a bubbling vat of acid. In the back of her mind, a small voice tried to tell her this couldn't be happening, it wasn't true, but she quashed the weak emotions of denial. It *had* happened and she'd face it head-on.

Her comments were for Kate alone. "Six years? For

what he did to me? To the others? To your partner? *Six years?* And you agreed to that? Without even telling me—then or even later, when he was let out?"

"I didn't want to take the agreement, but it wasn't just my call. And lives were at stake! Yours. Dillon's. Adam Scott had made it clear that he wasn't going to go away without taking you with him. Morton gave up Scott and Trask Enterprises—bank accounts, records—we had no choice."

"There's always a choice. But six years—why not seven? Ten? Or one? Why put him in prison at all if he was so *fucking* cooperative?"

We had no choice.

"Dillon knew," Lucy whispered. The air rushed from her lungs and she could scarcely breathe. Everyone knew—everyone except her.

She rose shakily from the chair, hands on the table to steady herself. She would not faint. She would not have a panic attack. She would *not* cry.

She needed to get out of there.

"I'm going to Patrick's," she said without looking at anyone. She didn't want to see the pity in their eyes, pity that she hadn't known, that she'd been treated like an unpredictable child. She understood deep down that her family had only wanted to protect her, but ignorance was not protection.

"I'll drive you," Kate said.

"No. I'm walking." She went to her coat and put it on.

"It's snowing."

"I need the air." She turned and asked Agent Armstrong, "Why was Morton in Washington?"

"That's what we're trying to find out," Armstrong

said. "Ms. Kincaid, I understand you need a few moments, but we do need to talk."

She nodded stiffly. "Tomorrow."

"We'll come by in the morning—"

"No. I'll come to your office."

Kate began, "Lucy, I don't—"

Lucy whipped her head toward her sister-in-law. "I don't care what you think, Kate. Not now." She sounded so cruel, her voice sharp and unfamiliar. But it was the only way she could maintain her composure. She turned back to Agent Armstrong. "D.C. Regional?"

"Yes." He handed her his card. Lucy pocketed it while eyeing the FBI agent.

He showed no pity. His entire body was hard and rigid, but that told her he was military. He stood like her brother Jack, with that ready-to-act stance that was deceptively casual. Everything about him was no-nonsense, which made his baby-blue eyes stand out even more.

"Tomorrow morning," she repeated, then turned and left the room.

FIVE

Patrick's townhouse, which coupled as the newly opened Rogan-Caruso-Kincaid East office and his residence, was just six blocks from Lucy's place, on a narrow tree-lined street off M Street. It was sandwiched between an embassy for a country smaller than the state of Rhode Island and a private residence. It wasn't far, but between the snow and the icy wind, the walk seemed longer than her daily mile trek to the Metro.

She rang the bell and waited, so cold and wet on the outside that the heat of betrayal had cooled, replaced by sorrow and uncertainty. Eventually, she'd have to sit down with Kate and Dillon to discuss their keeping her in the dark about Morton, as well as his murder. But not tonight, not when the pain of the secrets they'd harbored was so raw she could scarcely keep her past firmly locked down.

Morton had been *here*, in D.C. Her home. Even with the District's violence and crime rate, she had felt safe here because she'd unfailingly taken proactive steps. She had family and friends. She had a job and a future. But he'd been *here*. What if she'd seen him? What if he'd come to Washington because of her? Because he wanted to hurt her again? What if he intended to harm Dillon or Kate or the rest of her family?

Her stomach twisted and her skin flushed. She swayed on her feet and put her hand on the doorjamb to steady herself. Her hands were red from the cold. She'd left her gloves back on the dining-room table. That oversight made her pause as she stared at her shaking hands.

The door opened and she righted herself, not wanting Patrick to see her in such a sorry state.

It wasn't Patrick who opened the door.

"Sean."

Sean Rogan smiled with half his mouth, revealing his dimples. Lucy had wondered, from the time she'd first met Patrick's business partner, if he'd perfected the impish, boyish charm in front of a mirror. "You sound disappointed. Aren't you happy to see me?"

"No, I just—yeah. Sorry. Is Patrick here?" Her voice sounded panicked. Damn, she had to get her emotions together. She didn't want to fall apart in front of Sean. She barely knew him.

She didn't want to fall apart at all.

In a blink, Sean's entire demeanor changed from casual flirt to serious business.

"I thought you knew he left for California this morning."

How could she have forgotten? There was no one else, no one she trusted who knew her whole story. Where would she go now? The only option was back home.

"Lucy, you're shaking." Sean took her arm and pulled her inside, shutting the door behind her.

She tried to apologize for disturbing him, but no words came out. Her cheeks burned in the warmth of the house, reminding her how cold she was.

"You're frozen."

She tried to unbutton her coat, but her fingers were

stiff and numb. Sean reached over and quickly undid the buttons and slid the wet wool coat off her arms, tossing it on the coat rack by the door.

He frowned when he saw her red hands, and took them both into his. He was dressed in just jeans and a white polo shirt, but his body was a virtual furnace. The heat from his hands felt both wonderful and painful as her skin thawed. He brought her hands to his mouth and blew hot air on them, his black hair—longer on top—falling across one eye. He said, "I'm so sorry, Luce, I must not have heard the bell the first time."

"I only rang once. I walked here."

"Walked?"

"It wasn't far."

"From Kate and Dillon's place? That's half a mile and you're not property dressed." His bright blue eyes assessed her as his hands rubbed her arms. "What happened? Are you okay?"

"I'm—" Her mouth quivered. *No no no no no!* She didn't want to cry in front of Sean Rogan, not him, not her brother's partner. Not in front of anyone. She should have gone to her room. Why had she come here anyway?

You forgot Patrick was gone.

"I have to go," she said.

Sean ignored that statement and led her down the wide hall to the back of the house, where a fire raged in a brick fireplace that took up half of one wall. He seated her on the large hearth. "This should warm you up."

Unable to speak, she nodded, averting her eyes. The fire was too hot, but she sat and stared at the flames, willing herself not to cry.

Please, God, don't let me break down now.

Sean moved away, and Lucy breathed easier. She'd get her emotions together, find a way to lock the past back where it belonged, and phone for a taxi.

She had so desperately wanted to talk to Patrick. Maybe that was the answer—fly to California.

Right. Leave her job, her volunteer work, miss the WCF fund-raiser on Saturday. Fran would be disappointed. Lucy didn't run away from anything. She hadn't run six years ago even when she longed to disappear, and she wasn't about to do it now. And what for? She wasn't in danger, only hollowed out from the lies told by her family. She had no energy tonight, but tomorrow she would regain her strength.

She glanced into the kitchen, where Sean had his back to her, thankful he'd given her some space. She didn't want to make small talk with him, no matter how nice he was to look at, nor did she want to explain why she'd walked through what might turn into a blizzard to visit the brother who she'd forgotten was working three thousand miles away.

Lucy rubbed her hands together in front of the fireplace and tried not to think about what Sean must think of her lunacy. The last hour, from the minute she walked into her house and saw those two FBI agents talking to Kate, had drained her and she couldn't stop shaking.

Sean brought two mugs to the fireplace and handed one to her. "This will warm up the inside."

"What is it?" She looked inside. Teeny marshmallows were floating on top. "Hot chocolate?"

"When Patrick took us to dinner last month, I remembered how much you loved the chocolate mousse for dessert. This isn't as rich or tasty, but I hope it'll do in a pinch."

Tears rolled down her cheeks and she squeezed her eyes shut. Her hands shook, and Sean took the mug from her hands and placed it on the hearth, next to his. "Lucy—" He put his arms around her and she leaned into him. The more she fought the tears, the more her body shook.

"Let it out." Sean smoothed her hair back. "It's okay, Lucy, you're safe here."

Safe. He knew. Why was she surprised? It wasn't a secret; she just didn't talk about it. But he worked with Patrick; of course he'd know about her past. It wasn't a big secret, just not discussed.

Would she ever be able to escape her past? Six long years and it had followed her to D.C., to her new life.

Followed? No, that wasn't right. Her past was as much a part of her identity as her future. She couldn't escape it, because what had happened six years ago had molded and shaped every decision she'd made since, the big and the small, whether she realized it or not.

A sob that sounded nothing like her vibrated in her chest and Sean pulled her closer. "I—" she began, then stopped. She took several breaths, rubbed her eyes with her right hand, swallowed the apology that automatically sprang to her lips. She was stunned that she didn't feel embarrassment for crying in front of Sean. It was not as if she knew him all that well. But maybe, somehow, that was better. Her family would be pained; they would tell her everything was going to be okay. And in her head, she knew that she would get through this, that she would find a way to forgive Kate and Dillon, because that is what family did. They forgave.

But not tonight, and maybe not tomorrow, because right now, things were not okay. She felt as though her heart had been ripped out of her chest, the heart that trusted her family to protect it.

"Lucy, I'm right here if you want to talk. But you don't have to," Sean said.

She nodded against his chest and closed her eyes. Now that the tears had stopped, she focused on breathing normally. Sean smelled like soap, an unfamiliar brand, mixed with maybe a hint of aftershave.

Suddenly and acutely, Lucy became aware that Sean Rogan was not her brother. Why didn't she feel awkward being held by a handsome stranger? He wasn't really a stranger—she'd been over here many times since Patrick moved to D.C. from California—but somehow, this felt more intimate. More personal. A man she had barely admitted, even to herself, that she was attracted to.

Something shifted inside, and she slowly pulled away from Sean, feeling much colder. Right now she couldn't deal with everything she'd learned tonight plus the feelings that had been developing since she'd first met Sean. One thing at a time.

She sipped her hot chocolate, appreciating having something to hold in her hands. "I'm better."

"Good." He picked up his mug and drank. "Lukewarm."

"It's delicious," she said. "Do you mind if I stay for a little while? I won't get in your way. I just don't want to go home right now."

He cocked his head, then said, *"Mi casa es su casa."*

Sean watched Lucy closely, weighing his options. He wanted to push her into telling him what had chased her from her house into the storm, what had happened to make her more upset than he'd ever seen her. But if Sean knew anything, it was how to read people. Lucy would talk when she was ready, but if he pushed her she'd close up. He could afford to be patient because he had no doubt that she would open up to him.

He sipped his tepid chocolate more to encourage Lucy to drink something warm than because he wanted it. He followed her eyes as she looked around the large, re-modeled great room.

"I really like what you guys did here," she said. "You opened up this room, didn't you?"

"Yeah—we took down that makeshift wall that sepa-rated the sunroom from the family room and reinforced the roof."

She smiled. "It's comfortable. And now you can enjoy this incredible fireplace from the kitchen, too."

If she wanted small talk, that was fine with Sean—whatever worked to make her comfortable. He walked her around and showed her some of the smaller changes he had made to the space, her honest praise making him admire the room with new eyes.

The bell rang twice and Sean frowned. He'd almost gotten Lucy to relax, and now the interruption had her tense again.

"Stay put," he said, absently rubbing her arm. He glanced at her as he left the room. Except for the circles under her eyes, she masked her emotions well.

He ran a hand through his hair as he strode to the front door and glanced through the peephole. A slender blonde in a black trench coat and scarf stood shivering on the doorstep.

Kate Donovan?

He'd met Kate only once, when she and Dillon invited him to their house for dinner last month right after he and Patrick opened RCK East. The only thing that would bring anyone out on a night like this was an emergency. And by Lucy's distress, she was the emergency.

"I'd say I was surprised," Sean began as he opened the door.

"Lucy's here then?" She stepped in and in a low voice said, "I remembered Patrick was gone right after she left and I had to get rid of the agents."

"Agents?" he asked.

"She didn't tell you?" Kate straightened and clammed up. "I need to talk to Lucy."

"If she wants." The only thing Sean knew about whatever had upset Lucy was that she didn't want to go home, and now there were FBI agents involved?

Lucy's dream of becoming an FBI agent was well known, but Sean couldn't imagine that if she were turned down she'd be violently upset to the point that she'd leave her house in the snow without gloves and walk half a mile. Or that she'd be shaking so hard he expected her to shatter. Anger, he could see. Maybe even tears. But not the physical pain he'd seen on her face when he'd brought her into his house.

Kate glared at Sean. "Excuse me, Sean, but this really isn't your business."

"Lucy made it my business when she landed on my doorstep."

"To see Patrick, not you."

"What's your problem?"

"I don't have a problem, Sean, I'm just trying to protect my sister."

Sean hadn't heard Lucy walk down the hall, until she said, "Protect me?"

Kate walked over to her. "I am so sorry, Lucy, about everything, but you can't—"

Lucy was shaking her head the minute Kate started speaking and interrupted her. "Don't tell me what I can't do, not now."

"You're not speaking to Noah Armstrong without a representative. I'll go with you—"

"No." Lucy turned abruptly and stormed back to the family room. Kate followed, Sean right behind her. Lucy stood with her back to them, facing the fireplace.

Kate said to Sean, "Sean, tell her she can't talk to the FBI without a lawyer or someone to look out for her interests!"

Sean raised an eyebrow. "You just said this wasn't any of my business."

"Dammit, this isn't a joke!"

Lucy turned around and confronted Kate. "Damn straight it isn't a joke. You lied to me. You had plenty of opportunities to tell me about the plea agreement and you didn't. You didn't even tell me Morton was released from prison!"

"I said I'm sorry, and I am, but—"

"But?" Lucy shook her head. "But you were only trying to *protect me*? Ignorance is not protection!"

Morton. Sean froze, working double time to keep his anger from showing. He knew exactly who Roger Morton was. He knew all about Lucy's kidnapping and rape the day of her high school graduation.

"He's out of prison?" Sean asked.

Kate put her hand up to silence him, and he was getting irritated. "Sean—"

"With all due respect, Kate, security is my specialty."

Lucy said, "Morton is dead. He's been out of prison

for six months and no one told me!" She pointed a finger at Kate. "I had a right to know. He was *here*!"

Sean had a hundred questions, but now wasn't the
time. He crossed the family room and stood next to
Lucy. "Lucy, you can stay here as long as you need."

Kate said, "That's not the issue. Sean, you know she
can't talk to the FBI without a lawyer."

"Why does the FBI want to talk to her?"

"Morton was killed in the marina right across the Potomac," Kate said. "I had to answer their questions as
well, considering my history with that bastard. I drove
down with Dillon to Richmond last Friday, then flew
back Sunday night, and Dillon has been at Petersburg all
week. We're clear as soon as Noah verifies our alibis."

Lucy gasped. "They don't think I killed him!"

"I doubt it, you were pretty convincing that you didn't
know he was out of prison, but Lucy, I know how the
system works. Why answer questions you shouldn't
have to answer when it has nothing to do with the murder? They're just going to pump you for information,
and you don't know anything that can help."

"Stop," Lucy said. "Just stop trying to shield me. You
know something, Kate? I can see why Dillon would keep
the truth from me. And the rest of my family, for that
matter. I don't think any of them have truly, deep down,
stopped thinking of me as a victim."

"That's not true—"

"But," Lucy interrupted, "you?" She shook her head.
"I expected more from you. Of all people, you didn't
coddle me. You supported my career choices; you took
me to the gun range and taught me everything you
knew. You've always been straight with me. At least,
that's what I thought. Now I don't know what to think.

How many other times you lied to me. Kept information from me. Justified it . . . how? All I can come up with is that you thought I would fall apart. When it really mattered, you thought I'd break."

"No—"

"Then why not tell me?"

Kate didn't answer. Sean put a hand on Lucy's back. She was vibrating with her anger.

"Why, dammit?" Lucy demanded.

Kate had tears in her eyes. "I didn't want you to know how we all fucked up! No one should have agreed to those terms, but we were desperate. We were running out of time, and that bastard knew it. We made a huge mistake, but I don't know that we could have done it any differently. If we hadn't gotten the information when we did, Adam Scott might have succeeded in his plan to kill Dillon and grab you again. I don't know. It's easy to second-guess, but I'll tell you something: Dillon didn't know about the plea agreement until after the fact. Don't hold it against him. It'll tear him apart."

Tears streamed down Lucy's face, and Sean put his arm around her to steady her. She leaned against him. "But you still told Dillon, right? He knew?"

Kate nodded.

Lucy shook her head and half walked, half ran from the room. Kate brushed her own tears from her eyes and glared at Sean. What had he done to warrant her wrath? He was on Lucy's side.

"I'll make sure she gets home safely," he told Kate.

"I need to explain—"

"Not now. Give her some space, okay?"

Kate rubbed her temples with all her fingers and nodded.

"Tell me what happened."

"That bastard was supposed to stay in Colorado. He came to D.C. last week and ended up with a bullet in the back of the head."

"Execution?"

She didn't comment. "His body was found Saturday morning. The FBI got the case yesterday when the police ID'd the body and noted he was on federal probation."

Sean's mind ran through possible scenarios. Kate seemed to know what he was thinking and said, "Stay out of it, Sean."

He didn't respond. Of course he wasn't going to stay out of it. In a roundabout way, Morton's murder affected his business. Patrick was his partner, and Lucy was Patrick's sister. That made the entire case his domain, and nothing Kate said was going to deter him. That she even tried proved she didn't know him.

"I'll bring Lucy home later tonight," he said. "But a word of advice—I don't think she wants to hear any more excuses or explanations. I'd stay out of her way and let her work through it herself, or you're going to dig yourself into a deeper hole."

SIX

Brad Prenter glanced at his watch. Tanya was late.

He didn't like that. She'd already pissed him off with her indecisiveness. He had a very busy life and he always arrived on time—why couldn't his date reciprocate? Strike one.

He glanced around the busy club, anger gnawing in his gut. All these kids, mostly college students, laughing, yakking it up. Flaunting their freedom. He used to be one of them.

When had his life gone to shit? It was that bitch, Sara Tyson. Accusing him of rape. Like he needed to *rape* a woman to get laid. Women wanted him. Always had, always would. He came from a wealthy family; he always paid for dinner, drinks, even concerts and the theater—and not the cheap seats, either. He was attractive, with a good body, and he was great in bed. The women he screwed always told him how good he did them. Even Sara, but then she'd gone and had a mental breakdown when her roommate walked in on them doing it doggy-style. Went all psycho and said the alcohol made her do it. Bull-fucking-shit. If her roommate wasn't such a fucking interfering prude, he could have talked Sara out of charging him with rape.

It was Sara's word against his. Everyone had seen her

hanging all over him at the club. The cops hadn't even been able to prove *he'd* been the one to put the Liquid X in her drink. His attorney said he'd get off, that there was no way the judge would even let it go to trial.

But that damn text message Sara sent to her roommate did him in, and then Maggie came forward and said he'd done the same to her and the old fart of a judge caved.

Lying bitch.

Two years and four months. In *prison.* He couldn't finish his last semester and now was back in college to get his degree even though he was twenty-five and should be working for his dad's brokerage house and making his own money, rather than living off his meager trust. All because little hot Sara thing didn't want her friends to know she was a slut.

Brad glanced at his watch again. Eight-fifteen. "Shit, where is she?" If she'd gotten cold feet, he'd be livid. She'd already changed the place on him at the last minute, and because he sensed she was a flake, he'd checked his email right before he came and she hadn't contacted him again to cancel or say she was running late.

Bitch.

The bartender approached and gestured toward his empty beer mug. Brad nodded and said, "And a shot of JD." He needed it after being stood up.

"Bad news?"

"The hot chick I'm supposed to meet is late," Brad complained.

The bartender poured the shot. "The one you met on-line?"

Brad had forgotten he'd talked to the guy earlier,

when he'd been excited about Tanya—so excited he'd arrived early. "You should have read the messages she sent me. And the photos—if she's half as horny in person, it's going to be a wild night."

Tanya hadn't sent him photos, except the one head shot. And she wasn't explicit in her messages, but Brad could read between the lines. Why else would she meet him if she didn't want to get laid? That's how these on-line games were played. Dance around it, but when the girl agreed to meet face-to-face, that meant getting down-and-dirty.

"Hope she makes it, dude."

She'd better.

Brad looked around the room. Lots of couples and groups. Groups of guys, groups of girls. He'd just have to wait. The time would come.

He reached into his pocket and fingered the plastic vial with his special homemade Liquid X. Just to loosen her up. Girls liked to play this coy game. Two dates, three dates, leading him on, jerking him around. Get hot and heavy, then say no when he slipped his hand down her pants: They always said yes by the third date, but why should he have to wait that long? He was so tired of it, and after prison he was through with playing stupid games.

Brad drained the shot of JD, savoring the burn as the whiskey slid down his throat. He watched the crowd. A couple was bickering near the door. As he watched, the guy yelled at his date—Brad couldn't make out what they were saying—then left. The girl—a blonde, possibly twenty-one or she had a fake ID—stared after her boyfriend in shock. As Brad watched, she drained the drink in her hand, turned on her glittery heels, and strode purposefully over to the bar, standing next to Brad. She smiled at the bartender and put the glass down. "Another, pretty please?"

Brad might not even need the Liquid X to loosed up this babe. "Hey," he said.

She glanced at him in blatant appraisal, but acted nonchalant. "Hi." She scanned the crowd and sighed.

"Your boyfriend leave?"

"He's *not* my boyfriend. Not anymore."

"His loss."

"Exactly." She nodded her head to emphasize the point.

Her name was Ashley; she went to GWU, majoring in public administration. *Boring.* They chatted a bit, and Brad sensed immediately she wanted to fuck him. He saw it in her dark eyes, the way her tongue licked her lips, the way her nipples felt when he brushed against her thin black sweater.

Someone bumped Ashley from behind and she pressed her full body against Brad. She smiled, a bit nervous. Brad was experienced enough to know that she'd have to be real drunk to come home with him without a little urging. College girls thought they appeared less slutty if they had to be talked into spreading their legs. *I never do this. I never sleep with a guy on the first date. I never . . .*

It was all bullshit.

Brad would simply speed up the inevitable. He'd paid a hooker the day after he got out of prison, but he wasn't doing that again. He'd been counting on Tanya to show, and he would have his turn with her soon. She'd regret standing him up.

He'd had a lot of experience slipping drugs into his

dates' drinks. It had become harder as some bartenders watched with eagle eyes, but in a bar this crowded he could manage, no problem.

She said something, and he pretended he couldn't hear over the noise. She leaned closer. "Are you at GWU, too?"

He shook his head. "American U."

"Grad school?"

He *should* be in grad school by now. All because of those lying bitches, he'd had two years of his life stolen. He lied and said, "Law school."

She was impressed. "Wow. I'm only third year. Still don't know what I want to do, but there are a lot of options in D.C. with a public admin degree, don't you think?"

While she was talking, he brought his own drink to his lips, sipped, then as he brought it down he used a finger to squeeze the teeny vial of Liquid X that he'd pressed against the side of his glass. Several drops fell into her margarita, which she held at chest level. Even if she was watching his hand, she wouldn't have been able to see anything. If she saw the drops hit her drink, she might assume it was condensation from his glass.

"You have plenty of time," he said. "You should have fun. It's college."

She smiled and took a long swallow of margarita. "You're absolutely right."

"Do you want to go outside?"

"It's freezing."

"They have heaters on the back patio. It's hot in here."

"Sure," she said and smiled brightly, sipping her drink.

"Want another?" Brad asked.

"I'm good—I don't want to get *too* drunk!" she giggled.

Too late for that.

Brad led her out back, his hand rubbing her shoulder.

It was fucking cold outside, but the snow had stopped and the heat lamps took the chill off. Ashley slipped on her coat, however, and said, "Are you sure you're not cold?"

"Naw," he lied. He wasn't planning on staying here long.

There were a few other people outside, but not many—mostly people coming out for a quick smoke before heading right back in. Brad watched the blonde finish her drink, hiding his smile. She staggered a bit, and he put his arm around her waist.

"Whoopsie," she said and giggled.

He kissed her hard on the lips, and she froze. He didn't let her first reaction stop him, because he knew women. They always played these fucking games. He reached up her shirt and squeezed her breast—dear God, it felt incredible. He wanted her, he wanted her now, but he'd get her back to his apartment. Or at least to his car. No, dammit, he had the Porsche tonight. She could give him a blow job, then he'd take her home for a good fuck.

His cock was already hard, but at the thought of her mouth on him he groaned and pressed his body firmly against Ashley's so she'd know exactly what he had in mind. She could say no, right now, and he'd walk. He smirked as he bit her lip. She wouldn't say no. He could practically feel the drugs coursing through her body. She was hot, she'd do anything. He was ready for anything.

"Let's go," he said.

She hesitated. "I don't know—it's so fast—"

"Come on. Just a blow job. I won't do anything you don't want me to do."

She didn't say anything, her face confused, and he took her hand and led her out the back gate of the club into the alley. He'd parked half a block from the rear exit, and in five minutes her tongue would be doing anything he wanted . . .

"Ashley!"

Brad hesitated, then kept walking. He didn't want to get into a confrontation, but dammit, he wasn't letting the bitch just go back to her boyfriend when she was all primed to be fucked.

"Ashley, dammit!"

"My boyfriend," she said, slurring her words.

Fuck fuck fuck.

He stopped and turned around.

The prick who'd walked out on the blonde nearly an hour ago didn't take his eyes off him, but said, "Ashley? What's going on?"

"Go away," she said.

Brad quickly assessed the boyfriend as harmless. He said, "You left; she wants to come with me."

"Not anymore, buddy," the prick said.

Brad's jaw tightened, and he said to Ashley, "You want to go with him?"

"No."

"I don't want trouble," Brad told the guy, "but the princess doesn't want to go with you."

"Ashley," the guy said, his voice stern, "you come with me right now or I'll tell your dad about your fake ID."

"Excuse me?" Brad said.

"She's seventeen."

"No way." He dropped his arm from around the girl and stared at her. No way she was seventeen. But . . . he wasn't certain. He didn't care how old she was—she was definitely old enough to screw—but now the situation was fucked. Her boyfriend could identify him.

"Ashley?" he questioned.

She pouted, but didn't say anything.

Brad wanted to strangle her. "You can have her." He pushed the bitch toward her boyfriend. "Fucking tease."

"Jerk," Ashley said, but Brad didn't know if she was talking to him or her boyfriend, and he didn't care. He wanted a warm body to screw, to do exactly what he told her to do, and he was going to have to find a hooker, because no way he was going to jerk off.

He barely heard Ashley arguing with her boyfriend as he walked down the alley toward his car. Damn fucking *jailbait* tease.

SEVEN

I am the teacher. The master. The keeper of truth, justice, and the American way.

Silently, my laugh cuts into the night as I wait, watching the dark house. Superman? Yes, I am a superhero. I do what no man has the balls to do.

I educate females, as much as the stupid, vacuous, weak creatures can be taught.

Females disgust me.

Foul, pathetic things, they lie as easily as they breathe. Their hair is rarely the shade God intended. The false colors embellishing their faces are a physical testament to their continuing lies. The jewelry on their necks, in their ears, on their fingers—diamonds and sapphires and gold—catches the light and shines, but none of those baubles can compare to the simple unadorned beauty of a perfect gem.

The mask that females wear is a lie. When they look in the mirror, they lie, even to themselves. When they look at me, they lie. With their eyes, their mouth, their hands.

They lie with their bodies. They lie with their words, their fingers, their thoughts. Women think they are invincible, that they can do whatever they please, that they can lure men in with their falsities and gimmicks and then enslave us. We're always giving, giving, giving . . .

money, a house, a car, jewelry. They take, take, take, and the lies pile up.

I am the keeper of the truth. I expose deception, one by one by one, until they accept the truth. Until they get on their knees and obey.

They die so I can live. The ultimate sacrifice for love. The punishment for betrayal.

I watch and wait because I am patient. The house is dark again. I arrived late tonight, but now I have time to wait. Watch. Wait. Tick. Tock. Time passing. My time wasted. Months of my valuable time wasted! And why?

My anger grows, a real, living being that taunts me. Fills me with heat that is both fearsome and welcome.

She thinks you're nothing.

I consider leaving the anonymity of my car, walking into her yard, and waiting for her. When she comes home, I will slit her throat.

My vision darkens and for a moment I see nothing. I want her to understand that her actions have consequences. I can't teach her if she is dead.

Lights cut a swath in the foggy night, blurry and indistinct. The car slows, stops.

Lucy Kincaid is home.

My heart pounds in my chest, then it skips a beat. She is not alone.

She is with a man.

The female who deceived me, is sitting in her driveway with a man.

She is a tricky bitch. But no one has my patience. No one has my skill.

Lucy Kincaid will be my next pupil.

If my one transgression taught me anything, it is to never again act on impulse. I will not take her now.

I am a careful planner, every detail practiced, improved, perfect. For years, such organization has served me well. It is a testament to my fortitude that I have been tricked only once by the lying gender into acting too soon.

She plays a dangerous game, catching my attention with her lying, whoring ways and setting me up. But I am far smarter than a mere female.

I watch the man get out of the car, open her door, and walk her to the entrance.

I want to kill them both, though she lied to him as certainly as she lied to me, the whore.

But I do not have the luxury to make a mistake. I must control this powerful impulse. I breathe in the cold January night while my hands clench the steering wheel. Peace settles on my soul.

I see the truth. I am the keeper of the truth.

The man leaves, and I consider again going inside to confront her.

But I must prepare for the whore. And that means taking care of unfinished business.

I leave Georgetown and drive the forty minutes to my house. Or what would take forty minutes but for this weather. The longer it takes, the more frustrated I become. Because my student is waiting for me.

Finally, I am home.

I walk across the new-fallen snow and unlock the front door of the old house I love. The familiar smells make me smile. The plastic of the runners that line the floors to protect them. The lingering scent of bacon from this morning. The lavender from the dried flowers Grandmother hung everywhere. The flowers are gone, but the smell remains.

My home. My sanctuary.

I walk across the floor, the old boards creaking with each step, comforting. I open the door to the basement and turn on the light. Mice scurry across the dirt floor, faint, light movements that also comfort me in their familiarity. The female cries out, whether from the mice or the light I do not care.

The stairs are new. I had to rebuild them when two planks split the week I returned, after being gone for so long. Very little has changed in this house. The stairs. The basement. And of course, the cage.

She sits in the corner of the large pen, arms hugging her legs, chin on her knees. She can't stand in the cage, but she can sit up, which I think is quite generous of me. And there is room to crawl and even stretch out—it is eight feet square, four feet tall.

She looks at me with large, fearful eyes. Fear, not defiance, the way it should be.

"I am ready for my lesson, Teacher," she says.

Too bad she must die to make way for the new student. It took her only three days to learn the proper way to greet me in the morning. She has been with me for twenty-seven days, and I have—had—high hopes for her.

Maybe I can keep her awhile longer. A day? Two days?

I take out my key ring and insert the small key into the master lock. She flinches when the lock clicks, but doesn't move until I say, "You may come out now."

She crawls to the opening but waits until I open it, reminding me that I will miss this one. She would have lasted longer than so many of the others. I picked well, this female. So obedient. So eager to please.

"Stand," I command.

She rises, her legs shaky, but I do not help her. She has lost weight with me, but she was too fat to begin with. A woman of her size—five feet four inches—should be between one hundred twelve and one hundred twenty pounds. She had been much more than that.

"Go," I tell her, and she starts up the stairs. I am behind her. At the top she waits for me, as she has been taught. She is looking at the kitchen table.

"Aren't we—"

I backhand her. She falls to the floor and lies there, her hand on her mouth.

"I didn't give you permission to speak, Female," I say. "Get up."

I have been gone since breakfast. It is now after midnight. I know she is hungry, but I do not care.

The female rises and stands. I say, "Go," and motion her toward the living room.

She walks and I follow. I open the closet door in the entry and remove my long coat. I take my shotgun from the rack above the door. "We're going to walk," I say. "Open the door."

She turns the knob. A gust of icy cold blows in and she shivers. She opens her mouth, but no words come out because she knows better.

She knows better than to ask for a coat or shoes.

I let her squirm for a moment, wondering if she'll break a rule and ask. She doesn't. I say, "Retrieve your house slippers and your coat."

The female turns to the closet and does as told.

"Good girl," I say. When she is dressed, I command, "Go."

She obeys me, and I smile. I am a wonderful teacher;

my students learn what others would say is impossible to teach. But this proves what I have always known: a woman's place is to be obedient to man.

She walks through the fresh snow, her hands rubbing her arms through the thin coat she wears. She glances at me but dares not speak. Her face reddens from the cold; her lips become tinged with blue. We do not walk far, only to the empty barn less than fifty yards from the house. Not even the length of half a football field. But I acknowledge that it is cold and she is surpassing my expectations by not complaining.

I am right to keep her alive for a few more days.

I take another key and unlock the large padlock on the barn door. I push up the metal latch and the wind blows the door inward. We step in and I close it behind us, latching it from the inside. It is still cold, but not windy, and my female says, "Thank you."

"Thank you" is the only phrase she's allowed to say without permission.

I nod, and motion for her to walk to one of the stalls on the right. She obeys.

"Step inside," I command.

She hesitates. The last time we were in the barn it was for punishment. She raises her hand.

I say, "You may speak."

"What did I do to displease you?" she asks, her voice quivering from cold and fear. I prefer the fear.

"You are a woman," I tell her. I motion toward the saddle on the wooden sawhorse. She knows what to do. I do not have to instruct her again.

I don't like to repeat myself.

She whimpers, but bends over the sawhorse and exposes her bare ass to me.

I smile.

I take the paddle off its hook and stare at her backside.

You will behave. You will learn your lesson! I think I shout the command, scream it, but I don't say a word.

I smack her and she cries out. It does not matter how loud she screams; no one will hear her. I hit her ass with the paddle again, the slap of wood on flesh arousing.

But I will not put my penis in this vile woman. I have not touched any of them like that. I do not know where they have been. I will take care of my needs later.

First I must punish this female.

I hit her over and over, faster and faster, and she's screaming and crying. One last smack and the sawhorse falls over and she lies there, sobbing, her backside bloodied.

"Get up," I tell her.

She doesn't. I grab her and pull her to her feet. She cries out in pain and falls to her knees.

"You will crawl back to your cage," I order her.

I raise the paddle.

She begins to crawl. I open the barn door and she crawls through the snow.

I smile.

Even the most stubborn females can learn to obey.

Even Lucy Kincaid.

EIGHT

Though after meeting Kate Donovan Noah didn't think she was a viable suspect, he still took the time to clear both Donovan and her husband, Dillon Kincaid, of Morton's murder first thing Friday morning. At his desk, he glanced through the reports and statements again. Their alibis were airtight—not only were they out of town, but they'd had dinner with the warden of Petersburg Federal Penitentiary on the night Morton was killed.

A rock-solid alibi didn't mean that Kate hadn't hired someone to ice the rapist. But nothing in her financials, or her husband's, or Lucy Kincaid's, indicated that they'd hired a hit man. Noah passed the financials over to an analyst for further scrutiny but didn't expect to learn anything different.

It wasn't out of the realm of possibility that Kate knew the sort of guy who would take down a prick like Morton out of the goodness of his heart, but that was a stretch. Noah was a good judge of character. He generally believed the worst in people until they proved otherwise, yet Kate simply didn't hold up as a cold-blooded killer. Had she known Morton was in D.C. and wanted him dead, Noah suspected she would have done it herself, and his body would have never been found.

Abigail walked in a few minutes after nine with two cups of coffee. "Didn't know how you liked it," she said, putting his cup down and dumping packets of fake cream and sweetener from her pocket onto his desk.

"Black," he said. "And thanks."

"Should you ever decide to bring me coffee, I drink mine light. Very light."

"Duly noted."

"Anything juicy? Smoking gun? Alibi didn't check?"

He shook his head. "The Kincaids—Kate and Dillon—check out. Morton was killed with a nine-millimeter—Kate has her service pistol, a Glock .45, and a personal firearm, a .38 revolver. Her husband doesn't have a gun registered to him. Lucy Kincaid is licensed to carry, owns a .22 and an H&K .45. Not that any of those facts means squat, considering their connections to RCK and law enforcement—and buying a gun on the street would be easy for anyone who knows even a fraction about the underground that Donovan does."

Abigail laughed humorlessly. "It sounds like you want one of them to be guilty."

"No, I just don't assume that they're innocent."

"Whatever happened to 'innocent until proven guilty'?"

He just stared. In his three short years with the FBI, most suspects were guilty.

Abigail shook her head. "Come on, Armstrong. Kate Donovan had nothing to do with Morton's murder and you know it."

"I'm inclined to agree."

"Did Lucy Kincaid come in yet?"

"She called this morning and said she'd be in at ten."

"I'm surprised Kate is letting her come alone."

"I suspect that Lucy does what Lucy wants to do."
Noah didn't think Lucy had faked her reaction when
told that Morton was out of prison. It was too raw. He
supposed she could be an extraordinary actress, but he
didn't see it. In fact, in Lucy he saw a rare quality: the inability to lie.

Half the night, he'd been thinking about what she'd
said and how she'd reacted. She'd been on his mind
when he woke this morning after four hours sleep. He'd
come in early to finish reading the files and financials
that had landed on his desk at eight a.m. And he'd done
more research on Lucy Kincaid.

Out of all the suspects, had Lucy shot and killed Morton, she would have gotten away with it even if she'd
called the police and confessed. No jury would have
convicted her after hearing what she'd suffered at the
hands of Morton and his sick partner.

Noah honestly didn't know exactly what to make of
Lucy Kincaid, which made her both suspicious and intriguing. Her FBI file was surprisingly thick—and he'd
been able to access it only after Hans Vigo cleared him.
Few people knew that she'd killed Adam Scott, pulling
the trigger six times, emptying a .357 revolver into his
chest. It disturbed Noah, showing him that she could
and would kill if threatened.

Six bullets was overkill.

Except he hadn't been there. And if he'd learned anything in the military, it was to avoid the shortsighted
criticism of the politicians and media sitting high and
mighty—and safe—in the states, second-guessing command decisions when they didn't understand the immediate threat.

Morton had been killed with a single bullet to the

back of the head. The point of impact told Noah that the killer knew exactly what he was doing and where to aim.

Executions were for betrayal or money. And depending on the criminal enterprise, they were carried out in a variety of ways. A single bullet suggested a calculated hit. It seemed impersonal. A hit or business.

Could Morton have been killed for a reason completely unconnected to his past criminal enterprises? Or by someone upset that he'd turned state's evidence? Who had suffered when Trask Enterprises went down?

"Abigail, can you run a list of all Trask Enterprise employees and associates? Current address, records, anything you can get."

"What are you thinking?"

"The method. Bullet to the back of the head. It's cold and impersonal."

"Kicking his balls wasn't impersonal," Abigail commented.

"Yes, but the killer, or killers, had privacy—the marina was deserted. No security cameras in the area. They could have beaten him to death. Tortured him. Shot every limb and made him suffer. If it was personal."

"Remind me not to get on your bad side, Armstrong."

"There's one thing I don't understand yet," Noah continued. "Why was he here in D.C.? He had to have a reason. It seemed sudden and unplanned. Any word on the motels?"

"Still searching. If he used an alias, we're screwed unless some manager recognizes him. We're checking both his name and his cousin's name."

"What about someone who hasn't checked out?"

"Already ahead of you. We're working that angle."

Noah's instincts told him the reason Morton was in D.C. related directly to his murder.

The Denver field office was interviewing everyone who'd associated with Morton since his release. "No word yet from Guardino?"

"It's eight in the morning in Denver. I'll start nagging in an hour."

Noah's phone buzzed. "Lucy Kincaid to see you."

Right on time. "Thanks, I'll be right there." He nodded to Abigail. "Let's get this over with."

Lucy was alone. Kate Donovan hadn't won the lawyer battle. "Thanks for coming down, Ms. Kincaid."

She nodded. Noah led her down the hall to a small conference room. Lucy was a very attractive woman and seemed more mature than her years—her twenty-fifth birthday was next month, but she had the air of a woman with experience and confidence, who didn't let people push her around. At the same time, her body language—tight, controlled, with minimal facial expression—told Noah she kept her true self bottled inside, that her exterior was a shell. He'd seen that yesterday when she first walked into the dining room—how hard she struggled to rein in her outburst after learning that her sister-in-law had been lying to her for six years.

Lucy Kincaid was intriguing, and perhaps a bit mysterious.

"We're simply going to confirm your statement yesterday, and ask a few more questions," Noah explained as he gestured to the chair across from him. "Can I get you any water? Coffee?"

She shook her head. "No, thank you."

Abigail sat at the table and smiled. "We didn't get a

chance to formally meet yesterday," she said to Lucy as she extended her hand. "I'm Abigail Resnick. I've worked with Dr. Vigo on several cases. He speaks very highly of your brothers. All four of them."

Lucy's lips curved into a hint of a smile. "Likewise."

"Do you mind if we record our conversation?" Abigail asked.

Lucy shook her head, her smile gone.

Abigail pressed "record" on a small digital recorder and said, "This is Special Agent Abigail Resnick and Special Agent Noah Armstrong with Lucia Kincaid, regarding case file 201101120197. Ms. Kincaid, do you consent to have this interview recorded?"

"Yes," Lucy said.

"For the record, Ms. Kincaid, you voluntarily agreed to come to FBI Headquarters and answer questions pertaining to the investigation into the homicide of Roger Morton?"

"Yes," Lucy said.

Noah took over the questioning. He confirmed everything she'd said the night before, that she didn't know about the plea agreement nor did she know Morton was out of prison. Lucy was to the point and professional. Knowing what Noah now did about Lucy's trauma, his admiration for the woman grew.

But he couldn't let that cloud his judgment.

"When was the last time you saw or spoke to Mr. Morton?"

Lucy visibly tensed, and responded curtly, "Six years ago last June."

"Ms. Kincaid, thinking back to the time when Mr. Morton held you captive, can you remember anything—

something you saw or something you heard—that might help us track down his killer?"

She was wrestling with an answer, and finally said, "I'd like to speak off the record."

Noah almost said no. Then he nodded to Abigail, who paused the recorder. "You're free to talk."

Lucy waited several seconds before she spoke with thinly veiled anger. "After my kidnapping and rape I spent months trying to forget, trying to put everything I saw and heard and felt out of my mind. And I couldn't do it. When I gave up, when I thought I would have to learn to endure the nightmares and the anger and the fear and the deep, never-ending humiliation, it all finally began to fade. I don't know how long it took, but I let it go. I let every memory disappear.

"Now, all I remember are snippets of that Hell, and I refuse to put myself back there. Not for this, and most certainly not for Roger Morton. I didn't kill him, I don't know who did, but I'm not grieving. He was a disgusting, vile rapist who took pleasure in hurting women. He should never have been released from prison. I'm glad he's dead."

She nodded to Abigail, who hesitated, then turned the recorder back on.

"To answer your question, Agent Armstrong," Lucy continued as if she hadn't just spoken, "I don't remember much about those two days, and nothing that would even hint to who killed that monster."

Sean had spent the last fifteen minutes convincing Lucy's brother Patrick that he didn't need to fly back to D.C.

"Patrick, I'll keep watch over her. I promise." It

wouldn't be a hardship for him. Sean only wished he could have found a different reason to spend time with Lucy. "The bastard's dead. I don't think she's in any danger."

"I don't know." Patrick was torn, and if this job weren't so important he would have already been on a plane back.

"Call her," Sean told him. "I'm sure she'll tell you to stay at Stanford, do the job. They asked for you specifically."

"I seem to recall they asked for anyone but you."

"There're not many people out there who can do what we do with computer security."

Patrick sighed. "I'll finish the job—unless Lucy needs me. Then Duke will have to do it on his own."

"Fair enough."

"Keep me in the loop," Patrick said.

"I promise."

Sean said goodbye and hung up as he retrieved his email.

He smiled when he saw the message from Jayne Morgan, the RCK research guru. He wished he could have convinced his brother Duke to let him take her to D.C. as well as Patrick, but Duke put his foot down. Both Patrick and Sean were computer experts, but Sean's skills were in circumventing the law. One of the primary roles of RCK East was computer security. Sean could hack into virtually any system, but he didn't have the experience on how to fix the breach. Patrick had the technical background to secure the system, just like Duke. When Patrick started working for RCK in Sacramento last year, they'd hit it off—and both of them had wanted to get out of the shadow of their older brothers.

Sean read all the documentation Jayne had retrieved on Roger Morton, Adam Scott, and the Lucy Kincaid kidnapping.

Since his release from prison, Roger Morton had been living in Denver. Until he'd come to Washington, D.C., for an unknown reason, risking his probation to do so. According to the plea agreement Sean now had a copy of, one slip up and Morton would be back in prison for life. What was so important that he'd risk life in prison when he'd been given a virtual get-out-of-jail-free card? And what did he know, or what had he done, that got him killed?

Money or revenge.

Revenge was the easy answer, but revenge pointed to the Kincaids, not Morton. Lucy had been a victim, and her entire family had a justifiable reason to want Morton dead. But would they do it?

Sean thought not. If one of the Kincaids had killed Morton, why would they have lured him to D.C.? If he'd come to D.C. on his own and Kate or Patrick had seen him, they would have put him back in prison.

Jack Kincaid, on the other hand, had the ability, training, and personality to kill. With more than two decades in the military, then working as a mercenary, Jack would know how to make Morton disappear.

Sean made a note to research Morton's other victims. Maybe one of them had the wherewithal to kill. But even as he began the research, he knew that if he uncovered something down that road, he wouldn't turn it over to the Feds. He couldn't see any justice in punishing a victim when the criminal got out of prison so unfairly. It was enough to send most sane people over the edge.

Was Morton out for revenge? Had he come here to

harm Kate or Lucy for their roles in putting him behind bars? He'd gotten off practically scot free, so Sean didn't see why he'd risk his freedom for revenge, but then again he didn't understand men like Morton in the first place.

After revenge came money. Though Adam Scott had been the brains behind Trask Enterprises, Morton had carried out his plans. He probably knew everything there was to know about the illegal porn business. How would a guy like Morton make money if he was being watched closely by the Feds?

He'd go underground. He'd been used to a certain lifestyle working for Trask, he'd been in prison for six years, and if he came to D.C. for business—for *money*— it had to relate to his experience. Previous life, previous contacts.

Money. For people like Morton, it was always about the money. Revenge took too much planning, setup, and hatred. He'd violate his probation for money, not revenge. Reading Morton's rap sheet made it clear he cared most about money, getting laid, and demeaning women.

Sean suspected he was heading into dangerous territory. He was attracted to Lucy, and he feared his feelings would taint the evidence he had before him. Would he see what was important? He wasn't a cop; he couldn't be that fair. He didn't want to weigh the scales of right and wrong, giving criminals more rights than victims. To him, people like Roger Morton were scum and didn't deserve the rights they took for granted. Why was it that in the system, the criminals had all the rights? Where was justice?

He didn't understand what Lucy Kincaid saw in the

FBI, or why she wanted to be a cop in the first place, being forced to work within stringent rules that protected the bad guys more than they protected the innocent. But she wanted it—and there was nothing he admired more than deep passion.

He'd been enamored with Lucy Kincaid from the night Patrick first introduced them, a month ago when they flew out to sign papers on the new RCK East house and close escrow. The three of them had eaten pizza on the floor of the empty kitchen. Perhaps it went farther back than that. To the first time he'd seen her, when she came to visit Patrick and Jack in Sacramento more than a year ago. He'd watched her through his window, the way she moved, the way the jeans she wore hugged her long, lean legs.

Of course the first thing that attracted him was her looks. Neither tall nor short—he'd peg her at five foot seven, but with legs that made her seem taller—physically, she was just his type. An hourglass figure, curvy in the right places. Athletic. And when she relaxed, Lucy had the most beautiful smile. But it wasn't just a perfectly proportional body that enticed Sean, it was the whole package: her long black hair, her large brown eyes, and her brains. Her intelligence, passion for justice, and determination put Lucy Kincaid in a league all her own.

He knew about her past, of course. What Patrick hadn't told him he'd learned through his own research. Nothing that wasn't public—he wouldn't do that to Lucy. And how she persevered after going through Hell showed the world she would never act the victim or martyr.

Looks, brains, and commitment. Lucy was dedicated

to the future she was making for herself—of seeking justice for those who couldn't do it for themselves. He admired her drive.

Focus was one thing that Sean lacked. At least, that's what Duke always told him. That he'd tried everything in college because he didn't know what he wanted to do. Which was partly true. He understood Lucy's need to learn new and different things, her moving from the sheriff's department to Congress to the morgue.

He only wondered if she would grow bored with the FBI, hampered by its slow process, the excruciating paperwork, and all those rules. Sean wouldn't survive under such conditions. Lucy—maybe. And while he understood her motivation and he admired her dedication, he would have loved to have recruited her for RCK. She would be such an asset to the company.

But more than anything, Sean wanted to make her smile. He wanted to show her that there was more to life than 24/7 work. That those who worked hard should play hard, that she deserved to have fun.

But she wouldn't have fun until the situation with Morton was settled.

Sean continued reading the files Jayne had sent, and began to plan.

NINE

Only minutes after Lucy Kincaid left the FBI office and Noah went back to his desk, Abigail exclaimed, "Eureka!"

"Gold?" Noah asked.

"If you're looking for a sleazy, flea-infested motel, then yeah, gold. The Triple Tree, outside Dulles. The manager said a guy matching Morton's description paid cash for three nights on Thursday. He signed in as Cliff Skinner—Morton's cousin—and never checked out." Abigail grabbed her keys. "I'm going to check it out, get a confirmation on the ID, see if he left any belongings in the room, last sighting, the works."

Noah glanced at his messages. "The SSA in Denver called while we were in with Kincaid. I'll see what she's found. Call when you're done and we'll compare notes."

"You should have the full list—names and current contact info—on Morton's associates before the end of the day. I dropped Rick Stockton's name when staff balked at the amount of work needed to make the file current. Worked wonders."

"Good—I want to clear this as soon as possible."

Abigail leaned against the side of his cubicle. "You know, I might not be all that sad if we didn't close it."

Noah stared at his new partner. He didn't like the direction of this conversation. "Morton was a scumbag, but we need to know who killed him. Punishment is up to the U.S. Attorney and the court system, not us."

"We've done what Stockton wanted—cleared an active FBI agent, Kate Donovan. We know she didn't do it, and nothing in her finances suggests she paid a hit man."

"Not all hits are for money."

"You're going dark side here. Donovan doesn't work in the field; she can't let someone off in exchange for a hit, or screw with an undercover op."

"All I'm saying is that there are a lot of unanswered questions. Morton was up to something—there's no other reason he would come to D.C. in violation of his probation unless there was something big going down. We need to know what that is. There's more here than a simple murder."

"You got me there. Maybe he left a diabolical master plan for world domination in his motel room." She winked.

"Let me know if you find it."

After Abigail left, Noah picked up the phone and called SSA Monica Guardino.

Guardino answered the phone brusquely, and it was obvious by the background noise that she was in the field.

"Armstrong in D.C. returning your call."

"Your dead guy was a prick, just want you to know."

"I know. What did you find?"

"Morton was re-creating his old enterprise," Guardino said. "His cousin Mr. Skinner, being cooperative after I pointed out he could be considered an accessory, said Morton maintained a studio apartment his probation officer didn't know about. We popped the lock, found a high-end computer and dozens of boxes of pornography—DVDs and photographs mostly—including some photos that I'd wager my pension are of underage girls. But the kicker is, our e-crimes expert says Morton was downloading the DVDs and preparing them for Internet file sharing. Something about minimizing file sizes for bandwidth issues. The whole how-tos and why-fors are a bit over my head, but I trust my guy. I can hook you up with him—"

While Noah was technically competent, high-end cybercrimes were beyond his scope. "If you could box up everything and send it to me, I'll have our cybercrimes team go through the files with a fine-toothed comb."

"Already started boxing the files."

"Excellent. Any chance you can get it on a military transport today?"

"Where's the urgency? Isn't this a low-life scumbag murder? Hardly a top priority."

"It's top priority for Assistant Director Rick Stockton," Noah said.

"Well, shit, Armstrong, you didn't say the director's office was involved."

"I appreciate your help," he said. "I owe you."

"I may take you up on that. But I have more," Guardino continued. "Morton was broke. We went through his finances—he had less than three hundred dollars in his bank account. His cousin paid him for working in his autobody shop, but not much more than minimum wage, and all his money is accounted for. Nothing in or out that is suspicious."

"Any sign he had money stashed elsewhere?" Noah asked. "He's well-versed in money laundering."

"No luxury items, no trips, no cars. The only thing he spent money on was this computer system, and it's in line with what he earned. He even had the receipts in his file cabinet."

"So was he going to run his operation from there?" Noah wondered out loud.

"Can't say, but he definitely had something going on. You want us to boot up the computer? See what we can find?"

Noah considered letting Denver work that end, then decided against it. He didn't know what was on the computer, and while he trusted the field offices completely, after talking to Lucy Kincaid this morning he wanted to keep any files that may have her information as private as possible. The fewer people who saw them, the better, if Morton had anything on her he'd planned to exploit.

"No, but thanks."

"Good—it looks like it'll take a shitload of time."

Time. How was Noah going to convince the cyber-crime squad that this case was a priority?

"Thanks, Monica, I appreciate the help. Let me know when the transport is scheduled so I can send an agent to collect the evidence."

"Bring a truck," she said with a half-laugh. "We'll dig around a little more, but I think this is the bulk of what he was up to. If you need me, call."

After Noah hung up on Denver, he called Rick Stockton. He was surprised when the assistant director himself answered.

"This is Special Agent Armstrong," Noah said. "Do you have time for an update?"

"A few minutes," Stockton said.

"The Denver regional office found a computer and files of pornography; much of it they suspect is illegal or child porn. On the surface it looks like Morton was trying to re-create the enterprise he ran with Adam Scott six years ago. I asked Denver to box everything up and send it to me on a military shuttle."

"Good. We need to confirm exactly what he was up to and who he was working with. The last thing I want is another Trask Enterprises. We're overloaded as it is."

"I'm concerned that this case is going to take a lot of manpower, and my cybercrimes unit is swamped right now." During the last staff meeting, Noah had listened to the SSA of cybercrimes relate their multitude of cases, many of them involving children in jeopardy. Unless there was something similar in Morton's data, Noah couldn't in good conscience pull them, even if he had the clout. "I don't feel comfortable pulling weight when they're dealing with extremely time-sensitive crimes."

"Agreed," Stockton said. "What about Kate Donovan? Is she in the clear?"

"She was out of town, and no way she or her husband could have killed Morton. Her alibi checks out and there are no signs suggesting she or any of the Kincaid family took out a hit on Morton. Lucy Kincaid claimed she didn't even know he was out of prison, and I believe her."

"How would you feel turning the computer evidence over to Kate?"

Noah leaned back in his chair and frowned.

"Kate Donovan?" he asked unnecessarily. "While so

far everything checks out, I can think of ways she could have had a hand in it—"

"What do your instincts tell you?"

"I prefer to deal in facts, sir."

"So do I, but sometimes absolute definitive proof is unattainable. Her alibi checks, her financials check, and she knows more about Trask Enterprises and Roger Morton than anyone in the Bureau. She can assess the data and route it to the appropriate field agents. She's not working in the field while teaching at Quantico; she can devote her time to this. I can flex my muscles with the cybercrimes squad, but they won't be able to devote the same time to it."

"Understood." Noah didn't know how he felt about bringing a former suspect into the investigation.

"I'm not suggesting you let her into every facet of your investigation," Stockton continued. "That's your call. But as far as the computer data and tracking goes, she's the best we've got, and she'll work it till it's done. Better yet, she's part of the Quantico cybercrimes unit and has access to the fastest computers we have."

"Yes, sir."

"Good work. Shoot me and Hans a brief summary via email, and call me if you need anything."

"Yes, sir." Noah hung up. He wasn't wholly comfortable with Rick Stockton's suggestion—which sounded more like an order—but he didn't see any other option.

Reluctantly, he called Kate Donovan. When she answered, he said, "It's Noah Armstrong."

"Is Lucy okay? When did she leave?"

"Yes, and nearly an hour ago."

"Are you sure she was okay?"

"I didn't turn the screws on her; it was a straightforward and civil interview." Noah had been impressed with the lady. She'd held up well on the surface, even when the questions touched on sensitive areas. But she'd been tightly wound, and he wondered just how well she'd *really* held up. She was a private, controlled person, and in Noah's experience, they were the type who exploded big when it was least expected.

"When I said I wanted her to have an attorney, I didn't mean that she had anything to hide," Kate explained.

"I know that, Kate. I'm calling about a different matter. The Denver office found a computer and extensive collection of pornographic files, including child porn, in Morton's apartment. It'll be here tonight, but my cybercrimes team can't get to it immediately, and there may be data on his computer that will give us an idea of why he was here and who might have killed him."

"You're going to have to push cybercrime. That's Robeaux, right? I know him well. I'll call him—he'll do it for me."

She spoke with complete confidence in her ability to have her will be done, and Noah smiled in spite of the feeling Kate acted as if this was her case. "He's good, I agree, but his unit is overwhelmed right now. Rick Stockton authorized you to be the point person on this. I'd like to bring the evidence to Quantico tonight."

"Me?" She paused. "So you cleared me."

"Your alibi checks; so does your husband's."

"And Lucy?"

"I believe her." Her alibi—that she was home alone—would be virtually impossible to prove.

"When will the material be here?"

"I'm not sure—late. They're still boxing it."

"Let me know when, and I'll send a team from Quantico to the airfield to retrieve the evidence, log it in, and secure it in our lab. We'll start first thing in the morning."

"Thank you."

"No thanks needed. I want to know exactly what Morton was up to, and I swear if he has a partner I'll find out who he is and lock him up for the rest of his life."

The last thing Lucy wanted to do was go to WCF Friday afternoon, but neither did she want to go back home and feel sorry for herself. She made herself stop at a nearby deli and eat. She hadn't been able to eat anything that morning before going to FBI headquarters. She hoped she'd done the right thing because truly, she had nothing to hide. She hadn't killed Roger Morton, though she couldn't have honestly said she *wouldn't* have if he'd confronted her.

Her stomach was still in knots from her hour-long interview with Agent Armstrong. Both he and Abigail Resnick had been professional and they didn't seem as though they thought she had anything to do with the murder, or that she knew anything about Morton's activities even six years ago. She just wanted to keep the past buried, but it came back and slapped her in the face once again.

She couldn't finish her sandwich, her stomach still uneasy, so she walked the short block to WCF. Though the sun was peeking out between clouds, it was still cold, and she pulled her coat tight around her.

When she stepped into the WCF building, she was surprised that the place wasn't packed. Fran was in the conference room by herself, checking the fund-raiser name tags against her master list.

"Where is everyone?" Lucy asked.

"I had lunch brought in and we finished everything we needed to, and since they're all working on Saturday, I gave them the afternoon off."

"You're really done?"

"Just last minute details left. I'm triple-checking the guest list. The last thing I need is a major donor with a misspelling."

Lucy tried not to show her relief.

Fran looked up from the list and frowned. "You look tired."

"I didn't sleep well last night." Lucy considered telling Fran about Roger Morton. Fran knew about her past, and was one of only a few who Lucy could talk to about what happened. Fran was one of the most steadfast, loyal people Lucy knew—and she didn't treat Lucy like a victim. If anything, she pushed her harder, knowing that hard work gave Lucy intense pride.

But with the fund-raiser on Fran's mind, Lucy decided to wait until next week. Morton would still be dead, and maybe a few days was what Lucy needed to re-distance herself from her past. Right now, it felt too raw, too real—and she didn't want to talk about it anymore.

She was already embarrassed about crying all over Sean Rogan last night. Except . . . she wasn't. He hadn't talked much, but what he did say had calmed her. Then, he'd stood up to Kate when she tried to bully him into letting her take Lucy home. He'd agreed that Lucy needed an attorney before talking to the FBI, but he'd also said he trusted her to make the right choice for herself. That kind of support—that deep faith in her decisions—was surprising, especially from someone she hadn't known for long. In the month she'd known Sean, he'd been more fun than serious, but last night she'd seen another side of him.

"I didn't hear from Cody," Lucy said instead, taking the name tags that Fran had verified and sorting them into alphabetical order. "Did Prenter go up in front of a judge this morning? Did they send him back to Hagerstown?"

Fran stopped her chore and frowned at Lucy. "I thought Cody would have told you—Prenter didn't show."

"He didn't?"

"He could have suspected a setup. Sex predators have a sixth sense about cops. It wouldn't be the first time, and it won't be the last. But we have far more successes than most organizations doing what we do."

"But Prenter believed me."

"Maybe he pegged Cody. Lorenzo looks like a cop."

"But Cody's done this dozens of times! He knows the drill. And if Prenter had pegged either me or Cody, he would have contacted 'Tanya' to gloat or taunt or threaten. He wouldn't just be quiet about it. It's not in his personality—his mouth got him in big trouble at the trial."

"Lucy, just because you have a psychology degree doesn't make you a criminal psychiatrist," Fran said. Lucy blinked, surprised by Fran's comment. Fran immediately backtracked. "I didn't mean that to sound so harsh. You know I think your predator tracking program is the best I've seen—it's going to give law enforcement amazing tools to find these guys when they go to ground. It's just—I don't have to explain to you the difference between online communication, where comments can be considered before typed, and face-to-face conversation. These guys are good at hiding their true identity. So maybe you're right and Prenter would have taunted you if he ID'd Cody as a cop. Or maybe you're wrong and Prenter wants to disappear and not do anything to get himself tossed back into prison. Maybe his car got a flat tire. For one reason or another, he didn't show."

"You're right. Maybe I should reach out."

"I don't think that's a wise idea. If he does suspect you're a cop or working with the cops, he could get violent."

"He doesn't know who I really am."

"True, but if he sets up another meet, he may ambush our volunteer cops. If he contacts you, go ahead, keep it going. But don't initiate contact, okay?"

Lucy reluctantly agreed. She didn't like being so passive and reactionary.

"I have good news—you remember that case you worked a few months ago? The seven-year-old girl who was exploited by her father on the Internet?"

"In Atlanta? I'll never forget."

"He pled out yesterday when confronted with additional evidence the FBI found on his computer and the medical evidence of abuse. Eighteen years."

"That's terrific. Did they find her mother?"

"Sadly, no. She'd been a drug addict for years—she could be dead, or she could be so strung out she doesn't know her name. But they did find her maternal grandmother, who's overjoyed to take custody of the girl."

The child would need counseling and love, but Lucy

was confident that with enough of both, and a strong will, she would survive and lead a normal, happy life.

Normal. Was anyone who'd been abused considered normal? Victims never truly forgot their abuse. But they could develop strategies to live with it, to tolerate the pain and the memories—never easy, but essential if any of them were to find even a modicum of peace in the future.

Fran gave Lucy a spontaneous hug. "We need to celebrate our victories. If Prenter contacts you, let me know. Otherwise, I'll see you tomorrow night, okay? Go home and rest."

"I will. Thanks." Lucy gathered her bag. She glanced out the window and noticed the sun was gone and a chill wind tore down the street. She was so tired and drained from her near-sleepless night, she decided to grab a taxi.

The fucking bitch hails a taxi.

I watch Lucy open the rear door. She pauses and looks across the street, right at me. She doesn't see me; I am in the deli—the same deli she ate at earlier this afternoon.

That ignorance angers me, yet somehow I am thrilled. I cannot explain the exhilaration rising in my chest. I despise being ignored, yet she doesn't truly ignore me, does she?

I know Lucy Kincaid. I know where she lives. I know where she works, where she gets her coffee, where her brother lives, where she runs in the park.

She gets into the taxi and it drives off. Taking her home? Taking her to dinner? I do not know, but I am patient.

Her family makes me nervous. A brother who is a pri-

vate investigator. A sister-in-law who is an FBI agent. This is why I am cautious—I cannot afford to make a mistake.

Should I walk away and wash my hands of Lucy Kincaid? I could easily kill her and run, but would they hunt me down? Her family? The organization she works for? Can I defeat them? I want to believe I can, but I'm not an idiot.

I am patient, but my time is valuable. I keep a log of the time she has cost me. That time will be repaid.

No one understands the concept of time as I do. I sleep exactly six hours every night. No more, no less. I exercise for twenty-two minutes each morning, followed by four minutes in the shower. And while I understand the need for flexibility, if I am not disciplined, how can I expect my females to be disciplined?

I am the keeper of truth, and I will not forget her betrayal. I will forget no betrayals. They will all be disciplined in turn. They will all be nothing, not even a speck of DNA. Which seems appropriate since they are merely females; worse, females who do not obey.

But Lucy Kincaid is by far the most disobedient woman I have come across. I need to act wisely or else I should disappear.

But walking away from her is not an option. What kind of man would I be if a female scared me off?

I consider my options. I can take her almost anytime I want. I let two good opportunities pass me by because I do not want to be hasty. Rash action leads to mistakes, and because of her family, I cannot afford to err. I need a plan.

No woman will defeat me. She started this game. She

is the mightier-than-thou female who does not know her proper place.

I do not fear Lucy Kincaid. She is no threat. The men in her life are potential threats, but by the time they figure it out, if they can, I will be gone.

This situation presents a certain challenge.

I exit the deli and walk to my car. Ideas flood my brain: how and when to take her. I must have as much time with her as possible to teach her. All the time she has cost me will be repaid with her obedience, or it will be repaid with blood.

TEN

There was a time when Sean could have gone either way—become a criminal mastermind or choose the law-abiding road. If he'd ever doubted that staying more or less on the side of the law was the right choice, he didn't now.

Sean drove to the east side, the most depressed part of D.C., with his notes on known Morton and Scott associates who lived in the greater D.C. area. Their criminal enterprise had lasted nearly two decades, and while several of their associates were dead or in prison—and a few appeared to have cleaned up their act—most were still criminals ranging from petty to Mafia.

He had time to hit at least one today. Because she was the easiest to track down, he chose the lone female on the list.

Former prostitute Melinda Winslow had been released from prison six months ago after serving three years for possession of heroin with the intent to sell. It was her fourth conviction in eleven years. According to the information Jayne sent to Sean, she'd been a regular "star" at Trask Enterprises. When Trask closed up after Scott and Morton went underground following the murder of federal agent Paige Henshaw—Kate Donovan's partner—Winslow lost control of her addiction and had spiraled farther downward.

When she answered the door of her hovel, Sean nearly left, certain he had the wrong person. Melinda Winslow was thirty-six; this woman looked fifty on a good day.

It was not a good day. If drugs didn't kill you outright, they certainly sucked the life out of you.

"Well, fuck me, you pricks can waltz in here whenever you fucking please? Pig."

"Hello, Ms. Winslow," Sean said, mildly amused. "I have a few questions, if you don't mind."

"Like I can? Last time one of you tossed me back in jail because I wouldn't give you a blow job, and fuck that."

She thought he was a cop, and Sean did nothing to dissuade her. He didn't always see eye-to-eye with law enforcement. Some cops were just fine; others were too black-and-white for his taste. And some were, as Ms. Winslow so ungraciously stated, simply pricks.

"I don't want to see you back in jail."

She snorted, then rubbed her wet nose with the back of her hand. Sean wouldn't be touching her or anything in her filthy apartment.

"I have only a couple questions, like I said. May I?"

"Like you need to ask." She flung the door open, knocking a teetering stack of yellowed tabloid newspapers off a sagging bookshelf. She didn't seem to notice, stepping over the fallen rags.

Sean stepped in, keeping his hands to himself. "You had a business relationship eleven years ago with two men—Adam Scott, also known as 'Trask,' and Roger Morton."

At the mention of the names, her pasty face paled even

more, then she thrust her chin out. "I haven't seen them. Trask is dead, I heard. Roger in prison. I wouldn't talk to him if he were the last john on the planet."

"You were an employee of Trask Enterprises, correct?"

She cackled. "*Employee.* You know what I was. They paid me for sex tapes. It was legal, all legal—at least on my end it was."

Sean highly doubted she reported her income to the Internal Revenue Service, but he didn't say anything.

"I didn't know what they were doing on the side. I fucking swear to God."

"You associated with them for how long?"

"A few months. And then—a few times here and there when I needed the money. They paid more for hard-core action. But—shit, Trask nearly killed me once while getting off. Roger gave me two g's to keep silent. Told me I was lucky I wasn't dead, and not to come back or call. I didn't. That was years ago. I went to jail after that, in Minnesota, for drugs. Cleaned myself up." She nodded in pride. Sean noted the plethora of empty wine jugs around the apartment, and the stale smell of human body odor and spilled alcohol. Maybe she didn't shoot heroin anymore, but she was still slowly killing herself.

"Did Roger contact you within the last six months?" he asked.

"No. And if he tried, I'd tell him to go to Hell." She glared at Sean. "I thought he was in prison."

"Yes, ma'am, he was. He was released on probation in July."

She laughed, a hearty laugh, and Sean saw for a brief moment that she had once been a beautiful woman. "Probation? After the shit he did? I got three fucking years for drug possession, and he got what? Five? Ten? For prostitution, murder, drugs, and fuck knows what else."

She pulled down the collar of her T-shirt, revealing her neck. "See this scar?"

Sean saw a two-inch scar at the base of her throat. His jaw tightened as his protective instincts surged.

"Roger did that to you?"

She shook her head and let go of her collar. "Trask. I thought I was dead. But Roger watched and then later he paid me. I heard they made a fortune on that tape of Trask fucking me. Roger did everything for that bastard. We all knew Trask was a psycho, and Roger covered for him. So why'd he get out?"

"Because the justice system is fucked."

Sean dropped fifty dollars on her sofa and left, unable to stay another minute.

To say what happened with Morton was due to a messed-up justice system was the world's greatest understatement. Winslow wasn't a saint, but no one deserved to be treated as she had been, nearly killed in such a vicious manner. Adam Scott was the psychopath, but Morton had watched from the sidelines, helped clean up Scott's messes, kept the damn trains running on time.

Sean slid into his black GT, shooting a glance at the teenage boys eyeing his ride. They didn't bother him, and a glance in the rearview mirror showed him why. He looked ready for a fight.

He squealed into the street, maneuvering the muscle car as if it were an extension of himself. Driving usually gave him peace, but right now he felt nothing but deep, acid-building anger.

When Melinda Winslow showed him her scar, he pictured Lucy. He didn't want to, he had never seen any scars on Lucy, but that didn't mean they weren't there under her clothes.

Sean found the nearest Beltway on-ramp. He needed to get on the highway and floor it. Right now, he sorely missed Northern California where he knew all the back roads he could virtually fly on when he needed to let off steam. Here, there were too many people, too many cars, in too small an area. He headed south toward Virginia in search of a long country road.

Winslow had spoken bluntly of her attack, but she hadn't considered it an attack. She hadn't been raped. Stupidly, she'd gone into the situation willingly, for money. Sean pitied her after seeing the fear in her eyes as she recalled nearly dying. Eleven years ago and she was still terrified.

It was the matter-of-fact answers, her language, her acceptance of the shit life handed her and her own culpability in her situation that had Sean's head spinning. Lucy was the exact opposite. She had been kidnapped and wasn't a willing participant in Adam Scott's sex games. She'd been tortured, tormented, raped, and nearly killed because Adam Scott was a sadistic bastard who got off by hurting women.

Lucy hadn't spoken of her ordeal with more than a few vague details, but he hadn't expected her to. The murder of Roger Morton was bringing it back up to the surface. He could see that in her eyes, in the tension that filled every muscle. But he hadn't put her in the role of a victim because Lucy never once acted like a victim. Until last night, when she'd cried and he'd held her. Sean would do anything in his power to take away her anguish.

He hit 395 south and moved smoothly around traffic, grateful that the intermittent sunshine had dried the roads from the snow earlier that week. It was three in the afternoon and rush hour was just starting, but he would stay ahead of it. He picked up speed, trying to block Winslow's words from his mind, trying to stop picturing Lucy in her place.

Lucy was the strongest woman he'd ever met. She had to be to accomplish so much in such a short time, with the weight of her past sitting on her shoulders. But dammit, she shouldn't have had to suffer at all! No woman should have suffered at the hands of Scott and Morton. The justice system was fucked, and Sean wanted to hit something.

But he wouldn't. His release was driving, and he drove until his heart rate slowed back to normal, until he'd calmed himself enough to remember that both men were dead, they couldn't hurt anyone again, they'd never touch Lucy.

The radar detector hidden in his dashboard beeped rapidly, and he instantly slowed down—shit, he was going ninety-five?—to seventy, maintaining complete control of his GT. But it was too late. The trooper came up behind him and flashed his lights.

Sean pulled over, not holding his breath that he'd be able to talk himself out of a ticket.

But he would have fun trying.

ELEVEN

Lucy had avoided Kate last night and this morning, but her sister-in-law was waiting for her when the taxi dropped her off at four-thirty Friday afternoon.

"Lucy—" Kate said as Lucy started up the stairs.

Lucy didn't want to talk about yesterday or Morton or her FBI interview or Kate's lies, not right now. Her raw emotions could easily spill out and she didn't want a fight almost as much as she didn't want to cry. She was so drained from her confrontation with Kate yesterday, she didn't want to say anything she couldn't take back.

"Can we do this tomorrow?" Lucy was already thinking of ways to avoid Kate all weekend. She would have to talk to her; she couldn't live here and expect to evade the inevitable conversation. She simply didn't have the energy at this moment.

Kate tucked her straight shoulder-length blond hair behind her ear, tilting her head up to look Lucy in the eye. "Lucy, I just—"

"The FBI interview went fine. I'm not a suspect. That's what you want to know, right?"

"I know, I spoke to Noah."

Lucy felt like an outsider, that once again Kate was

working behind her back and keeping information from her.

"Terrific."

"He didn't tell me anything, just that you did great and weren't considered a suspect. I need to talk to you about something; it's important. Please. I have to leave in ten minutes—and I want you to have all the information I have."

Lucy frowned, torn, but reluctantly followed Kate to the kitchen, her curiosity stronger than her sense of betrayal.

Kate's jacket, laptop, and keys were all on the table. "I'm heading to Quantico to process evidence in the Morton case."

"They're letting you work on it? Isn't that a conflict of interest or something?"

"Denver FBI found a computer and files at Morton's apartment, and on the surface it appears that he was re-creating Trask Enterprises. Everything has been boxed up and sent to Quantico. Noah got clearance from headquarters to let me process the computer data and create a timeline of Morton's activities. I'm supposed to figure out whether he had a partner, what he was specifically up to, and to assess the data to determine if there is anyone in jeopardy."

Lucy sat at the table, unsure of how she felt about Kate's news. Relieved that strangers weren't involved. Angry that Morton had the freedom to exploit women and children. And a hint of fear at one word: *partner.* Kate pulled out a chair and sat across from her. "Lucy, I will not let your name out. If there is anything in those files related to you, I will take care of it."

Lucy knew exactly what she meant. For years, Lucy

had known—though her family never talked about it—that Kate had been sending viruses to computer servers that hosted a digital copy of Lucy's attack. She had a program running that could find and identify the file based on size, name, or date and when she verified that it came originally from Trask, she uploaded the virus. Though the virus destroyed only that specific file, it was highly illegal and would get Kate fired and likely prosecuted. No one had given Lucy any details, and if questioned, Lucy couldn't truthfully answer that she knew what Kate was doing.

It wasn't the risk to Kate that had Lucy tense; it was the sudden realization that this would never end. That her rape could come back any time, not just in her thoughts and nightmares but publicly, on the Internet. That each time it did, she became more desensitized to her own pain and suffering. As if that girl wasn't her, she hadn't lived through it. Her emotions were already suppressed in nearly everything she did. Kate had long ago told her it was compartmentalization, something that most cops did when confronted with a tragedy or a case that was emotionally disturbing. Child murder, a grossly violent crime, any number of things that were difficult to process without losing control. And Lucy had done the same thing by being able to detach herself from her kidnapping and attack.

But the lack of emotion had transcended into other aspects of Lucy's life. She emotionally distanced herself from relationships, from friendships, and even from her family much of the time. The biggest problem with her relationship with Cody was that she didn't *feel* anything. She enjoyed spending time with him, she liked him, but she didn't *feel* anything inside, love or pleasure or commitment. It was as if she were a puppet acting and reacting the way she thought she was supposed to, but watching herself from the outside, a director, not able to truly live free and enjoy life.

"Lucy?" Kate reached out, her hand inches from Lucy's but not touching.

"I want to help," she said. "I can go through the files with you. I know how it works, I can—"

Kate was shaking her head. "No."

"Dammit, stop trying to protect me!"

"It's not my call. My assignment is limited to Morton's computer and digital files. Noah Armstrong is the lead agent on this case and I'm not going to make waves, because he'll pull me and then I'll have no inside information. And you're not an agent yet, Lucy. I refuse to jeopardize your chances."

"I don't care," Lucy said, knowing it wasn't true. She *did* care about being accepted into the FBI. "Some things are more important."

Kate smiled. "Lucy, you're good with computer data tracking—really good—but I'm still better."

Kate was trying to lighten the conversation.

"I feel helpless."

"You are the least helpless person I know. Other than me," Kate said.

Lucy sighed. "I understand. But please, Kate, promise me one thing. This is important." She wanted Kate to know how absolutely serious she was.

"If I can, I will."

"Don't try to protect me anymore. I want to know everything you learn about Morton's operation. Unless it's directly related to national security and you'll be tried for treason if you breathe a word of it, I want to know. Especially if it's about me."

Lucy saw the conflict in Kate's eyes.

"I'm a big girl, Kate. I've faced much worse up close and personal. Bad news is not going to break me. Do not keep shielding me from the truth because in the long run, it will hurt both of us."

After Kate left, Lucy set the security alarm and went up to her room to check her messages. Specifically, any messages for "Tanya." She still didn't understand why Brad Prenter hadn't shown.

There were none.

She pulled up all her chat transcripts with him and reviewed them again. What if she'd inadvertently sounded like a cop? She didn't have a badge, she wasn't a cop—local or federal—but because of her extensive training with Fran she had the mentality of a cop.

Nothing that she read, even critically, made her sound like anyone but who she pretended to be.

Maybe he had a family emergency out of town, and why would he bother to cancel a date with a girl he'd met online?

She was overreacting to everything. It was this crap with Morton.

She showered, then went downstairs to make something to eat. She didn't feel hungry, but she had a headache that felt like a hunger headache.

She surveyed the contents of the refrigerator, then the pantry. Nothing looked appetizing. She picked up a banana from the counter and had just taken a bite when her cell phone rang.

It was Cody.

"Hi," she said, quickly swallowing.

"Fran told me she talked to you about Prenter."

"That he didn't show?"

"I don't know what happened, but I had Angel with me. She was inside, I was out. We stayed two hours. Not even a sighting."

"Did he see you?"

"No, he didn't show. Sorry, Lucy."

"I didn't get a message from his chat profile yesterday canceling. I just checked tonight and no contact. I was thinking he might have had a family emergency, or maybe a better offer," she added jokingly.

"I think he made Tanya out as a cop. Sexual predators can smell cop, especially those as savvy as Prenter."

Lucy didn't believe it, but she wasn't surprised Cody sounded like Fran. "He didn't think I was a cop."

Cody sighed audibly. "He didn't show and he didn't contact you. It's happened before. You're not the first. Considering the success you've had over the last few years, I'm surprised. But it's not unusual."

She supposed Cody was right—there had been several parolees who had never shown, and Prenter wasn't even the first of hers—but she hadn't had the same feeling about the others as she did about Prenter. She'd thought for certain that she had him.

Prenter bothered her more than most of the parolees. There were some who had more victims, some who were more violent, but Prenter was a handsome college student who had used his looks and money to his advantage. He didn't look like a predator. He looked like an all-around nice guy. But even more than his deceptive appearance, he had a callous disregard for the welfare of

the women he drugged. That went part and parcel with
rapists in general, but he'd shown no remorse, no sympathy for the girl he left in a coma because he'd overdosed her. He'd denied it, had never been convicted, but
the evidence was there—it was simply inadmissible. He
didn't even pretend to care about her fate. It was all
about *him* all the time. He thought his money could get
him out of every jam. And until Sara Tyson testified, it
had.

Lucy wanted him back in prison in the worst way. To
give justice to the girl who could no longer speak for
herself.

"Lucy?" Cody said. "You still there?"

"I didn't tip him off."

"It's not an accusation. We'll get him back in prison.
I'll find another way."

"Before or after he rapes another woman?" she
snapped. She instantly realized that was unfair. Cody
had volunteered countless hours with WCF, often after a
long shift. "I'm sorry. I didn't mean to sound like a
bitch. I'm frustrated, but it's not your fault."

"You are never bitchy, Lucy. I understand how you're
feeling. Prenter will see justice again. I'm not going to let
this go. But you have to stand down. If he doesn't contact you soon, we'll know he thought he was being set
up. But he doesn't know it was *you*. I'd never let you do
this if your real identity could be uncovered."

"I'm not worried about that." And she wasn't—she
had enough safety protocols on her personal computer
to rival the FBI, thanks to Kate. Nothing was foolproof,
but even if Prenter had the extraordinary skills to track
her communications as "Tanya," he would get only as
far as WCF—not Lucy, personally.

"I think you should let it go, let me take care of it."

Lucy didn't know if she could let Prenter go, so she didn't say anything.

Cody said, "You'll be at the fund-raiser tomorrow, right?"

"Fran would have my head if I weren't. See you there." She hung up before Cody asked to take her. She had been planning on going with Patrick, but since he was out of town she was simply going to take a taxi because she didn't like driving in snow or ice.

She finished her banana and poured a glass of milk. Hardly a meal, but she couldn't eat more. She itched to send Prenter a message, but maybe Cody was right. She'd give him the rest of the weekend to contact her. If he did, she could play the offended date—why should she talk to a guy who'd stood her up?

She had other things to worry about that were much more important than Prenter. She wished Kate had let her help with Morton's computer files, because being proactive might allow her to forget, at least temporarily, that she was in limbo. That she had no real job, simply an internship with the D.C. Medical Examiner's Office. That she was waiting for a slow-moving bureaucracy to grant her an interview, to get her to the next step in the too-long application process for the FBI. The more she sat doing nothing of substance, the more she realized how alone she was. Even with her family, her friends, her job, and her volunteer work, Lucy was very much alone.

Sean decided at the last minute to check in on Lucy and clue her in to his plans. That was a lie, he supposed, because she'd been on his mind all afternoon and stopping by seemed to be inevitable.

She answered the door dressed in sweatpants and a faded blue Georgetown T-shirt, the bulldog mascot prominent. Her hair was wet and loosely braided down her back, the end over her shoulder. "Sean?" she said, her surprise evident in her tone.

"Can I come in for a minute?"

"Of course." She closed the door behind him. It hadn't snowed all day, but when the sun disappeared the temperature had dropped dramatically—and it hadn't been warm to begin with.

"Is Kate here?" Sean asked.

"No—did you want to talk to her?"

Sean didn't know if it was his own wishful thinking, but he thought he detected a hint of disappointment in Lucy's voice.

"I came to talk to you."

Lucy put up a shield, so obvious to Sean that he practically saw the veil fall over her expression. She walked down the hall to the dining room, but Sean said, "Let's go in the family room. A little more comfortable, don't you think?"

She shrugged but led him back. He'd been to the house a couple of times with Patrick. It was far more formal than the RCK house, though the family room was cozy and well lived in.

Lucy sat Indian style on the chair closest to the fireplace, not an open hearth like at RCK, but enclosed and functional, designed to heat the house.

"Well, I thought we should celebrate," Sean said as he sat on the couch, "but I forgot to pick up champagne."

"Celebrate?"

"I talked myself out of a speeding ticket."

Sean grinned widely and Lucy smiled, just a bit. "You did?"

"Yep, the trooper was a hard sell, but that's simply a new challenge."

"How?"

"My charm and wit."

She laughed, then covered her mouth as if she'd surprised herself.

"I can't give away all my secrets," Sean said. "But I did want to talk to you about something."

His tone, though he tried to keep it light, gave him away, and Lucy's good humor quickly dissipated. She was exceptionally perceptive, even to the subtlest signs. It was unnerving, and Sean almost didn't tell her what he was up to. But her family had kept her in the dark for years; he wasn't going to start this new friendship—this *relationship*—with deception.

"Patrick called me earlier and wanted to fly back, but I convinced him to stay in California and finish the job."

Lucy rubbed the back of her neck. "I talked to him late last night and told him not to come, that I'm fine. Morton's dead; he can't hurt me."

Physically was the unspoken word. "That's what I said, but Patrick's concerned and asked if I'd kind of keep an eye out for you. I wanted to be up front about that, because I promised him I would."

She frowned but didn't say anything.

Sean continued. "One of the things we're concerned about, from a security perspective, is that we don't know why Morton came to D.C. It probably has nothing to do with you, but because he was killed nearby, and we don't know what he was up to, I'm going to look into Morton's death. On the q.t."

Lucy had to have heard Sean wrong. Her stomach churned uncomfortably, her light dinner now feeling like a lead ball. She could understand Patrick asking Sean to check up on her, that didn't really bother her that much—in fact, it bothered her not at all—but what did that really have to do with Morton?

She said, "I don't get it. Why?"

Sean leaned forward, his forearms on his thighs. "It's my job, it's what I do best, Lucy, but I don't want to do it behind your back. I'm not going to interfere with the FBI investigation, but some of my research may cross paths with theirs, and I don't want you to be surprised."

She shook her head. Nothing about this would end well, she was certain of it. "I can't have you crossing *any* paths with the FBI. It could hurt my chances getting accepted."

"I have many contacts, and the FBI has many limitations."

But maybe it wasn't just that Sean might get in hot water with the Bureau. It was that he would be digging into *her* life and *her* past. It would be inevitable, even if Morton's murder had nothing at all to do with her.

Except that wasn't the case. Kate was at Quantico now because Morton had been starting Trask Enterprises all over again.

"Lucy?"

"The FBI found evidence in Denver that Morton was re-creating a new online sex website," she said quietly, unable to look Sean in the eye. "Kate's going through the files at Quantico."

Sean didn't say anything. Her stomach tightened even more, and she thought she might be sick. She didn't want to talk about any of this with Sean, but she didn't see how she could avoid it.

"Luce." Sean took her hands into both of his. She stared at their joined hands, a warmth spreading through her, relaxing her better and faster than any of her panic-control techniques, as if he were drawing her tension into him.

"You're not alone. Kate is good at her job, you know that. I'm good at mine. I can find answers. At the very least, we need to know if you're in any danger."

"The only danger I'm in is of being humiliated and exploited on the Internet," she said bitterly.

His hands tightened around hers. "I won't let anyone exploit you."

She jerked her head up and stared at Sean. She had never heard him sound so venomous. Every time she'd seen him, up until last night, he'd been witty and seemingly lighthearted. Smart, but shallow.

He had far more depth than she'd thought. It made her wonder if his typical carefree attitude was his protective shell.

"The FBI isn't going to let this case go. Kate won't let them."

"I agree. But it won't hurt if I sniff around. Quietly."

"Just don't get in trouble." *And don't get me in trouble.*

"I'll do my best," he said, trying to sound casual but failing. "Patrick said there's something you need to do tomorrow. Said if you won't cancel, I should go with you."

"It's a fund-raiser for WCF, the victims' rights group I volunteer for. You'd be bored."

"But you're going?"

"I have to. And honestly, whatever Morton was here for, if it was to hurt me—he's dead. I don't know any of his other cronies, so I highly doubt anyone is after me. There's no reason."

"I agree, but humor us, okay?"

She nodded. She hadn't wanted to go alone, anyway.

"Good. Now, how formal?"

"Business attire."

"And here I thought I could wear my tux. I bought it for my brother's wedding and haven't worn it in two years."

Suddenly, there was nothing Lucy wanted more than to see Sean in a tuxedo. He would look good in anything, but a tux would be . . . incredible. "That might be a tad too formal," Lucy said.

"Another time." He smiled at her and Lucy knew he was talking about them, a date—her and Sean. Just the way he smiled, the way his blue eyes brightened mischievously, the way his fingers began to tap on the palm of her hand, she realized he was flirting. Subtle, but she couldn't miss it. She was speechless.

She couldn't just stare at him. "You want to drive tomorrow or shall I?" Lucy asked Sean.

He looked at her with mocked indignation. "I always drive."

She raised an eyebrow. "You do?"

"I'm a guy. You have brothers, you must understand that it's our right. Isn't it in the male code book? Men always drive?"

He said it with such a straight face she couldn't help but smile. "What if I drive your car?" she asked.

Now he really did look pained. "My car?"

"What, you don't let anyone take it out?"

"No." He was serious about that one. "I might let you drive it someday," he said cautiously. "But not tomorrow."

"I'm going to hold you to that."

"Yeah, I thought so," he grumbled.

TWELVE

Lucy had heard Kate come in late, and hoped she'd get a chance to talk to her about Morton's files first thing in the morning, but while Lucy showered, Kate left. She'd sent her a text message on her cell phone:

I'll be at Quantico all day. We'll talk later. Love you, sis. —Kate.

"Kate." Lucy shook her head, her smile more bittersweet than happy. She loved her sister-in-law so much, which made the lies that much harder. She had to find a way to forgive her, and Dillon, or she wouldn't be able to live under the same roof. More than that, she didn't want this distrust to become a chasm between them, but she didn't know how to get rid of it. It was easy to *say* "I forgive you," but it was much harder to feel it. She prayed time would help.

She went downstairs and heard the thump of the newspaper hitting the front door as she poured a cup of coffee. Lucy rarely read the paper, but her brother Dillon was old-fashioned, maintaining a subscription to a physical newspaper rather than reading online the way Lucy and Kate preferred. The papers had stacked up in his study, and Lucy picked the Saturday morning paper off the stoop to add to the five that were already there. She couldn't miss the small headline in the bottom right corner.

American University Student Killed in Robbery
Possible drug deal gone bad. Story B-3.

She brought the paper to the kitchen table. Normally she didn't care about drug-related crimes, but since a student from a nearby college was involved, it piqued her interest.

The story was shocking.

WASH DC—In a crime all too common in DC, an American University student was gunned down at approximately 9:45 p.m. Thursday night on the 900 block of T Street.

Bradley Harper Prenter, 25, had been at Club 10 prior to the murder, according to DC police. He left with a woman at approximately 9:30 p.m. According to witnesses, a man who appeared to know the woman confronted Prenter in the alley, but an eyewitness who asked to remain anonymous said that after a brief confrontation, Prenter left the alley alone. The man and woman, who authorities are looking for as possible witnesses, left in the opposite direction. Police sources would not confirm nor deny the eyewitness account.

Prenter was shot at point-blank range and was missing his wallet when a couple walking their dogs found him lying next to his vehicle, a late model Porsche.

Prenter was convicted of two sexual assaults in 2008 and was paroled three months ago from the Maryland Correctional Institution at Hagerstown. One DCPD officer who spoke on condition of anonymity said possible drugs were found on his person.

"Our lab is testing a clear liquid packaged in small, plastic vials that were found on the deceased."

When pressed, the officer stated that the packaging was similar to how date-rape drugs such as ketamine, Liquid Ecstasy, or Rohypnol might be packaged.

Police are looking for any witnesses who may have spoken to or seen Prenter at the club, or who may know the woman who was seen leaving with Prenter. Please contact DCPD Hot Tips line.

Liquid date-rape drugs. Lucy dry heaved, waves of first fiery heat then icy cold coursing through her nerve endings. Her skin turned clammy, and she stumbled as she stood and ran to the bathroom, fearing she'd get sick.

Her stomach tightened painfully, but she put her head between her legs and breathed deeply until she felt the sensation pass. She ran cold water into the sink and washed her face, drenching a paper towel and putting it on the back of her neck.

She wanted a shower, the urge to scrub herself clean almost overpowering. But she'd showered only thirty minutes ago, and she wouldn't give in to this unnatural obsession with cleanliness. Instead, she washed her face and hands long enough for her fingers to turn red. Her stomach ached and she leaned against the counter, willing herself to pull it together.

She needed to get a grip. How could she be an FBI agent when a news article could send her into a tailspin? *Focus*.

Prenter was robbed. D.C. was a violent city. How

many murders last year? Two hundred? More than one every other day. One forcible rape *each* day. Robbery and assault was astronomical, dozens every day.

Club 10.

Why was he at Club 10 when he was supposed to be in Fairfax meeting her fictitious cyber-ego? By 9:45 when he was killed, he should have been on his way to jail. What happened?

Cody would have told her had he known, wouldn't he? He was a D.C. cop; how could he not know?

But he didn't work homicides specifically. He was patrol, so even if he'd heard about the robbery he'd have no reason to ask about the victim's identity.

She had to talk to him, but she needed more information about the murder.

Lucy dressed quickly and left. She needed answers. Though it was Saturday, the morgue was still open to employees, and often the autopsy file included a copy of the police report. Having a plan settled her stomach and gave her the determination she needed to get through the rest of the day.

And, despite her alarm, she was more than happy to have something to focus on other than Roger Morton and what Kate found—or didn't find—on his computer.

Noah Armstrong wasn't surprised that Kate Donovan beat him to Quantico Saturday morning. She hadn't wanted to leave last night, but he'd convinced her that if she didn't get a couple of hours' sleep, she'd be no good to him. By the time they had all the material transported to Quantico, logged into evidence, and processed it had been nearly two a.m. Now was not the time to cut corners. If Morton had indeed been working with a partner and that partner was setting up an illegal porn site, if they didn't preserve the chain of evidence, some creep might walk on a technicality. Nothing they found in these files would be admissible if they screwed up the basics.

Kate understood that, even though it obviously frustrated her.

"When did you get here?" He put his briefcase down on the small worktable in the corner of the windowless cave where Kate worked. The room was large but packed with electronics and computers, some working, some not, all taking up space. Noah would go stir-crazy down here; Kate seemed in her element.

"Seven," she replied, fixated on the screen in front of her. It was running through numbers and letters at a great speed; she couldn't possibly be reading anything.

"What are you doing?"

"Breaking Morton's code. It's not a complex one; I have a program that will have it soon—it's only been running for ten minutes. I copied the drive first, so I'm not even working off the original data in case he has a Trojan set up to erase data. But he was never that smart back then. Trask was the brains."

"Trask?"

"Adam Scott. He went by the name Trask."

"What about the disks?" Noah asked. "Do you want me to get started on them?"

"I set Hans up next door."

"Dr. Hans Vigo?"

"Yeah—that's okay, right? You said you were working with him."

Noah didn't have a specific problem. "You could have asked me first."

"I should have. I'm sorry." She glanced at him. "Really. But this case—I made a huge mistake six years ago when I was part of the plea agreement. I have to find these answers, for Lucy. I'm not taking over, and I'll try not to step on your toes, but Hans is one of the few people I know who can view the data on multiple levels—risk assessment of the victims, legal or illegal porn, child endangerment. Plus he knows the players from the years I was tracking Adam Scott and Roger Morton before Paige was killed."

"I understand." He sat down in a metal chair next to Kate. "I need to follow up on something today, but I need to know for sure that I can trust you."

She looked at him. "If you didn't trust me, why did you let me work the data?"

"Because I heard you were the best."

Her lips curved up slightly. "True."

"So I need you, but I also know you have a history with Morton and a relationship with his victim. Whatever you find, I want to know. Everything."

She nodded, but Noah couldn't read her blank expression to discern if she would hold to their agreement. "I can tell you from looking at the physical files that he was copying disks manually onto his computer. He had a system that is very straightforward—after he viewed the disk and presumably imported it, he marked it with a code. 'X' is straight, soft-core porn. 'XX' is straight, hard-core. 'XXX' is violent hard-core, possibly nonconsensual. 'WC' is webcam, probably hidden webcam or homemade sex tapes. The 'WC' is rated by the fetish—up-skirt, hidden videos, et cetera. It's become all the rage now for teenagers to record themselves having sex and post the tapes on the Internet." She shook her head.

"They really don't understand what they're doing with their future."

She handed Noah a sheet. "Hans wrote that when he got here a few hours ago. It gives us a cheat sheet of priorities."

"What's 'P' stand for and why is it in red?"

"Anything with a 'P' means a minor likely under the age of fourteen is involved. Hans sent those immediately to our child pornography task force. They can run them through their offender database, which will save us a lot of time and give us a better chance to save some of them. However, Morton wasn't creating these files. He was creatng a clearinghouse of sorts, which makes tracing the evidence to the source next to impossible."

Very little riled Noah; crimes against children was one of the few things that made him see red. While the FBI and local law enforcement had made great strides in investigating and prosecuting child pornography, the sheer number of cases was staggering. If they couldn't identify the victim or the offender, there was little they could do except put the images in their database in case they popped up again. Working cybercrimes against children was emotionally the hardest job in the Bureau, hands down, and one of the few squads that agents could transfer out of without difficulty.

Kate said, "I'm not going to do anything stupid, Noah. I understand the trust you've placed in me, and believe me that I want to stop whoever Morton was working with as much as you do. The legal way."

Noah stood. "I hope to be back before long. When Abigail went to the motel yesterday, the part-time clerk was there. Today the manager is back, and he's the one who checked Morton in. I hope he has more information, but yesterday we got squat."

Though Lucy's internship was part-time Monday through Friday, most full-time morgue staff rotated shifts, so she knew nearly everyone who worked there. She always made it a point to talk to everyone, even though her position wasn't permanent. She found that she could learn far more about a job, the *real* job, if she befriended people.

She also learned that no one cared about the details of why she wanted to look at files, so when she walked into the intake room to pull the file on Brad Prenter no one questioned her. If someone had, she'd have come up with something plausible—such as making sure she'd filled out forms right. But no one questioned what she did.

The autopsy had been done yesterday afternoon, and she was correct—the body was scheduled for pickup by a local funeral home on Monday morning. Because it was a homicide, all evidence was in the evidence room. Clothing and other contents on Prenter's body were still in the drying chamber. They had to dry the clothing and then comb it for any trace blood evidence. The articles would be packaged for possible trial.

Crime scene photos and the corpses that surrounded Lucy when she worked at the morgue didn't bother her, but this was different: in a weird way, she had known Brad Prenter. He'd been out Thursday night because he thought he was meeting her alter ego, Tanya. A chill went through her body, causing the hair at the base of her skull to rise as she opened the file and saw a picture of his body on the autopsy table. A DVD was attached to the file—homicide autopsies were routinely recorded.

She couldn't view the DVD without breaking the evidence seal, so she put that aside and read the report. Three entry wounds to the abdomen fired from two to four feet away. No exit wounds. Bullets had been sent to the laboratory, standard procedure for ballistics testing. They'd also go to the FBI to add to their database and run against other ballistic reports to determine whether the gun had been used in a previous crime—solved or unsolved.

According to the pathologist, the wounds to the torso were fatal—the liver had been hit, a lung, and the stomach—but the killer had also shot Prenter in the back of the head at an angle that would have had Prenter on his knees. He died instantly from that final shot.

Three bullets to the front, then one in the back. Lucy closed her eyes to picture a possible scenario. Killer faces Prenter—either Prenter knew him and didn't try to run, or the killer startled him and shot him without giving Prenter the chance to run. Prenter falls to his knees, suggesting a low-caliber bullet. Higher-caliber bullets would most likely force the victim back, not down.

Then the killer walked around and shot Prenter in the back of the head. To ensure he was dead.

But Prenter would have died *anyway*. Probably in minutes. Had Prenter known his killer and the killer feared he'd say his name? Was the overkill to make sure he died before his body was found?

A copy of the evidence log was in the file, including the whereabouts of each piece recovered. Items found on Prenter's body were here at the morgue or the lab, though from experience Lucy knew that some personal effects and drugs would be separated and sent to the laboratory or evidence room. Vials found in his pants had been sent to the lab for analysis, but the results weren't back yet. Blood samples—they'd done a standard tox screen in the autopsy room and already had his alcohol content, just barely legally drunk, low enough that he shouldn't have been grossly intoxicated.

A copy of the initial police report was included, but not any of the follow-up investigation. Damn, she really wanted to see the rest of the police report and hoped Cody would get it for her. Was it asking too much? She hoped not; she didn't want to abuse their friendship, but she had to know what had happened with Prenter.

Something felt very wrong, and until she knew the circumstances surrounding his murder she wouldn't let it go.

THIRTEEN

Sean left the city early Saturday morning and drove an hour to an assisted living facility in Baltimore to meet Dustin Fong, another former employee of Trask Enterprises, who had been with the company longer than any other employee.

Fong could barely remember his own name let alone who Roger Morton was. The staff nurse said he'd been shot in the head and left for dead four years ago. He had no memories and while he could function on a minimal level, he had the attention span of a five-year-old. His only visitor was his sister, who came the first weekend of every month from her home in Maine. She'd been there on Sunday, January 2, and before that Saturday, December 4.

Sean crossed him off his list—he'd been promising on paper, but if he had any valuable information, it had been destroyed by the bullet. Roger couldn't have gotten anything from him. Had the sister been in D.C. during the window of time Morton was there, Sean would have tracked her down, but it didn't seem likely. He sent Jayne at RCK West an email to check out Danielle Fong Clements and her husband, Bruce, just to cover his bases, but neither name had come up as a possible associate of Morton or Scott, then or now.

Sean drove back toward the city, stopping at a club in Silver Spring owned by Sergey Yuran, a known trafficker. Yuran brought in whatever was in demand from Russia: prostitutes, drugs, or weapons.

Sean's brother Duke would never have let him talk to Sergey alone. But one thing Sean had that Duke didn't was the ability to hide his emotions and play the game. Duke wouldn't have been able to disguise his loathing of the criminal. Though the club didn't open for another couple hours, the door was unlocked. Sean walked in, face blank, leaving his judgment at the door.

He assessed the club within seconds; five booths were occupied, but the scarred, good-looking blond man in the back sitting with an illegal Russian—Sean could tell simply by how she responded to a stranger walking in—was Sergey Yuran.

There were four bodyguards in the room at every entrance and one next to Yuran. Overkill, in Sean's opinion, but it would give Yuran the sense of complete control in any situation because he had multiple shields. It also told Sean that Yuran was paranoid. He tucked that tidbit away for future use as he approached the largest of the four and handed him a business card. "Sean Rogan to see Mr. Yuran."

The bodyguard told him to stay, and Sean obeyed. Now wasn't the time for sudden movements or disagreements.

He didn't make any pretenses of ignoring the exchange, but watched the bodyguard approach Sergey Yuran and hand him Sean's business card. Yuran had a poker face, but his feet gave him away. They went from crossed at the ankles to flat-footed under the table. No other part of his body registered a reaction. He spoke low, in Russian, and the bodyguard returned.

"Mr. Yuran asked if you have a death wish."

"No sir, I do not." He didn't elaborate, and instead waited for the bodyguard to ask the next question.

"What business do you have with Mr. Yuran?"

"Personal," Sean said.

The bodyguard stared and didn't move. This game could go on all day, and usually Sean would enjoy the challenge, but he didn't have the time.

"I want to know if Mr. Yuran had Roger Morton killed last Friday night. If so, I'd like to shake his hand and thank him. If not, I'd like to know who did, so I can shake their hand."

His blunt response had the bodyguard show a rare, albeit brief, look of surprise. He left Sean again, though two guards moved in to flank him.

When the big guy returned, he ordered Sean to turn around and submit to a search. Sean complied. He wouldn't get near Sergey Yuran with a weapon. "As long as I get them back," he said.

"If you live, you will," Big Guy said.

Fair enough.

Sean was relieved of his .45 and his backup .22. When the guy was done, Sean said loud enough for Yuran to hear, "You missed the H&K blade. Inside right pocket of the jacket."

He couldn't help himself, but it cost him. He was searched again, then a fist connected with his right kidney. He winced and closed his eyes a moment for the pain to pass.

The bodyguard led Sean to Yuran's table. The Russian

girl was gone. Whatever papers Yuran had been reading had also disappeared.

"You have balls, Mr. Rogan," Yuran said in a heavy but understandable Russian accent. Sean knew it was fake. Yuran was Russian, but he'd been born and bred in the U.S.A.

"So I've been told." He didn't sit until the bodyguard motioned for him to do so. When he did, the guard moved to prevent him from suddenly leaving.

"Do you know who I am?"

"More or less."

Yuran said, "Your brother put a hit out on me ten years ago."

"You must have come to an agreement. You're still alive."

Sean had no idea which brother Sergey Yuran was talking about. It could have been Liam, since Liam was in Europe, but Liam wouldn't have put out the hit. He'd most likely have killed Sergey himself, if he felt strongly about it, but Liam didn't feel strongly about much of anything. He didn't see Duke putting a hit out on anyone, even a cold criminal like Yuran, but Duke had surprised him in the past. Kane? The most likely.

But Sean didn't ask. He knew whom to get the answer from later.

"Why do you come to speak to me?"

"Roger Morton was killed last week in Alexandria. Friday night, around midnight, take or leave."

"If I had killed Mr. Morton, there would be no body to find."

"I have no doubt. I didn't think you killed him. He was in D.C. to meet with someone regarding a special business opportunity, similar to the business he ran with his dead partner, Adam Scott. You might know him as Trask."

Sergey laughed heartily. "Ahh, Trask. He let women control him. Just because you kill a woman doesn't make you a man. I suppose it was—what do those God people say? Divine providence? *Fate?*—that had one of his girls killing him in cold blood."

Sean had to use every ounce of control not to react to Yuran calling Lucy one of Scott's "girls." Whether Yuran knew anything about Lucy or not, Sean didn't know, but he didn't want her on his radar. Yuran was watching Sean like a hawk while pretending to be more interested in the scantily clad female bartender working behind the bar.

"Why you come to me?" Yuran asked, sipping his drink. "Why risk your life? I could kill you and no one would find your body. It would be extremely satisfactory to send your head overseas."

It *had* been Liam. What was he up to? *Ten years ago?* But that was a story for another day, because Sean had to focus on finding Morton's killer and making sure that Lucy wasn't in danger.

"Your name popped up as a former associate of Trask Enterprises. I'm not interested in your business. I'm only interested in finding out who Morton was meeting in D.C."

Yuran was quiet, assessing Sean with a blatant interest, running through every possible scenario in his head. Sean knew because he often did the same thing.

"I have no reason to help you, Mr. Rogan."

"Of course you do. It'll be your good deed for the year."

"I don't do good deeds."

"Might as well start now."

He knew something. Sean felt it in his bones. Yuran stared at him for over a minute, then said, "I didn't kill Roger. He wasn't worth a bullet. But I did hear about a new venture. It wasn't Roger asking, however."

When Yuran didn't continue, Sean barely restrained himself from prompting the Russian. There had been a subtle shift in the bodyguards behind him, but Sean didn't feel that the threat level had been raised.

"Word came down from a scumbag named Ralston. I heard he was spreading the offer far and wide, and I don't appreciate competing for business. I had Johan follow up—" Yuran looked at Mr. Big Guy. "What did you learn, Johan?"

"Ralston was full of shit."

Yuran smiled. "Someone put the word out and used Ralston to do it, but when I showed interest, it dried up. Frankly, Mr. Rogan, if I may be blunt, I wanted to gut the prick for wasting my time. But I have a heart."

Sean smiled and Yuran smiled back. Coldly.

"Thank you for your time, Mr. Yuran."

He stood. Big Guy didn't budge until Yuran nodded so faintly Sean almost missed it.

"Mr. Rogan."

Sean turned back to the trafficker.

"Tell your brother Liam I haven't forgotten."

A chill ran up Sean's spine. He gave Yuran a faint nod, then retrieved his weapons.

When he reached the door, Yuran said, "The only reason you're alive is because I know you haven't seen your brother in fifteen years. Make it another fifteen."

* * *

Lucy met Cody at the Starbucks on M Street during his lunch break.

"What's wrong?" he asked, sitting down as soon as he saw her.

"I need to talk to you about Brad Prenter's murder."

He stared at her with cop eyes, assessing, curious, and a bit worried. "You saw the paper."

"Why didn't you tell me?"

"I didn't know until this morning."

"Did you know he was shot four times? Three times in the abdomen and once in the back of the head?"

He straightened. "How do you know that? It wasn't released—" He caught himself. "You went to the morgue."

"I read the autopsy report."

"Why on earth would you do that? You could have asked me."

"I wanted more information before we talked. He was supposed to be at the Firehouse, not Club 10. Doesn't that seem suspicious to you? That Prenter was supposed to meet a girl at one club, and ends up twenty miles away and across the river at about the same time?"

"How do you know it was the same time?"

"Because he was killed between nine-thirty and ten. The article stated that he was in the bar hitting on a girl before he left with her—"

"Lucy, we talked about this last night. I thought we'd agreed that he had pegged the date with 'Tanya' as a setup."

"I don't know." She frowned and stared at her coffee cup.

"Lucy?"

She glanced at him.

"Even though it's popular, Club 10 is in the center of six blocks of bad streets," Cody said. "There's a mugging practically every night. Even two homicides just last month. They found drugs on him—I haven't seen the lab reports, but maybe he was trying to score, and it went south. Do you know how many drug-related murders we have in D.C.?"

"I know, but—" She sighed. Maybe Cody was right. There was a logical explanation.

"Would you feel better if I looked into it?"

She nodded. "I'd appreciate it."

"What do you think happened?"

"I don't know. I just want to know why he was at *that* bar. Why he stood Tanya up. If I tipped him off, I need to know how I did it. I went over every chat transcript with him last night—I don't see it."

"Send them to me. I'll take a look. And maybe it wasn't you—he could have spotted me."

"Thank you," she said. "Even if you just find out he goes there all the time—that's good enough for me. Or if he got a better offer. Whatever, there's a reason, and I need to know."

"Your curiosity will make you a great FBI agent."

She smiled. "I still haven't heard back about my interview."

"You will. You know how slow those bureaucrats can be." He reached out and squeezed her hand. "I'll see what I can find out about Prenter's death, and I'll bet there's a logical explanation as to why he bailed on 'Tanya' and went to Club 10."

Robbie "RNR" Ralston lived in a third-floor flat of a tiny row house in a decrepit area on the edge of the D.C.

limits. Sean rapped on the door, then stepped back, listening for movement inside. He heard nothing, but something felt strange. He shivered. He squatted in front of the door and pressed his fingers to the crack between the door and the floor. The air was ice cold—colder than it should be even if the guy was keeping his heat low to save on the bill. In this cold spell, even with blue skies, if Ralston had turned off his heat, he probably hadn't been home for quite a while.

Sean considered trying to find someone to let him in. He could talk himself in and out of nearly any situation, but a rental property this small probably didn't have an on-site manager and he didn't want to prolong the situation. He pulled out his lock pick and popped the old lock in seconds.

As soon as he slipped in and closed the door behind him he knew exactly why the apartment was so cold—every window had been cracked open an inch. He pulled his gun, though he suspected that if anyone was in this apartment, he was dead.

The front room was cluttered but neat. However, the computer on a small desk against the far wall had been smashed. The hard drive had been removed; the shell of the CPU was open and exposed. There were only two rooms in the apartment, and Sean found Ralston, long dead, on the bedroom floor, shot in the back of the head. On the bed was a half-packed suitcase.

"Fuck," Sean muttered. He pulled out his phone and stared at it. He considered, just for a second, calling the D.C. police, coming up with a plausible excuse for his presence. But that would prolong the inevitable. Ralston was connected to Morton, which made this murder likely connected to Morton. Which made this murder connected to Lucy.

The apartment had been kept cold to slow the rate of decomposition and minimize the smell to avoid quick discovery. Why? To avoid connecting this murder with Morton's?

He dialed Kate Donovan. "It's Sean Rogan. I would have called the cavalry, but I don't know who's in charge of Morton's murder investigation."

"What's going on?"

"I was doing my own side investigation and came across an associate of Morton's. He's dead." Sean glanced at the body. "A very cold stiff."

FOURTEEN

Noah had spent more time than he'd planned at Quantico talking to Kate and the cybercrimes task force about the files they'd recovered from Morton's computer. That had been followed by a conference-call briefing with Hans Vigo and Rick Stockton. When he finally broke away well after the lunch hour, Abigail had a sandwich waiting for him, which he ate during their drive to the Triple Tree Motel near Dulles Airport.

The manager, Paul Grunelli, was a scrawny guy in his fifties with stringy, thinning gray hair and the aroma of a heavy smoker. He looked up from his television when Noah and Abigail entered the motel's small, dingy office.

"Room?" he asked.

Noah flashed his badge. "Questions."

Grunelli turned back to the television with a shrug. "Ask."

"Turn the TV off, please, Mr. Grunelli," Abigail said.

"I don't want to miss—"

"We can ask the questions in the quiet interview room of FBI headquarters, if you'd prefer," Noah said.

"Fuck," Grunelli mumbled, but he turned off the television. "What?"

Abigail slid a picture of Morton across the counter.

"This man registered early in the morning on January sixth, according to your logs. He paid for three days in cash up front, used the name Cliff Skinner. Do you remember him?"

Grunelli shrugged.

"He never checked out," Noah added.

"Oh, him." He narrowed his eyes at them. "Weren't one of your people here yesterday picking up his crap from the room?"

"That would be me," Abigail said. "But your relief manager hadn't actually seen Mr. Morton, said you'd checked him in and had been working that weekend. He was in room 103—you can see it from your chair there."

"If the blinds are open," Grunelli added.

Noah didn't have patience for the back-and-forth with a jerk like Grunelli. "Morton was killed in Alexandria less than two days after he checked in. We're retracing his steps. When did you see him?"

"Dead, eh? Well—he checked in at eight-something on Thursday, which I noted in the log. And he was gone most of the day after that. Came back that night, then left again Friday morning. Didn't see him after that."

"How did he get here? Taxi?"

Grunelli shook his head. "Car."

"Rental?" They hadn't heard back from the rental companies yet.

"Probably, I didn't check."

"Did you write down the plates?"

"Why would I do that?"

"Oh, I don't know, many motels do it for security, so only guests park in their lot."

Grunelli barked out a laugh. "Like I have that problem. Don't know the plates, can't tell you the make. It was white, that's all I remember. Foreign sedan-type. Like a Toyota Corolla or Honda or something."

Noah made a note to stop at Dulles, the most likely place that Morton had rented a car. The analysts had looked for a rental, but if Morton used a name other than his own or Cliff Skinner, they might not have tracked it down yet. Sometimes face-to-face interviews could yield better information, faster.

"And the last time you saw Morton was when he drove away on Friday morning. What time?"

"Before lunch. I don't know when. He'd paid up; I didn't think much about him until he didn't check out on Sunday. By three, I had to haul my ass to his room. He wasn't there. I boxed his stuff and that was it."

"Did Morton have any visitors while he was here?"

"No." Grunelli frowned and looked down.

"Do you remember something?" Abigail asked.

"The car. I thought I saw his car in the lot early Saturday morning. I mean, real early, like two or three. I was outside having a smoke, upstairs on my deck—the owner gets all anal about me smoking inside. It was fucking cold, but I couldn't sleep. And I saw the car. I hadn't heard it come in, so I was like just watching and smoking and this guy left room 103."

"Morton?"

"No. Another guy. Not as big as Morton. Different shape, but I couldn't tell you if he was taller or shorter or whatever. It was dark. I just knew it wasn't the guy who rented the room, and he got into the white car and drove off. That was the last time I saw the car."

"And you weren't suspicious?"

"Hell no. The guests here have people come and go all

the time. As long as they're not loud or fighting, they mind their business and I mind my business."

"And you're certain it was the same car?"

He shrugged. "No, but I don't get many people driving brand-new cars into this place, unless it's a rental, and most of the guests here don't drive rentals, either."

When they stepped out of Grunelli's squalid office, Noah said to Abigail, "Contact Vigo and get an administrative warrant in the works for the rental agencies. Once we ID the company, we'll want all the logs and GPS tracking, if they have it."

"Most do these days."

"It should be pretty straightforward." Noah pulled out his phone. It had vibrated several times during his conversation with Grunelli.

"Donovan has been ringing me." He called Kate right back. "It's Noah."

"Robbie Ralston, one of Morton's closest associates from the old days, is dead."

"Ralston?" Noah didn't remember the name.

"He was a low-level pimp, but provided a steady stream of girls for Trask and Morton back when Trask Enterprises was mostly legal. I ran him while waiting for you to call me back. He served a few years in prison, was on disability, and get this—he had a ticket bought and paid for to Miami last Sunday."

Noah was confused. "He was killed in Miami?"

"No, he was killed in his apartment. He never made the flight."

"Send me the information—I'll head over there immediately. Who's on scene?"

"No one yet. I have an ERT unit standing by."

"Why didn't you call the local police?"

"Sean Rogan found the body."

Rogan? "*What?*"

He must have sounded as pissed off as he felt, because Kate quickly said, "Talk to him. He called me because he didn't have your number." She paused, then said, "Sean's looking into Morton's past because my family asked him to."

"And you *knew*?"

"I just found out. After all, Patrick is his partner, and Patrick is out of town and worried about the situation. Sean called me as soon as he found the body. He's not screwing around."

A Rogan in the middle of his investigation was not what Noah wanted.

"Noah?"

"Where's Rogan now?

"At the scene."

"I'm on my way."

Sean stood outside Ralston's building while the FBI's Evidence Response Team did their forensic work upstairs. He supposed he had Kate to thank that he wasn't officially detained, but while he waited for Agent Noah Armstrong to arrive he called Jayne instructing her to dig deeper into Ralston and Morton's history, focusing on shared connections. Clearly, Ralston's murder was no coincidence.

Why had Sergey Yuran sent him here? Did the Russian trafficker know that Ralston was dead? Had he killed him when the deal into the online sex trade went south? It didn't seem to be up Yuran's alley—he was ruthless, but this wasn't his M.O.—and the smashed computer was a sign that Ralston had information that the killer didn't want getting out.

Or was there something more here? Who else had Ralston talked to about Morton's deal? And who ultimately bought into the scheme? Had Morton and Ralston cut out an unknown partner? Taken the money and run? Ralston had the suitcase, Morton had violated his probation—there was something just out of reach. He needed more information. But there was no doubt in his mind that Morton and Ralston's murders were connected. He'd inspected the body and the guy had been dead for several days. The cold apartment slowed decomp, but Sean knew enough about forensics that the coroner could account for ambient temperature and give a good range for time of death.

An elderly black woman with a small Pomeranian in her purse and a canvas grocery bag over her shoulder turned the corner and walked slowly down the damp sidewalk toward Sean. He covered the distance quickly and said, "Let me help."

She smiled, revealing perfect teeth that didn't quite look real. "Thank you, young man." She handed him her grocery bag.

Sean put his hand on her elbow. "Where are you going?"

She gestured toward Ralston's building. "The first-floor apartment on the right."

The entrance was only about 150 feet away, but it took several minutes to reach the front stoop. The little dog stared at Sean but didn't bark. "Cute dog." Not his type of pet, but he figured the woman was a possible witness.

"She's a little bitch, but I like her."

Sean suppressed a grin.

The woman glanced at him as she climbed the front step. "You're not from here."

"No. There was a homicide upstairs."

She shook her head and sighed. "I'm not surprised. Two B or Three D?"

He raised an eyebrow. "Three D."

"Robbie. I hadn't seen him this week."

"Did you know he was planning a trip?"

"He don't like me."

"Why not? He must not have been friendly."

"He don't like blacks. He tolerated me. I own this building." She winked, then took another step and leaned against Sean. Her hand was tight with arthritis.

"Doesn't the grocery deliver?"

She laughed. "Here? Naw. I go out once a week, and my granddaughter comes by every Wednesday to take me to bingo and brings my medicine and groceries. But sometimes I need a few other things. Look in the bag."

Sean did. There was a fifth of Scotch—good stuff, too, not the cheap rotgut—and a pack of Marlboro Lights, along with a small steak.

"Missy won't buy me liquor." She shook her head in disgust. "It's not like I'm an alcoholic—one shot a night. And she won't buy me steak, neither. Says it's not good for my arteries. And don't get me started on the cigarettes. I'm eighty-nine years old, dammit, and I don't much care if I see ninety. I don't think one damn cigarette a day is going to kill me."

"I'm Sean Rogan," he said as he helped her onto the final step. "I'm a private investigator, and very pleased to meet you, Mrs.—"

"Tessie. Call me Tessie, everyone does. You have questions about Robbie?"

"I do, in fact."

He held open the door that led to the small lobby of the row house. She walked to the door with 1A painted in white.

"Who's upstairs? I didn't see any police cars."

"The FBI."

She turned and craned her neck up to look at him, eyes wide. "The FBI? Well, Robbie did get himself into a little situation, didn't he? Was he playing both sides?"

"Both sides?"

Tessie laughed. "He was an informant, you know. Used to be, anyhow. Come on in, I'll tell you all about him. Did you know he used to be a pimp? Yep, I've lived here forty-six years, Robbie moved in—oh, nineteen ninety-three. Four? Was in prison once, but paid his rent so I aired out his place once a week."

"He paid his rent from prison?"

She shrugged. "His cop did."

His cop. Sean was very interested in who this cop was, and what kind of information Ralston gave him that paid the rent on a place for however many months Ralston was in prison.

Tessie continued as she pushed open the door. "He'd get drunk and *blah blah blah*. Didn't know what to believe, but after a while I learned to tell his bullshit from the truth."

Sean stepped into her immaculate but overheated apartment. He'd hit the jackpot with information and hoped Agent Armstrong didn't get his panties in a wad about him talking to a potential witness. But one thing Sean knew about Feds is that they didn't share information, and if he was going to help Lucy he needed to know everything they knew.

Noah walked upstairs to Ralston's third-floor apartment and met Agent Dale Jarvis, the head of the ERT unit. "What have you learned?" Noah asked as he assessed the apartment.

Jarvis walked Noah through the scene. "No sign of forced entry. As you can see, the computer is destroyed. The UNSUB removed the hard drive from the box and smashed it. We've collected all the pieces, but most of the circuits and chips are completely destroyed. There's no salvaging it, but we'll run it by our tech people. They've been known to perform miracles, on occasion."

"I'll get a warrant for his ISP to check browsing history and any external storage sites he might have."

Jarvis looked around the room. "And the place was searched, but not extensively. Possibly the killer was looking for something and found it." He walked down the short, narrow hall to the small bedroom. Ralston's body was prone at the foot of the sagging double bed. A suitcase was open on it.

"He had a plane ticket for Miami he never used," Noah said.

"No sign of defensive wounds, but my guess is he was pushed down." Jarvis gestured toward the victim's hands with a laser pen. "He fell or was pushed while holding something—and if you follow the likely trajectory . . ."

Noah followed the thin red beam to the base of the open closet, where several bottles of pills had rolled to a stop. One had opened, spilling small, oval-shaped pills every which way. Jarvis pointed behind him. "The bathroom is there. The vic grabs his meds, comes back to the bedroom, walking toward the closet, is pushed down from behind. Drops the pills, is shot without hesitation."

"Why do you say that?"

"The vic didn't move his hands; they are laying as someone would fall."

"Silencer? Wouldn't someone in the building hear a gunshot?"

"Yeah, that's my guess. We'll know more when we get the bullet out. It's in there. Two entry wounds, but they're close. Based on the location, either bullet would have done the job."

"Pro?"

"Silent entry, no disturbance, bullet to the back of the head and destroyed computer?"

Noah nodded and left the bedroom. "Find anything else? Motive?"

"You know what I do about his background. He has no arrests since his last stint eight years ago. On disability. Kept under the radar."

"Abigail is running a full background on him, pulling financials, travel—he was an associate of the dead guy at the Washington Marina."

"I heard." Jarvis looked at him pointedly. "Hard not to hear when the assistant director himself takes an interest in the case."

So much for discretion. "What did Rogan say about finding the body?"

"Said the door was unlocked."

"Right."

Jarvis shrugged. "Could have been, or he's good at picking locks."

"I'd go with the latter."

"He noted that the apartment was unusually cold, saw the computer destroyed, and checked on the well-being of any occupants."

Why had Sean Rogan been here in the first place? "Where is he now?"

"Downstairs."

"I didn't see him."

"He said he'd wait for you." Jarvis looked out the window. "His car is still here."

"I'll find him."

Sean thanked Tessie for the coffee and cookies—he had a weak spot for homemade sweets, and the oatmeal cookies were amazing—and stepped into the small lobby. He saw one of the ERT guys coming down the stairs.

"Hey Rogan, Agent Armstrong has been looking for you."

"I've been right here." He attempted to sound innocent.

Sean followed the ERT dude out to the street. The coroner's van pulled up and double-parked. Sean tried to pick out Noah Armstrong among the assembled agents. It wasn't hard when one suit strode over with a tight jaw. "Where have you been?"

"It was cold outside," he said, not liking the instant hostility of the Fed. "The landlady invited me in for coffee." And an earful. "Agent Armstrong, I presume."

The Fed nodded curtly. "Why were you here in the first place?"

"As I told Kate, I'm just making sure that Lucy Kincaid is safe. Do you know why Morton was in town?

Whether he had a partner? Whether he was working with Ralston?"

"We're pursuing all leads, but I will remind you that this is a federal investigation."

"I might have some information that can help in your federal investigation."

"I'd suggest you share any and all information pertaining to this matter. I don't have to tell you that withholding information from law enforcement is an obstruction of justice, and your P.I. license isn't going to protect you. You're on thin ice here, Rogan."

Sean frowned. This guy was a lot more hostile than he should be. He seemed to not like Sean at all, which was unusual because Sean usually made a good impression—unless he didn't want to.

"Look, Armstrong, we're on the same team, for the most part. We both want to make sure that Lucy isn't in any danger from whatever shit Morton was doing in D.C. before he got himself killed."

"What is your interest in this other than your association with the Kincaids?"

"My interest? It's my business. But you know that already."

"What were you doing in Ralston's apartment?"

Sean forced himself to relax. "I knew that Ralston was one of Morton's associates and wanted to talk to him, that's all. Like I said, my job is to make sure Lucy isn't in danger. I needed to assess whether any of Morton's associates were a threat to her."

"You're her bodyguard."

"I wouldn't say that."

"What *would* you say?"

"Exactly what I did say. Roger Morton died in the

same area where one of his victims lived," Sean said firmly. "That's not a coincidence. If he had plans to harm Lucy, or had a partner—I need to find out."

"That's my job."

"No, your job is to find out who killed the bastard. My job is to make sure Lucy is safe. It's what I do, hence the 'protective services' after 'Rogan-Caruso-Kincaid.' "

"You all think you're above the law," Armstrong said.

"What?" Sean had sensed that Armstrong didn't like him, but this sounded as though he *knew* him.

Armstrong didn't respond, but said, "Did you touch or take anything from the apartment?"

"No—just the doorknob." He grinned. "Scout's honor."

Armstrong wasn't amused. "I'd appreciate it if you'd leave the investigation to me, and guard Ms. Kincaid's person, instead of attempting to interview my witnesses."

Sean wanted to leave and let the Fed try to get the information about Ralston out of Tessie. That was his job, right? But that kind of knee-jerk reaction was what had gotten Sean in trouble in the past, and he was trying to curb the tendency.

So he bit back his initial reaction, and said as casually and conciliatorily as he could, "I had an interesting conversation with the landlady. She's known Ralston for nearly twenty years."

"You talked to a witness?"

"I helped her with her groceries. We chatted."

Armstrong stared at him in disbelief. "Chatted."

"She invited me in for cookies."

"And milk?"

"Coffee." Sean grinned. Playing with Mister Special

Agent Armstrong was getting fun. "I can introduce you if you'd like."

"Cut the crap, Rogan."

Sean straightened, mimicking a soldier at attention. Just the facts. "The last time Tessie remembers seeing Ralston was Wednesday night, when her granddaughter walked in after their weekly bingo date. However, she heard him in the lobby Friday morning arguing with another man. She didn't go out—she was still in her pajamas—but she was getting ready to call the cops when the visitor left and Ralston stomped up the stairs."

"Friday," Armstrong said flatly.

"She also knows a lot about Ralston's rap sheet, which I'm sure you've already pulled. But the one thing you might not know yet is that Ralston was an informant."

Sean hid his enjoyment as he watched Armstrong react to the information.

"Informant."

"Do you ever speak in complete sentences?" Sean jibed.

Armstrong stepped forward, a vein pulsing in his jaw, and Sean didn't budge, but he realized there was something more going on between him and Armstrong than he knew.

"What branch were you in?" Sean asked, changing the subject.

Armstrong didn't blink. "Air Force. Ravens."

Security force. They worked heavily in South and Central America, where Sean's brother Kane had the strongest influence. Had his oldest brother messed with this former Raven?

"You were never in the armed forces," Armstrong said with disdain.

Sean needed to call Duke to find out . . . but he didn't want to pull in his brother. It had been hard enough to get Duke to let him and Patrick open up RCK East and slide out from under the auspices of their controlling brothers. He'd find out more about Noah Armstrong through his own sources. And whatever the problem was, it had nothing to do with Lucy or this case.

"No, I never served. But I do fly."

"Do you?"

"You probably already know that."

Armstrong didn't comment.

"Ralston was an informant for the D.C. police for years, as long as Tess has known him. The cop's name was Jerry Biggler. Know him?"

"No. But I will."

FIFTEEN

Sean was speechless when Lucy came to the door wearing a royal-blue dress that somehow managed to be both modest and sexy as hell. It had a high neck and revealed little flesh, but it hugged her shapely and athletic body as if it had been created just for her. The skirt swirled around her calves as it would on a dancer. With her hair pinned loosely back, she was, simply, stunning.

"Thanks again," Lucy said as if *he* were the one doing her a favor. She set the alarm and locked the door.

Sean found his voice. "Hey, beautiful, my pleasure."

She hesitated before putting her keys in her purse, and Sean mentally hit himself. That sounded like such a line. A line he'd happily use on any of his previous girl-friends, but Lucy was nothing like them, and he wasn't going to treat her like the flavor of the month.

Sean lowered his voice. "I really mean it, Lucy, you look amazing." He reached up and touched one of her thick curls. Her hair was soft and shiny, and her lips—he knew he'd better not think about her full, painted lips right now.

"Thank you." She smiled, and he relaxed. He wanted to give Lucy a fun night out, even if they were going to a fund-raiser for a victims' rights group. He intended to convince her to go for dessert afterward.

He opened the passenger door for her, and she said, "Chivalry isn't dead. I thought my brother Dillon was the only one who still opened doors."

"I don't do it for just anyone," he said as he closed the door. She might have thought that was a line, but it was the truth.

As soon as he pulled away from the curb, Lucy asked, "About what you said yesterday, looking into why Roger Morton was in D.C.—"

"Let's not ruin this evening." He wanted to tell Lucy about what he'd learned, and about Ralston's murder, but he didn't want her to be upset or preoccupied with Morton tonight.

"Not knowing is worse than knowing."

"I haven't learned anything important." He hesitated, then said, "I narrowed down all Morton's known associates within a hundred-mile radius who are still alive and not in prison. The three I spoke to don't know anything."

Lucy glanced at him, her narrow eyebrow raised. "And they told you the truth?"

"Yes," he said. "I'm a Rogan."

"Is that like having a golden lasso?"

"Naw, I don't look so good in blue shorts with stars."

"You don't have to do this."

"I know." But he did. He couldn't explain it to Lucy, not yet—he wasn't sure he could explain it to himself. But Sean despised bullies, and Roger Morton had been a bully. Whoever killed him was a bigger bully, and that person was a potential threat to people Sean cared about: his partner, his business, and Lucy. The entire Kincaid family had treated Sean like one of their own, from Jack to Patrick to the brothers and sisters he'd met when he went to San Diego to help Patrick with a project last summer. Sean had a large family, but they weren't like the Kincaids. His family was spread all over the world—Kane in South America, Duke in California, Liam and Eden in Europe.

He couldn't help but wonder wistfully if his parents hadn't died in a plane crash, would his brothers and sister have ended up in the same places they were today, or would they have been as close knit as the Kincaids? Probably not. All of them, from his parents down to him, had wanderlust. Only Duke had stayed at home, and that was largely because he'd taken on the responsibility of raising Sean, then a teenager, after the crash.

"Sean?" Lucy said, breaking him from his melancholy thoughts.

"There's one more thing," he said reluctantly. "One of the contacts I was trying to make is dead. Ralston. They haven't narrowed the time of death, but he missed a flight last Sunday. I'll figure out how it's connected."

"But—"

"Tonight, let's just put it aside, okay?"

She sighed. "Okay."

He didn't think she'd be able to banish all thoughts of the situation from her mind, but at least he could work double time to distract her.

"Sean, thank you. I appreciate your attention."

It took Sean a second to realize she wasn't talking about his personal attention, but his professional interest in Morton's death. He didn't want Lucy to think of him only in a business context. He was good at reading women in general, but he was having a harder time knowing what Lucy was thinking. She kept a large part of herself closed off, and he needed to find a way to get her to open up to him.

At the Omni Shoreham Hotel, Sean bypassed the valet parking and parked his GT himself.

"Is no one allowed to touch your car?" Lucy asked as he opened her door.

"*Especially* not valets."

Lucy glanced at Sean and her anxiety about the new information about another dead body faded. Sean winked at her and took her hand as she stepped from the car. Lucy felt that not-so-subtle tingle she'd had earlier when she first opened her door and saw Sean in the tailored dark-gray pinstripe suit, the cerulean tie nearly matching the blue of his eyes. He was breathtaking, and she wasn't used to physical attraction. She admired good-looking men in an intellectual, *"Yes, he's attractive,"* kind of way. But with Sean Rogan, her body reacted before her mind, responding to his voice, his touch, the way he looked at her, before her thoughts could catch up that maybe he was flirting. And that maybe she liked it.

Sean draped her wool coat over her shoulders in a gesture that was as timeless as it was endearing, yet she didn't sense that he was being calculating. He took her arm as they walked through the lobby toward the fundraiser.

"Give me the rundown," Sean whispered as they approached the bustling reception room. "Who's who and all that."

Lucy looked around. "There's Fran Buckley, the director of WCF. She retired from the FBI several years ago. Senator Paxton introduced us when I interned with him, and I started volunteering."

"You interned with a senator?"

"He was on the Judiciary Committee, and I wanted to learn everything I could about how Congress impacted federal law enforcement and criminal justice issues."

"For your FBI career," Sean said.

"Pretty much. I didn't particularly like working in Congress, but I learned a lot."

She scanned the crowd. "There are several elected officials here, the deputy mayor, and a lot of law enforcement—we have several cops who volunteer for WCF when off-duty. The chief of police is here. That pretty blonde next to the buffet? She's Gina Mancini, Fran's *über*-efficient assistant. She's talking to Donald Thorne, one of our top donors. I don't know who the other couple is with them."

"Okay, overload," Sean said.

"You're in luck, it looks like they're getting ready to start the speeches. And it won't take long; Fran likes to mingle. That's when she says she raises the most money—one-on-one."

"Would you like a drink?"

"Thank you. Red wine, please."

Lucy watched Sean stride to the bar, where he comfortably chatted with the bartender. He could walk into any room, any situation, and make friends. Lucy couldn't remember ever being so comfortable or carefree—though carefree wasn't quite the right word for Sean. He was alternately serious and driven, then light and fun. She wondered who the real Sean Rogan was, and if she'd find out.

After Fran briefly spoke about the state of WCF and gave her thank you's, she introduced the chief of police, who gave a speech on crime stats and sex crimes in D.C. and the surrounding area.

Sean returned with her wine. He was drinking beer from the bottle, and she grinned. It fit him, sleek suit notwithstanding.

"Make a new friend?" she asked, nodding toward the bartender.

"Everyone has a story," he said. "Some are really interesting." He whispered, "Who's that going onstage?"

"Aubrey Lewis. Her daughter was killed by a repeat sex offender two years ago. Senator Paxton introduced legislation to tighten restrictions on sex offenders, and she testified before Congress. She's amazing."

After a brief, moving speech, Aubrey introduced Senator Paxton.

Jonathon Paxton, sixty-six, played tennis and golf regularly and took his health seriously. He walked onto the small stage, gave Aubrey a hug, and took the podium. He began with the story of how he got involved in WCF. It all started with the murder of his daughter more than two decades ago.

It was hard for Lucy to give her full attention to the speeches while Sean was standing so close to her. He wore a subtle aftershave or cologne that had her inching closer, trying to figure out what it was. When he leaned down to whisper in her ear, she shivered.

"Look at that couple," he said quietly. "Mr. and Mrs. Andrew Valerio; they own VT Communications."

"You know them?"

"They hired RCK a couple of years ago to test their security. Took me seventeen hours, but I broke in."

"You should talk to them. I don't know them personally, but they've been supporters of WCF for years."

He shrugged. "They don't know me."

"But—"

"Duke always works with the clients."

"How'd you know it was them?"

"I saw their photo once."

"Good memory." She glanced up at him, surprised at how close his face was to hers as they quietly chatted in the back of the room.

Suddenly, it felt as if a thousand ants were crawling under her skin. She glanced around the room but didn't see anyone staring at her. Still, she couldn't shake the feeling that there were eyes upon her. She rubbed her arms, and Sean put his arm around her.

"Lucy?" he questioned.

She didn't answer, pretending to listen to the senator's speech. She pretended to ignore the people glancing not-so-discreetly at her. Her story wasn't a deep, dark secret. She'd spoken to schools, written fund-raising letters for Fran, even testified in the Judiciary Committee in support of Senator Paxton's legislation that had been dubbed "Jessie's Law." She never enjoyed it, always felt tainted, and worse, hated that people pitied her, that they thought she'd been a stupid, irresponsible teenager. No one would ever say it out loud, but many held her accountable for putting herself in a vulnerable position.

She'd agreed to meet her attacker in a public place because she'd believed it was "safe." She'd thought he was a college student named Trevor Conrad. She'd been wrong.

Applause signaled that the senator was done speaking, but Lucy was still on edge. She said to Sean, "Want to get out of here?"

He took her hand. "You're shaking."

"I'm just cold."

He stared at her. "Lucy, what's really wrong?"

She froze, tilted her chin up, and stared him down. "I just told you." She tried to pull her hand away, but Sean held on.

"Lucy, something has you spooked. Tell me."

Lucy didn't want to share anything with Sean. She tried to put him back into the role of her brother's partner, but she'd already gone far beyond that. And the way he was looking at her implied a much more intimate relationship than a business one.

"It's personal," she said, hoping she made clear by her tone that their relationship wasn't. Even though she wasn't sure how she felt about that, either, or exactly how attracted she was to him.

She felt comfortable with Sean, and she liked that he was smart. But he was also into his toys. His car. His pool table. Patrick had even told her he had a plane he flew all the time. She was too focused on her career and her future to get involved with anyone who wasn't equally devoted. The best thing was to put distance between them so she could think clearly.

Not that he was interested. Or she. Or . . .

"Lucy."

She jumped, and Sean squeezed her hand as she turned to face Fran. "Fran."

"I didn't mean to startle you." She smiled at Sean. "I'm Frances Buckley, WCF's director."

Sean extended his hand and smiled his award-winning grin, melting Lucy's resolve to flee from him.

"Sean Rogan," he said.

"Patrick's partner," Lucy explained.

"Very nice to meet you," Fran said, giving Lucy a

smile that showed her approval of Lucy's choice in escort. Lucy resisted the urge to explain to Fran that they were just friends. That might be hard to prove, since Sean was still holding her hand.

Sean said, "The room is crowded. I hope they're all paying customers."

"Even in this tough economy, we were able to surpass what we raised last year."

Lucy saw Cody stride into the room and scan it, spotting her just after she saw him. He walked over. "Lucy, can I talk to you privately?"

Lucy felt a distinctly protective shift in Sean's posture, and Cody glanced at him with stern eyes. "Sean, this is my friend Cody Lorenzo, with the D.C. Police Department. He volunteers at WCF. Can you give us a moment?"

"Go ahead." Sean dropped her hand, but Lucy felt him watching her follow Cody outside the ballroom into the hall.

"What's wrong? You're agitated."

She couldn't imagine he'd be this upset that she'd come to the event with Sean.

"Tell me the truth, Lucy. Did you change the meeting place with Prenter?"

She blinked several times, switching her focus. "What? Why on earth would I do that?"

"Before I came here, I stopped by Club 10. Prenter boasted to the bartender that he was going to get laid, that he was meeting a hot blonde who liked to talk dirty online."

"That's bullshit and you know it. Fran has a copy of all my transcripts!" Cody hesitated, and Lucy grew enraged. "You think I could have played the game that far?"

"No, not under normal circumstances, but if the chats weren't getting what we wanted out of him, maybe you pushed a little too hard, got in too deep. I'm not blaming you, Lucy, but—"

"Hold it. What makes you think it was me? Maybe he was chatting online with someone else. I did not change the meeting place, nor did I talk about anything sexual. Read the damn logs—I flirted, nothing more. Why don't you believe me? Why would you think that Fran would have allowed it?"

"You're sharp. You could have changed the logs. Or logged in from home and not copied the transcripts."

She shook her head and squeezed her lips tight. That Cody could think she was capable of such a thing! He knew exactly who she was and where she'd been in her life. He knew what had happened to her, and why her volunteer work was so important. She would never jeopardize her career with the FBI or Fran's trust in her by crossing the line with a suspect.

Cody reached out to her. "I'm sorry, Lucy—I had to ask."

"You didn't ask. You accused me. And you shouldn't have had to ask in the first place! You should have known that I would never do anything like that. There is a logical explanation: Prenter was meeting up with another woman. Or he was lying through his teeth. You know how these rapists are, embellishing the truth to make themselves feel powerful and in control. It was a fantasy in *his* head, not one I deliberately put there."

"You're right, I just—"

"Leave it." She took a deep breath and forced herself

to calm down. Maybe she was overreacting, but his accusation had stunned her. "Did you learn anything else? About the man and woman Prenter argued with in the alley?"

"No, I came here directly from the bar. I'm really sorry, Lucy." He glanced toward the reception.

"Are you upset that I'm here with Sean?"

"No," he said, but she didn't believe him, and he made no pretense to convince her that he was being truthful.

She nodded, still shredded inside over Cody's accusation. Jealousy was another burden she didn't need. "Excuse me, I'm going to the restroom."

She walked briskly down the hall. The feeling that someone was watching her was strong, and she suspected that Cody was staring after her, feeling guilty.

Lucy pushed open the door and was relieved that no one was inside. She walked into the small powder room off the main restroom. She leaned against the vanity counter, arms holding her weight, forcing herself to breathe slowly. She stared at her hands. Her nails were cut short but neat. Clear polish kept her nails strong and provided a finished look. Her fingers were long and slender, and she'd always imagined she should be good at piano, but the five years she took lessons proved she had no musical talent. These fingers flew over the computer keyboard, though, almost with a mind of their own, telling lies to sexual predators, enticing them through words to lure her. She had no guilt about how she helped put predators in prison.

Her arms, like her legs, were lean and muscular from spending hours at the gym. But no amount of physical strength could have prevented her from being kidnapped and raped six years ago. She'd been attacked from behind, grabbed and injected with a drug that had immediately weakened her muscles. Only street smarts might have prevented the attack, but she would never know. She had none then, and now? She imagined every scenario where someone could get the drop on her and she did everything she could to protect against it, but nothing was foolproof.

After that first year, Lucy realized she couldn't live in a plastic bubble. She refused to be a victim for the rest of her life. She was angry with herself, and angry with the men who had abducted and hurt her. But even the rage had faded, because she would not allow them to control her emotions from the grave.

Her family didn't understand why she wanted to walk in the darkness by being a law enforcement officer, by chatting with sexual predators online, why she continued to read and research and learn everything she could about the men and women who committed horrid crimes. They thought that because she'd been a victim, she should find a career completely unrelated to crime. Her mother wanted her to be a teacher. Her father wanted her to go into linguistics, just as she'd planned in high school. Even Dillon, her own brother who was a forensic psychiatrist and worked every day with criminals, was skeptical of her decision.

But if not her, then who? Who else had the passion and the resolve to dedicate their life to putting these bastards behind bars?

Already she'd had some success, times when she knew she'd helped someone. When she'd spoken at a local high school and a fourteen-year-old girl came up to her afterward with a story that was all too familiar: a thirty-seven-year-old man had befriended her online and wanted to have sex. That man had been arrested two weeks later when the girl and her mother helped the cops locate him. Or the twelve-year-old boy who had almost run away with his online boyfriend, until Lucy had proven to him that his fourteen-year-old cyberpal was really a sixty-two-year-old pedophile.

And there were the people she'd helped who she'd never know. The kids who listened silently to her talks, pretending to ignore her; the ones online whom she'd scared straight; the women and children who wouldn't be victimized because she'd helped put a predator where he belonged.

So it was worth the watchful eyes, the whispers behind her back, the wrong-headed belief by the ignorant that she'd asked for it, she was to blame, she was different from them. That predators didn't go after just anyone, they only went after *other people*.

The door opened and she straightened, glancing in the mirror to see who was entering.

Sean.

"You're in the wrong bathroom," she said.

"Not unless you are." He walked over to her and placed his hands on her shoulders. He held her eyes in the mirror. She didn't want him to see her like this. Her self-doubt leaked through her expression, and it mattered to her that no one, especially her friends and family, thought she was on edge.

"I'm fine."

"I know." But he still held her shoulders, giving her a slow, firm massage. "You're tense."

"I don't like fund-raisers."

"Something happened out there. Tell me."

"Nothing happened." She looked down at her hands, which were still pressed against the marble countertop. She closed her eyes and let herself relax under Sean's thumbs. The knots in her muscles loosened and she sighed.

"Lucy."

When he didn't say anything else, she opened her eyes and saw he was staring at her, his mouth a firm line.

"Cody accused me of falsifying some data. That hurt. We've been working together for a long time, and—" She sighed.

"I understand. But that wasn't what I was talking about. Right before we talked to Fran, something happened. Tell me."

She stared at him. How could he have such a single-minded purpose? And what could she say?

"It's—just—" How could she explain it to him? She certainly didn't want to talk about her past. "I don't like being the center of attention, and I don't like people watching me."

"Who?"

"No one, everyone, I don't know. It was just that creepy-crawly feeling you get when someone is looking at you on purpose, you know? It's ridiculous. I know when I come to these things that I'm practically on-stage."

Sean edged closer. "You need to trust your instincts. How long have you felt this way?"

She couldn't look at him anymore. A rush of humiliation flooded through her. "Six years."

"But this is different."

"No—yes—I—"

Was it different? Lately . . . "I don't know. It's my

nerves. It's been a stressful few months, with the FBI application process and then Roger Morton's murder, and the Brad Prenter situation—"

"Who?"

The door opened and two older ladies walked in, startled to see Sean standing with Lucy. Lucy cracked a sly smile. "Busted," she said.

He took her hand and led her out, giving the ladies a low bow as they left. As soon as the door closed, he steered Lucy to the side and said, "Is this Prenter guy harassing you?"

She shook her head. "No—I didn't know him. He was a college TA who drugged and raped a student. He was killed in a robbery this week. That's been on my mind, too."

"Divine justice."

"Maybe."

"Lucy, you have solid instincts, so don't dismiss these feelings as being some neurosis. Trust yourself."

"Thank you."

"For what?"

"Having faith in me."

"Who doesn't?"

She didn't answer because there wasn't really an answer. Her family supported her, but they were always watching out for her when they didn't think she knew. She wasn't ignorant, and she picked up on their protective vibes. "You want to go?" she asked.

"I'm ready when you are."

"Now." They started down the hall to the coatroom.

"Can I interest you in dessert?" Sean asked lightly.

"You mean the buffet wasn't enough?"

"You didn't eat anything."

"I wasn't hungry."

"I know a place," Sean said cryptically. "Do you trust me?"

She hesitated. Not because she didn't trust him, but so many emotions were jumping around inside and she wasn't sure she could keep a lid on them.

"It's beginning to snow."

Sean glanced at her. "Are you kidding? A few scrawny flakes aren't going to deter me from treating you to the most incredible strawberry cheesecake east of the Mississippi."

"Cheesecake?" Her stomach growled and she put a hand to her mouth.

"I heard that," he said. He took her hand and kissed it. It was a spontaneous gesture, and Lucy tried to convince herself it was a kiss of friendship, but a warm sensation ran up her arms to the base of her neck as they walked to the car.

SIXTEEN

Sean walked Lucy to her front door. She was vibrant, her cheeks red from the cold, her dark eyes sparkling from the cheesecake sugar rush, topped with a glass of champagne.

Sean was pleased with himself that he had been able to distract Lucy after her earlier attack of nerves. Two hours later, she finally seemed relaxed.

He hadn't forgotten what she said, however. She thought someone was watching her. He didn't discount it as a personal defect the way she had. With all the stuff going on with Morton's murder, maybe someone was paying too much attention to Lucy.

"Thank you so much, Sean." Lucy sighed contently as she unlocked the door. They stepped inside, the light snow still swirling around. "I'm so glad we went out for dessert." She reached over to disarm the alarm.

"Anything for you, milady," he said with an accent and half bow. He wanted to kiss Lucy, but he hesitated. Hesitating was unlike him. What was wrong with him? He never had a problem—*ever*—in showing a woman he was interested.

But Lucy wasn't any woman. He'd known that from the first time he'd met her.

And she was his partner's sister. Patrick was his friend *and* business partner. He hadn't told Patrick he was interested in Lucy.

And she wasn't the kind of woman he usually dated. He liked dating girls who liked to have fun, just like him. Skiing, spontaneous trips cross country in his plane, skinny-dipping in a lake. His ex-girlfriends were generally nine-to-fivers or trust-fund princesses with no devotion to anything but themselves. He liked that, because that meant he never felt guilty when he broke it off.

None of those girls had lasted more than a few months.

That Lucy was special couldn't be more obvious to him, but Sean knew himself and had never shied away from the truth. He screwed up relationships right and left. Not at the beginning—he had courtship down to a fine science. But after the romance wore off, he became bored with the monotony of the same old, same old. Different girl, same problems. Superficial desire that wore off quicker with each passing woman.

There was nothing superficial about Lucy Kincaid, and absolutely nothing superficial about his desire for her.

"What's going through that mind of yours?" she asked.

"I want to kiss you," he said before he realized the words left his mouth.

"Do you usually ask first?"

"No."

She tilted her chin up defiantly and looked almost angry, her dark pupils widening. "Then don't ask."

Sean put his left hand on the back of Lucy's neck, her

long, soft hair luxurious in his fingers. He searched her face for any reticence, any doubt. Her expression was serious and for a second he thought he'd misunderstood her, that she wanted him to back off. Then her full lips parted just a fraction, and he leaned down and kissed her.

She tasted sweet, like the cheesecake and champagne they'd shared. He'd intended to give her one warm good-night kiss with a promise of more, but he didn't want to let go. He wanted to taste more of her, to feel more of her. He gently pressed his body against Lucy, her back bending as her head dipped back to continue the long kiss.

Her hands found his biceps, then inched up to his shoulders. Her thumbs held his neck, attaching him to her as much as he kept her close to him.

Any other woman, and he'd be moving this dance to the bedroom. But Lucy wasn't a one-night stand. He was confident in his powers of seduction, but he didn't want to push too fast. He wanted—*needed*—to do this right.

But she fit so well against him, he didn't want to stop.

Yet if he didn't, he would make mistakes. He knew it as certainly as he knew that the sun would rise over the Atlantic tomorrow.

He slowly pulled his lips away, holding her close. He looked down at her face. Her eyes were closed, but they opened the moment after he broke the kiss. She appeared bewildered, like she didn't know where she was, as if she'd been lost for the last few minutes. She licked her lips, then glanced down and stepped back demurely, almost as though embarrassed. He pulled her back to him and kissed her lightly, showing her that there was nothing to be embarrassed about.

"I'd like to take you on an official date," Sean said.

"A date?" she repeated.

"Tonight wasn't official. This was . . . filling in for your brother."

"I—"

"Tomorrow."

"Tomorrow?" she repeated.

"I'll pick you up at ten a.m."

"Ten." She shook her head and glanced down, sheepish. "I have church. I usually go to nine o'clock Mass. How about eleven or so?"

He almost said he'd pick her up at eight-thirty for church, but he hadn't stepped inside a church since his parents' funeral fifteen years ago. "I'll pick you up there. Ten, okay?"

She nodded. "Holy Trinity. On Thirty-sixth between—"

"I know where it is." He kissed her again. "Ten in the morning." He kissed her one last time. "I'd better go before we let any more snow inside."

Lucy had forgotten she'd opened the door, and stared at the puddle of melting snow that had blown in through the crack. "I'd better clean that up before Kate sees it," she said, then smiled at Sean. "You're a distraction."

She kissed him spontaneously, surprising herself. "Thanks again." Her insides were light and airy, a far cry from the way she'd felt only a few hours ago. She should be freezing standing on the small covered stoop, but she was anything but cold.

"My pleasure, ma'am," he said with a warm grin, his dimples showing.

She smiled and closed the door behind him. She waited, listening for his car, until it had started and driven off.

Lucy couldn't remember a time when she'd felt so comfortable with someone. When she'd felt so attracted. Maybe because tonight hadn't been a date, there hadn't been any pressure on her to act normal. Everything they said and did was almost spontaneous. For the first time in a long, long time, she felt like a typical woman.

He'd asked her out on a date. An *official* date. When was the last time she'd dated anyone? Cody? That wasn't right. She considered, and realized that while she'd gone out with one or two men since breaking it off with Cody, she'd eased herself away from any potential commitment after the second date. She'd been with Cody for nearly two years—it had been comfortable and normal, until he proposed and she realized she didn't love him. She couldn't imagine being married to him— or to anyone. The thought of marriage left her cold and panicky. Odd, considering her parents had an incredible, forty-five-year marriage—and counting.

But Lucy wasn't normal, and she knew that. Her past would always be part of her. While she'd learned not to let her past control her, it colored all her decisions, leading her down this path in front of her. The FBI. Fighting predators.

Why shouldn't she enjoy the company of Sean Rogan? Didn't she deserve a little happiness?

She vowed to have fun tomorrow, no matter what. She probably wouldn't have a choice—Sean had a knack of getting to the heart of whatever was bothering her and turning it around without making her feel foolish.

Lucy's romantic thrill ended when she glanced at her computer and remembered what Cody had said earlier.

"Did you change the location?"

He'd been so positive, which meant the bartender had been convincing, which meant that the bartender was simply repeating what Prenter said. That he was meeting a hot blonde.

It wasn't "Tanya" who'd talked dirty to him. Prenter was obviously embellishing—he was a convicted rapist who had an inflated sense of ego.

But Prenter *was* at another bar at the same time he'd told her online identity to meet him at the Firehouse in Fairfax. The more she thought about it, the more she convinced herself that he'd been working a couple of women online, and the "hot blonde" who talked dirty had given him a better offer than the more reticent "Tanya."

She sat down at the computer and logged into her "Tanya" account. With a little work, she could find every person with whom Prenter had chatted. It might not be completely legal—it would require hacking in as an administrator, but that wasn't difficult since she knew all the protocols that this particular site used.

Most likely Prenter had ditched "Tanya" for a better prospect; it was the only thing that made sense. Maybe it had been that girl from the alley, the one he may have drugged.

She frowned as her computer query yielded no results. In fact, she couldn't find Prenter on the site at all. His profile was gone. Deleted. Had the police secured it? If so, there should be *something* that showed that his account was here, but locked. There should be a record of his chats in the admin area, even if they didn't have any data. It was common for users to lock their profiles when they didn't want strangers contacting them. His screen name should be here—but it wasn't.

Lucy logged out and tried to create an account using his log-in. It was available to use, which meant that no other registered user in the chat community had it, locked or unlocked.

Why would the police delete his account? It made no sense. Not for what on the surface appeared to be a routine homicide. And so quickly? He was killed only forty-eight hours ago.

Lucy shut down her computer, but it took her a long time to fall into a troubled sleep.

I watch her bedroom light turn off. Her room is dark. She is alone.

Except for the woman in the house, who I know to be a cop. A federal cop.

The house is owned by Dillon Kincaid and Katherine Donovan. They are married. Married—that pussy-whipped bastard let the bitch keep her maiden name. Now I do not wonder how Ms. Lucy Kincaid turned out to be a lying, whoring killer, with role models like that.

It is war. Us against them. Most men are pleased to give in to the demands of females. Let them work. Let them play. Let them do whatever fucking damn thing they want! Let them cheat, let them lie, let them leave.

I close my eyes and the rage flows through my veins, my sustenance, nurturing my needs as I remember.

Rosemarie.

I love you, Rosemarie.

I loved you through your lies and tricks. Did you al-

*ways know you would disobey? I gave you the world
because I wanted you to stay with me, and still you left!*

You pretended to love me, but you loved your friends
more. You pretended to be with me, but when you cried
out you called his name.

I miss you, Rosemarie.

Father knew best, and I should have listened. He lived
through the same thing, but I thought you would stay if
all you depended on came from me! If your dreams and
hopes and needs were fulfilled by me, you would never
leave. I worked day and night for you! You lying, cheating whore, you used me like every woman uses man.
Like Eve used Adam, like Delilah used Samson, like
every other woman in the world used man.

But you were weak. All women are weak. All women
need to be taught to obey.

To stay.

To beg.

To fetch.

Like the bitches they are.

I am one of the few left. The only one who understands that until women once again know their place,
our society, our future, is gone. All women should be
trained by me. Only the most obedient will survive.
Only those who do exactly what I say will live.

I have not yet found any worthy.

I will come for you, Lucy. Very soon.

SEVENTEEN

The morning sky seemed an even more vibrant blue in the icy cold, and while last night's snowfall had been cleared from the roads, the delicate blanketing of white across small yards, parked cars, and roofs sparkled in the sun. The walk to Holy Trinity usually allowed Lucy a chance to reflect, but today the quiet and subtle beauty of winter gave her no peace of mind. She walked into the church late and slid into the back row.

Her lack of sleep showed in her lackluster responses to the Mass. She thought through possible scenarios as to why Prenter's account had been deleted. An account *could* be accidentally deleted, but that seemed too coincidental. Or Prenter himself might have deleted it to avoid a trail of evidence. That was more likely, but why? Because he'd planned to drug and rape "Tanya"?

That went against type. He hadn't gone to any lengths to cover up his rape of Sara Tyson, which yielded physical evidence that had aided in his conviction. Still, he could have learned from that experience and become more cautious.

After communion, Lucy knelt and prayed, pushing all thoughts of Prenter from her mind. Someone knelt next to her, and she automatically shifted away while glancing at the person. She didn't like being snuck up on.

"Cody," she whispered.

"I'm sorry about last night."

"Shh." She wasn't going to argue with him in church, even if he was apologizing.

Ten minutes later, Mass was over, but Lucy didn't leave. She turned to Cody after the recessional and said, "Prenter's chat account was deleted."

He looked confused. "Why is that important? Lucy, anything could have happened to his account. The police could have locked it."

"It's been deleted."

"They could have archived it, then deleted the public copy."

"There are no archives on that site, except for private messages. I never sent him a private message."

"I think you're making a big deal over nothing."

At first Lucy was enraged—it wasn't *nothing;* then she noticed Cody's brow was furrowed. He was at least thinking about her concerns.

"I need to know what happened, Cody. I have run the scenario every way I can think of and some are plausible, but I need to know."

"Why is this important to you?"

"Because—" Why was it? Why did she care? She glanced at the corpus of Christ suspended on the wall behind the altar.

She'd killed Adam Scott and didn't regret it. He'd deserved worse, but her lack of guilt had bothered her for years. She'd talked to her brother Patrick about it, only him, and he'd dismissed it. *"You feel guilty because you don't feel guilty about killing the man who raped you, who nearly killed Dillon and Kate? Don't."*

Lucy had become desensitized by the violence in the world around her. She'd experienced pain and humiliation, she'd killed a human being, and she was immersed in an online world where sex predators were the norm, where they constantly hunted for victims. She didn't want to take murder in stride, even the death of a convicted rapist.

"I don't want to take anyone's death lightly," she said.

"I understand." Maybe he did. "I'll look a little deeper."

"Thank you."

"Want to go for breakfast?"

Sean. She glanced at her watch. It was already after ten. "I have plans," she said.

"Oh, maybe a rain check then—" Something over her shoulder caught Cody's attention and he straightened into his alpha cop stance.

She looked behind her and saw Sean walking toward them. Her heart quickened when he caught her eye and smiled.

"You didn't tell me you were seeing someone," Cody said, his voice hard, as if she were cheating on him.

"I'm not," she said automatically.

"You were with him last night."

Cody didn't believe her. She wasn't sure if she believed herself, either. "I mean, it's not serious." *Yet.* "We're just . . ." Why did she have to explain anything to her ex-boyfriend?

Sean came up to them, putting his hand on Lucy's back. "Officer Lorenzo," he said in greeting.

"Rogan." He said to Lucy, "I'll call you if I learn anything." Then he left.

"Did I say something?" Sean asked.

Lucy shook her head. "He's my ex-boyfriend."

"How long ago?"

"Over a year. Sorry—I don't know why he's acting so strange."

Sean raised his eyebrow. "You really don't know?"

"Know what?"

"He's still in love with you."

She shook her head and looked toward where Cody had walked out, but he was gone. "I don't think so." *Was he?* No, she didn't think so. *Maybe.*

"Luce, I'm a guy, I can tell." He kissed her lightly on the lips. "Tell me he doesn't have a chance of getting you back."

She let Sean's words sink in, her eyes widening. "He doesn't."

"Good." He kissed her again. "You look tired."

"I didn't sleep well."

"Hungry?"

"I could eat."

"You'll need the energy for what I have planned."

"What is that?"

"It's a surprise." He took her hand. "Let's go."

"You're going to burn out," Noah said to Kate when he walked into the computer room at Quantico at noon on Sunday.

She shot him a glare that might be described as the evil eye. "*You're* here."

"It's my case."

"It's my family."

Noah wasn't going to win this battle. "Abigail spoke to the regional vice-president at the rental company, faxed him the administrative subpoena, and he said he would give us the GPS logs tomorrow morning if possible—it's a holiday, but he's working on it."

"Good."

Kate was back staring at the computer. "I have something, too. I have a list of every email address in Morton's address book. I still haven't recovered the messages themselves, but I'm getting closer."

"How do we match those up to real people?"

"Some are easy—names attached to the emails. Some are harder, but I know some tricks."

"What about going to the ISP?"

She glanced at him, eyebrow raised. "So you're not as technically incompetent as you act."

"I know the basics."

"Internet service providers are less likely to turn over any private customer information without a warrant—they're not as friendly as the rental company. So we need probable cause, such as an email exchange that is obviously criminal in nature, or that we can show is criminal based on other evidence. Here's a list of everyone I've found so far—I highlighted those who are in Morton's file as being a known associate."

"I'll pull addresses and see who's local," Noah said, feeling the familiar excitement in his gut telling him this was a turning point in the investigation.

"I have dozens I haven't identified yet. The second list are those I have names for but aren't on Morton's associate list. That's a little longer. My guess, those are the people who sent in disks for his porn site."

"Why are they doing it? Morton didn't have money to pay them."

"Some people send in for free—those are usually amateurs who do the up-skirt videos or home movies. Some people have a deal with the site to be paid per view, so when someone watches the video they get paid. Trask had recorded more than half of his own material—he used prostitutes, drug addicts, anyone who'd do anything for a couple hundred dollars. But *he'd* make tens of thousands of dollars off the recording."

Noah shook his head. "And that's all legal."

"Most of it is, and he worked damn hard to keep Trask Enterprises off the radar. But Adam Scott was a sick bastard, and he couldn't help himself—he killed women for pleasure, and that's what tripped him up. It was when he started killing online that we could finally pursue him." Kate rubbed her temples. "Sometimes, the system is fucked," she mumbled.

Noah didn't exactly disagree with her but still thought their system was the best in the world. In his ten years in the Air Force, most of it in the Ravens security force, he'd been in dozens of countries and had seen the worst governments and justice systems in existence.

Noah sat at an extra terminal and pulled up the names Kate had identified. "There are only two who are local—both with criminal records. And one is already dead."

Noah looked at Andrew "Ace" Shuman, who'd been in and out of prison most of his life. Prostitution, racketeering, assault. According to Morton's file, Shuman had been a bodyguard. His official title with Trask Enterprises was "Head of Security." He'd been out of prison for three years and seemed to have kept his nose clean, but as Noah knew, most were criminals for life: career criminals—few changed their stripes, they just got better at hiding.

"I'll talk to Shuman," Noah said. "He knew Ralston and Morton."

"Shuman is a piece of work, and dangerous," Kate said. "I had a couple of run-ins with him, but couldn't nail him for anything substantive. He was in prison before Trask went into hiding—assault, I think. I tried to get him to turn on Trask, and he wouldn't."

"Good to know. He sounds like a possible."

"Oh yeah, if Morton pissed Shuman off, there's no doubt Shuman could kill him. But why?"

"That's the million-dollar question."

"Anything on Ralston?"

"ERT is processing the evidence. His computer was trashed, the hard drive destroyed."

"The killer didn't want us to find anything."

"They haven't narrowed time of death. The autopsy is scheduled for later this afternoon. The killer left the windows open; the apartment was a friggin' icebox. But the ERT said he'd been dead for more than forty-eight hours, and the last witness we spoke to saw him coming home Friday night at approximately six-thirty in the evening."

"So the big question is whether he was killed before or after Morton," Kate said.

"I don't think that really matters. He was dead before his flight left on Sunday morning. I'd like to find out what kind of information he gave to policeman Jerry Biggler."

"Biggler?" Kate frowned.

"Ralston was a CI—a criminal informant. He talked

only to Jerry Biggler, a D.C. cop who died of a heart attack six months after he retired—back in 2006."

"You think Ralston was murdered because he'd been
an informant? Why *now*? It doesn't make sense."

She was right, but Noah suspected there was something here. He just hadn't been able to figure it out yet.

But he would. He always did.

EIGHTEEN

I *watch her skate on the ice with her boyfriend.
She laughs at something he said. Lucy Kincaid is having
fun.*

*Lucy Kincaid is a whore. I saw her sex tape. I know
exactly who she is. She's a liar. And a killer. A whoring,
lying killer.*

*I close my eyes and concentrate on breathing. Con-
trol. Need control. Slowly I breathe in. Hold it. Release.
In. Out. Calm down.*

*I repeat the deep breathing until I regain my compo-
sure. Acting out of anger, in public, would be unwise. I
do not want to go to prison. I could kill her now, but
I would be arrested.*

*I will kill her, and I will not be caught. They won't find
her body, because there will be nothing left to find. Just
like the other females.*

*I allow the images to flood my mind. They make me
smile. The women I trained. How well they learned to
obey as a good wife should.*

*But like all females, when I gave them the chance to
make the right decision, they always chose the wrong
option. They all lied.*

Lucy Kincaid is the worst of the lot. She is the poster

girl for all that is wrong with the female of the species. Did she think she was equal to men? Superior? That she could kill without punishment? That she could entice me with her snake tongue, trying to convince me that she was someone she wasn't?

Rosemarie lied as well. She told me she would never leave. Some women leave in mind, some in body. Rosemarie had been everything to me. Perfect. She did everything I told her. I gave her everything in return for her obedience. I loved her. I loved her!

Vixen! She tricked me. The lying, cheating whore deceived me.

My father had warned me, but I did not listen because I believed I had learned from his mistakes.

Father knew best . . .

I never allowed another woman to deceive me, until Lucy Kincaid said she was someone she wasn't.

She slips and her boyfriend grabs her before she falls to the ice. My hand wraps around the cold grip of my gun. I want to shoot her now. Pull the nine-millimeter from my pocket and press the trigger. One bullet, two bullets, three bullets, four . . . the entire clip. Watch her blood spill onto the ice. Watch her blood spray across her boyfriend's too-pretty face. Watch Mr. Pussy-Whipped Boyfriend look down in horror at his dead whore.

He, too, has been deceived, has he not? He will learn, just as I have, that no woman is trustworthy.

Maybe it would be better if I kill her boyfriend first. A bullet in the right part of his skull would force his brains out on the ice, all over her. She would stare, horrified, at the headless corpse. Then I would walk over and tell her he died because of her. I would tell her who I really am and why she will die.

Because she is a Jezebel. A liar. Pretending to be someone she is not.

I need to hear her pleas for mercy. I need to taste the tears on her face. I need to see her break. I need to smell her fear. I need for her to obey.

Calm. Down. Breathe.

I take my hand off the grip of my gun because I am too tempted to pull the trigger.

I breathe easier now as I watch Lucy Kincaid rub up against her boyfriend. He is being led by the whore, given to weakness because of her deceit. He may have to die, but that is not my first choice. Only if he interferes.

I must be strong. This is the wrong place for action. I already draw looks because I don't have a child or a wife on my arm. It is time for me to leave.

I'm watching you, Lucy. From now until the day you die.

Lucy had never been ice-skating before.

After brunch, Sean took her to an outdoor skating rink in Arlington. Lucy argued.

"I barely know how to roller-skate."

Sean said, "But you ski, right?"

"Not well. I'm still on the bunny slopes."

"Skiing is next, then. It's all about balance."

"There's a huge difference between ice and snow. Ice is hard. It hurts more when you fall."

"So don't fall."

She glared at him. "You think this is funny."

He feigned offense. "I take my playtime very seriously."

She sighed. "I don't know," she said, looking out at the rink, dominated by kids who could skate rings around her. "Maybe we should go to a pool hall. I can play a wicked game of pool—"

"After. Now sit so you can put on the ice skates."

Lucy watched dozens of people on the ice as she pulled on her skates. Most knew what they were doing; some were struggling and holding onto the railings. A little peanut of a girl whizzed past her in a swirling short pink skirt and matching sweater, gloves, and scarf. She did a spinning thing that had Lucy thinking future Olympic Gold Medalist.

Lucy feared she'd break a bone.

Sean was already laced up before Lucy had started. He bent over and quickly tied up her laces. "I don't think this a good idea," she said.

"Scared?"

"No, but—"

"Chicken?"

She glared at him. "I'm not chicken, but—"

"Then prove it."

"I am going to embarrass myself," she said under her breath. Sean helped her to her feet and she added, "There's no way I can walk on these skates."

Sean picked her up.

"What are you doing?" she cried, panicked. "You can't carry me with skates on."

He laughed as he walked—on skates—to the entrance of the rink. "You'll be gliding across the ice like a pro by the end of the day."

"Or frozen from falling on my ass."

"I'm not going to let you fall." He set her down on the ice. She grabbed the railing, her legs spreading into a split.

"Sean!"

He laughed again, grabbed her biceps, and pulled her to standing. "Pretend you're dancing."

"This is not dancing."

"I said pretend." He held her at the waist, facing her forward, his chest pressed against her back. "I'm going to lead, okay? I'll steer you forward. You can hold onto my forearm if that helps."

She held on tight.

"Skating is all about balance and movement. Let your thighs do the work."

"We're moving!" She squeezed his arm as it tightened around her waist. The little girl with the future Gold twirled by as if she were floating. "I swear, she did that to make me feel inferior."

"Probably."

"I wasn't serious."

"I was." He kissed her on the cheek. "Now stop comparing yourself to the other children and focus."

Lucy took a deep breath, the cold air feeling both amazingly refreshing and icy in her lungs. Sean gently moved them forward as he steered her. "Do you feel my legs move?"

She did, and swallowed, acutely aware of Sean's thighs pressing lightly against the back of hers, first the right, then the left, in a sensual rhythm that both calmed and excited her. She moved at his direction, and soon they were skating, slowly but steady.

"Hey, I'm skating!" She grinned widely, nervous but proud of her accomplishment.

They skated around the rink twice as Lucy gained confidence. "Okay, I'm going to let you go," Sean said, "but I'll be right behind you."

"No—"

But he'd already dropped his arms. She glided forward, trying to keep the same rhythm, but she went too far to the right, overcompensating and turned 180 degrees. She grabbed at the railing, but it was too far and she fell on her butt, her feet shooting out from under her.

"Shit!"

Sean laughed.

She glared at him. "Stop laughing." Then she smiled. "I'm such an idiot."

He held out his hand and pulled her up with one smooth move. "Okay, we'll try something else in the dance family."

Facing her, he held her waist and started skating backward, pulling her along with him instead of pushing her forward. "You're going backward!" she exclaimed.

"Would you rather?"

She shook her head and put her hands on his shoulders. They moved fluidly along the edge of the rink. Or, rather, Sean steered them perfectly, seeming to know by instinct and quick glances back exactly where they were on the ice, and where everyone else was as well. Lucy rediscovered her rhythm, and they glided smoothly around the rink, as close as they could get without fully touching, Sean's movements seemingly effortless. Their flowing dance became more than two friends skating, as the banter subsided and Sean kissed the top of her head.

Then her lips. Lightly, sweetly, showing a deep affection that surprised her.

"I'm proud of you, Luce."

She cleared her throat. "Why?"

"New experiences."

"I suppose I'm willing to try anything once."

"Once?" He frowned and looked worried. "You're not having fun?"

"I'm having fun. Much more than I thought I would. You're pretty amazing."

He grinned and winked at her, then kissed her cheek and nipped her ear playfully. "I am, aren't I?" he teased.

"My, what a large ego you have!"

"All the better to impress you with, my dear."

Lucy raised an eyebrow and glanced around Sean to make sure no one was in their way. She turned suddenly, in a full circle, surprising him, and he tried to regain control, but she'd gotten her "skating legs" and spun him until he fell on his butt. She grabbed the railing to keep from falling and laughed.

"So that's how it is." He grinned. "You'd better watch yourself, Ms. Kincaid, because payback is a bitch."

"I can hardly wait." She surprised herself with how easy it was to joke with Sean.

He got up easily enough and pushed her against the railing. His blue eyes sparkled with humor as he said, "You won't know when or where, princess."

"I'm so scared," she said, suppressing a giggle.

He kissed her, opening his mouth slightly, warming her lips, sending a shiver through her body. His hands were on her face, his leather gloves cold but she barely noticed. He held her there, holding the kiss. His body pressed against hers and she was effectively trapped against the sidewall but didn't panic, didn't feel anything but the powerful presence of Sean Rogan.

He sighed, put his forehead against hers and whispered, "How about some hot chocolate?"

She nodded, because suddenly she couldn't talk.

They left the rink and returned their skates. "Thank you, Sean," Lucy said and kissed him spontaneously. "I haven't had this much fun in a long time."

NINETEEN

Andrew "Ace" Shuman was a foul-mouthed ex-con and there was nothing Noah would have liked more than to find a reason to arrest him.

"Fucking Feds," Ace said when he opened the door and saw Noah and Abigail standing on the stoop of his beat-up post–World War II cinderblock house. Noah hadn't pulled out his badge yet. "My parole was up eighteen months ago, I don't got to talk to you." He leered at Abigail as his eyes skirted up and down her body.

Noah showed his badge. "Special Agent Armstrong, my partner Special Agent Resnick. We're here to ask you questions about the murder of Roger Morton."

Telling him right off the bat that this was serious—a capital offense.

Shuman scowled. "Roger *Morton*?" He leaned against the doorjamb. He didn't invite them in, and Noah wasn't sure he wanted to step into this pigsty. He'd spent a winter at Fort Dix in New Jersey, and this cold sunny day didn't bother him, but Abigail was trying to stop herself from shivering, so Noah got down to business.

"When was the last time you had any contact with Morton? In person, email, phone?"

"That motherfucker's dead?" Ace sounded skeptical.

Noah nodded curtly and waited for an answer. When Ace wasn't forthcoming, he added, "You're an ex-con. You have a history with Morton. Don't make me come back with an arrest warrant."

"Bullshit, you can't arrest me for squat."

"I can and will compel you to answer my questions. As I stand here, the FBI is reading every email sent to and from Morton in the last six months. We know you and Morton corresponded."

"Then read them and get back to me," Shuman said and started to close the door.

Noah put his foot forward to prevent the door from closing. "I've had a long week, and you're making it longer. Deputy Chief of Police Richard Blakesly is a personal friend of mine. One call and he'll make your life miserable. You won't be able to step out without a patrol car on your ass. You won't be able to go to a bar, the grocery store, or walk to the corner without a Baltimore P.D. officer asking you what time it is.

"Morton had child pornography on his computer. You emailed him something. And if there is any hint that you sent him illegal porn, we'll raid this place top to bottom. One stray picture, and you're back in prison. And everyone there will know you get off on naked kids."

Ace stepped forward, his face dark and dangerous. "Fucking prick, I don't go for kids."

"Please hit me," Noah said, not moving.

Ace wrestled with his anger.

Noah pushed. "I know you talked to Morton; I want to know what it was about. Why was he in D.C. last week?"

Ace spewed a chain of profanity that would have had

the most foul-mouthed Marine blush, but Noah kept a straight face.

At the end of the rant, Ace said, "I didn't know Roger was dead, but I thought something was up because he never came by when he said he would."

"When was that?"

"He said he had a business proposition. He was supposed to come over last Saturday."

"What did he say about the business proposition?"

"Okay, this is the God's honest truth. After he got out of the pen, he contacted me, said he had to watch his ass, but he had a plan and might need me to head up security. Asked if I was interested. I was. Didn't hear squat from him for months. Then out of the blue he said he was coming to D.C. and would see me on Saturday. If things worked out, he'd have startup capital and would need my help."

"Startup capital for what?"

"He didn't say, but I heard around that someone was putting together a new online sex club. Live webcams, quality videos, chats. Sounded promising."

"And that someone was Roger Morton?"

"Don't know. That was just the grapevine, a friend of mine talking big. But when I heard from Roger, I thought about that."

"Who is this friend?"

"Now that, I ain't saying."

Noah took a risk. "Robbie Ralston?"

Shuman shrugged.

"Ralston is dead, too."

Shuman couldn't hide his reaction. "Robbie's dead?"

"Was he the big talker?"

"Might be. But he wasn't smart enough to do it on his

own." Shuman paused, then added, "I'd rather take my chances in prison than fuck with certain vodka-swilling shits, if you get my drift."

Noah got it, all right.

"Thank you, Mr. Shuman."

Ace laughed. " 'Thank you Mr. Shuman'? That's a fucking hoot." He winked at Abigail.

In the car, Abigail said, "You have friends in high places."

Noah blinked. "Excuse me?"

"The deputy chief of police? What are the chances?"

Noah shrugged and turned the ignition. "I don't know. Richard Blakesly was my first lieutenant when I joined the Air Force. He's still there."

"You bullshitted him?" Abigail grinned. "Pulling one over on a con like Shuman, I'm impressed."

"I didn't have time for his games, and I had no cause to haul his ass in. Nor did I want to spend an hour in the car with him." Noah turned onto the main road and headed back toward D.C. "Morton and Ralston were playing a dangerous game."

"Of course. They're dead."

"I was thinking of the vodka-swilling shits Ace Shuman alluded to."

"You'll have to clue me in."

"Sergey Yuran is a Russian trafficker. If it's in Russia—drugs, people, weapons—he can get it."

"Yuran?"

Noah nodded. "He's the only Russian who's on Morton's associate list. According to Kate Donovan's notes, he supplied Trask Enterprises with a steady stream of prostitutes for their sex tapes. If Morton crossed him?"

He stopped. Something didn't feel right about this.

"What?" Abigail pressed a moment later.

"I don't know. I don't know Yuran well, but Morton's murder seems sloppy to me."

"Sloppy? One bullet and he's dead."

"Yeah—but Yuran is better than that. Still," Noah said, turning onto the freeway, "Morton was into something that got him killed, and that means someone even more dangerous is involved in whatever plan Morton had up his sleeve."

"Where to now?"

"Yuran. I have to call it in, I'm sure one of our people is watching him closely. I don't want to risk any existing undercover op, but he knows something or Shuman wouldn't have seemed so nervous."

Driving back to D.C., Noah called Hans Vigo to learn the status of any investigation involving Sergey Yuran. By the time Hans returned his call, he was pulling into FBI headquarters.

"You were right to call," Hans said. "Immigration has had him under surveillance for months, and they don't want us involved at this point. I did, however, get some information out of them. Good news, bad news. Or good news, neutral news, depending on your point of view."

"Give it to me."

"Yuran and his key men are all alibied for last weekend—they were in New York City."

"Doing what? A human trafficking convention?" Noah added sarcastically.

"They didn't say, I didn't ask. Immigration is touchy these days."

Noah said, "He could have put a hit out on Morton."

"True, but there's no whisper of that. According to my source, Morton and Ralston aren't even on their radar. There are no signs that Yuran is even looking into the online sex trade; he prefers to deal with live people."

Noah didn't think that Shuman was blowing smoke up his ass. "My source says Yuran was a possible source of capital to launch the venture."

"That may be possible, but only from a money perspective. Yuran has been known to loan money, at huge cost. You think that's why Morton and Ralston were killed? They didn't pay up?"

"No," Noah admitted. "That doesn't feel right—there's no sign that either of them had any cash, even for a short time. Yuran isn't an idiot; he wouldn't kill them without a reason."

"I agree. I think Yuran is a dead end, but I did ask my ICE contact to research the matter. How many emails were exchanged between Yuran and Morton?"

"One."

"Doesn't seem like a good bet. Does Kate have the content yet?"

"No. Anything else?"

"Yeah, the neutral-to-bad news."

"I thought you gave me the bad news."

"Because you didn't close your case? That'd be too easy. But you should know that Sean Rogan paid a visit to Sergey Yuran yesterday."

Noah tensed. "Rogan?"

"Stayed for twenty-seven minutes. Went to his bar before it opened. The timing suggests it was right before he found Ralston's body."

"Yuran sent him there?"

"Doubtful—Ralston was an associate of Morton's, Sean was working the case like you were."

"Obstructing justice."

"I'm saying, you might want to use Sean and RCK where you can. They have a little more freedom than we do."

Hans wasn't explicitly giving him an order, but it felt like one. Noah didn't want to cross that line. Bringing in a private consultant was one thing, but a gray-area firm like Rogan-Caruso-Kincaid? "I think I'll just ask Rogan what he and Yuran talked about, and then tell him to stay the hell out of my case."

"I understand; I'm just giving options," Hans said.

It wasn't an option Noah cared to exercise—except as a last resort.

TWENTY

Cody confronted Lucy outside the Medical Examiner's Office on Monday morning. "You lied to me."

Lucy blinked rapidly, at a complete loss. Her head ached from lack of sleep, the wind had picked up, making her colder than she already was, and that awful pinprick sensation of being watched had returned.

He shoved a piece of paper into her gloved hand. It was a printout of a message from Prenter's social networking account—the deleted account—forwarded to Prenter's personal email.

The original message was from Lucy's "Tanya" account:

change of plans—i have an errand in dc can we meet at club 10? can't wait!! ☺ xoxo Tanya.

Lucy read it five times before Cody yanked it out of her hands. "I didn't send it," she said.

"I don't believe you."

She stared at him, heartbroken that he thought she was lying. A curdle of fear twisted in her stomach as she realized someone had used her account to send Prenter to Club 10. Where he'd been murdered. "You've known me for over three years. You don't trust me?"

"Are you denying this is your account?" He waved the paper in her face.

"No, but—"

"Your secure WCF account?"

"Cody! Stop interrogating me like I'm a suspect."

He didn't say anything, but glared at her.

"I didn't send that message," she repeated.

"Then who?" He shot out the question as if she were a hostile witness.

"I don't know!"

Lucy's mind ran through every possible scenario she could think of. "It's not impossible for someone to have hacked my account."

"Someone would have to have known who you were."

"No—not necessarily. If someone got hold of Prenter's emails—hell, Cody, he had them forwarded to his personal email, anyone could see my log-in name! Maybe one of his ex-girlfriends was pissed off and didn't want him seeing someone else. Maybe—"

"Listen to yourself!"

"I'm trying to figure out how someone used my account—or masked their account to look like mine—to send him to the bar where he died. Maybe it's just a co-incidence." As she said it, she realized this was no coincidence. The decision to send Prenter to Club 10 was deliberate and calculating. Less than two hours later, he was murdered in the alley. Quietly, she asked, "What do you think, Cody?"

He ran a hand over his face. "I don't know what to think, Lucy."

"The murder was purposeful. Did you read the autopsy report? Four bullets, remember? Three in the stomach, one in the back of the head. That sounds professional, right? Not a drug dispute gone bad."

Lucy began to shake from more than the cold.

Cody grabbed her hand. "If you're in trouble, tell me. I will do everything in my power to help you, but you have to tell me the truth."

"Trouble? I'm not in any trouble!"

"Did someone ask you to send that message? Or maybe you gave someone access to your account? Who are you trying to protect? Tell me!"

"No! Cody, what are you thinking about me?"

"Then you told someone."

"I told no one! I'm the one who told *you* that I thought something was odd about Prenter's murder. I came to *you*, remember?"

"Maybe to see if you'd screwed up."

Lucy stepped back, pulling her hand from Cody's tight grasp. It became clear that Cody thought she had conspired to kill Brad Prenter.

"Please," Cody pleaded. "Let me help you."

"You don't believe me." She bit back the bile of betrayal that burned her throat and said in a shockingly calm voice, "If I were going to set Prenter up, I wouldn't send you to another bar. I wouldn't have let you know that I had him on the hook. I wouldn't have him killed in your jurisdiction, since you knew I was working him online. And I certainly would never have come to you to look into the odd circumstance of his murder."

Cody slumped, the truth of her words hitting him, but as far as Lucy was concerned she could never trust Cody again. "I—I'm sorry," he stammered.

"How could you think I am capable of doing such a thing?"

He didn't say anything, and Lucy knew exactly why he'd believed the worst of her. Her hands came up to her mouth and she swallowed a sob.

It was because she had killed before. Six years ago she'd shot Adam Scott at point-blank range. Few people knew the whole story, but Cody did. When she and Cody had been dating she had told him about her past.

She turned and walked away, as fast as she dared on the icy sidewalk. Cody called after her, but she ignored him. She called her boss on the way back to the Metro station, told him she was ill, and headed home. Tired, cold, and sick at the loss of a friend.

But under it all was a simmering anger that someone had used *her* to kill Brad Prenter. She had to get home and look through all her records and accounts and figure this out before whoever killed him realized she was suspicious.

Unfortunately, with Cody looking into Prenter's death, it might be too late.

In the back of her mind, Lucy knew that if not her, someone else at WCF would have worked on Prenter. WCF had dozens of volunteers, but only a handful of paid staff. Fran ran background checks on everyone. Some of the volunteers had tragedy in their own lives; others were retired law enforcement; others were active in public safety and used their free time to help. All had to pass a security check, but they weren't foolproof.

Lucy couldn't tell Fran unless she was certain. It would devastate the director to think that her organization had been used to kill a rapist. Their donors, their funding would dry up. All the good work they'd done in the past would be scrutinized. The active cops associated with them could be in jeopardy. Like Cody.

The people Lucy worked with didn't kill predators, they put them in prison. It sickened her to think that their work might be tainted because one person wanted Prenter dead.

When Lucy arrived home, she smelled the roses before she saw the bouquet on the table next to the stairs. Red roses in a clear glass vase. She saw the card on the table next to it with her name. On the notepad next to the phone, Kate had scrawled, "These were delivered as I was leaving. Gorgeous! I want the scoop when I get home."

The tension from her contemplative Metro ride and walk home began to fade. She opened the card.

I had a terrific time at the ice rink yesterday. I'll see you soon.

He hadn't signed it, just added a scrawl of something illegible. She smiled and smelled the flowers. Roses had never been her favorite, but today they were. Sean had quickly become important to her. She'd liked him when Patrick first introduced them but thought Sean wasn't at all serious. His car, his plane, his computer toys—he seemed to be all about his stuff. But the last few days spending time with him, getting to know him better, kissing him . . . she felt a peace and comfort she hadn't felt for a long time, and a deep attraction that surprised her. Sean might appear frivolous on the surface, but Lucy saw a depth of character and raw intelligence that was as captivating as his Irish charm and good looks.

She reluctantly put the card down. She hadn't ditched

work to sit around, but needed to find out exactly what had happened to Brad Prenter.

His killer knew how WCF tracked paroled sex offenders and sent them back to prison to complete their original sentence. Did someone in WCF have a vendetta against Prenter?

The most logical explanation was that one of his victims had gone after him.

Lucy went to her room and logged onto her computer. She could access WCF files from home, though she rarely did. She pulled down Prenter's criminal records, though she knew them by heart, just to reread and make sure she hadn't missed anything.

He'd been convicted of raping Sara Tyson. Two other women came forward to testify against him, and Lucy didn't know why they hadn't filed charges. Lack of evidence? The judge had allowed the testimony, but as Lucy reviewed the transcripts she realized that their testimony had been limited. They spoke only to facts that could be corroborated by a witness—both of them had appeared intoxicated at a public place and Prenter had taken them home. Prenter never denied having sex with them, but said it was consensual. They had likely been drugged—hence the appearance of drunkenness—but there was no proof; however, it looked bad to the jury that Prenter on two occasions had taken advantage of a drunk college student. Coupled with the proof that he'd drugged Sara Tyson, the jury had convicted him.

Lucy further researched Sara and the other two women. All had graduated from college. None of them lived within a hundred-mile radius. One was engaged to be married, and Sara attended law school in Texas.

Not in Prenter's file, but in Lucy's personal notes, was

the information about his high school girlfriend in Rhode Island.

Evelyn Oldenburg had come home late on Saturday night from a house party. Her parents were asleep and didn't hear her come in, but her younger brother said he'd heard the garage door close at 1:40, over an hour past her curfew. He didn't want to get her in trouble, so he didn't say anything. The next morning, her mother went to wake her and Evelyn was unresponsive. The girl had vomited on the floor next to her bed, indicating that she'd likely been conscious when she came home. The parents and paramedics believed it was alcohol poisoning, and her best friend, Sheila, tearfully confirmed that she'd driven Evelyn home in Evelyn's car, then Sheila had walked to her own house.

It was what happened between 11:45 and one a.m.—when Sheila couldn't find Evelyn—that was suspicious. No one, not even the police or hospital staff, had thought that Evelyn had anything but alcohol poisoning. Drug tests came back inconclusive. Further tests confirmed that she had ingested an unknown anabolic steriod—similar but not identical to GHB.

Evelyn had no signs of violent rape but did have signs of recent sexual intercourse. No DNA had been found on her person, but the rapist could have worn a condom. In addition, Sheila had found Evelyn naked in a backyard hot tub. The water and heat easily could have destroyed evidence.

Prenter had been at the party, and Sheila gave a statement that he'd been with Evelyn the entire night—until they disappeared at 11:45. He was nowhere to be found when Evelyn turned up in the hot tub. Other witnesses corroborated the fact. He said they'd had consensual sex, and Evelyn's own diary confirmed that she was considering having sex with Prenter. But he said he left at midnight.

While the police suspected Prenter of drugging her, they had no evidence, and Prenter graduated from high school and went off to college.

Homemade Liquid X coupled with alcohol most likely sent Evelyn's system into shock, but it couldn't be proven. She slipped into a coma, where she remains today—eight years later.

Lucy did a deep search of Evelyn's family. Her brother, Kyle, was a freshman in college on the West Coast. Her parents still lived in Providence, and Evelyn was living in hospice care. Her father was a bank manager, her mother a teacher. They lived modestly. The mom had a Facebook page, and Lucy read the archives, heartbroken and uplifted at the same time. Most of the time, Mrs. Oldenburg was positive, but last year on Evelyn's twenty-fifth birthday she'd written:

Happy Birthday Evelyn: We had so many hopes for you and your future. You were bright and smart and beautiful and a dreamer. I will never stop hoping for a medical solution, or praying for a miracle.

Lucy didn't notice the tears running down her face until they dropped onto her desk. She felt the mother's pain. Her brother Patrick had been in a coma for nearly two years, all because of an explosion that Adam Scott had rigged. He'd been alert after the explosion, but pressure on his brain had necessitated emergency surgery, and he hadn't woken up for twenty-two months.

She wiped away the tears, furious with Brad Prenter

and angry with Evelyn's peers who hadn't told the complete truth. *Someone* knew what happened at the party. If Brad Prenter was innocent of drugging her, he'd still slept with a girl who was obviously intoxicated and unable to give informed consent.

She couldn't see the Oldenburgs going after Prenter using such an elaborate ruse as WCF's parolee project, but she certainly understood how ordinary people could kill.

She pulled the binder where she kept every sheet on every predator she'd worked on at WCF. Not all of them were part of the parolee project—some were predators luring kids on the Internet whom she'd identified and referred to law enforcement for investigation and prosecution. But the bulk of her work was on the parolee project.

There were twenty-seven special cases in which she chatted with paroled sex offenders. They'd been identified through a variety of means, but most were creatures of habit and walked in the same cyber-circles. Once a sex offender's preferences were identified, he rarely deviated from his preferred victim type. Lucy's computer program helped identify those types and where on the Internet the predator was most likely to lurk. WCF monitored numerous message boards and chat rooms looking for keywords and phrases. If someone sparked the interest of WCF staff or volunteers, they'd track the screen name and, if possible, the email. They'd compare that data with known parolees, and if there was a match, that sex offender was targeted.

Most of these guys had already broken their parole by returning to chat rooms, but most judges would not put them back in prison for that. Overcrowding and cost controls in the criminal justice system were a huge problem, and law enforcement didn't have the time or manpower to follow up on every paroled sex offender who logged into a chat room. WCF selected only high-risk repeat offenders, sexual predators who should never have been let out of prison.

Of the twenty-seven Lucy had worked on, nine hadn't taken the bait. Predators were notoriously good at sniffing out police activity. Seventeen were arrested and returned to prison. There was no trial, since they were all in violation of their parole. And when it came to sexual predators, most judges simply revoked their parole when they crossed the line. However, two parolees had a judge who felt the violation wasn't severe enough to warrant reincarceration. They were still on the streets.

Frustrated that she didn't have an answer, and not wanting to go to Fran without something tangible, Lucy wondered whether there was another connection to Prenter. Perhaps he'd pissed off someone in prison. But she needed greater access to information.

Her sister-in-law wasn't home, which was good because Lucy needed to use her computer.

Kate had access to public and prison records through her FBI credentials, and Lucy knew her password. Whether Kate knew she had access or not, Lucy didn't know, but Kate probably never thought she would use it. Lucy could legally obtain the information she needed on her own, but it would take time to jump through the hoops and fill out the request forms, and time was not on her side. Not when Cody Lorenzo thought she had been party to murder.

One by one, Lucy went through the names on her list and using Kate's access to federal records, wrote down which prison they had been incarcerated in and the year they would be released, who their cell mates were, if any, and any problems they'd had in prison. When she had all the information, she'd cross-reference it to Prenter, his victims, and WCF employees and volunteers and see if there was a connection that wasn't obvious.

There was nothing that seemed unusual. Next, she used Lexis-Nexis to search newspaper archives, wondering if the parolees who had been no-shows had gone to a state prison or a county jail on unrelated charges.

Lucy checked each name.

Tobias Janeson was dead. Murdered in Raleigh, North Carolina.

She felt the blood drain from her face. One by one she looked up each of the nine parolees.

It didn't take Lucy long to learn that seven of the nine men she thought hadn't shown up for their "date" were, in fact, dead.

And each had been killed the night Lucy had set them up to be arrested.

TWENTY-ONE

Lucy hugged Sean tightly as soon as he arrived. He'd either run or sped the six blocks, because it took him less than five minutes.

"What has you so panicked?" Sean asked quietly, though his eyes were deadly serious.

"I need to lay it all out for you," she said and led him to the dining table, "otherwise you won't believe me."

"Of course I'll believe you."

Last week it was two FBI agents shaking her foundation, but she'd gotten through it. Now? It was far worse. She reached for Sean's hand.

"Lucy, tell me."

"I've volunteered with WCF for nearly three years," she began. "We've had so much success—taking hundreds of predators off the Internet and putting them in prison." Lucy realized she was stalling—at the fundraiser the other night, if Sean hadn't already known this, he would have picked up the basics then.

"And. Well." She drank half a water bottle. "Another WCF project focuses on high-risk repeat offenders on parole. We know that fifty to eighty percent—depending on which study—of sex offenders who target children or teens and are paroled will be arrested for a like crime within three years. Those are the ones who are caught.

We find them in chat rooms popular with their target victim, and wait for them to contact one of us. We create a profile that fits their preferences, and it rarely takes longer than three months to identify and locate them. Most of these guys, by virtue of talking online with a minor, have already violated parole, but because of overcrowding, we usually need more than that to put them back in prison. We need them to try and meet up with a potential victim.

"I was involved in twenty-seven of these cases," she said. Then added, "Twenty-eight. Brad Prenter was the latest parolee we targeted. He had a strict parole—no alcohol, mandatory AA meetings, for example—and was easier to put in a situation where he'd break parole. I chatted him up in a popular college chat room. He made a move immediately; I drew it out until the time was right. Then I set it up for last Thursday at the Firehouse Bar & Grill in Fairfax.

"Cody Lorenzo takes many of these cases when he's off duty. But Prenter didn't show Thursday night. He was killed in a robbery outside a different club." She slid over a copy of the autopsy report to Sean. "I pulled the autopsy report. Look at those entrance wounds. Three in the abdomen, one in the back of the head. Then I found out that Prenter's online account was deleted. Wiped. Gone. I couldn't get it back. Cody found out from the bartender that Prenter was meeting someone at the club that he'd met online, and then he found an email in the police investigation files that came from my alias 'Tanya' sending Prenter to the other bar. He thought I had written it." She hesitated, then added, "On purpose. To kill Prenter."

Her bottom lip quivered, but she bit it to control her emotions.

Sean said, "Sit down."

"I can't—"

Sean grabbed her hand and pulled her into the seat next to him. "Why would your ex-boyfriend think you had done something like this?"

"I—he knows I killed someone before."

Sean's expression turned stony. "Adam Scott?"

"Yes, I told him when we were involved. And—and he thought—" She shook her head, unshed tears burning the back of her eyes. "He apologized. But I am capable of murder—"

Sean pulled her to him. His eyes flashed, darkened, and he said in a stern voice imbued with restrained fury, "That wasn't murder."

Then he kissed her. It stunned her, the intensity of his lips, the way his hand grasped the back of her head, holding her to him. He broke it off just as quickly, and before he could shield his emotions, Lucy recognized the rage in his expression.

"Lucy, did Cody tell you he was arresting you? Investigating you?"

She shook her head. "He thought I was protecting someone, but—"

"That bastard. Do not talk to him alone again."

"He knows I had nothing to do with Prenter. I pointed out all the reasons why it couldn't be me. He understands that now."

"He's a cop, Lucy. Do not talk to him alone about Prenter or the WCF—promise me."

She agreed. "Someone used *me* to kill Prenter. They

used *my account*." Her voice cracked and she willed herself to remain calm.

"If Prenter's account was deleted, how did Lorenzo get hold of the email?"

"Prenter had auto forwarding to his personal email. The police printed a copy from his cell phone."

"Is it traceable back to you?" Sean asked.

"No—it's nearly impossible to trace. WCF has blind accounts. If someone was really good or had a warrant, they might be able to follow an active account back to the source, which would be *Women and Children First,* not me personally. But Cody knows all my account names, and knew the name I used with Prenter."

Sean was thinking, his body deceptively relaxed, his eyes looking right at Lucy, but she could tell he wasn't seeing her.

Lucy was so torn up by the situation, she couldn't stop talking, trying to figure it out. "At first I thought it was personal—that someone who knew one of Prenter's victims had killed him," she continued. "I looked into each of them, and their families, which I didn't want to do."

Sean's eyes focused and he stared at her. "Because they were victims."

It wasn't a question, and she nodded, relieved that Sean understood exactly how she felt. "No matter how sensitive or well trained the police or the prosecutor, rape victims always feel violated by the criminal justice system. But I did it because I thought one of them used me."

"And?"

"Nothing. Maybe you can find something more—"

"You don't even have to ask. And I'll be exceptionally discreet."

She knew he would—another reason she was glad she'd called him. "But then I thought, maybe Prenter was killed by someone else—a drug deal, since we know he had date-rape drugs in his possession. And since he was released recently from prison, some prison battles spill out into the streets. So I ran all his cell mates against his victims, Prenter and his family, and all staff and volunteers at WCF. I added in all other parolees targeted by the WCF and everything came clear.

"Out of twenty-eight parolees targeted, most were in fact reincarcerated. Ten had never taken the bait—they were no shows. Seven are dead. Eight, including Prenter."

She took a deep breath. "They all died the night I set them up to violate parole. Murdered. One hit-and-run. Three stabbings. And with Prenter, four shootings. Twenty percent of the guys I set up were murdered that same night."

Sean turned her head to face him. "What do those eight have in common?"

She said, "Nothing, other than they're convicted sex offenders who were paroled early."

"Are they local?"

"No—Prenter is the only one in the greater D.C. area. They're all over the Eastern seaboard. Even one who was paroled in California. WCF has contacts in law enforcement all over the country."

"What about their crimes? Rape?"

"Prenter was the only one who was in for rape. The others were child predators. But," she added, "one of Prenter's victims was raped when they were both in high school. She's still in a coma from the homemade Liquid X he overdosed her with."

"Where?"

"Rhode Island. I looked into her and her family. I don't see them being involved, but maybe . . . I needed to talk this out with someone before I talk to Kate."

"You can't tell Kate."

Lucy frowned. "She's smart. She'll see the whole picture. If anyone can keep a lid on something, it's Kate. She didn't tell me about Morton's plea agreement, and it's not like she hasn't kept her own secrets from the FBI."

"You think that now that Kate has her life back in the FBI with her position at Quantico she can keep the lid on a vigilante killer?" Sean asked.

"I need more information," Lucy admitted. "I need to know who was assigned to each parolee."

"It wasn't your ex?"

She shook her head. "We have several officers who volunteer to help WCF in their free time. Cody is one of five or six in the greater D.C. area, and that doesn't count other regions."

"I need their names. I'll do my own investigation."

Lucy's stomach felt queasy, but she agreed. She couldn't imagine any of the men and women she knew at WCF could be party to vigilante murder. While they all wanted justice, they were all wards of the court. Cops. FBI agents. A correctional officer. One of them wouldn't kill in cold blood, would they?

"I'll run a deeper comparison of each parolee and see if there is something in common that isn't obvious," she said. "The program I'm developing has all the data points already identified; it's just a matter of picking which victims to compare."

Sean asked, "How are you going to find out who was assigned to each case?"

"Fran will know," Lucy said. "I'll talk to her—I need to be there at three anyway."

"No," Sean said forcefully. "You don't know that Fran isn't involved."

Lucy stared at him, slowly rising from her chair. "This is *Frances Buckley.* Former FBI. Head of WCF. She's not a killer!"

"Vigilante killers are a completely different breed than sex offenders or serial killers or mass murderers."

"You don't have to tell me that!" She understood criminal psychology. She'd lived it.

"No, I don't," Sean said quietly.

Lucy put her hands on the table and closed her eyes, head lowered. She didn't know what to think. This was *Fran,* her mentor. A woman she wanted to emulate, in her dedication, her compassion, and her rock-solid emotional control. Fran had taken Lucy under her wing from the beginning, and Lucy loved her like a sister. Like a mother.

"Lucy?" Sean sounded concerned, and Lucy bit back her emotions. She was not going to lose control.

"You're right. I can't tell Fran, not yet. I'll get the information on my own."

"Be careful."

Sean rose and wrapped his arms around Lucy from behind, putting his chin on her head.

"Lucy, I know this is hard for you."

Hard? It was hell, but she'd gone through hell before. She would survive, even in the face of betrayal. Because the only other option was to go to bed and pull the covers over her head and cry. If she hadn't done it six years ago, she certainly wouldn't do it now.

"If she's involved, that means she used me and my computer program to target those men. I developed my database to help WCF better assess the dangers of individual predators. She encouraged it, helped me with details, helped me input data. She's my friend." Her voice cracked.

"And it's very likely she's done nothing wrong." His tone said he didn't believe it. He turned Lucy around and touched her cheek tenderly. "But you still have to be cautious. Maybe you shouldn't go into the office. Can you hide your feelings on this?"

"I've done it for years, Sean," she said. "I'm going in. It's the only place where we'll get the information we need. Then, we'll have to talk to Kate."

"Okay. I'll go with you."

She almost said no. "And what would I tell Fran?"

"Can't you show me around the office?"

"For a couple of hours?"

"I'll drop you off; you give me the grand tour. I have a few tricks up my sleeve. Then I'll leave and watch the building while you work, pick you up when you're done."

"What kind of tricks?"

"Legal-ish tricks."

Lucy stared but didn't say anything.

"I think it's best you don't know," he said.

She crossed her arms and continued to stare, frowning.

Sean raised an eyebrow. "No need to get testy. I'm going to bug the office."

"You're not bugging Fran's office."

"We're not stealing corporate secrets. We're trying to find out who at WCF used you to target and kill sex offenders. I think it's pretty damn important to get the right information, don't you?"

Sean's casual posture painted a false picture. An undercurrent of anger still coursed through his voice. He added, "If the killer learns you figured this out, you're in danger. I need all the information I can get."

Lucy didn't know what was the right thing to do. But deep down she was humiliated and angry that she'd been used in this deadly game.

"And," Sean said, "you need to tell your ex to keep a lid on this. If you trust him."

"All right," she said. She looked at the clock. "I need to get my files and laptop."

"I'll wait."

Sean watched Lucy walk out of the room and when he was certain she was out of earshot, he called Jayne in Sacramento.

"Jayne, I need you to run some people for me, complete background."

"Hold on a sec, okay?" Without waiting for him to answer, she put him on hold.

Half a minute later, a male voice said, "Sean?"

"Duke?"

"I told Jayne the next time you called, I wanted to talk to you. You don't have any active cases. What's going on?"

Even three thousand miles away, his brother was second-guessing him. They'd had this conversation a hundred times—and Sean had thought that after he'd worked several complex cases both on his own and with Patrick, Duke had finally accepted that he was a grownup capable of running an investigation without his big brother's guidance and micromanagement. But it wasn't until Duke—reluctantly—agreed that Sean and Patrick could open RCK East that Sean thought he had truly changed.

"Do I need permission to use Jayne?" Sean asked.

"No, of course not, but—"

"Then why are you doing this?"

"Patrick told me about Roger Morton's murder. The FBI is investigating, and we have a delicate relationship with federal law enforcement and need to finesse any parallel investigations."

"And you think I don't know that?" Sean didn't particularly care about finessing any relationship with the FBI, but he wasn't burning bridges, either.

"I just want to be kept in the loop."

Sean decided to save this battle with Duke for another day. He didn't have the time or inclination to fight now. "This is unrelated to Morton. There's a vigilante group targeting sex offenders, and Lucy Kincaid is unwittingly in the middle of it. They used her to set up their victims, and I need some deep background checks."

"Who knows about this?"

"No one except you, me, and Lucy. And possibly a local cop. He's the first I want to check out. I don't think he's involved, but he has access."

"Give me the names. I'll take care of it personally."

"For now, two—Cody Lorenzo, a D.C. cop, and Frances Buckley, the director of WCF. She's former FBI." Because he'd assured Lucy he'd be discreet with Prenter's victims, he'd take care of those himself.

"Got it. I'll run these and call you later."

"Duke—"

"What?"

"If you want to talk to me about how I'm running RCK East, call me. Don't put Jayne in the middle of it."

Duke didn't say anything for a moment. "Fair enough. But you have to understand—"

"No, I don't have to understand anything about your lack of faith in me. I'm twenty-nine. You were running Rogan-Caruso when you were twenty-nine. I thought this move was a positive step, that it proved you trusted me—"

"I do, Sean."

"Not when it matters." He hung up.

Lucy came back into the dining room with her laptop packed into its case and a thick file folder. "I'm ready." She tilted her head. "Are you okay?"

"Yeah. Just a disagreement with my brother."

"Business or personal?"

"Both."

She nodded in understanding. Sean leaned over and kissed her lightly. "We're going to find out exactly what's going on. Trust me."

"I do."

Duke had known him his entire life and didn't completely trust him. Lucy had known him for a few weeks and was putting her future in his hands. In *their* hands, because she was just as involved in this as he was. Sean wasn't about to let her down.

They walked down the hall and she gestured toward a vase of red roses. "Thank you," she said as she opened the alarm panel.

"For what?"

"The flowers."

Sean halted mid-step. He stared at the roses, as if the answer of who sent them was printed on their petals. He said flatly, "I didn't send you flowers."

"But—" Lucy's voice caught when she saw the truth in his expression.

Sean looked at the table and saw the card. Fury and fear raced through his bloodstream as he read the brief message.

I had a terrific time at the ice rink yesterday. I'll see you soon.

"I didn't write that. Who knew we went skating yesterday?"

The panic that crossed Lucy's face was tangible.

"No one," Lucy whispered. "No one."

TWENTY-TWO

Lucy was wrapped up in her own thoughts as Sean drove to WCF. She hated feeling like a victim again and vowed she *wouldn't*. She wasn't a victim. She'd fought back six years ago, and while she lost a couple of rounds, she'd won the battle. She'd *survived*. She'd *prospered*. She had a life and a future and family.

Someone watched you yesterday at the ice rink. Some sicko saw you with Sean. Saw you kiss him. Dirtied what was pure and fun.

Her stomach heaved and she closed her eyes, prayed that Sean couldn't see her inner turmoil. But when her eyes were closed, memories of what Roger Morton had done to her flooded her mind: flashes like a camera, others watching as she was raped and beaten.

She couldn't bear the thought that her affection toward Sean had been tainted by a voyeur. *A stalker*. Pain seared her, physical angst, until she could hardly breathe.

The flowers and card told her he was a stalker. Her mind knew it and rebelled against it, angry and ready for action. But the intangible spectator, watching her as if she were a show, fueled the ember of pain that she still harbored deep inside.

Intellectually, Lucy could tell herself that she wasn't a

victim, that she was a survivor and everyone involved in her attack was dead. She could repeat the mantra endlessly, but it didn't change how her stomach felt, or the prickle across her skin when people looked at her, or the way her throat tightened when she let her guard down and the memories flooded in unexpectedly.

It had all been better, until now. Kate's lies, Morton's death, the stalker. Everything felt real again.

The car stopped before she realized they were already at WCF headquarters.

Sean said, "I wouldn't have sent you red roses."

She opened her eyes and looked at him. He reached out and put his hand on her cheek, then ran his fingers through her hair.

"I would have sent multicolored daisies, dozens of them in yellow and white and blue and purple and pink and every color I could find."

"Why daisies?" she whispered.

"Because they would make you smile, then laugh, and you would smile again every time you looked at them. Every time you saw a daisy, you would think of me. Because no one else would give you such a whimsical bouquet of flowers."

He pulled her the short distance toward him, meeting her halfway, and kissed her. It started soft, as if he intended to give her a quick, supportive kiss. But it didn't end. His mouth pressed against hers, confident, calm, but insistent. His hand held her neck, his fingers moving in small circles like five dancing fairies, easing her tight muscles. Her lips parted as she relaxed, her nerves calmed, and she leaned into Sean, her right hand finding his face, the rough stubble beginning to push through his skin. She rubbed lightly, the sandpaper texture alluring, then her hand moved to his soft, thick hair, savoring the contrast.

Sean kissed her repeatedly, as if to assure himself that she was here, and she returned the urgency, her internal pain and fear retreating deep inside, behind locked doors, where she prayed it would stay.

He reached down and unbuckled her seat belt, then pulled her as close as possible with the console separating their seats. Lucy put her head on Sean's chest and closed her eyes, feeling peace and safety and hope.

Somehow, they would find the answers. And whatever those answers were—whoever was responsible—Lucy would survive. She'd survived worse.

Before she had her family. Now . . . she thought she might have something else. Someone else.

"Lucy," Sean said quietly in her ear, "are you okay with this?"

"Giving you a tour so you can bug WCF offices? I don't know. But—I understand why you have to do it. But as soon as I get the files I need, we go to Kate, right?"

He smiled. "Right, but I wasn't talking about WCF. I was talking about us. About me. You. This." He kissed her.

She licked her lips, then firmly kissed him back, showing him that she was very okay with *this*. "Actions speak louder than words."

"Maybe I just want to hear how much you like me." He grinned devilishly. "I have a very sensitive ego. It needs constant reminders that I'm worthy of you."

He said it playfully, but Lucy heard just a hint of awe and apprehension in his voice, as if she were special and he really did need to know how she felt.

"I like you," she assured him. "You're wonderful. You're worthy of me. Let's get this over with and take our mutual admiration society home."

"Before we go upstairs, call Kate. We need to know about the flowers."

Noah needed daylight.

He'd been holed up in Kate's windowless computer room at Quantico all day. While he understood the need for the added computer power, he didn't understand why they couldn't have set up anywhere else. His cubicle at regional headquarters had a window.

"Your tension is suffocating me," Kate said.

"How do you work in here?"

"I've had worse. You can leave—I'll call you when the files are uncoded."

Kate was running a program to re-create every email that had passed through Roger Morton's account. She needed to keep on top of it to prevent hiccups, and she was simultaneously grading tests from the current session of FBI recruits. Running this program had taken nearly three days. Noah would never have survived in cybercrimes.

Noah had decided to work from here rather than his cubicle downtown because he was still uncomfortable about pulling in someone to help who had such a twisted history with the victim. But Kate had been nothing if not professional. A bit hotheaded at times, but sharp.

"Where's Abigail?" Kate asked.

"She's been working all day on getting the GPS data from Morton's car. It's a federal holiday, not that you were looking at the calendar or anything."

"I don't see you taking the day off, Armstrong."

The phone blinked but didn't ring. Kate answered it. She listened for a minute, then said, "I didn't see the logo on the truck. The delivery guy was five foot eleven, wore black pants, navy-blue jacket, red turtleneck underneath. Probably a sweater as well; I couldn't see because the jacket was bulky. Green cap—white words . . ." She closed her eyes. "GW Florist. He had a long blond ponytail. . . . Yes, of course I'm sure it was a guy. Lucy, what's wrong?"

The edge in Kate's voice had Noah turning his attention to her phone conversation with Lucy.

Kate said into the receiver, "Don't leave the house. . . . Dammit, Lucy!"

Kate stood and paced as far as the phone cord could go. "I want to talk to Sean. . . . Listen, Sean, I'm coming home as soon as I can. I don't like this at all. . . . I can't believe you let her go to WCF! . . . You'd damn well *better* keep an eye on her." She slammed the receiver down.

"Is everything okay?"

"Just peachy. Lucy has a—"

"One sec," he said as a new message popped up on his screen. "The ballistics from the Ralston homicide came back. No match to anything in the database."

"Did they check it against Morton? That was recent—"

"They did. No match."

Her computer beeped, and Kate turned to the screen. She grinned widely. "I'm a genius." She pressed a few buttons. "It's printing now. We have a lot of reading to do tonight. I want to take it home."

"So is there something wrong?"

"You heard the call."

"Couldn't miss it."

"It's Lucy. I think she has a stalker. I need to follow up on some roses that were delivered. I'd assumed they were from Sean. They weren't."

After Lucy gave Sean a "tour" of WCF offices and he'd planted bugs in the conference room and Fran Buckley's office, he left her there with the admonition not to leave the building until he returned. Then he drove back to Georgetown to GW Florist.

Sean walked into the small shop on Wisconsin. It was empty, except for a young female clerk behind the counter. He walked up and smiled.

"May I help you?" she asked.

Sean had considered different ways to get the information about who sent the flowers. Often, retail businesses wouldn't share private customer information with just anyone. And while he could often flirt information out of women, it wasn't a guarantee and he'd get only one chance.

He pulled his wallet out of his front pocket and opened to his private investigator's license. "Sean Rogan, private investigator. I was retained by a woman who is being stalked. This morning, she received one dozen red roses delivered by one of your drivers. There was no signature, but the message disturbed her greatly. Do you have records of who ordered such a delivery?"

She looked closely at his identification and frowned. "I'm not supposed to give out any information."

"I understand. I'll file a police report on her behalf and they'll come back with a warrant." He pocketed his ID.

"I don't know—well, I only work afternoons. I can call my mother, who owns the store."

"Do you keep records of deliveries?"

"Of course."

"I have the name and address the flowers were delivered to."

She nodded. "I can look it up by delivery address."

Sean gave her Lucy's address and waited a minute while she typed. "Yes, we have one dozen long-stemmed red roses going to that address this morning."

The tension in his stomach increased tenfold. "Do you have a name?" That he kept his voice professional was a testament to his training.

"Mr. Lorenzo was a walk-in customer and paid cash," she said.

Sean straightened. "Lorenzo?" he snapped.

She fidgeted and stepped back. "Y-yes," she said. Sean must have sounded furious, because she looked like a doe caught in the headlights.

"Cody Lorenzo?" he said, forcing himself to sound calm.

"Yes."

What was Lorenzo up to? After accusing Lucy of getting Prenter killed, maybe—*maybe*—Sean could see him sending flowers to apologize. But there was no *I'm sorry* on the card. What was he doing watching Lucy at the ice rink? Why send a cryptic message? The cop had to know it would disturb her.

Yet it happened far too often—ex-boyfriends, and sometimes ex-girlfriends, unable to let go, resorting to stalking. And Lorenzo was a cop—they had access to information the average John Q. Public didn't. When a cop turned stalker, it rarely ended well. They often used their resources to bully their victims.

Sean would not let Lucy be bullied by anyone, particularly Cody Lorenzo.

"Mr. Rogan?" The clerk bit her bottom lip.

Sean attempted to smile but wasn't sure if he pulled it off. "Thanks. I may need to talk to the person who helped Mr. Lorenzo this morning, in case I have more questions."

She handed over a card for the shop, with a number on the back. "That's my mom's number. She'll also be here tomorrow morning."

"Thank you for your time." Sean handed her his card. He was still fuming about Lorenzo, unable to figure out what he was up to—other than scaring Lucy—but on his way out, some long-stemmed white daisies caught his eye.

Sean turned back to the clerk. "Can I get one of those daisies in a bud vase?"

TWENTY-THREE

Lucy was silent as Sean drove back to her house. She couldn't wrap her head around the fact that Cody had sent her the flowers.

He must have followed them after church. It would also explain her intense feelings of being watched for the past couple of weeks. But they'd broken up last year! Why now? Because of Sean?

She felt ill. She'd trusted Cody—was her judgment about people that bad? How could she not know the truth when she saw Cody all the time?

She looked at the daisy in her hands and took a deep breath, doing her best to accept that Cody was stalking her.

Sean said, "The good news is that when confronted, most stalkers will sulk but stop their harassment. Lorenzo has a lot to lose; he'll back off."

"You're probably right," she said quietly.

"You going to be okay?"

"We were friends. I thought so anyway. How could I be so wrong about him?"

"This isn't about you, Lucy, I don't have to tell you that. It's about him."

In her head she understood that, but her heart told her she was an idiot to have trusted Cody for so many years.

To have dated him. Slept with him. He'd been so good to her.

I will not cry.

Sean stopped his car in front of her narrow house. "Come here," he said, taking her hand, kissing it, then kissing her lips. "We'll fix this. I promise. I know it hurts, but you're strong, Luce. I'll talk to him—"

She frowned. "He'd see that as a threat and dig in his heels."

"I don't think so."

"Stalkers aren't always reasonable."

"He gets out of line even an inch, we go to his boss. Right now, we don't have enough. While you and I think the message was disturbing, he could argue that it was innocuous. So we put him on notice and go from there."

"Okay." She was still worried about Sean confronting Cody, but right now she couldn't explain to Sean that she needed to be the one to talk to Cody about the flowers and unsettling message. She knew exactly what to say.

"Neither of us is going to let that guy intimidate you," Sean said, then kissed her again. "You're okay?"

"In many ways, I'm relieved it's Cody. I know him, and while I don't understand what he was thinking, I can handle the situation much better than an unknown variable."

They went inside. Though she had agreed with Sean, it didn't make sense that Cody would send her flowers, then accuse her of conspiracy to commit murder. What possessed him?

Kate was sitting by herself at the dining room table with a beer and stacks of papers in front of her. She looked up at Sean and said, "Did you find who sent the flowers?"

"Cody Lorenzo."

Kate stared in stark disbelief. "Cody?"

"That's what the florist said. Paid cash."

"That fucking bastard. Dammit! I need to talk to him—"

"I am going to do that," Sean said.

"I don't think that's a good idea," Kate said. "Considering . . ." her voice trailed off, but her eyes went to Sean and Lucy's clasped hands.

"Kate, with all due respect, I can handle Lorenzo."

"What about me?" Lucy said, frustrated. "This is between Cody and me. I'm not saying I'm going to do something stupid and confront him in a dark alley, but I think I need to be the one to talk to him." Sean opened his mouth, but Lucy cut him off before he could speak. "I understand your reasons, and you're right, except that I've known Cody for three years, and I can find out what's going on."

"You're not seeing him alone."

"I'll invite him over here. You both can be in the kitchen eavesdropping, but I will talk to him. Agreed?"

Neither Sean nor Kate liked the idea, but then Kate said, "Lucy has a point. Cody has been a friend of the family for a long time."

"Fine," Sean relented, but didn't sound happy.

Lucy dialed Cody's number on her cell phone. His voicemail picked up. "Cody, it's Lucy. Call when you get this message. It's important." She hung up, her stomach still unsettled. "I'm going to change," she said. She just needed a few minutes alone. "I'll be down in ten minutes."

Sean watched Lucy walk up the stairs. She'd reacted as he'd expected, if a bit subdued.

When Lucy was out of earshot, he asked Kate, "What do you think about this Lorenzo?"

"Sit down," Kate said.

Sean was surprised at the command. He sat, though he didn't like being ordered to do anything.

"Cody wasn't happy when Lucy broke up with him," Kate said. "But that was over a year ago. I can't see her remaining friends if he was actively pressuring her to get back together."

"Maybe that's why he's following her. He hasn't gotten over her leaving him."

Kate considered. "This was the first time he's made such contact. He was satisfied in the role of friend until—" She stared pointedly at Sean.

He resisted squirming. Kate's unspoken question asked about his intentions, and he wasn't surprised.

"So he sees Lucy and me together and he flips out and sends the flowers."

"I don't know why he didn't sign the card," Kate said. "I don't see why he wants to scare her, when his goal—at least I'd think it had be his goal—would be to win her back."

"Maybe he's looking to run in and protect her. Trying to scare her so she feels she needs a cop around."

"What am I? Chopped liver?"

"You know what I mean. The macho protective crap."

"You do pretty well with the macho protective crap," Kate said.

Sean frowned. "That's not the same thing."

Kate grinned, and Sean realized she was baiting him. She said, "Lucy's right, though—Cody needs to hear it from her. She'll make him understand. And if he crosses the line, I'll come down on his ass so hard he'll move halfway cross the country just to avoid me."

A man's voice came from the doorway. "Remind me never to get on your bad side, sweetheart."

Sean turned and saw Dillon Kincaid—Kate's husband and Lucy's brother—standing in the doorway, a suitcase at his feet.

Kate jumped up and ran to him, throwing her arms around his neck and kissing him long enough that Sean averted his eyes. "I thought you wouldn't be home until after midnight," she said.

"I came as soon as we found the bodies," he said.

"I'm so sorry, Dillon." They exchanged a look that said more than words could, and Kate added softly, "The families deserved to know the truth."

"What's going on with Lucy?" Dillon walked over to the table and shook hands with Sean. "Good to see you again. Patrick said you're helping keep an eye out for Lucy while this Morton situation is hammered out."

"Yes, sir," Sean said.

"Thank you," Dillon said.

"I'll let Kate fill you in on what's going on. I know you have some catching up to do. I'm going to check on Lucy."

Sean knocked on Lucy's door and heard her mumble something, but he didn't know whether it was "come in" or "go away."

He walked in.

Lucy's room was large, the same footprint as the

garage below, but with dormer windows protruding from the slanted ceiling. It was relatively neat, though her bed wasn't made and she had stacks of books and notebooks on every available surface, as well as two tightly packed bookshelves. She was sitting on the far side of the room, in an oversized chair.

"I'll be down in a sec," she said.

She'd been crying, but the tears had dried up. Her face was splotchy, and she sat with her knees drawn up to her chin, looking out one of the dormer windows. There was nothing to see—the overcast sky blocked the moon and stars, though the city lights would have blocked most of them anyway.

Sean closed the door and walked over to her. Lucy glanced at him, a sliver of anger slicing through her anguish.

"Dillon's here," Sean told her.

"Thanks."

She stared at him, her dark eyes bright with emotion that she was trying her damnedest to hide. What was she trying to hide from him?

He squatted in front of her chair, trying to understand what she was thinking, what she feared the most. Not the stalker—she was more angry and upset about Cody Lorenzo than scared. It was something else . . . something more than her ex-boyfriend. It was personal. It was about Lucy.

She glanced away, obviously uncomfortable with his scrutiny. What did that say? That she was scared about his feelings for her? Or her feelings for him? Did she fear he'd walk away because of what happened in her past? Or that he was here only because of it?

How could he convince Lucy how much he cared?

He reached out for her hands, which were clasped around her knees. He pulled her up.

"Sean, I—"

He kissed her lightly, then picked her up and turned around, sitting down where she'd been, but with Lucy on his lap. "I see why you like this chair," he said. "I may never get up."

"How do you know I like it?"

He smiled, and motioned to all the books surrounding it. He ran his hand down her face, through her thick hair, holding the back of her head firmly, and kissed her again. This time, he kissed her warmly, using his tongue gently but with purpose, slowly and methodically. The tension in Lucy's body dissipated and a sigh vibrated in her chest. He had one arm around her back, between the thick armrest and her body; the other he moved from her hair to her arm, then down, slowly, purposefully, to her waist and cradled her.

Lucy couldn't remember the last time she'd felt such peace, comfort, and yearning. Sean kissed her softly, over and over, no rush, no pressure, just the constant affection flowing through him. She absorbed it, relishing the embrace. She felt wanted, desired. But what gave her the butterflies in her stomach was Sean himself. The way he made her feel both protected and trusted, the way he looked at her as if they shared a secret. The way he touched her. Not just here in the chair with his arms wrapped around her like a hot, muscular blanket, but all the time. With a touch on her hand. When he pressed against her back. Brushing against her arm, as if to make sure not only that she was there, but that she knew *he* was there. He was the most tactile person she'd ever met. Sean Rogan was also extremely confident—he knew he was smart and attractive, but didn't flaunt it. But when he touched her, it was almost to reassure himself of something. What? That she was here? That she wasn't walking away? That she wanted him to touch her? It was endearing and thrilling and even a little scary, but in an exciting way.

"I wish you could hold me like this all night," she whispered.

"I don't think I could simply kiss you all night long."

She swallowed, old fears returning. "What made you think I was talking only about kisses?"

"Why do you sound defensive?"

"I'm not—" But she was. Her greatest fear when she was falling for someone, when she wanted to make love, was that he would shun her. The first time she'd found someone she cared enough about to sleep with, it had been awkward and uncomfortable and he had broken up with her shortly thereafter. It was as much her fault as his, because she should have known she wasn't ready—and that he hadn't loved her enough to be patient.

Cody had been wonderful. Sweet and warm, but always cautious. Too considerate. Too careful. Which made Lucy think that he couldn't dismiss the fact that she'd been raped. And thinking back to their relationship, could she have predicted he'd start following her? That was two strikes—two men she'd cared for who ended up being nothing like who she thought they were.

And what about Sean? Was he who she thought he was? Was she blind, foolish, a total idiot? She hadn't seen the Cody as Stalker thing at all. What didn't she see in Sean?

She wanted someone to make love to her, and only her. To not think about anything but the two of them, at that moment in time. She wanted to erase the past and not think about the future for that sliver of bliss that she knew was possible, if only she could find the right person.

"Talk to me, Lucy."

She didn't want to put a voice to her feelings, for fear they would chase Sean away. How could she explain them to him without sounding stupid? Or whiny?

"Do you want to make love to me?"

He stared at her. "Is this a trick question?"

"Not right this minute—but in general. If we were alone, would you make love to me?"

"Why are you asking me this? Do you think I'm pressuring you? I'm not—I just can't stop touching you."

"I like that."

"You're confusing me, Lucy. Tell me what you're really thinking."

She closed her eyes. Maybe, if she wasn't looking at him, it would be easier to explain.

"I want to be normal," she said. "You make me feel beautiful and wanted, but I fear . . ." She hesitated. Swallowed and gathered the courage to tell Sean the truth. "I fear that you'll treat me different because of what happened to me. I don't want to be different. I want you to treat me like you would any other woman you desire, not like I'm going to fall apart or have a panic attack. I want to be just like your other girlfriends."

Sean didn't say anything, and Lucy knew she'd said too much. After all, they'd had only a few days to get to know each other, a few days tarnished by murder and stalkers and vigilantes. Hardly a strong enough foundation on which a new relationship could grow.

She tried to get up, but Sean wrapped his arms tighter around her.

"Look at me, Lucy."

She turned to face him.

"You're *not* like my other girlfriends. Don't tense up on me; you're going to hear me out. You're not like them. That's a good thing. But it has nothing to do with your past. *Nothing*." He shook his head with a half-smile. "I've dated airheads. Beautiful women who have little motivation or drive to do anything profound or meaningful. They're shallow. You're anything but shallow."

"Then why me?"

"I grew weary of superficial women a long time ago, but I didn't know how to get out of the cycle. Didn't really want to. And then I met you, and you've been on my mind ever since."

"Ever since last week? I brought a lot of drama into your life."

"Last week? What about last month, when we had dinner at RCK on the kitchen floor? What about last year?"

"Last year?"

"You don't remember? When you flew to Sacramento to visit Patrick and Jack, you came by the RCK office one afternoon and I was sitting in my office. Patrick introduced us."

"I remember, but that was like two minutes."

"I was instantly drawn to you. I knew then I was tired of the life I'd created. I didn't know I'd be moving out here, though I did hope to see you again. But you never came by after that, and Patrick said you'd just broken up with your boyfriend, and I really didn't want to be mister rebound guy. Not to mention you were three thousand miles away."

"Now I'm six blocks away."

"Much better." He kissed her. His hand touched the soft skin under her chin, then moved to the back of her neck so he could hold her closer, so he would convince her he meant everything he said.

"I can't promise you that sometimes you won't think I'm treating you . . . *different* . . . as you say. Everything that happens to us becomes a part of us. The good, the bad, and the ugly. It shapes our future, our destiny. But what really matters is what's in here." He put his hand on her chest. "I would do anything to wipe away what was done to you; I would do anything to take away your memories and pain and fear. But deep down, you're Lucy Kincaid. Smart, beautiful, compassionate. Your compassion and drive are boundless. You *are* different, but not only because of what happened. You're different because you care. You want to make a difference in the world, by helping others find peace in theirs. There's so much in *here*," he pressed her chest firmly, "that makes you special."

She couldn't help but smile just a bit, her cheeks flushed.

"I want to be with you, Lucy." He kissed her, his hand moving to cup her full breast. "And if I have to make love to you to prove it, then I guess I'll make the sacrifice." He smiled. "I'm willing to sacrifice quite often. I think you're kind of stubborn, you might need constant reinforcement that I find you not only beautiful, but incredibly sexy."

She wrapped both arms around his neck. "You're amazing."

"I know."

"And arrogant."

"I'm a Rogan. It's in the genes."

"I like it."

Lucy relished Sean's attitude. She enjoyed how he touched her breast, how comfortable he was with his body and with hers. His confidence made her more confident.

She leaned forward, shifting on his lap slightly so she was sitting firmly on top of him. She kissed him on the neck, little wet kisses up to his ear, then to his mouth where she kissed him fully, her body moving as if it had a mind of its own.

He had his hands on her waist, his hands moving under her shirt, touching her bare skin. They were so warm, almost hot against her cool flesh, as they moved to her breasts and stopped, holding them, his fingers moving in a light, sensual massage at the top of her demi-cup. When his thumbs rubbed against her nipples, she gasped in surprise at the flash of heat that shot through her body.

"Lucy," Sean groaned, hugging her tightly, giving her a long kiss that left her breathless. He reluctantly pulled his lips from hers and said, "We should get back downstairs, or I'm going to get in trouble for something that we're not even doing."

It took Lucy a second to figure out what he meant.

She smiled, enjoying this new feeling, this new relationship with this man. She hadn't been expecting it, and yet . . . she wasn't going to question or analyze what she felt, especially now. "I almost forgot we're not alone in the house."

"That might not stop me next time."

TWENTY-FOUR

When Lucy came down the stairs, she spotted Dillon in the dining room talking on his cell phone. She waved a greeting. Even after learning what happened with Morton's plea agreement, it was good to see her brother home.

Dillon stared at Sean for a beat too long, and Lucy turned away, a bit sheepish, realizing that Kate probably already told him everything. Not only about Morton and the stalker, but also her involvement with Sean. A lot had happened in the time he'd been gone.

"I think I'll make some coffee," she said as Sean followed her into the kitchen.

Sean kissed her on the cheek. "Don't worry. Your brother will soon love me," he whispered in her ear.

She suppressed a laugh. "You think Jack will, too?"

Sean feigned fear. Maybe he wasn't pretending. "He liked me before you fell for me; maybe that'll mean something." He winked at her.

Dillon walked in and said, "Kate told me about Cody. I'm so sorry, Lucy."

Dillon didn't mean to quash her good mood, but reality dampened her spirits.

"Yeah," she said. "Me, too." What else could she say? She was so drained right now that sleep was the only thing on her mind. But she suspected that the minute she lay down, she'd be running over every conversation she could remember between her and Cody, trying to identify signs she'd missed.

She rinsed out the coffee carafe and went about the business of making coffee, needing something to do with her hands.

Sean asked, "Where's Kate?"

"On a call in her office."

"I'm going to grab my laptop out of the car," Sean said. He caught Lucy's eye. He was thinking about the listening devices at WCF. She'd almost forgotten that she'd let him plant bugs earlier that evening.

After Sean left, Lucy thought Dillon was going to discuss having boys in her room—even though she was hardly a teenager anymore—but instead he said, "I'm really sorry we kept the plea information from you, Lucy."

She scooped coffee into the filter. "I know. I'm not angry about it anymore, Dillon—you were gone for that part." She glanced at him. "I just wished you had trusted me to be a grownup."

"I do—"

"But back then I wasn't?"

"Back then I wanted to protect you."

She took a deep breath. "You can't protect me. No one can. Life is like that. We just do the best we can. And I refuse to live in the past. I'm not the girl I was six years ago."

"I know that."

"There's only so much we can do to protect ourselves and our loved ones. Unless we live in a panic room twenty-four/seven, we'll never be one hundred percent safe one hundred percent of the time. But you know what puts us all in danger?"

"What?"

"Lies. Lack of information. Good intentions. I should have known that Morton was free, because then I would have had the *information* I needed to protect myself. If I had run into him without that knowledge, I would have been stunned. That hesitation could have been my undoing."

Dillon's blue-green eyes looked at her with the unconditional love of family. "Don't underestimate yourself, Lucy."

"I don't."

She poured water into the reservoir, closed the lid, and turned the coffeepot on.

"But—" he prompted.

"I'm human. I can be shocked."

"I'm really sorry."

"I know, and I forgive you. I know that everything you did, you did because you love me." She walked over and kissed his cheek. "That doesn't make it right, but it makes it understandable. And I do love you, too, Dillon."

She leaned against the counter and watched the coffee slowly drip into the carafe.

Dillon said, "You went ice-skating yesterday?"

"Surprised me, too."

"And you like Sean Rogan?"

She rolled her eyes. "What do you think?"

"I think you're answering my questions with questions because you don't know." Dillon leaned against the counter next to her.

"Damn. Serves me right; I have a shrink for a brother."

"You could be a shrink, too. Just a few more years of school."

"I'm done with school."

"And?"

"And I really like Sean," she said quietly.

"Why does that scare you?"

"I can't talk about this with you."

"Because I'm your brother?"

Right. That sounded so stupid. "Do you believe that you can really like someone, deep down know that someone is different and special in a way you don't think of everyone else, after just a few days?"

Dillon smiled. "I knew I would spend the rest of my life with Kate after two days. And I had it worse than you."

"Worse? How so?"

"I had Jack as competition."

"*Jack?*" Lucy laughed. "I don't see Jack and Kate together *at all*."

"They have a lot in common," Dillon said, not finding the same humor that Lucy did. "The way they think, they way they distrust, the way they process information. There was a point where I believed if I had to make a stand for Kate, I didn't know if she would choose me. But I would have done it. Even though I was scared stiff she'd pick Jack."

Lucy thought a moment. "I didn't know Jack was ever in the running," she said. "Jack and Kate *are* alike in some ways, but Kate has always wanted—needed—stability. Trust. Honesty. She plays the tough, no-nonsense FBI agent, but at her core she's a quiet

homebody. She's happiest when she's here, at home with
you. It gives her peace."

Dillon looked straight ahead with a half-smile on his
face. "I really love her."

"I know. That's why you made her marry you, even
though she gave you every excuse why that was a bad
idea."

"She's stubborn." Dillon glanced at Lucy. "Why don't
you trust your own feelings?"

"I don't know." She glanced down the hall to where
Sean was working in the dining room. She remembered
what he'd said, the promises he gave. How she was different, but not in the way she'd thought. "I think I realized that falling for someone who is almost part of the
family—Patrick's partner—creates a lot of problems, especially if things don't work out."

"Or it creates a lot of benefits if it does work out. You
and Patrick have a terrific relationship. Sean is his closest friend since the accident. And Sean is smitten."

"Oh, God, you sound like Dad."

Dillon laughed and hugged her. "Don't over-think
everything, Lucy. I have that problem, too. Maybe it's
the curse of having a degree in psychology."

Sean brought his laptop into the dining room and set
it up so he could see anyone who approached the entrance. He glanced at the papers Kate had been reading
when he'd first walked in with Lucy over an hour ago—
they appeared to be emails from Morton's computer. He
didn't have time to read them now; he had to ensure his
bugs were operable and recording.

They'd have to tell Dillon and Kate about Prenter's
murder and the possible connection to Lucy's work at

WCF, but first Sean needed more information. Lucy had uncovered little of value while she went through the WCF files. She verified that no one person had been assigned to all eight parolees who had been killed, which made sense considering that the murders were all over the country. The one apparent connection was that each assigned cop reported that the felon didn't show—and the parolee was killed miles from the original stakeout.

Sean put in his earbuds and logged into his server where the recordings were archived. He focused on the recordings from Fran's office. After Lucy explained the operation, he knew nothing happened in WCF without Fran Buckley's knowledge and consent. It would hurt Lucy, but Sean read people well—and his gut told him Fran was somehow involved.

The first sounds recorded were of Fran working at her desk—typing, on the phone in a boring conversation—but he didn't want to fast-forward for fear he'd miss something. Talking, typing; then he heard Cody's voice.

"Fran, we need to talk."

"Come in," Fran said.

A door closed. Shuffling of a chair.

"Brad Prenter is dead."

"Cody—"

Sean sat upright and replayed the last minute of the recording to make sure he hadn't missed anything. He glanced at the time stamp. Five-fifteen. Right after he picked up Lucy.

Lucy walked into the dining room with a tray of coffee, cream, and sugar. "You like yours cream only, right?" She narrowed her gaze. "What's wrong?"

He paused the recording and glanced at Dillon stand-

g behind Lucy. "Lucy—I'm listening to the bugs we
lanted."

"What?" She put the tray down, the dishes rattling.

"You planted *bugs*? You mean listening devices?" Dil-
on asked, too surprised to sound irritated.

Lucy bit her lip. "I was going to tell you and Kate, but
hen this all happened tonight with Cody . . . remember
he parolee project I told you about at WCF? One of the
uys we were tracking was murdered. Someone used my
ccount to set him up."

Kate stood in the doorway next to Dillon. "What the
ell are you talking about?" she exclaimed.

"Sit down," Lucy said. "I have a lot to tell you."

TWENTY-FIVE

When Lucy was done telling Dillon and Kate every
thing she knew about the parolee project, Kate swor
and Dillon stared at his sister with his deep-thinkin
gaze. But Lucy didn't know exactly *what* he was think
ing, and she felt so tiny she wished she could go to be
and hide under the covers. She hated that she'd bee
caught in the middle of something like this—that
might have been Fran using her, she didn't even want t
think about it.

"Say something!" she finally said.

"This is fucked," Kate snapped.

Lucy had to agree with Kate, but right now Dillon
opinion meant more to her. It always had.

"Dammit, Dillon, tell me I was a stupid idiot, sa
something!"

Dillon's expression softened. "You're not stupi
Lucy."

"Naïve, then."

He shook his head. "I've interviewed hundreds of co
victed criminals. And there were some I knew, if the
ever got out on the streets again, they'd rape or kill.
knew it *here*." He punched his stomach. "But there wa
nothing I could do except testify to make sure the

stayed in prison for their maximum sentence, and hope—pray—that they'd die before they were released."

"I didn't kill anyone. I didn't know," Lucy said, her chest tightening. "You can't believe I did!"

"Of course I believe you, Lucy."

"Then what are you saying?"

"I can easily understand how someone could plan such an elaborate project. It would be someone with a strong moral center, and because of circumstances—probably a traumatic event—they've twisted that morality to justify murder."

"The vigilante syndrome."

Dillon nodded. "When the system fails, someone has to uphold justice."

"So someone is killing for what they consider noble reasons," Sean said.

"And they're smart—they're not targeting all parolees, but they've selected a choice few. That takes restraint, intelligence, premeditation . . . but *who* they're picking is important."

Sean asked, "What about opportunity?"

Dillon shook his head. "I don't think so. It's premeditated. Vigilantes have a strong sense of right and wrong, but what they think is *right* and *wrong* is viewed through distorted lenses."

Lucy added, "They think the world is in anarchy, law enforcement and the criminal justice system ineffective. They justify their actions—they are simply doing what the government can't or won't do."

"They justify murder," Kate said. She rubbed her eyes. "Damn, I can almost understand that. I would have killed Trask to stop him."

"That's not the same thing," Dillon said, "and you know it. Trask was a killer evading authorities."

Lucy said, "There are many law-abiding citizens who aren't violent, though they have some traits in common with vigilantes. They fight nonstop for tougher laws, swift penalties, strengthening of the death penalty, more resources for law enforcement."

Dillon concurred. "They strongly support restrictions on freedom in the name of public safety, and often report friends and neighbors who they think are breaking the law. They don't have the psyche to kill."

"But," Lucy said, "those with a strong sense of vigilante justice coupled with the ability or psyche to take a human life, usually because of violence in their past, can cross the line."

Did that make Lucy more likely to kill in cold blood. She'd killed Adam Scott because he'd hurt her, he would have killed her, and he would not have stopped with her. She tracked parolees because they should stay in prison for their crimes. Was she on the path of developing such a twisted sense of justice that she could justify cold blooded murder?

A chill ran through her body, cold goose-bumps rose on her flesh. Sean looked at her, but didn't say anything.

Dillon leaned forward, his expression intense, so wrapped up in his own analysis he didn't notice Lucy's discomfort and self-appraisal.

"They have taken their crusade beyond the law, and almost to the people themselves. Because really, would most people shed a tear for a child molester who's killed in a hit-and-run? Or a rapist who's shot to death in an alley?"

Sean said, "Then why not just declare war on the worst of the lot and kill them all?"

Dillon said, "Public relations. Motive. Opportunity. Vigilantes don't want to be stopped. Also, the targets have some meaning for them personally. They may be targeting an area—for example, criminals who get off on a technicality in one jurisdiction—or they may be targeting individuals who committed a specific crime, like child molesters."

Lucy cleared her throat. "I ran all eight victims, and I can't see a commonality."

"Do you mind if I look?"

Lucy handed over her files. "I used my program; maybe there's a flaw in extrapolating the data. I thought—"

Dillon glanced at the files. "Your program is brilliant, Lucy. It's the best thing I've seen that melds science with psychology." He tapped the first page. "I already see the problem."

"What?"

"Take out Prenter." He handed her back the files.

She stared. At first she didn't see anything because the report had been run with Prenter's data and stats. She'd need to rerun everything without Prenter, and then . . .

"Oh!"

"You see it, too."

"Yes. All seven were convicted of molesting a minor female they knew."

"It's more than that. The rapist had authority over their victim. A pastor. A stepfather. A father. Two uncles. A teacher. Prenter doesn't fit the profile. When you take him out, it creates a pattern."

"But we can't take him out because he was killed in

the same way—meaning he was on parole and targeted by the WCF."

"I didn't say I had all the answers, but I think whoever is selecting the parolees to target is focusing on convicts who committed a crime similar to one perpetrated on someone they loved."

Kate said, "Prenter was in a position of authority as well—he was a teaching assistant who raped a student."

"Not a minor student," Dillon said. "Sara Tyson was nineteen, correct?"

Lucy nodded.

"She was still young," Kate said.

"And," Lucy said, "there is the victim they couldn't tie to him, his ex-girlfriend who's in a coma because of a near-lethal dose of homemade X. Anyone who was involved in Prenter's case knows about her. But it was never allowed into the court record."

"How do you know it's not in his official records?" Kate asked.

"WCF has backgrounds on all the predators we identify and monitor. But—" She frowned.

"What?" Dillon prompted.

"He was seventeen at the time. His juvenile record is sealed, and the judge refused to unseal it during his trial."

"Then how do you know about the girl in the coma?" Dillon asked.

"From my briefing at WCF. Fran has a lot of contacts—she could have spoken to the original investigating officer in his hometown. Or even the D.C. detective in charge, because they would have uncovered it in the course of investigating Sara Tyson's charges."

"He's different," Dillon said. "Something about Prenter doesn't fit the other parolees, though maybe you're right and it goes back to his first victim."

Sean looked at Kate. "You might want to leave the room."

She glared at him. "Why?"

"I bugged Fran Buckley's office. It's a digital bug; everything is sent to a blind server that I can retrieve. I don't actually need to listen live." Sean glanced at Dillon. "It's a gray area."

"I believe it's illegal," Dillon said.

"It *is* illegal!" Kate exclaimed.

"I'll dispute that. I'm not stealing corporate secrets, nor am I using these tapes to incriminate her in a criminal investigation."

"It's fruit from the forbidden tree," Kate said.

"All the more reason for you to leave the room," Sean said pointedly.

Lucy bit her lip. She hadn't seen Kate this angry in a long time. Her sister-in-law stood abruptly and left. A moment later her office door slammed shut.

"I'm sorry," Lucy said to Dillon, "but someone is setting me up, and I couldn't sit by and let it happen."

"Kate knows that," Dillon said. "She's not angry with you. I think it's the situation—she hates when an investigation gets out of control. She finally has her life back. She doesn't want to cross the line again. The FBI isn't big on second chances, and third chances? Forget it."

"I don't want to put Kate in a difficult position," Sean said, "and I didn't want to bring her in at all until we had something." Sean caught Lucy's eye. "You okay with this?"

She nodded. "Play it."

Sean turned up the speaker on the laptop and cued the recording.

A moment later, Fran's voice came through surprisingly clearly. She was talking to Gina, her assistant, about following up on donor commitments from the fund-raiser.

Then Fran was on the phone with someone—they heard only her end of the conversation, but it sounded like it was the hotel manager of the event and they were settling some details. Sean fast-forwarded, then said, "This is about seven minutes after the assistant left."

On the recording, a door closed. "Do you have a couple of minutes?"

It was Cody.

"Of course," Fran said. "Is something wrong?"

"You could say that. Brad Prenter is dead."

"I know, I read about it—"

"I think you know more about it."

Lucy sucked in her breath. Sean took her hand and squeezed.

"Cody—"

Cody sighed loudly enough for the recording to pick up the sound. "I'm sorry, I just—I don't know anything anymore."

"Tell me what happened. I really don't understand what you're getting at."

"Someone used Lucy's chat account—the same account she used to talk to Prenter—to send him to Club 10. He was shot and killed a block away."

"That couldn't have happened."

"But it did. I have proof. At first—God, Fran, at first I thought it was Lucy, because it was her account and I know how meticulous she is. She'd never give out her

password. And she was so focused on Prenter because of
the girl in the coma. She'd told me when Prenter was
first added to our list that Evelyn Oldenburg never got
justice."

"Lucy?"

"I thought she was working with someone."

"You didn't accuse her—"

"I feel like shit. I can't believe what I said to her, but
she didn't have anything to do with it. Not just because
of what she said, but she just wouldn't. I should have
known from the beginning, but I got sucked in by the evidence."

"What evidence?"

"The police found a message on Prenter's cell phone
that had been forwarded from Lucy's 'Tanya' account
that sent Prenter to Club 10 instead of the Firehouse,
where my partner and I were waiting for him."

"I'm still not sure what you think happened."

"Someone used Lucy's online identity to send that
message to Prenter."

"You mean someone from WCF sent him to that bar."

"And killed him."

Silence. A long moment later, Fran said, "You're accusing one of my people of murder?" She sounded both
angry and upset, though her digital voice, without benefit of facial expression, also sounded flat.

"Yes, I am."

"I don't know what to say." A chair rolled on hard
plastic. "I don't believe it."

"We need to go through everyone's background reports. I think someone here has a connection to Prenter
and took advantage of WCF to kill him. Someone with
sharp computer skills, because this individual also went

in and completely erased Prenter's chat account. Gone. The only reason I found this message is that it had been automatically forwarded to Prenter's personal email, which was on his BlackBerry. It's in the police report."

"Do the police think that someone at WCF is involved? Or Lucy?"

"No—they don't even think it's connected. They're focused on finding the man and woman he argued with in the alley."

"Fill me in—I'm not up to speed on this case."

"Prenter told the bartender he was waiting for a woman he'd hooked up with online. About forty minutes after he arrived, a girl came up and hit on him—the bartender said she'd come in with another guy, but they fought and he left. They talked for a while, left about fifteen minutes later. The girl's boyfriend confronted them in the alley, according to a witness, and the girl left with her boyfriend. Less than five minutes later, Prenter was shot and killed next to his car. Four bullets."

"Robbery?"

"His wallet was taken. Not his Porsche—and he had his keys in his hand."

"Maybe the shooter got scared. Heard someone."

"And not take the fastest available transportation? Leave on foot? I don't think so. I think the wallet was taken to cover up a hit. I think Prenter was intentionally targeted, and whoever did it had access to our computers."

Fran said, "Our charter isn't a secret. It's not like we broadcast what we do to the world, but we don't keep it to ourselves, either."

"Shit." Cody was walking—pacing—the room, his

voice getting louder and fainter as he moved away from the bug. "Fran, this is serious."

"I agree. Let me look into it. I'll be discreet, of course—I'll have Gina pull every computer log from every computer and we'll see who logged into the chat room to send the message after Lucy logged out on Wednesday afternoon."

"That's good, but I think you need to review the background reports again, find out if there is any connection to Prenter."

"I will." She paused. "You said you told Lucy?"

"I had to—she's the one who asked me to look into Prenter's murder in the first place."

"*Lucy?*" Silence. "Why would Lucy ask you to look into Prenter's murder?"

"She saw the article in the paper, then pulled his autopsy report. She said it looked suspicious. I was placating her at first, but when I read the file I realized she was right. This whole thing is suspicious."

The door opened and Cody's voice sounded as if it was in a tunnel. "I'm sorry, Fran. If you find out who, we'll handle it internally."

"Thank you, Cody."

The door closed firmly.

"Damn," Fran said.

There was complete silence.

Dillon said, "There's something wrong with that conversation."

Sean nodded. "No mention of going to the police. Fran's first reaction, I'd think, after disbelief, would be to inform the authorities."

Lucy disagreed. "The parolee project is in a gray area.

It's not technically entrapment, but Fran didn't want it getting out to the public because of the potential for bad press. Her entire life is WCF. If she thought someone on the inside was using the organization for their own agenda, I don't know what she would do—except everything she could to protect the group."

"But this is murder," Dillon said.

The digital recording registered a loud noise, then files slamming and papers ruffling.

Fran's voice, "Dammit, where is it?" More movement, a loud, long sigh of frustration. "I just don't believe this." Sounds of the filing cabinet opening, a furious perusal of papers, then silence for a good two minutes. Lucy thought Fran had left, then there was a jingle of keys, followed by a door slamming shut.

Sean looked at Dillon. "I should have found a way to bug her purse."

"Not Fran," Lucy said, not wanting to believe it. She looked at Dillon.

"You think it's her, too," he said quietly.

She nodded, blinking back tears. "It's what you said earlier—about why vigilantes target certain criminals. Fran's younger sister was repeatedly molested by their uncle. They lived in virtual poverty, their mom worked two jobs, Fran worked nearly full-time in addition to school so she could save money for college, and no one knew what a sick pervert the uncle was."

"Most repeat child molesters are well versed at keeping their victims quiet," Dillon said. "A combination of treats and threats, and by the time the child outgrows both, they are made to feel so guilty—convinced that they are to blame for the abuse—that they never talk about it. How did Fran find out?"

"When her sister was strangled by the uncle. The day she started her first menstrual cycle, he raped and killed her. He told the police she'd lost her innocence and he had to stop her from turning into a whore." Lucy spoke matter-of-factly, but the case bothered her deep down in a place she kept sealed.

"There's another difference in these targets," Dillon said, looking at Lucy's spreadsheet.

"Right—they're spread out. No two in the same city."

"Or, if you look at it another way, Prenter is the only *local* parolee who was killed. That's one more reason Prenter doesn't fit with the others."

"You mean different killer?" Sean asked.

"No, same killer. Or same group—I'm certain there are at the minimum two killers, but most likely three or more people involved, for a conspiracy this large. They targeted Prenter for a different reason, otherwise they wouldn't have risked hitting so close to home—not just D.C., but a *personal* hit. We need to look at all his victims. I think one of the people involved is related to one of his victims. When he got out, that individual used their position in the group to put Prenter on the list, even though he didn't fit their profile."

"I've looked at the victims," Lucy said. "Nothing jumps out. I asked Sean to look deeper."

"Good," Dillon said.

"We need to talk to Cody," she said. "He'll help, tell us everyone he spoke with. Maybe something will ring a bell."

"Lucy," Sean said sharply. "Cody has other problems. He's stalking you."

"Maybe he didn't mean to make the message sound so disturbing."

"And what about all those times you thought some-one was watching you? That didn't freak you out?"

"Yes, but—"

"Do not make excuses for that man!"

"Ease up, Rogan," Dillon said.

Lucy shook her head. "Sean's right." She had to accept the fact that Cody had tried to scare her. "Cody followed us from church to brunch to the ice-skating rink—I didn't tell him where we were going because I didn't know. It's just so hard to put him in the role of a bad guy."

"Did he call you back?"

She shook her head. "I'll track him down tomorrow morning."

"Not alone," Sean said.

She glanced at Sean. She understood that he was worried and being protective, but the tension coming off him was palpable. He'd been so understanding earlier, but now he was acting just like her brothers.

She raised an eyebrow at him and, keeping her voice cool, said, "I don't have a death wish, Sean, and I already have four overprotective brothers—I don't need another one."

He ran a hand through his hair. "I'm sorry."

"I appreciate your concern, though, and I promise I won't cut him any slack, okay? But I think Dillon should come with me when I talk to him. Less testosterone."

"Gee, thanks," Dillon said, lightening the conversation.

She rolled her eyes. "You know what I mean."

TWENTY-SIX

Abigail hailed Noah as soon as he turned down the aisle of their squad's cubicles early Tuesday morning. "I got the GPS data."

"We were supposed to have it yesterday."

"Yeah, and I harassed the poor CEO mercilessly all day even though there is no immediate risk to life or limb for this data."

"Sorry." Noah rubbed his eyes. "Kate and I split Morton's emails. I still have a headache."

"Learn anything?"

"Quite a bit. Our victim from Saturday, Robert Ralston?"

"I remember."

"If I'm reading these messages right, he's the one who first contacted Morton. Morton got out of prison, sent a few emails letting people know he was around, and then nothing—until the first week of August, when Ralston sends Morton a message."

Noah put down his files and pulled the summary he'd typed out at home. "August sixth, Ralston asks Morton if he's interested in a new game plan, that Ralston wants to retire to Florida but doesn't have any money. Morton responds that he's broke, too, and he hates being a mechanic. Ralston says he'll see what he hears, but he's not a techie."

"Morton bought his computer a few weeks later."

"I think that was incidental—he needed to earn the money to buy it, and after seven weeks working he had the funds. He immediately started going to all the online porn sites. Possibly doing research on how the technology and offerings changed."

"Or maybe he was just a horny bastard after spending six years in prison."

Noah shrugged. "Then Morton contacts Ralston in late September and says he has a new game plan—same phrase Ralston used—and would be ready in a few months. That's about the time he started collecting porn and archiving it on his computer. A lot of the tapes and disks were older. I don't know what his plan was—nothing in the messages give any details. But he had a lot of webcam films and our techs say it's obvious one or both participants didn't know they were being filmed."

"Blackmail, maybe?"

"Possibly. And he would need money for equipment, setup, planning, and then of course the blackmail angle, if that's what he was doing. Or, he could simply have been creating a voyeur site. I don't know if we'll ever learn the truth, considering both Ralston and Morton are dead."

"Until whoever killed them launches the venture."

Noah nodded. "We don't have Ralston's emails, but he must have been doing some work for Morton, because he gets back to Morton in late November and says he found a 'game-player.' "

"Why didn't Morton come out here then?"

"I don't know. I can't find any other messages from

Ralston until late December. I'm wondering if they might have talked on the phone, and Guardino in Denver is going through Morton's records. There were no 202 or 703 calls, but in this day and age disposable phones could have any number of area codes, Morton could even have had one we didn't find. Our analysts are going through Ralston's phone records. Something is going to match up but it's going to take time."

"So in December Ralston says what?"

"Pick a time and place. But get this—Morton didn't tell Ralston when and where. There are no more communications from them."

"Then you'll love what I have here." Abigail grinned like the Cheshire Cat and spread a greater D.C. map on his desk. "I mapped out everywhere Morton went in the rental car from the moment he drove out of the Dulles Airport parking lot. And two of his stops? Ralston's apartment."

Noah followed Abigail's finger as she traced her pencil mark. "He was busy those two days."

"Yes, he was."

Noah scanned it. In addition to Ralston's apartment, it included the Washington Marina where he was killed. He arrived there at 11:23 p.m. He died at approximately midnight. His body hadn't been moved. At 11:59 p.m. the car left. "He went to the meeting—possibly to hook up with the money people for his new 'game plan'—and they killed him. Took his car and went back to his motel—why?"

"If we're going with the blackmail angle, maybe that was how he was going to fund his new project—and he blackmailed the wrong person."

Noah considered. "He doesn't bring the incriminating

evidence, so the killer goes to his motel to look for it. Then drives the car to within blocks of Dulles Airport."

"No—the car went one other place." She put her finger down.

Noah's mouth almost dropped open. "Back to Ralston's apartment?"

"You know what I think? I think the killer was looking for something."

"That would support the blackmail theory."

"Morton didn't have it on him. It wasn't in his car, it wasn't in his motel—"

"So they went to Ralston."

Abigail nodded. "And killed him. *Then* they left the car in the warehouse near Dulles at four-thirty in the morning."

Blackmail. It could pay enough to fund Morton's "game plan."

"How did the killer get to the marina if he drove away in Morton's car?" Noah pondered.

"He came with Morton?"

"Unlikely. Unless they were meeting someone else."

"So the killer has a partner. Or took public transportation."

Noah considered. "Or, Ralston went with Morton."

Abigail frowned. "But if Ralston and Morton were working together as closely as they appeared, why go back to Morton's motel after he was killed? The manager's description, though vague, doesn't come close to fitting Ralston. If the killer wanted both of them dead, why take Ralston back to his apartment?"

"Maybe Ralston was scared, trying to buy time."

"It's possible."

But something was missing. It seemed too convoluted

a plan, but until they knew who Morton was meeting and what Morton was supposed to exchange for the money he expected to get, they wouldn't know.

"Did you check taxi and limo companies?"

"No licensed driver took anyone out to the marina that night."

Noah tapped his finger on a mark in Somerset, Maryland. "What's this? It looks residential."

"I haven't checked it out yet; I just got this an hour ago."

"He drove there Thursday night."

His computer beeped, telling him he had a new email. He glanced at it, then did a double-take. "Here's something new," Noah said.

As he opened up the message, Abigail looked over his shoulder. It was from one of their analysts.

Agent Armstrong,

Per your instructions, I retraced Roger Morton's steps prior to his arrival at Dulles. Under his name, there was no travel. Under his cousin's name Cliff Skinner there was only the ticket from Denver to DIA. However, there was a charge to Skinner's credit card for a round-trip ticket from Dulles to Seattle on January third, returning on January fourth, under the name Robert Ralston. I contacted the airlines and they confirmed that the ticket was issued and used.

Let me know if you need anything else.

—Sandy Young, Analyst II

"Ralston went to Seattle? What for?" Abigail asked. Noah didn't respond. Morton paid for the ticket, but

Ralston did the travel. One day, overnight, why? What was Morton's connection to Seattle?

He replied to Sandy:

Thanks Sandy. See what you can find on Ralston in Seattle. If he got a rental car, hotel, under his name or Skinner. Noah.

"Curiouser and curiouser," Abigail said.

Noah agreed. "Let's go check out the location in Somerset." He started walking, then stopped so abruptly that Abigail nearly ran into him.

"I see a flash of brilliance," she said.

"Seattle. It was in the files Stockton gave me. It's where Adam Scott and Morton took Lucy Kincaid after they kidnapped her."

"You think it's connected?"

"I doubt it's a coincidence."

Noah turned around and went back to his computer. He quickly sent a message to Assistant Director Rick Stockton and Hans Vigo, who would be able to get answers faster.

TWENTY-SEVEN

Sean pulled up as close to the employee entrance of the D.C. Medical Examiner's Office as he could get, double-parking because there was no street parking available. He wasn't about to let Lucy walk far, not until they knew what Cody was up to. And whether Fran Buckley or the people she worked with were dangerous. Lucy hadn't agreed or disagreed with Dillon and Sean's belief that Fran was behind the vigilante group, and Sean didn't push. She'd had a lot dumped on her in the last few days, and he wanted to give her the room to come to her own conclusions. She'd get there.

Lucy said, "I could get used to having a car service. Sweet car, hot guy, door-to-door service."

"Shouldn't that be 'hot car, sweet guy'?" Sean teased. He kissed her grin. "Be careful, Luce. Remember, if Cody comes by, call your brother or Kate. And avoid Fran until we figure out if she's involved in this."

"You don't have to tell me twice."

"I'm just worried." He touched her face. She looked tired, and he said, "You know, when this is all over you deserve a vacation. A three-day weekend anywhere my plane can take us."

She smiled mischievously. "Anywhere? I don't think you should give me such freedom."

"I said anywhere, I mean it. What time do you get off?"

"Three."

"I'll be here."

Sean watched Lucy until she entered the building, then made sure that no one followed her before the security door closed.

He drove back to Lucy's house. Kate had emailed him earlier and asked that he come by at ten.

When Kate opened the door she looked at her watch. "You're an hour early," she said.

"It didn't take long to pick up Lucy, take her to work, and get back here."

She closed the door behind him. "Coffee's in the kitchen."

Sean followed Kate down the hall. Like Lucy, she looked exhausted. Her hair was still damp from her shower, and thick sections fell in her face. She impatiently tucked them behind her ears.

Dillon was sitting at the kitchen table reading a thick file. A man of about fifty with glasses, a slight paunch, and graying hair sat across from Dillon.

Dillon glanced up. "Sean," he said, gesturing to the stranger, "this is a good friend of ours, Dr. Hans Vigo. He's FBI."

"Vigo." Sean knew that name. "You're the profiler?"

"Good memory." Hans shook Sean's hand. "We haven't met."

"No, but my brother Duke—everyone at RCK—speaks highly of you."

"How is Duke?" Hans asked.

"Same as always." Sean had been inching closer to see what Dillon was reading.

Kate stood next to Sean and said, "It's Fran Buckley's personnel file from the Bureau, Mr. Nosy."

"Is that why you asked me here?"

"No, Noah Armstrong wants to talk to you."

Sean abruptly turned to her. "You're setting me up to talk to a Fed?"

It was Hans who answered. "You were seen on a surveillance tape entering a restaurant owned by Sergey Yuran. Considering his name has come up in the course of this investigation, we need to know what he said."

Sean frowned. "If I learned something that would have helped, I would have shared the information with Agent Armstrong on Saturday."

Sean didn't feel comfortable talking to the FBI about something that could get him in hot water—he stood by his decision. He considered calling Duke for advice on whether to pull in a lawyer, but quickly dismissed the thought. He wasn't going to lean on his brother every time he came head to head with law enforcement. He was a big boy, he would make his own decisions, and he knew he hadn't been out of line in talking to Sergey Yuran. There was no way Yuran would have spoken to a cop, and if it was true he was under surveillance, Armstrong wouldn't even be able to get in there. Shaking the trafficker down for the murder of a scumbag like Morton was way down on the priority list from trafficking in guns and human beings—which told Sean that Noah wanted this meeting off the record, hence here at Kate's house. Maybe the Fed wasn't the "by-the-book" hardass Sean had thought when he met him on Saturday.

Yet, every time Sean had spoken to cops in the past it had come back to bite him in the ass.

Before he'd been kicked out of Stanford, Sean discovered one of his professors liked child porn. Sean exposed his repulsive obsession so everyone would know what kind of pervert he really was. The Feds promised nothing would happen to Sean if he told the truth about how he'd hacked into the professor's system and what initially tipped him off. Sean told the truth. Next thing he knew, Stanford expelled him for hacking into the school database. Duke had said the FBI did what they could, and Sean was damn lucky he wasn't in prison. They'd agreed to expunge the record; however, Sean was certain his FBI file was an inch thick. The incident with the sick Stanford professor wasn't the only time he'd been in hot water when trying to right wrongs.

Kate said, "Sean, you'd better watch yourself around Armstrong. He's good, and he doesn't like interference."

"I didn't interfere with anything."

"Showing up at Ralston's apartment wasn't interfering?"

"I'm not going to rehash this. You know why I was there. I didn't screw with his investigation."

Hans said, "No one is looking to get you in trouble, Sean."

Sean didn't know whether to believe him, but Duke thought Hans Vigo walked on water, and that couldn't be said of a lot of people, so Sean gave the profiler the benefit of the doubt.

"All right, but if Armstrong arrests me, you'd better be the one to post bail."

Hans smiled. "I give you my word."

Sean relaxed marginally and went to pour himself coffee.

Hans said to Dillon, "Switching gears, is there anything in Buckley's file that puts her on or off the suspect list?"

Sean glanced at Hans. Hans said, "Dillon called me last night and told me about Prenter's murder and Lucy's concerns about a setup with parolees."

Sean frowned. "Is this going to be a problem for Lucy? She's in the middle of the FBI application process."

"I'm well aware—I gave her a recommendation. And nothing she's done is going to affect my recommendation. I can't honestly say how this will play out with the Bureau, however."

"But we can't keep it secret," Kate said. "This kept me up all night—Morton was on federal probation. But he was shot in the back of the head, just like Prenter and several of the other parolees Lucy discovered last night."

Kate's theory stunned Sean. He hadn't considered that the Morton homicide was connected to WCF.

He said, "You think the same people killed Morton as killed Prenter and the other parolees?"

Hans said, "I'm quietly pulling all the files—we're dealing with multiple jurisdictions here—to see if there's something that connects the killer to the victims. Different manners of death, and so far no ballistics matches. I'm looking for other patterns, such as that they all were killed after dark. They all were in public. None of the crimes were solved.

"No one brought him out using WCF's system," Hans continued. "It would have been extremely easy to put him back in prison for the rest of his life if someone found him violating his parole by traveling to D.C."

"Go directly back to jail, do not pass go," Kate mumbled, sitting next to Dillon, a hot cup of coffee in her hands.

"They wanted him dead," Hans said. "Not back in prison."

"But that still doesn't explain why they brought him here and didn't gun him down in Colorado," Sean said.

"Noah learned this morning that Ralston flew to Seattle three days before Morton arrived in D.C.," Hans said.

Sean looked at him blankly. "Is there something important about Seattle?"

Dillon said, "It's where Adam Scott and Morton took Lucy after they kidnapped her. To an island off Seattle."

Sean's skin crawled. "Why was he there?"

"We don't know," Hans said, "but the SAC in Seattle is on top of it. He's been part of this from the beginning."

Sean walked to the kitchen counter and topped off his mug, even though he didn't particularly like coffee. He needed something to do or he'd go right now to retrieve Lucy.

"Why can't you just haul Fran Buckley into an interview room and ask her?" Sean said, growing impatient with speculation and incomplete information. "We know she's involved. I just can't believe seven sex offenders—eight, including Morton—could be killed without her knowing exactly what's going on."

"I agree," Hans said, "but we don't know the extent of the vigilante group, and we don't know if she's the ringleader or one of the underlings. We bring her in too early without solid proof, we tip our hand and her partners disappear. We need something more—"

"Like what?" Sean interrupted.

"A connection."

Well, that was vague. Sean frowned and looked over Dillon's shoulder. "Where's her FBI service record?"

"I haven't gotten that far."

"She's retired. I'll bet she still has a lot of contacts. What squad did she work on?"

"How do you know so much about the FBI?" Kate asked, taking the folder from Dillon.

"Duke married a Fed. Domestic Terrorism. Jack's married to one as well. We have several former Feds— FBI, ICE, DEA, pick your acronym—working with RCK. I pick up on things."

Dillon said, "She retired ten years ago—five years early."

"But she had twenty years. That's not uncommon," Hans said.

"Kate, did you know Fran when she was still in the Bureau?"

Kate shook her head. "We weren't in the same office— I was in the Washington Field Office my entire six years before I went underground."

Kate flipped through Fran's service record. "She spent her first three years in Philly, ten years in Richmond, then her last seven in Boston as an SSA."

She continued to flip through pages, then exclaimed, "Oh shit."

Sean watched the blood drain from Kate's face. He'd never seen the unflappable Fed look scared. She handed Dillon the file with shaky hands.

"Look at her stint in Richmond. Right before she left. Dillon—it's the connection."

Sean looked over Dillon's shoulder, but nothing obvious jumped out at him. "What is it?"

Kate stared at Hans. "I didn't know Mick Mallory was in Richmond."

"Who's Mick Mallory?" Sean demanded.

"I don't know where to start," Kate said.

Dillon explained. "Mallory went undercover in Trask Enterprises working for a rogue FBI agent. Deep cover. He became one of them."

The blood in Sean's veins froze. "You don't mean—"

"He went too far by not turning Trask in when he could have, but his boss wanted very specific information, and Mallory was under extreme stress. When he was still an active agent, he'd been in deep cover in a joint FBI-DEA op. His cover was blown and the target killed his wife and young son." At first, Sean detected a hint of sympathy and understanding in Dillon's tone, but that disappeared as he continued explaining what happened to the disturbed agent.

"Mallory lost everything he cared about, and was put on administrative leave, but he couldn't let it go," Dillon said. "He went after the target and the situation ended in bloodshed. Two agents were seriously injured in the process, and every suspect was killed. The information the FBI and DEA needed about their operation died with them. Mallory lost his job, laid low for a while before he was recruited to infiltrate Trask. He justified his actions because the reward—putting Trask and others in prison or the grave—was all he could see. And that bastard Merritt used him!" He hit the table with his fist.

Sean had never seen Dillon Kincaid so angry. He nearly stepped back in surprise. Kate put her hand on Dillon's arm. His hand covered hers. "Don't," she said quietly.

Hans said, "Merritt's dead. Either a car accident or

suicide, six months after the whole thing went down. He left a detailed journal of everything he'd done and ordered Mallory to do. Mallory was deemed suicidally depressed and put in a mental health ward for eighteen months."

"Great. First Morton gets an easy six years in federal prison, then this prick Mallory gets the psych ward? Big fucking deal when people are dying." Sean would never understand the criminal justice system. It wasn't usually those whose lives were on the line who screwed everything up—lawyers and politicians were the problem. Cops did their job, but in the end, whether someone went to prison or not was as much deal brokering as anything else.

"Mallory was shot and left for dead when Trask figured out that he'd sent me information about Lucy's location," Kate said.

"You mean this guy sat by while Lucy was attacked?" Sean had never seen red before, not like this.

"Calm down, Sean. You weren't there," Kate snapped.

She was right. But dammit, he cared deeply for Lucy! Knowing that some rogue federal agent had allowed her to be brutally raped and did nothing to stop it made Sean sick and angry.

Dillon said, "If Mallory and Fran Buckley got together, this sort of vigilante operation might just appeal to both personalities."

Hans agreed. "If Mallory is involved, it would explain why Morton was a target. If he thought Morton was falling into his old tricks, then Mallory would certainly go after him."

"I think Mallory would have gone after him no matter

what," Kate said. "That still doesn't explain why Morton was in D.C., or why Ralston went to Seattle."

"Where's Mallory *now*?" Sean asked.

"We don't know," Kate said. "He disappeared after he got out of the hospital."

"We need to find him," Hans said.

The doorbell rang and Kate got up to answer it.

Hans leaned forward and whispered, "Dillon told me about the listening device you planted. Let's keep that quiet."

Sean looked at Hans differently now. He was no typical federal agent.

Kate returned with agents Noah Armstrong and Abigail Resnick.

"Morton went to Somerset, Maryland, the night he arrived in D.C.," Noah said without preamble. "He parked on Eucalyptus Street, and Abigail and I interviewed every neighbor who was home this morning and ran the property records for the houses within one hundred yards of where Morton parked. No one matches a name on any of Morton's contact lists, but there are a couple of rentals and we're contacting the owners of the properties."

Abigail said, "I'm going back tonight to talk to anyone we missed. He was there for twenty-five minutes, so he must have had a reason."

"Maybe it was a prearranged meet on the street or in his car or a park," Kate said. "Not in someone's house."

"Unlikely," Noah said. "The neighborhood is established and well maintained. Someone would have noticed a stranger, and he was there just after eight in the evening. But anything's possible." Noah turned to Sean. "Rogan, we need to talk about Sergey Yuran."

Sean tried not to bristle at Noah's official tone. He
didn't trust Mr. Law and Order. Noah Armstrong was
too black-and-white for his taste. But the faster they
shared information and found Morton's killer, the better
off Lucy would be. If Morton's murder was connected
to the other dead parolees as he and Kate had specu-
lated, all Lucy's problems would be solved and Sean
could take her away for a few days.

"I went to see him on Saturday."

"Why?"

"He was one of Morton's known associates. I knew
who he was—not personally, but RCK has worked rescue missions all over the world; we know the players in
human trafficking. It was an obvious place to start."

"For *me* to start, not you."

"He would never have talked to you and you know it.
Criminals like Yuran have the system gamed, which is
why there's surveillance on him. My guess, it was ICE.
I'm surprised they shared with you."

Noah bristled. "Who told you that?"

"I spotted them."

"I highly doubt that."

Sean didn't comment. He'd only further irritate the
Fed. "If he'd had information about Morton or who
killed him, I would have told you."

"You're not a cop; you don't know what's going on in
this investigation or what questions to ask."

Sean raised an eyebrow. "All he said was that he'd
heard about a guy looking for an online sex trade expert
and he put out some feelers, then nothing—said the guy
disappeared or lost interest. He smelled something
wasn't kosher, so didn't pursue it."

"Dammit, Rogan, you're screwing up this investigation right and left!"

"No, I'm not," Sean said firmly. "Yuran didn't trust the source because it didn't come through his normal channels."

"And you believed him? Yuran runs one of the biggest Russian Mafia organizations in the greater D.C. area."

"I know all about Yuran. There was no reason for him to lie to me. I'm not a cop, and I wasn't after him."

"He could be involved in Morton's murder. Morton and Ralston were *executed*."

"Common among the mob, but it's not Yuran's M.O."

"And you *know* this," Noah said flatly.

"I do my research."

"I'd like to know where you get your information."

"That's confidential."

They were at a standoff, but Sean wasn't budging. He'd done enough research into Yuran to be confident he didn't have any interests in the online sex business. If he thought there was anything there, he'd have given up his information, but Sean wasn't burning his brothers because they did him a favor that was bordering on illegal.

"You're getting under my skin, Rogan. I should hold you for questioning."

Sean stood. "If you're accusing me of a crime, this conversation is over."

"Let's start with interfering with a federal criminal investigation."

Sean started toward the door. "Call my lawyer."

Kate said, "Sean don't go."

"I'm not playing the power game with a Fed. I've been burned before." He glanced at Noah, who stared at him.

"You can't stay out of trouble," Noah snapped.

Hans said, "Noah, stop jerking Sean's chain."

"I think it's more like he wants me on a leash," Sean mumbled.

"Truce," Hans said. "We're on the same team here."

Hans was right. Sean didn't have to like Noah Armstrong, but he should have been smarter than to allow the cop to get under his skin.

Kate tapped Fran Buckley's personnel file. "Vigilantes targeting parolees. Morton fits."

Sean turned to Kate, stunned. "What are you doing?"

"It's connected, Sean." She gave him a look that told him to back down. Reluctantly, Sean did, but he inwardly fumed. He didn't trust Noah Armstrong not to quash Lucy's dream of becoming an FBI agent. If he thought Lucy had any knowledge of these murders, she was done.

Hans spoke up. "Lucy uncovered a string of vigilante murders tied to the victim's rights group Women and Children First. She brought the information to Kate and Dillon, and they asked for my profile of the players who may be involved."

Sean had liked Hans Vigo from the minute they met, and now his estimation of the profiler was even higher. The seasoned Fed was brilliant, telling the truth without giving details that might put Lucy's application in jeopardy.

"You're saying Morton was killed by a vigilante?" Noah asked.

Hans nodded and gave Noah a rundown on what Lucy had discovered, Brad Prenter's murder, and the other dead parolees. He concluded, "According to

Lucy's detailed records, of the twenty-eight cases she worked on, most were reincarcerated, but eight are dead."

"Being dead doesn't mean—"

Hans interrupted. "They were all killed on the night they were supposed to be arrested."

Kate said, "There are several people at WCF doing the same thing, but Lucy couldn't access those records."

"It would reason," Hans said, "that the ratios—about four to one—would hold across all staff. I doubt Fran Buckley was only using Lucy for this project."

Noah sat down as he processed the information. Sean walked to the kitchen and leaned against the counter, where he could watch and listen. "You have proof of all this?"

"We have proof that the eight men all died the night they were suppose to be arrested," Hans said. "We also know that someone hacked into Lucy's WCF account and sent the last victim, Brad Prenter, to a completely different location than she had arranged."

"Where does Morton fit into all this?" Noah said.

"Right before you arrived, we found a connection between Buckley and Morton," Hans said.

Kate asked, "Do you know former FBI Agent Mick Mallory?"

Noah shook his head, but Agent Resnick spoke up. "I remember Mallory. After his family was killed by a perp, he lost it. Went under deep cover with Adam Scott's criminal enterprise, none of it sanctioned by the Bureau."

"Mallory is a bastard with his own sense of right and wrong, but he helped us find Lucy," Kate said. "Mallory fucked up. He was in so deep, he'd been party to several crimes, and still his handler pushed him."

Dillon reached out and took her hand.

Hans said, "Mallory worked in the Richmond office with Buckley for two years."

Noah didn't say anything for a long minute. "How long ago?"

"Nearly twenty years. Mallory was a new agent at the time in Buckley's Violent Crimes squad."

Noah rubbed his eyes. "What do you think, Hans?"

"I think both Buckley and Mallory are capable of murder under the right circumstances."

Noah looked up at the ceiling. Sean could practically read his mind, though his face was stoic. He was running through the case, weighing the evidence against the supposition.

Finally, Noah said, "We need to bring Fran Buckley in for questioning and track down Mallory. I don't suppose you know where he is?"

"No," Hans said. "We just made the connection this morning, haven't even started looking."

Noah glanced at Abigail. "Can you get a current address on him?"

"Will do."

"About Fran," Kate said. "Pulling her in may not be to our advantage."

"Why's that? Hans said we had proof that someone at WCF killed those parolees."

"No," Hans corrected, "we have proof that the parolees were killed the night they were set up to be re-arrested by volunteer cops. One more thing to consider—their personalities."

"Explain."

"Buckley and Mallory are not leaders. Mallory has always taken orders. He was in the military, he went undercover and had a lot of leeway, but always acted at the direction of a superior. He never did his own thing. Even when he was undercover at Trask, he did it at the direction of a high-ranking FBI agent. Buckley runs WCF, and on the surface you might think she's a leader, but she was an SSA for seven years in Boston and didn't do well in the role. I've read her employee reviews and she relied heavily on her superiors for even the most minor decision-making. To the extent that after three years, while she retained the rank and salary of an SSA, she was effectively demoted into a nonsupervisory role. She's good at doing her job, but not at giving direction."

"You're saying there's a third person," Noah said.

"I think that it's highly likely. I'm not one hundred percent certain—Mallory has the capability of being a leader, he's just never done it." Hans steepled his fingers and looked up at the ceiling. "If there's another player, a leader, then he's lost someone close to him. One of the victims will connect back to him. I need more details about the murders. Dillon made a copy of Lucy's files and I'm going to review them and see if there is another connection."

Dillon commented, "Do you think there are more than three people involved? For crimes like this—in seven different states—it seems like they'd need a network."

"It's a small group," Hans said. "A larger conspiracy wouldn't have been able to keep such control over their activities for this long. There is no evidence at the crime scene that ties in with any other crime. That tells me they have money to buy and dispose of guns. They use the gun once, get rid of it, get another. Travel—Mallory could easily be traveling around the country. No ties to the city he kills in, the perfect assassin. I'd imagine there is at least one other involved, but he would be someone Mallory trusts. Mallory is the key—he knows who's really in charge."

Sean considered what Hans said, his mind running through all the possible people who could have organized such an elaborate and successful vigilante group. He'd call Duke as he left. Between his brother and J. T. Caruso, they had contacts all over the country.

Noah asked Hans, "Who's the weak link?"

Hans weighed his thoughts carefully. "Frances Buckley, if interviewed properly, by a male in authority." He glanced at Kate. "No offense, Kate."

She waved off his comment. "I understand. She's old school, considers women equals, men as superiors."

"Not exactly," Dillon said. "I think she has contempt for women."

"Right," Hans said, nodding.

"I don't get it," Sean said. "She's fond of Lucy, or she's a damn good liar."

"You're right, Sean, about Lucy," Hans said. "Think of it this way. Fran is sixty. She joined the Bureau when few women did, when the mentality of the Hoover years was still dominant. She fought hard to earn what she had. Many of her contemporaries didn't, or chose professions where they weren't constantly butting heads with men. Right there she considers herself superior to most women—she chose the harder path.

"Next consider her chosen field since her retirement. Sexual predators. They prey on women and children. The weak, in her mind. She is protecting the weak. That puts her on higher ground. Couple that with crossing the line—not only is she *legally* working to protect the weak, she's doing more. She's risking her life and her freedom to protect other women and children—not herself."

"Maybe not so much contempt," Dillon said, "but a superiority complex. She's doing what others refuse to do."

"How do we make her talk?" Noah asked.

"Put Rick Stockton and Dillon in the room," Hans said. "Rick is the ultimate authority, only a step down from FBI director, and well known as being tough but fair. He plays the role of hard-ass. Dillon commiserates with her, understands her, even commends her. Strokes her ego, lets her know that she'll be admired and respected for doing the right thing in the face of overwhelming odds. No one understands the pressure she faces, et cetera."

Dillon asked, "Isn't this a conflict of interest for me?"

Hans shook his head. "Not with Buckley—and she'll feel comfortable with you because she knows you, knows Lucy. It'll work. But if we find Mallory? Stay far away from him."

"You don't have to tell me twice," Dillon said.

Noah said, "I'll call Stockton and get the warrants moving, then bring in Buckley." He put up his hand to ward off any more comments. "You say Lucy is suspicious. Do you think Buckley might know we suspect her?"

Hans nodded. "She could be in denial, but it won't last long—she'll start destroying evidence."

"If she hasn't already," Noah said. "We have nothing

else—no hard evidence, no forensic evidence, no witnesses."

"Lucy has a copy of everything she'd—"

Noah interrupted Kate. "A copy is good, but it's not the original database, and there's no guarantee that Lucy didn't manipulate or change the data. I'm sure she didn't," he added quickly, "but prove that to the U.S. Attorney's Office. We need all files, all computers, all backups—and if Lucy's circumstantial evidence is good enough for a judge, we'll get it before the end of today."

TWENTY-EIGHT

Noah had made it clear that Sean should make himself available but stay away from the investigation. Kate pulled Sean aside and said the best thing he could do for them was keep an eye on Lucy until they resolved the WCF situation. Sean agreed, but he had several hours before he needed to pick up Lucy from the Medical Examiner's Office. He couldn't sit around doing nothing, so he went home to do his own research.

Because two of the people allegedly involved in the vigilante group were former FBI agents, Noah was playing the investigation close to the vest. He'd briefed Rick Stockton, who was apparently on board, but everything else was off the books. They didn't want to tip off Mallory and Fran Buckley and give them a chance to disappear or destroy evidence. It would be extremely difficult to get a conviction, let alone an arrest, because they had no physical proof. Sean understood the pressure that Noah was under to get one of them to talk. Lucy's discovery about the parolees being killed was a big red flag, but there was no hard proof that WCF had anything to do with it. The only physical evidence she had came from Cody Lorenzo, who'd taken one email out of the police report. They needed to prove that someone at WCF had used Lucy's password, which means they needed the WCF records before they were destroyed, if they weren't already.

And connecting it all to Morton? They could connect the dots, but the dots were all over the place and the overall picture was still unclear.

Sean called his brother Duke and filled him in. Even when they had disagreements, like they'd had earlier in this investigation, when it mattered, Duke would do whatever it took to help. He said he'd shake some trees and see what fell.

"You should know," Duke said, "someone tried to run a background on you."

Sean wasn't surprised. "Who?"

"Don't know, but it came from D.C."

"The FBI?"

"I'd know if it was the FBI. This was private."

He wondered who it was. Lorenzo? Fran Buckley? Or was it unrelated to this case?

"I can be there first thing in the morning. Just say the word," Duke said.

"I have it under control. It's not a solo operation—the FBI is in with both feet."

"Be careful."

Sean hung up and did his own search for Mick Mallory. It didn't help that "Michael Mallory" was a common name. But Sean knew a few tricks and it didn't take long to find him.

By searching newspaper archives, he found the article about the bombing that had killed Mallory's family. Mallory's name had been left out of it, and the victim—Janice Blair—and her son didn't share Mallory's last name, but this was the U.S. and car bombings were extremely rare.

Sean couldn't find anything viable under Janice Blair or Michael Mallory or any combination of their names. He pulled up Janice Blair's obituary and noted that Janice was the only child of Margaret-Ann Blair of Herndon. It didn't take long from there to ascertain that the ninety-two-year-old woman was living in a rest home in Chevy Case, Maryland, but still owned property in Herndon. Sean had a hunch—if the mother-in-law was in a nursing home, who lived in her house?

It was noon. He had time to drive to Herndon and back before he had to pick up Lucy.

Sean went to his gun safe. He always had his nine-millimeter on him, but he liked the .45 best. He added a Taser and extra ammo and grabbed his keys. He was in his car when Dillon Kincaid drove up.

Sean almost sped off and pretended he didn't see him, but Dillon caught his eye.

He rolled down the passenger window to talk but Dillon reached in, pulled up the lock, and slid into the seat.

"I'm going on an errand," Sean told him.

"You're going to see Mallory."

"Why do you think that?"

"I'm good at my job."

"What? Psychic?"

"Psychic, psychiatrist, they're almost identical, aren't they?"

"So you've analyzed me?"

"Am I wrong?"

Sean didn't answer.

"I'm going with you."

"No—"

"Why? Because it's too dangerous and I'm not a cop?" Dillon shook his head. "Guess what? Neither are you."

"Do you know where he lives?"

"No," Dillon said. "I gather you already found him."

"Kate's going to kill me," Sean muttered as he drove off.

"Probably."

"Call her and let her know."

"That we're going to confront Mallory? She'll kill *me*."

"At least send her the address. We don't know for certain that Mallory is living there, but I don't want Noah Armstrong breathing down my neck, talking about obstruction of justice or any crap like that. I'm just feeling the situation out, not looking for a confrontation." Sean didn't know if that was the truth or not, but it sounded good.

Back at his cubicle in the FBI office, Noah quickly typed up the facts for Rick Stockton to push for a warrant for Frances Buckley and WCF. Stockton thought they had enough, but Noah was skeptical.

He went through the case methodically, glancing at both his and Abigail's notes. He sent it off just as Sandy, the analyst who was working the case with them, emailed him the list of property owners on Eucalyptus Street in Somerset, and the two cross streets. He glanced at the list, then did a double-take.

Biggler.

He looked at the map, and the house owned by David and Brenda Biggler was vacant and had been up for sale for the last four months.

It couldn't be a coincidence that Ralston had been an informant for *Jerry* Biggler.

Since Abigail was on her way back to Somerset, Noah

quickly sent her a message to check out the house and talk to the neighbors about the Bigglers. He then ran a quick background check on the two. He immediately learned that they were not married as he'd first assumed, but brother and sister. The house had been owned by their father, Detective Jerry Biggler, who'd lived there until he died.

Definitely no coincidence.

David Biggler, thirty-four, was a high school English teacher. *A teacher*. Noah pulled up his photograph. He looked like a nice kid, though he was only a year younger than Noah. Biggler had a degree in American literature from John Hopkins University.

Brenda Biggler, twenty-six, was an attractive blond nurse.

A teacher and a nurse. Maybe he was wrong about this.

He looked closer at their history. David Biggler graduated only four years ago. Noah looked farther back. Biggler had enlisted in the Marines when he turned eighteen. Spent eight years active duty. Came home after his dad died and went to college.

Noah reviewed his notes on Mallory. He'd been a Marine as well. Coincidence?

Was Biggler part of this whole thing? Was he with Morton and Ralston—or Mallory and Buckley?

But why on earth would Biggler either help his father's informant in a criminal enterprise or turn vigilante? Neither he nor his sister had any criminal record. David had been honorably discharged.

Noah considered what Hans Vigo had said about vigilante personalities and wondered if he was missing something in Biggler's background. Where was the mother? Divorced when David was fourteen. She went to Arizona and remarried. It didn't look like there was much communication between the kids and their mother, and it seemed odd that the father was given custody, especially more than two decades ago. He'd have to get an analyst to pull the case file, but there was no way he'd get it today.

It took Noah twenty minutes to find the connection, and he would never have found it if he wasn't looking for one, or if he hadn't talked to Hans this morning.

Four months before Mrs. Biggler filed for divorce, thirteen-year-old Nicole Biggler was raped and murdered by a known sex offender, released only three months before after serving four years for attempted rape of a fifteen-year-old.

Hans said that the vigilantes involved likely had lost someone to violence. Losing a sibling, coupled with the mother leaving, could have been the impetus that Biggler needed to turn vigilante. Just because he didn't have a record didn't mean he wasn't a killer. And just because he was a teacher didn't mean he couldn't turn violent.

Biggler's sister is killed, then his mother leaves him and his younger sister to the dad and moves nearly three thousand miles away. Biggler joins the Marines first chance he gets. Returns when dad is dying.

All the pieces by themselves made sense, but together Noah had a mess. Far too much conjecture and no solid evidence to link Biggler to Mallory or to Morton.

Noah leaned back in his chair and closed his eyes. He had a few options, but none of them appealed to him. He could go to the high school and pick up Biggler now or wait until school let out. He could get his current address and wait for him at home. Or, they could simply put a tail on Biggler, and see where he went and what he did.

The last option seemed the most viable. Once they had a warrant for Fran Buckley and WCF, the news would get out and Biggler might rabbit. Noah needed eyes on him before then. If he pulled him in too soon, Noah might tip his hand.

TWENTY-NINE

Mallory's mother-in-law's house was thirty minutes away in Herndon on a secluded parcel of land. "I'll knock," Dillon said. "He knows me."

"What makes you think he won't shoot you on sight?"

"Jack saved his life."

"Maybe he should have let him die."

Dillon hesitated. "Mallory is heavily burdened and made huge errors in judgment. But if it weren't for him sending Kate the longitude and latitude of the island where Lucy was held captive, we'd never have saved her in time. He nearly died because of it. He did the right thing."

"Too late."

"You're not going to get an argument from me, but he's not going to kill me."

"You can't be sure of that. It's been six years."

Sean didn't like the idea of Dillon taking the lead, but they were already far off the reservation in disobeying Noah Armstrong's direct orders to stay out of the investigation. Since Noah wasn't his boss, Sean wasn't taking it seriously, but they both knew that Kate could get some heat for their actions.

Dillon rang the bell. Sean peered into the garage. There was one car inside, but the garage could fit three.

There was no answer. Cautiously, they walked the perimeter of the house. The windows were covered by storm windows and the blinds were all drawn. Sean heard no movement inside. He put a small microphone in his ear and positioned a small amplifier close to the door.

Dillon motioned toward the device. Sean took out the earpiece and whispered, "It detects and amplifies sound and movement. Not foolproof, but it's worked for me before." He put the earpiece back in and listened for a good minute.

"I don't think anyone's home," Sean said, taking out his lock pick.

"We're not breaking in."

"Go back to the car then."

"Dammit, Sean!"

Sean popped the lock, then faced Dillon. "We're in and out. I won't take anything. You stand guard."

"Sean—"

"All we need is information."

Sean went inside and closed the door before Dillon could argue.

The house was extremely tidy, but there was a slight greasy smell. Sean checked the garbage in the kitchen. Someone had cooked a meal last night. No rotting food.

He searched the place quickly and saw nothing out of the ordinary. Then he went to Mallory's den.

A computer. That was all Sean needed. He'd promised Dillon he wouldn't take anything, but he hadn't said he wouldn't make a copy. He didn't even try to boot up the computer, but took out a pocket computer and carefully removed the covering on the hard drive. He then hooked up two wires to the motherboard and copied all the data on the computer, making a perfect replication. He replaced everything and was about to leave when he saw two framed photographs on a small table next to a reading chair. His heart nearly stopped.

The larger photo had been taken on a beach: a young, beautiful brunette with a toddler in her arms. They were smiling. Mallory's family.

But the second photo definitely had more interest for Sean. A younger Lucy, maybe nineteen. Just as beautiful as today, but her eyes were sad. The shot had been taken from afar with a zoom lens.

The fucking bastard.

Sean left and said to Dillon, "He has a picture of Lucy."

"Anything else?"

"No. But I have a copy of his computer."

"What did you do?"

"I didn't disturb anything. Just made a copy."

"Kate's going to kill me."

"We won't tell her. Unless, of course, we have to."

Sean looked back at the house as they drove off. Something was amiss—he had a strong sensation that Mallory was watching. Not from the house . . . Sean looked around the perimeter. There were plenty of trees and shrubs he could be hiding in.

He had an idea.

Dillon sat patiently in the passenger seat. How could he be so calm? The minutes ticked by and Sean wondered if he'd been wrong and Mallory hadn't been watching the house while he searched it.

No. Sean never doubted his instincts. When they hummed, he listened. And from the minute he stepped foot outside Mallory's house, his instincts had been beating the drums like John Bonham. Mallory had been watching. He was waiting for them to leave. For how long? Until he was sure they were gone. There were only two ways out of this neighborhood—on foot and by car. One entrance into the neighborhood by car. Could he have come on foot? In the ice and snow? Possible, but unlikely. And Sean didn't see Mallory as the type to be without transportation.

Of course, he could have a car stashed somewhere else. Or—

"You don't participate in many stakeouts, do you?" Dillon asked.

Sean glanced at him sideways. "I'm not a cop." He tripled-checked the custom GPS and driving system he'd designed, making sure he'd compensated for the road hazards. The icy roads were not his friend, and he hoped his car would help him control any pursuit.

"I'm familiar with RCK. I'm certain there are many times sitting still for long periods of time is necessary."

"I leave that to others. I'm the only one who hasn't been in the military. When you enlist, they teach you to be a statue."

"It's called survival," Dillon said. "Are you certain—"

"Yes. I'm certain." *I hope.* "I have that feeling in the pit of my stomach that I've learned not to doubt."

"That's good enough for me."

Sean glanced at his watch. "We have to leave in an hour to pick up Lucy in time."

"Kate can pick her up."

"No. Mallory'll be out before then. I'd rather keep Kate out of this until we absolutely have to involve her. She shouldn't be put in an awkward position between me and Armstrong." Sean trusted the Kincaids—he'd be a fool not to—but none of them were trained bodyguards. And while Sean didn't specialize in personal security, he'd had his fair share of protective assignments. He didn't like the idea that Lucy was at the Medical Examiner's Office without a guard, but if Mallory was *here,* he wasn't *there.* Still, Sean was nervous—if he was wrong, Lucy's life was at risk. He didn't care what Dillon said about Mallory not hurting her; Sean didn't believe it.

The bastard had a photograph of her in his office.

Sean had cracked the windows, even though the air was icy, to better hear a car approach. It was a quiet neighborhood. He closed his eyes and listened. Forced himself to be calm.

"You care about her."

It was both a statement and a question. Sean suspected after the last few days with Lucy that he'd be getting the third degree from more than one Kincaid.

"Yes," he said simply.

Dillon didn't say anything else, and that made Sean nervous. What did Lucy's brother really think of him? Was he assessing whether he was good enough for her? Whether he knew everything that had happened in her past? Whether he'd be scared away if the going got tough?

Dillon remained silent. Was it that easy?

Cold still air carried sound well, and Sean heard the car long before he saw it.

They were around the corner from Mallory's private dead-end street abutting the woods, and Sean had positioned his car in such a way as to be able to see through trees and shrubs anyone coming from the ten or so houses up Mallory's street.

A gray sedan.

Sean turned the ignition of his GT and the engine purred into life. "Seat belt," he told Dillon. He glanced over. "I should tell you I race cars. Amateur racing, but I'm good. Don't panic if it gets rough."

He waited until the sedan had reached the corner, then shot forward to block it.

Mallory braked, immediately reversed twenty feet turning 90 degrees, then drove forward, right behind Sean's car.

Sean anticipated the move and spun 180 degrees in pursuit.

"This is a residential neighborhood," Dillon said.

"I'm not going to hit anyone. I love this car."

But Sean would total it if it meant catching the fleeing bastard. He pressed the "2" on his GPS number pad.

"What's that?" Dillon asked.

"Questions later."

His GPS gave him a cutoff route, and the radar in the front of his car told the computer how fast Mallory was driving, and how fast Sean had to go to cut him off.

He made a hard left, leaving Mallory.

"What are you doing?" Dillon exclaimed.

Sean didn't answer. His eyes glanced left and right, looking for any potential dangers. Kids. Animals. Bouncing balls. It was a weekday, near the time schools let out, which demanded caution.

He glanced at the map, made a hard right up a hill, cut through a dirt service road, then floored it when he hit the main street. He'd lost time on the dirt road, which had turned into a muddy slush from the weather. He suspected that Mallory had slowed, just a fraction, when Sean's car was no longer in his rearview mirror, but he couldn't count on it.

His back wheels slipped on a patch of ice, but Sean maintained control of his car. He slowed, looking up the street where he expected Mallory to emerge. No one was there.

"Shit!" Had he miscalculated? No—but he could have misjudged Mallory. The killer could have turned around or hidden somewhere—in a driveway, perhaps.

Then he saw the car turn and head toward him, slowing as soon as Mallory saw him. Was he surprised?

"You'd better be right about Mallory," Sean said to Dillon.

"What do you mean?"

"Get out when I tell you."

Sean turned the wheel hard to the right, using the ice in a controlled slide, relying on his intuitive knowledge and impeccable maintenance of his car to ensure he wasn't going to hit a pole or jump the curb. He controlled his spin by keeping the tires in it, while his momentum kept the vehicle moving toward Mallory's car. Because this was the main road into the neighborhood, it was wider than the side streets, giving Sean the room he needed to play chicken with Mallory.

Mallory had to slam on his brakes to avoid hitting them, and he skidded, going into his own short spin before heading back the way he'd come.

In one seamless move, Sean stopped the car, put it in park, pressed the seat-belt release, and opened the door. He had his gun out, using his door as a barrier. He fired two shots into each of Mallory's rear tires. The car fish-tailed, turned, and stopped.

"Out!" he commanded Dillon. Mallory might shoot *him,* but according to Dillon, Mallory wouldn't shoot a Kincaid. Sean was counting on that.

Mallory was out of his car, his gun drawn, and then glanced over as Dillon opened the passenger door. "Mick," Dillon called out, "it's over. We know about the parolee project. We know about your connection to Frances Buckley. The FBI is getting a search warrant for WCF and Buckley's house right now." Dillon crossed in front of the car, putting himself in the line of fire.

"Dillon!" Sean called out. What was he thinking? Sean wanted Mallory distracted. He didn't want to give the guy an easy target.

Mallory shook his head. "You understand what we face, Kincaid."

"I do understand. But this is not the way."

"You have no proof."

"We have more than you know. There's only one thing I don't understand. Why the elaborate game of luring Morton here? It would have been so much easier for you to kill him in Denver. Does it have something to do with Ralston going to Seattle? Morton had something you wanted, didn't he? What was it?"

Mallory was thinking. Sean couldn't give him time to think. He stood up, gun aimed at Mallory's head, and approached the car.

"Don't," Mallory said, turning his gun toward Sean.

"You going to kill me in cold blood? Dillon, too? You

fucking prick. You have a picture of Lucy in your house. How dare you!"

Mallory tossed his gun out and put his hands up. Sean hadn't known what to expect, other than Dillon's psych-out, but he hadn't expected it to be this easy.

"I want to talk to Lucy."

"Fuck no," Sean said. "Assume the position. Dillon, search him and cuff him." Sean tossed Dillon a set of handcuffs.

"You're not a cop," Mallory said.

"I think you know exactly who I am," Sean said. "You did a background check on me. Someone tried to pull my data, now I know who."

Mallory slowly turned around and put his hands on the car hood.

Sean said, "I'm still alive. Does that mean I passed your test?"

"The jury's still out on you, Rogan," Mallory said quietly.

Dillon searched Mallory, found another gun, and handed it to Sean. He then cuffed Mallory and had him sit on the curb. Sirens were in the distance—the gunfire had most certainly alerted authorities.

"Dillon, I have to get to Lucy, in case there are others involved who aren't as friendly with the Kincaids as Mallory."

"No one will hurt Lucy," Mallory said.

"Excuse me for not believing you," Sean said, then turned back to Dillon. "You okay here?"

Dillon nodded. "Mick and I have some things to talk about."

Mallory stared at them. "Dillon, I have tremendous

respect for you, which is why I didn't shoot. But we're not talking."

"I can help you."

"Maybe I don't want help." He added softly, "Maybe I'm relieved its over."

THIRTY

It was a quarter to three when Lucy received a text message from Sean.

Your chariot is running late. I have good news. Don't leave without me, princess.

She smiled. Sean was a romantic at heart. And after the last few days, she really appreciated his attention.

The intake clerk entered the file room where Lucy was working. "Two police officers are here to see you."

She hesitated. Was it Cody? Had he brought a friend? He hadn't called her back; was this unannounced visit his idea of getting back to her?

"Did they say why?"

"No."

"Can you get their names for me?"

The clerk looked at her oddly, then shrugged and left.

Lucy took her time restacking the papers she'd been sorting and filing and carefully placed them back in the in-box. Her hands were steady, but her heart thudded so loud her ears were ringing. What did they want? Were they good guys or bad guys?

And were the bad guys *really* bad?

When she thought about it, was she more upset that

Prenter was dead or that she'd been used to kill him? What about the other parolees? Too many states no longer had an extensive parole system. They didn't track parolees, and they rarely detained anyone for parole violations anymore because the prisons were so overcrowded. Unless the parolee had committed a new crime, he rarely went back inside.

Correction. Unless he was *caught* committing a new crime. Another person had to be raped or robbed or killed before the parolee went back in.

The phone beeped and startled her. She picked up the receiver and the clerk said, "Detective Light and Officer Raleigh."

"Thanks, tell them two minutes. I have to log these files."

She hung up and bit her lip, relieved that she didn't have to confront Cody right now but curious about why a detective wanted to talk to her. Could Cody have told his boss about his suspicions? Whether or not he'd implicated Lucy, they could be following up on the Prenter murder.

Lucy had no feelings for the criminals who'd been killed, and that unnerved her. Was she that heartless? Sean had said she was the most compassionate person he knew, but she didn't see that in herself. Not when she didn't have even a sliver of grief for the dead felons.

The criminal justice system was far from perfect. Victims were often revictimized in the legal process. Parents of dead children were dragged through the mud during the investigation, their lives dissected by a judgmental society who cast blame on the families for the fate of their children. The media sat in wait outside their homes, outside the schools their kids attended, talking to friends and family, wanting to know how they felt, what they were doing the minute their child disappeared, why they weren't with them twenty-four/seven.

Lucy wanted to scream at the stone-throwing media who created fear on which criminals fed. Predators wanted to tear apart society, to have mothers and fathers separate because of their missing child; to have neighbors gossip; to have the police question fathers about having too much or too little affection for their sons and daughters. Question friends about how much attention they give. Question family, casting doubts, making brothers turn against brothers, wives against husbands, fathers against sons, mothers against daughters.

Sisters against sisters.

Lucy had been seven when her seven-year-old nephew—and best friend—Justin was kidnapped from his bedroom in the middle of the night. She was the youngest Kincaid; Nelia was the oldest and gave birth to Justin when she was in law school, but later graduated and became a corporate attorney. The middle sister, Carina, then in college, had been babysitting for Nelia that night.

Lucy was only a child herself, but the hateful accusations that grieving Nelia had thrown at Carina in the days that followed Justin's murder had been burned into her soul. Lucy heard the whispers that her brother-in-law Andrew had been sleeping with another woman the night Justin was kidnapped. Then, the gossip that Nelia had known about the affair and didn't care. That she worked late every night so she didn't have to see her husband.

Nelia had left San Diego and the family, and though

over time she'd begun to talk to most of them, nothing would ever be the same.

But the worst was when Nelia looked at Lucy and Lucy felt the regret pouring off her sister in tangible waves of agony.

Why was it Justin and not you?

She'd never said it, and she'd never admit that the thought crossed her mind, but Nelia had never spoken to Lucy since Justin's murder eighteen years ago. Not one word.

The file room door opened and Lucy whirled around. "Lucy, they're still waiting," the clerk said. "I took them to the employee break room because the conference rooms are being used."

"Okay, sorry, I'm coming." She took a deep breath. She didn't know how long it would take for Sean to arrive, but she could face the police. If they wanted to arrest her for setting up Prenter, she could argue with them long enough to give Sean time to get here.

Lucy didn't like relying on anyone other than herself, but sometimes just knowing someone was there, if she needed it, was enough to get her through the hardest times. But she could do this alone.

She stepped into the break room. One uniformed officer and a plainclothes detective stood to the side. Both were black, the detective tall and skinny, the cop tall and broad-shouldered. She felt smaller than she was.

"Hello, I'm Lucy Kincaid. I'm sorry to keep you waiting," she said with a smile, and hoped she didn't seem nervous.

"We understand, Ms. Kincaid. I'm Detective Light, this is Officer Raleigh. We're investigating a possible suicide that's hit the department very hard. It's one of our own."

Her skin burned, as if bathed in microscopic shards of glass.

Cody hadn't called her back.

"I'm sorry to be the one to tell you that Officer Cody Lorenzo died last night."

Her knees buckled and she reached for the table. Slowly she sat down and shook her head. No words came, though she had a hundred questions weighing down her tongue.

"You once had a romantic relationship with Officer Lorenzo, correct? His partner said you remained friends."

She nodded, still unable to speak.

Detective Light sat in the chair across from her. She couldn't read his expression. She could barely see anything, as if the room was fading away in front of her.

Cody was dead?

"When was the last time you saw or spoke to him?" Detective Light asked quietly.

"Yesterday," she whispered. She cleared her throat. Her hands were on the table in front of her, frozen. She stared at her short, unpainted fingernails attached to her long fingers and remembered her last words to him.

"Why would you think I could be capable of doing such a thing?"

She'd been so upset, so angry with Cody that he'd thought she'd intentionally set up Prenter, she hadn't even accepted his apology. She'd walked away knowing he was remorseful, but she hadn't cared. She couldn't see past her own emotional pain and overwhelming feelings of betrayal. That he'd used her act of desperation when she'd killed Adam Scott against her. Had she wanted him to feel guilty? Had she walked away hoping he'd feel bad about his assumptions?

She hoped she wasn't that shallow. Cody had remained one of her closest friends, even though she hadn't been able to marry him.

"Ms. Kincaid? Are you all right?"

She nodded, though she was far from all right.

A minute later, Officer Raleigh placed a Styrofoam cup of water in front of her. She sipped automatically but tasted nothing.

"What did you talk about yesterday? Was it personal?"

"No—it was about WCF." When they looked blankly at her, she explained. "We both volunteer at Women and Children First, a victim's rights advocacy group."

Raleigh said, "I've heard of it."

Lucy couldn't tell them about the dead parolees or Prenter, but what if that had something to do with Cody's death? She couldn't withhold information if it kept a killer free.

She asked, "You said *possible* suicide?"

"We're still investigating. We haven't made any official determination, but there was a suicide note."

"Cody didn't commit suicide," she said flatly.

"Why are you so sure?"

"He's Catholic."

"That's not always—"

"He wouldn't do it to his mother. His dad died of a heart attack when he was sixteen, long before I met him; his brothers and sisters all moved out of the area. He wouldn't do it to his mom. He wouldn't." She put her hand to her mouth and swallowed a sob.

Officer Raleigh unfolded a piece of paper. "This is a copy of the suicide note. The investigators are comparing handwriting samples."

Lucy took the paper and placed it in front of her. Dark spots on the paper, copies of the bloodstain, marred the bottom corner.

To whoever finds me, I'm sorry you have to see me like this. Forgive me.
To my parents, I have failed you. Forgive me.
To my colleagues, I have abused my position of authority. Forgive me.
To my Lucy, the truth will set you free. It set me free.
I'll see you soon.
Goodbye.

She couldn't stop shaking. She willed her hands to stop, holding them close to her body. Her stomach dry heaved and she dipped her head down. "Cody. Cody didn't write this." Her voice twisted on a cry at the end.

"You don't recognize the writing?"

"It doesn't look exactly like his writing, but it could be. I don't know. But it's the line about his parents."

"He might have been thinking about his entire life, and not recently."

She shook her head. "It doesn't sound like him."

"When someone gets so depressed they commit suicide, they're not always thinking straight."

"I just . . . Cody . . . why?"

The door opened and Lucy looked up to see Sean, his face hard, concern and suspicion in his eyes as he looked from the cops to her. He crossed the small room to Lucy. "Lucy—what happened?"

She stood on weak legs, and Sean put his arm around her waist to steady her. She leaned against him. "Cody's dead."

And then the tears came, and Lucy couldn't stop them.

THIRTY-ONE

When Noah learned that Mick Mallory was in custody, he left Abigail in charge of executing the warrant on Fran Buckley and WCF, and he and Kate went to the Washington Field Office.

He walked into an interview room and was surprised to see Assistant Director Rick Stockton there with Dillon Kincaid and Hans Vigo. But this case was already the most bizarre in Noah's three-year career in the FBI. He couldn't recall anything during his tenure in the Air Force that came close, either.

Dillon Kincaid's friendship with Stockton and Vigo notwithstanding, Noah stated firmly, "I told you to leave Mallory to me."

"I understand," Dillon said. "I apologize for any problems I may have caused."

"Are you protecting Rogan?"

"Pardon me? Protecting?"

"You didn't apprehend Mallory on your own, since the Herndon police drove you here with Mallory. You couldn't walk to where you arrested him in Herndon from Georgetown. I told Rogan to stay the hell out of my way—"

Rick Stockton said, "I'll let you handle the situation, Noah, as you see fit, but I have a meeting with the director at five, and I need to tell him something, even if it's that Mallory refuses to talk. We have sensitive media issues with two former FBI agents allegedly orchestrating a vigilante group."

"I apologize, sir." He used his military training to tamp down his anger. "Which psychiatrist is going in with me?"

"Hans," Rick said without comment. "And Kate. I'm sorry, Dillon, you're too close to the situation right now. If Mallory wants to talk to you later, that's fine, but I need my agents in there."

"No explanation necessary," Dillon said.

Noah asked Hans, "What do I need to know?"

"Mallory is extremely protective of Lucy Kincaid. He failed Lucy six years ago and couldn't—or didn't—protect her. When he survived, he sought ways to right wrongs. He needs to appease his guilt, but it will never be satisfied. Which is why he continues. Using Lucy as one of the lures through WCF."

Dillon said, "He sees it as letting her help, even though she doesn't know what she's doing for him. He's empowering her."

"Exactly," Hans concurred. "Lucy was able to put the bad guys back in prison, which gave her power and helped her develop a strong sense of justice and fairness. Getting Lucy to help the vigilantes was easy: she was predisposed to do anything *legal* to get those people off the streets. But our gang of conspirators never approached her to be an active member of the assassination team. Mallory's own guilt required a blood sacrifice, of sorts. He would most likely decide when someone needed to die, and Fran would target the appropriate felon. In fact, when we analyze the WCF files we'll likely see a pattern suggestive of a serial killer. At least one a month, escalating over time because Mallory's guilt isn't assuaged by his kills. In fact, his actions make him feel increasingly disconnected from humanity. He sees himself on one hand as a dark knight saving Lucy over and over because he couldn't do it right the first time, and on the other as a monster, a killer, and that is antithetical to everything he believes in."

"Morton doesn't fit the profile," Noah said. "And neither does Prenter—he didn't target children."

"Because Mallory chose those targets, not Buckley. And he didn't use Lucy for Morton—because Morton wasn't prowling the online chat rooms. He was too ADHD to sit for long in front of a computer. He needed physical communication, not virtual."

Kate said, "We don't have enough evidence. So far, the agents at Mallory's house have found nothing incriminating. No weapons, other than what was on him, but we already know that the ballistics don't match on any of the victims—and one of the victims was killed in a hit-and-run, and three stabbed. There's nothing to tie them together."

"We need a confession," Hans said.

"Mallory is tired of this," Dillon said. "That's what he told me while we waited for the police. I think, with the right approach, he'll be willing to tell you everything. You'll have to earn it. He's going to want you to be worthy of the information."

Hans nodded. "Excellent point. And if not him, once we have Biggler and Buckley in custody it'll be easier to get one of them to cave. What's the status?" he asked Noah.

"Abigail is executing the warrants on Buckley and

WCF. I have two agents each on Biggler's tail and his sister. His sister is in the middle of a twelve-hour shift at Mercy Hospital. We made contact with the principal at Biggler's school, who confirmed that he was still on campus. The students are gone."

"I don't see Biggler as a threat," Hans said. "And he's not going to leave his sister. If he suspects anything, he'll go straight to the hospital to talk to her. Let him. Then arrest both of them together."

"Why Brenda Biggler?" Kate asked. "I thought we were just looking at the brother."

"I read the Prenter police report, and it stated that a blond female left with the victim. That tells me that Biggler and Mallory are working with a woman, and she's the only one in the picture that we know about. If she's not involved, Biggler will confess so she doesn't get dragged into the mess. If she is involved, he'll try to negotiate leniency for her. His involvement with the vigilantes suggests that he's seeking justice for his murdered sister. So it stands to reason that he'd be protective of his other sister."

"And we need to find out why he brought Morton to D.C.—if he did, or if he took advantage of a situation," Dillon added.

"Do we know why Ralston went to Seattle?" Kate asked.

"No," Noah said.

"Mallory knows," Dillon said.

"You really think that Morton had something that valuable?" Kate asked.

"It could be information. This isn't about money—it's about revenge. For Lucy, and for the others."

"Information," Rick said. "If we didn't seize Morton's money when he was sent away, he would have disappeared right after he was released."

Noah said, "A hit list."

"Excuse me?"

"That's what this group is all about—taking out the bad guys who aren't in prison. What if Morton had a list of his associates?"

"Oh shit," Kate said. Everyone turned to her. "What if it's viewers? Everyone who paid to watch Trask videos. Morton swore that the credit card information was kept offshore in a blind account and they had no names, nor did they retain credit card numbers. He gave us the bank accounts, and our white-collar unit seized the money, we had no reason to believe he held anything back."

"You think he lied?"

"He was a fucking bastard, of course he could have lied. The best of our people went through the Trask Enterprises computer systems but found nothing useful. Yet it's possible Adam Scott found a way to hide the data. He was brilliant. A psychopathic killer, but brilliant nonetheless."

Noah nodded. "If Morton was trying to re-create Scott's business enterprise, he might use a customer list as an enticement for the money people."

"What would Mallory do with such a list?" Dillon asked. "There must be thousands of names. He can't kill all those people."

"No, but he can make their lives a living hell," Kate said. "Identity theft, destroying their reputations."

"Blackmail," Noah said. "Running a vigilante group

couldn't be cheap. Maybe he's looking for specific names."

Hans agreed, but said, "Money is a secondary benefit. This is about retribution. If blackmail was part of the game, they wouldn't keep the money. They'd funnel it to expand WCF or give it to other victims' rights groups or the international fugitive apprehensive program—proactive justice."

"We're pulling all the financials of WCF, and comparing the accounts with their nonprofit financial reports," Noah said. "I'll pull in someone from White-Collar Crimes to take a look when we have everything."

He motioned to Kate and Hans. "I'm ready," he said. "Let's go in."

"I'm going to observe for now," Hans said. "I think he'll be more defensive if a psychologist is in the room. He'll know we're out here, but not seeing us will make it seem like you're three agents—equals—talking about an unfortunate situation. I'll come in if I feel it necessary." He glanced at Stockton, who nodded his agreement.

Noah and Kate stepped into the interview room. Mallory sat straight in the chair, his legs shackled but his hands free. They were flat on the table in front of him. An untouched cup of water sat in front of him. He appeared almost serene, and he smiled when he saw Kate. "Marriage becomes you, Kate," he said. "I'm glad to see you happy."

"Does this face look happy, Mick?" Kate said.

"Actually it does. It's in your eyes. That no matter who or what you're facing, you have someone to go home to. I'm really pleased for you."

Kate released an exasperated sigh. "This is Special Agent Noah Armstrong."

Mick nodded at Noah, but said to Kate, "I never thought you'd be teaching at Quantico, though. You were always on the go, always moving. Sitting in a classroom must drive you up a wall."

"We're not here to catch up, Mick. So let's cut to the chase. This is Noah's case; it would really help if you answer our questions. Minimal fuss—you already know you're going to prison. Cush situation, too, because it'll be federal, and you're a cop, so you'll have a nice private room."

Mick shook his head. "I would never survive in prison."

"The guards will consider you a hero. They won't let anyone touch you."

"That's not what I mean."

Noah opened his notepad and put an end to the small talk. "We're executing a search warrant on your house, your apartment in D.C., WCF, and Frances Buckley as we sit here and chat. I have two agents following Biggler. Who do you think will crack first?"

Mallory said nothing.

Noah continued. "We have enough evidence to hold you. Simple possession of a firearm is enough."

Mallory smiled. "Any attorney worth half their pay is going to get everything tossed. Because you have nothing except circumstantial evidence. I know it. You know it. Rogan stopping by my house is one thing—he's a P.I. But whether or not Kate knew her husband and Rogan were paying me a visit doesn't matter, because no judge is going to buy that a civilian consultant to the FBI didn't know better."

"We've put together a file of all the parolees who were arrested on a parole violation through the WCF program, and all those who were killed."

"Fascinating."

"Prenter is the one who screwed you up. You would have gotten away with Morton. Unless of course ballistics on the bullet matches one of your guns, but I think you're too smart for that."

Mallory smiled and shook his head, as if he had a secret.

"But Prenter—it was Lucy Kincaid who figured it out," Noah said. "Isn't that damn ironic? After reading about Prenter's murder, she spent all weekend pulling together data that she'd saved on each of the parolees she chatted with online. Your people didn't grab his cell phone, where a message from her account—that she didn't send—sent him to Club 10."

Mallory wanted to say something but visibly restrained himself.

Noah let the silence draw out for well over a minute. But Mallory got himself under control, and Noah realized that silence wasn't going to get the killer talking. Some criminals couldn't stand the quiet, and after only minutes of Noah staring or taking notes would blab everything, as if in relief.

Mallory wasn't an idiot.

"The parolees, Morton, Prenter—I get those. Hell, I wanted to enact my own Wild West justice from time to time. You're probably thinking, no jury would give you the death penalty because you took out child molesters and rapists. Prenter? That might be a little harder, since he was a college kid convicted of date rape. But, a good lawyer—I suspect the government doesn't want this to go to trial at all—will probably settle it all out of court, because really, do any of us want a big fat spotlight on the flaws in our criminal justice system? Or a slew of copycat vigilantes?

"But," Noah continued, "there are civil cases. Even if you pled out, you'd have Prenter's very rich family suing you for all the sordid information and whatever money you have left. We'll have the press crawling up our ass for details. You wanted to protect Lucy? You just made her the star attraction all over again."

"Bullshit."

"Really, what do you think the press is going to write about when they find out that Lucy's rapist was one of the victims of the vigilante group that she was unwittingly working for? Her past is going to be headlines and it's your fault. We can do this either way, but if you give even a little thought to Lucy and what she's going to suffer through—again—then you'll talk to me."

Mallory clenched his fists. "I want to speak to Lucy."

"Never," Kate said.

"You want to know everything? I'll tell Lucy. I have nothing more to say to either of you."

Mallory leaned back and crossed his arms.

After several minutes of trying to get him to talk, but encountering only silence, Noah and Kate left the interview room. As he shut the door, Noah said, "Shit, that didn't go over well."

Hans shook his head. "It was brilliant. Perfect. Let's call Lucy."

"No!" Kate said. She glanced around the room. "Where's Dillon?"

"Phone call," Hans said. "Kate, he *will* tell Lucy

everything we want to know. He wants to explain it to her, to justify it. He wants her forgiveness."

"I'm not putting her through that."

"Kate, this is the only way."

"I don't like the idea either," Rick Stockton said to Kate, "but I agree with Dr. Vigo." He glanced at his watch. "I need to brief the director. Let me know what happens with Ms. Kincaid." He left as Dillon returned. The psychiatrist's face was ashen.

"What happened?" Kate asked, going to his side.

"Cody Lorenzo's dead. There was a suicide note, but the police are suspicious." He stared at Mallory through the one-way glass. "Cody was investigating Prenter's murder."

"You think he stumbled onto something?" Kate asked. "And Mallory killed him?"

"I didn't think Mallory would kill a cop," Dillon said, shaken.

Hans said, "Maybe he figured out that Cody was stalking Lucy. He was protecting her."

"Hans, I don't want to hear ever again that Mallory wants to 'protect' Lucy! He is a manipulative, righteous bastard who's playing God, even now!" Kate was livid.

Hans asked Dillon, "You said the police are skeptical that Lorenzo killed himself?"

"There was a suicide note with Cody's body, but there were errors in it—referring to his parents when his father died years ago, for example. They're checking with a handwriting expert now. When Sean picked up Lucy, he convinced them to send it directly to FBI headquarters for analysis, and they agreed."

Kate said to Dillon, "Mallory won't say another word. He wants to talk to Lucy."

Everyone turned to Dillon. When he didn't immediately say something, Kate exclaimed, "You can't seriously consider letting her!"

"Lucy's all grown up," Dillon said, his voice cracking. He stared at Mallory through the one-way glass. "She needs to make the decision. We can't do it for her."

Sean ached seeing Lucy so withdrawn. By the time he'd driven into his garage, she'd gone from tears into a trancelike state, her big brown eyes full of anguish. He'd do anything to erase her pain.

He'd sat her on the couch in the family room, then sat down next to her, her hands in his. "Luce, can I get you anything?"

She shook her head, but looked up at him, her eyes rimmed red. "Hold me?"

Sean pulled her into his lap and cradled her. She shouldn't have had to ask. He should have known she needed to be held, to be assured that she was safe when everything around her was crashing down.

Rare, deep anger burned his chest, directed at the bastard who was sitting in FBI headquarters right now. Mallory had started this chain of events. He'd started it when he turned vigilante. And all for what? Because of his fucking *guilt* that he hadn't defended Lucy six years ago?

Rage was foreign to Sean, and he couldn't explain the fury tearing him apart inside. The deep need to protect Lucy from this pain battled with his near-primal urge to pummel Mick Mallory. Vigilante justice was sounding good right now.

"Sean?"

He kissed her forehead. "You want something? Just name it."

"You're angry."

"No, I'm not."

"I can feel your anger." She put a hand on his chest and tilted her head back to look into his face. "I'm sorry to put you in the middle of this."

"Don't." He kissed her deeply, his hands splayed on her back. "Don't think." He kissed her over and over, no sweet savoring of her lips, but possession. His hands moved upward, touching her soft, tear-stained face. And he continued to kiss her, hating that his rage at both Mallory and Cody Lorenzo upset her.

"Do not apologize," he said, his lips skimming across hers. "Do not tell me you're sorry for anything." He kissed her cheeks, her chin, her neck, her ear. She tasted sweet and salty, and if she wore perfume it was subtle and floral, something soft and springlike and beautiful.

He whispered into her ear, "I'm here, Lucy. I'm not leaving."

Her arms tightened around his neck and she turned her head so she could kiss him. "I've been so lost," she whispered.

His chest tightened. That she could feel lost and alone when she had a family who loved her so much was a testament that she still kept her true emotions under lock and key.

A phone vibrated on the table in front of them, and Sean wanted to ignore it. He glanced at the caller ID and handed it to Lucy. "It's Dillon."

"Hello?" she said.

Sean could tell by the way her body began to shake that it was bad news.

"I'll be there in an hour." She hung up and said, "Mallory wants to talk to me."

Sean was shaking his head as she spoke. "No. No!"

"He'll tell me the truth. He promised."

"The guy is a freak! Did you know he has a picture of you in his house? Right next to his dead wife and son?"

Lucy flinched, and Sean rubbed her arms. "I'm sorry, I shouldn't have said that."

"You didn't tell me you were in his house."

"Dillon and I went out to Herndon and I searched his place. I knew he was watching—sensed it—so we waited until he left, then apprehended him. But—" He hesitated.

"And?"

"I left before the police came. Dillon didn't tell anyone I was there."

"They must know."

"Probably, but right now the important thing is *you*. The guy was obsessed with you. Maybe not in a sexual way, but it's so wrong."

"Sean, I need this to be over. I have to do it."

She was right, of course, but Sean didn't let her go. She straddled his lap and hugged him tightly. Slowly, she began to relax in his arms.

"I wish I could keep you here, safe, forever," Sean whispered.

"Hiding is never the answer. I can do this, Sean. Mick Mallory can't hurt me."

"You're amazing, Lucy. I've never met anyone braver than you."

She rested her forehead on his. "I'm not. I just can't sit in a corner, scared of dark shadows and creaking stairs for the rest of my life. I made that decision six years ago. Mallory isn't going to change that."

Lucy was the epitome of courage, but Sean didn't repeat the obvious. "I'm going to wash my face," she said, "then we should go. I'm relieved this will be over tonight."

THIRTY-TWO

"You don't have to talk to him," Kate said when she saw Lucy.

Lucy had admired Kate from when she first met her, for more reasons than Lucy had ever shared with her. But the primary reason was that Kate was willing to face evil and fight for what was right, that she could put her pain and her anger aside to do the right thing *all the time*, even when it came at great personal or professional or physical risk. She spoke her mind, and was more of a sister to her than her own flesh-and-blood sisters.

Lucy hugged Kate spontaneously—neither of them was demonstrably affectionate, and the physical display came as a surprise to both. "I love you, Kate. I don't think I ever told you that."

Lucy stepped back and Sean took her hand. He'd accepted her decision to talk to Mallory, even if he wasn't happy about it.

Lucy observed Mick Mallory through the one-way glass. He sat rigid, though he'd been there for several hours. His hands were on the table in front of him, shackles on his feet.

He was much older than she remembered. But she didn't really remember what he'd looked like. She'd blocked him from her mind the way she'd blocked what happened to her on the island.

There were only two things she remembered clearly from that time: when Dillon pulled her up from the filthy floor of the cabin and gave her his shirt to wear, and when she shot Adam Scott two days later.

Everything else was dark and fuzzy, and she preferred it like that.

But she'd know Mick Mallory if she saw him on the street. That he was living in nearby Herndon seemed unreal. She didn't hate him, and that surprised her.

He hadn't raped her.

But he watched.

He'd apologized.

He did nothing while the others hurt her.

He had nearly died sending Kate information.

He may have killed Cody.

Lucy might be able to forgive the past, if only because harboring lifelong anger and pain would destroy any chance of living a normal life. But what if Mallory had killed Cody because of her? Because she'd asked Cody to look into Prenter's murder?

Maybe it would have been better if she'd looked the other way. If she'd ignored her suspicions. Prenter was a rapist. Cruel, sadistic, he didn't care about the women he hurt, drugged them so they didn't remember, couldn't testify. Drugged them into a coma. . . . He was better off dead. She had no remorse that he was gone. No guilt. No grief. No sympathy.

Did that make her as cold and calculating as Mick Mallory?

Yet she would never have killed Prenter. She would never have killed any of those men, unless they were a direct threat. She'd never have thought of it . . . but she'd thought about killing Adam Scott. Not only thought about it, but took a gun from her father's safe and walked the three blocks to Dillon's house and shot the bastard who'd kidnapped her. Six times. She remembered it as clearly as if she'd shot him yesterday, felt the recoil of the handgun each time she pulled the trigger.

Maybe she was more like Mick Mallory than she thought. More like him than she wanted to be.

Cody was dead and even though he had been following her, he wasn't a rapist or a killer. Had he found something that incriminated Mallory? If that was the case, his death was for nothing—the FBI had found the connection to Mallory only hours after Cody died.

But if Cody had committed suicide, then he'd done it because of her. In her head she knew that if Cody was distraught enough to kill himself, he had a lot of problems. But in her heart she couldn't help but think that the way she treated him yesterday—that her inability to love him the way he wanted—that her rejection of his marriage proposal last year—that somehow, all that turned him suicidal.

She didn't know if she could face this every day as an FBI agent.

She asked quietly, "Do you know if forensics has a report on Cody's death? Suicide or murder?"

Noah said, "The D.C. police are giving our people full access. We have our best ERT processing all evidence. Our people are canvassing with the police to find any witnesses. We're talking to everyone whom Officer Lorenzo had contact with over the last seventy-two hours. We'll have an answer, but we can't rush it."

Lucy said, "I'm ready."

Noah started with her toward the door. She shook her head. "I need to talk to him alone."

"Hell no," Sean said.

She squeezed his hand. "I'm okay."

Noah agreed with Sean. "I'm not putting you in the room alone with that killer. He promised to talk to you, but he said nothing about being alone with you. We'd never agree to it."

Hans said, "Kate can join them. Mallory and she have a history. He may be more forthcoming with Kate in the room, Noah."

Exasperated, Noah ran a hand through his hair. "Okay. Fine."

Hans said, "Lucy, I'm confident you'll know what to say and do, but he did promise a full confession if you talk to him, so get everything you can out of him. Plus, we have a few questions for him—like why Robert Ralston went to Seattle. Why he waited until Morton was in D.C. before killing him. Confirm how they select their targets, and why Ralston was killed. Was Ralston working only for Morton, or playing for both teams?"

Lucy took a deep breath. "And why he killed Cody."

Hans nodded. "The minute you feel uncomfortable, you can leave. You don't have to stay. Even if you just need a couple of minutes, take them."

She nodded. "I'll do my best."

Sean turned her face to his. "I'm right here."

She gave him a smile that she hoped wasn't as weak as it felt, then stepped inside the interview room behind Kate.

To say Mick Mallory brightened when he saw her was an understatement. He sat straighter. He didn't so much as smile as open his mouth slightly in surprise and something that felt like awe. Lucy considered turning around and having Sean take her home. She didn't want to be in the same room with this man.

But there was no going back. She would face Mallory and get the answers they all needed. The answers *she* needed.

She sat down. Kate sat next to her. Lucy didn't take her eyes from Mallory's face.

"You wanted to talk to me."

"Thank you."

She shook her head. "I'm here so you will confess. I want the truth. *The truth will set you free.*" She intentionally quoted from Cody's fake suicide note. Mallory nodded, not flinching or showing any other reaction. He was cold. Colder than she remembered.

"I'm sorry," he said quietly.

"I don't want your apology. I want the truth. Start with why you have a picture of me in your house." She hadn't intended to start with that piece of information, but her mind had gone blank when she saw him sitting there.

He nodded and showed his first sign of discomfort as he reached back and rubbed the back of his neck, licking his lips at the same time. "I took that a year after I got out of the hospital. I came back here and didn't know what I was going to do. I wanted to kill myself, but didn't have the courage. Then I heard about the plea agreement between the government and Roger Morton, and my anger over that kept me alive. Guilt and vengeance fuels me; it runs through my veins. It's the air I breathe." He cocked his head. "You didn't know, did you?"

She shook her head.

"I wanted to see how you were doing, to make sure you were, I don't know, living as normal a life as possible.

"I shouldn't have tried to find you, but I couldn't help myself. I learned your schedule and waited one afternoon for you to leave one of your classes, I don't remember which one. You looked both sad and happy at the same time—I didn't know how that was possible. I was looking at you through a long lens because I didn't want you to see me. I didn't want to scare you. And I snapped a picture, without intending to."

For the first time, Lucy feared she'd been wrong about Cody—that he hadn't been the one stalking her. Trying to keep the anger out of her voice, she asked him, "Have you been stalking me?"

"No, I swear. The last time I saw you was at the WCF fund-raiser, but before then it had been a long time."

Lucy couldn't keep the shock off her face. "You were *there*?"

"Yes. You wouldn't have recognized me."

"You were in disguise?" Her head began to spin. She willed her breathing to even out.

"Pretty much."

"What about the skating park?"

He stared at her blankly. "I don't skate."

"No, at the skating rink in Arlington."

He shook his head. "Before Saturday, I hadn't seen you in over a year."

"Why were you at the WCF fund-raiser?"

"I'm not going to say."

"You said you'd tell me everything if I talked to you. I'm here. I'm talking. It's your turn."

Kate interrupted for the first time. "It might be helpful, Mick, if you tell Lucy about why you used her to lure parolees into a death trap. She deserves to know, don't you think?"

"Yes." He swallowed, his head falling into his hands. His shoulders rose, then fell. Again. Lucy did not feel bad for him, not even a sliver of empathy.

Mallory focused on Lucy. It was as if Kate wasn't in the room, though it was clear he'd heard her.

"After my wife and son were murdered, I lost my heart and my soul. Lost everything that was good, everything I loved. After the . . . *situation* where I was fired, Fran was the only person I could talk to. We kept in touch."

"That doesn't answer Kate's question," Lucy said. "Why did you use me?"

"We didn't. I never wanted you to know."

"Too late. I figured it out. But not until after seven parolees were killed—seven that I lured into public."

"Don't feel an ounce of remorse for those animals! They were all violent predators who are better off dead."

"Because you're a god? Is that how you see yourself?" Lucy asked.

"No, I'm sure I'm going to Hell. I figured I'd send some of those bastards there before I arrive." He paused, glanced at Kate, then turned back to Lucy. "Four years ago, Fran called me from Boston. She'd learned about a rapist who walked on a technicality. The bastard had been raping his niece from the time she was ten until she was fifteen. She committed suicide instead of telling her family that she'd had two abortions. They only found out after she died, from her diary. The judge wouldn't allow the diary to be admitted as evidence, and there was nothing else to prove he was a child molester.

"The situation reminded Fran of what happened to her sister. She went to Boston and killed him. In his own house. Then she called me to help her cover it up. So I did. I stole the creep's paintings and fenced them. He was quite a collector. Look it up—his name was Parker Weatherby." Mallory paused, then added, "I read the diary, Lucy. It was gut-wrenching. Fran should have gone after the fucking judge. When our own system fails the innocent!" He slapped his palm on the table and a startled Lucy leaned back.

Mallory looked pained that he'd scared her. He said in a rush, "After that, I had an idea. I needed to do *something* to stop these men. I only took a few hits a year to avoid patterns, I never charged more than my minimum expenses, and I rarely did a job in the same state twice. If the Bureau had figured it out, they weren't looking at me.

"It wasn't enough. I was so dissatisfied, but couldn't take on more. Not from lack of opportunity. And if I went after killers and rapists who got off on technicalities, like the prick up in Boston who Fran killed, the Feds would have figured it out pretty quickly. So I asked Fran to identify parolees for me to hit. She'd already started the lure program, it was successful, but honestly—why should these monsters go back to prison on the taxpayer's dime for two, three, four years to finish their sentence when we damn well know that the minute they get out, they'll be hunting for their next victim?"

"Did you know I volunteered for Fran?"

He didn't say anything at first.

"Don't lie to me!"

"I knew. I kept up with what you were doing."

"And that's not stalking? I suppose you've already rewritten the criminal penal code to suit your vigilante justice, so why not redefine stalking?"

"I'm sorry."

"I don't accept your apology!" Lucy took a deep breath. Her anger wasn't getting them the information they needed. "So you set these guys up. I copied the database and identified *seven* I was responsible for. Eight including Brad Prenter."

"You? Responsible? I killed them!"

"*I* set them up. How do you think that makes me feel? That I caused another human being to die?"

"You should feel relieved that they can't hurt anyone else, that they will never destroy another family."

In the back of her mind, Lucy realized that she *was* relieved they were off the streets. But she couldn't accept cold-blooded murder. If vigilante justice ruled, anarchy would soon follow.

"The system is far from perfect. But your way is not the answer. It's premeditated, cold-blooded murder. That makes you as much a monster as they are."

He looked pained. "I thought you would understand. You took justice into your own hands."

Kate jumped up. "Don't go there, Mallory, dammit!"

"It's okay, Kate." Lucy put her hand on Kate's arm without taking her eyes off Mallory. "I'll tell you the difference. Adam Scott raped *me*. He nearly killed *my* brother. He stabbed Dillon, who can no longer feel anything in his left hand. He's lucky he still has a hand! It was *personal*. He hurt me and people I love. I killed him." When she'd learned that Adam Scott had set explosives in Dillon's house, when she heard the explosion she later found out was in Jack's car, she didn't think. She didn't plan. She took one of the many guns in the house and ran the six blocks to Dillon's house. She saw Scott and Dillon fighting in the yard. There were no cops anywhere; there was no one to help. It was up to her.

Scott was such a sick psychopath, deep down in his core evil. He believed that she'd come to run away with him. He let his guard down, stepped toward her and said, "You're late."

She shot and killed him.

She said, "For six years, shooting Adam Scott has eaten me up because I don't feel any remorse for it."

Lucy took a deep breath, and before Kate or Mallory could say anything, she asked, "Why Prenter? He didn't fit the profile of the other victims."

"Yes he did," Mallory said, and left it at that.

"How?"

Mallory shrugged. "Figure it out."

"I'd rather you just tell me and stop playing these games. I'm sick and tired of it."

He didn't say anything, but stared at her, waiting.

"And Roger Morton? Why did you kill him?"

"You have to ask? I don't regret the killing of Morton. I'd dance on his fucking grave if I could."

Kate said, "I could have put him back in prison for life. Did you manipulate him into coming here, or did you learn he was coming here and then plan to kill him?"

"Prison," Mallory snapped bitterly, turning to Kate

for the first time. "Really. I prefer a bullet in the back of the head. Cheaper, faster justice."

Lucy said quietly, "So you killed Morton because he was a rapist and helped Adam Scott cover up untold murders. And he was walking free."

"I would have saved you if I could—"

Lucy raised her hand. "But you didn't. And that's the crux of it, isn't it? Because you didn't stop him from raping me, you needed to punish him because of *your* own guilt. You took a picture of me after deliberately getting my class schedule. You framed it and put it in your house. You knew where I worked and what I was doing. You lured Roger Morton here so you could kill him in my own backyard. And you say you're *not* obsessed with me?"

"Lucy, you needed to know he was dead. I wanted to give you peace."

"Peace." Lucy almost blurted out her accusations about him killing Cody, but she needed to do the one thing that Hans had asked her to do, not use this interview because she was battling her own guilt. "Why bring Morton here? You were a noble assassin," she said sarcastically. "Why have him come *here*? To where I live?"

"I had to."

"But why?"

Mallory didn't answer.

"Dammit, tell me!"

He was wrestling with something, she saw it on his face, but a moment later he sighed and his shoulders sagged.

"Adam Scott kept souvenirs from all his victims. Usually a piece of jewelry. Denise, the woman who helped

him, told me about it. She found the box in Scott's suitcase when we were on the island, and threw it away.
Scott found out and recovered it. Beat the living shit out
of her. I went to Seattle to try to find it but couldn't. I
had been working with Dave Biggler for two years, and
he knew Ralston, one of his dad's informants. The first
time I tried to get to Morton, it was to go to Seattle to
retrieve the box. We paid Ralston to plant the idea that
there was substantial cash, securities, and jewelry that
Scott hid on the island in a metal box with intricate de-
signs on it—I was certain Morton would know exactly
where it was."

"Why would Morton think that Ralston knew about
it?" Kate asked. "Wasn't Morton suspicious?"

"No. Ralston was a longtime cohort of Adam Scott—
and we told Ralston to say that the information came
from one of Scott's former security people who had a financial backer to create another Internet sex site."

"Wait," Kate said. "None of that was for real? All
those videos Morton was collecting was because of your
scam?"

"I would never have let them go live."

"You're fucking insane," Kate said. "You're the one
who gave Morton the idea to re-create Trask Enterprises!"

"No, he was already playing around; I just provided
incentive for him to act faster."

"But Morton didn't go to Seattle, Ralston did," Lucy
said, trying to get Mallory back on track.

"I didn't know he sent Ralston to retrieve the box.
However, I did learn that Ralston was keeping the box
for Morton."

"So you killed Ralston because of it."

"I killed Ralston because he was playing both sides. He thought he could get more money if he worked with Morton."

"Why did Ralston help you in the first place?"

"Because Dave asked him to and we paid him well. I should have realized he was a double agent, so to speak. Morton didn't show up with the box when he was supposed to on Thursday. So after the meet at the marina, I went to his motel. It wasn't there. I realized that Ralston had to have known where it was—Morton was carrying one piece of jewelry on him from the box, so it had to be *somewhere,* and Ralston was the only one Morton had talked to since he arrived."

"What sick reason could you want with Adam Scott's souvenirs anyway?" Kate asked.

Lucy knew. "You wanted to give the jewelry back to the families."

He nodded. "I have your ring, Lucy. I just didn't know how to give it to you."

She blinked back tears she refused to shed in front of Mallory. "You know, I almost understand. I don't agree with anything you did, but I understand. Everything. Except Cody. Why'd you kill him?"

Mallory looked like he'd been slapped, but Lucy continued without pause.

"He was a good man," said Lucy. He never hurt me, he never hurt anyone! He believed in what we were doing, putting the parolees back in prison. He was loyal to Fran. And you killed him because he found out about your cowardly vigilante group!"

Mallory was shaking his head and leaned forward. "No. No fucking way did I kill Cody Lorenzo. I swear on my wife's grave that I didn't kill him."

Lucy rubbed her eyes to stop her tears from leaking out. She didn't want to believe Mallory, yet everything else he said had the ring of truth, so why not this? But she'd rather believe that Mallory killed Cody than Cody killing himself.

"You didn't? Who'd you send to do it? Fran? David Biggler? Who did it?"

"It wasn't any of us, I swear to you, Lucy. I would never hurt someone you cared about. All I've wanted these last six years is your forgiveness."

Lucy rose from her seat and leaned forward. "I forgive you for what happened six years ago. But I'll never forgive you for what you've done since. I don't want my ring back. I don't want to see it or see you, until your trial."

She walked out.

Sean found Lucy sitting in the small lobby of FBI headquarters. He sat next to her and took her hand. She looked up at him, and he kissed her. "Kate and Dillon are going to be awhile and Armstrong and Resnick are headed out to Mallory's place to wrap up the search for evidence. They still can't find any guns."

"He probably got rid of them. It sounds like he would know exactly how to do that."

Sean hated how defeated Lucy looked. He wanted her fire back, the same fire that led her to pursue this investigation in the first place, that gave her the courage to confront Mick Mallory. "Come home with me, okay?"

"Do you think he killed Cody?"

"I honestly don't know."

Lucy closed her eyes and leaned back. "Neither do I. When I went in there I was so certain that he'd done it.

And now . . . if Cody killed himself, I can't blame any-one but *him*. And I don't want to."

"They'll know for sure by tomorrow whether it was suicide or murder," Sean said.

"Will they?" she asked.

"You know Forensics better than I do, but Noah said they are prioritizing this and hope to have a definitive answer in the morning. What do you think?"

"With ballistics, they know for certain more than ninety percent of the time—but it still could be inconclusive."

"I'll go with the odds." He kissed her on the forehead. "You'll have the answer tomorrow. Don't beat yourself up about it now."

"What about Fran?"

"She's in jail for the night. So is David Biggler. Armstrong said they don't have anything on his sister, but told her not to leave town. Mallory didn't give her up, so maybe she really wasn't involved."

"Or he's trying to protect her because she's a young woman. She's my age." Lucy hated Mallory, hated what he'd done, what he'd perverted in his twisted sense of right and wrong. That she'd somehow been the impetus for his decisions sickened her.

"You're exhausted, Lucy. Let's go."

"I am tired," she agreed.

Sean stood, pulling her up with him and wrapping an arm around her shoulder. "There's nothing more either of us can do tonight."

When Noah and Hans arrived at Mallory's house, it was after eight at night, below 30 degrees, with the promise of blizzard-like conditions by Thursday morning. The search team was done, but SSA Lauren Cheville had asked Noah to come out.

"I wanted you to see this," Lauren said. "Pictures simply won't do it justice."

He and Hans walked with Lauren toward the kitchen. "I thought the search was a bust," Lauren explained. "We found nothing to implicate Mallory in any crimes. But I remembered what you said, Hans."

"That he will have kept his guns."

"Exactly. I just didn't imagine that he'd have made it so easy for us to trace them—just hard to find them."

They followed Lauren into the basement, accessed by a door in the kitchen. The basement was damp with a moldy scent that made Noah sneeze. There was full fluorescent lighting and several workbenches, tools hung meticulously on peg-board lined walls, and canned goods lined a metal shelf. "We checked the basement earlier, did a complete sweep, but nothing jumped out. After we came up empty, I walked through the entire place again, thinking about where *I* would have hidden a gun collection. I knocked on walls and tables, and then found it." She motioned to an agent who was standing by a workbench. "Show them, Carl."

Carl knocked on one of the two six-foot-long workbenches. It was solid wood. He knocked on the other. It sounded hollow. "Watch this," he said. He extended his arms as far as they could go and reached under both front corners of the bench. "There's a special release— you have to press both at the same time and—*voilà*!"

The top of the bench popped open on a spring. Inside on the felt-lined hidden compartment were dozens of handguns—mostly nine-millimeters and .38s. Three rifles—an M21 and two M24s—were secured on the underside of the workbench lid. Several knives were also on display.

Each firearm had a name painted on the barrel in white.

"My God," Hans said. Even he appeared surprised, although he'd predicted that Mallory would have kept the weapons he used. "How many are there?"

"Seventeen nine-millimeters, ten .38 revolvers, and two Glock .45's," Lauren said. "This is a fortune in guns to be tagged and left for souvenirs."

"But it makes each murder that much harder to prove when the ballistics don't match up with anything else," Hans said.

Noah read the names. Most he didn't recognize. Then he saw Roger Morton next to Robert Ralston. "See those?" He gestured toward the guns.

"Can't miss them. Did you notice what's under each gun?"

"File folders."

"My guess? It's his justification for each murder—a list of their crimes, sentences, parole information. Mallory doesn't want anyone to think he's a monster, so he convinces himself that he's a savior."

Noah stared at the firearms and wondered what it would take for someone to turn vigilante—what was the trigger? For Mallory, the trigger had been the murders of his wife and son, coupled with his inability to protect Lucy Kincaid when she was kidnapped. But Fran Buckley—other people have been victims and lost family, and they didn't take the law into their own hands—why had Fran? What had been her trigger?

Nothing good was coming from this investigation. A cop was dead, lives were ruined, and Noah suspected it wasn't going to end with Mick Mallory's confession.

THIRTY-THREE

Lucy didn't know if it was the strange bed or the events of the day, but after three hours of an uneasy, dreamless sleep, she woke up and was unable to go back to sleep.

She sat up and considered reading, but she needed to sleep.

She didn't want to be alone.

She was wearing one of Sean's shirts, a worn, over-sized MIT T-shirt that hit her mid-thigh.

Maybe it was sleeping in Sean's shirt, wrapped in his scent, that had awakened her. With the idea she had, she was glad Patrick was still in California.

She walked silently down the hall to Sean's room. It was two in the morning, but his light was still on. Her heart flipped. He was working this late because of her. Trying to put all the puzzle pieces together, even though Mallory and Fran and Dave Biggler were all in jail.

Even superheroes needed rest, she thought, planning to say such when she pushed open his bedroom door.

Sean was asleep, wearing sweatpants and no top. He had two laptops open, one next to him and one on his lap, and a folder leaking papers lying on his chest.

Lucy quietly closed the door and walked over. She

didn't want to startle Sean—living with a family of cops she knew that wouldn't be wise—so she said, "Sean."

His eyes popped open. They were cloudy from sleep, but two blinks later he was fully awake.

"Luce—you okay?"

"I'm fine. You should go to bed."

"I will." He cleared his throat and closed his computers. "I was just monitoring the security system."

"There's no one out there."

"We don't know that everyone involved has been arrested."

"No, but why would they come after me?" She shook her head.

"Can I get you something?"

"No." She lifted the laptops off his bed, putting them on the dresser. He put the file folder on his nightstand. Without asking, she slipped under the blankets.

"Lucy—"

"I want to sleep here tonight. Is that okay with you?"

For a moment, she thought he was going to send her back to the guest room; that he'd give her an awkward excuse, but deep down not want to sleep with her because of her past. Because he didn't want to rush her or hurt her, and while she appreciated the sensitivities, they were excuses. Because if she were any other woman, he'd have climbed into *her* bed earlier.

Her old fears rose up, and she opened her mouth to give him an out, an excuse to save face, but then he kissed her.

And all her doubts, all her fears that she was less than perfect for Sean, washed away in his affection.

This was exactly where she was supposed to be.

From the moment Sean started working on his security system, he'd thought about Lucy and debated whether he should go to her room. Lord knew he wanted to, but she'd been so exhausted. He'd considered just holding her, telling her he wanted to simply lay next to her, but he suspected that wouldn't last. He wanted her, wanted to hold her, kiss her, make love to her.

He was thrilled she'd come to him. And now he wanted to make this moment perfect. Memorable. His mind wanted to go slow, but his body was in a rush. His body wanted all of her now, but he willed himself to take it slow. To be calm. In control.

He so much wanted to lose control with Lucy.

He savored her mouth, the faint mint from her toothpaste, the warmth from her tongue. He kissed her as they sank into his pillows, under the down comforter. Her hands were on his chest, her long fingers moving, but tentative. He maneuvered her hands away so that his bare chest pressed firmly against hers. He wanted her shirt off.

He remembered what she'd said earlier. That she wanted him to treat her like all his other girlfriends. But she wasn't like any of them. He'd meant it then, and he meant it even more now. He wasn't going to simply pull off her shirt—his shirt, he thought with a smile—to get to her full breasts.

Instead, he moved his left hand slowly up her shirt, feeling her body tense, then relax. He kissed her neck as his hand moved farther up, until he cupped her breast and gently massaged her soft skin. His thumb ran over a rough line, and for a second he thought it was a thick thread from his comforter; then he realized it was a scar that cut a wicked slash from one breast to the other.

When he touched it, she tensed again, and he wanted to tell her he didn't care, but talking about it was the last thing either of them needed right now. So he continued his sensual massage, over her breasts, across her back, returning to her breasts, skimming his fingers and rubbing his palms across every inch of flesh until he felt the sigh of pleasure in her chest, heard the small exhale of breath that told him she was enjoying his attentions.

"I want to take off your shirt," he whispered.

"Please," she said, putting her arms up.

He slowly pulled it off, glancing at her breasts as he did. He saw the scar, faint but long, and it took all his strength not to react. Not because the scar diminished Lucy in any way, but because he wished he had killed Roger Morton and Adam Scott himself.

Lucy reached up and turned off the light. "Luce—" he began.

"You don't mind, do you?"

"No." He wanted to look at her, but this time he would make love to her by her rules. Hell, he'd make love to her by her rules all the time. He kissed her, feeling her now-bare chest against his, and sighing with a contentment he usually didn't feel in any of his relationships.

He focused above her waist, but left no place untouched or unkissed. Her neck, her shoulders, her breasts. He kissed her stomach, then back up to the sensitive underside of her breasts, then skimmed his tongue across her nipples, up to the hollow of her neck. She gasped when he blew a breath where he'd moistened her skin, and he smiled. Then he kissed her again and felt her respond from deep inside.

Lucy had been nervous from the moment she slipped

into Sean's bed, but her nerves disappeared as Sean methodically explored her body. Her skin pulsed with his touch, wanting more, a feeling unfamiliar to her. She'd enjoyed sex, but always in the back of her mind were doubts. She always held back, always feared something bad would happen—that she would do something wrong. But tonight she craved Sean. She wanted him with her, his body against hers, his lips everywhere, his hands touching her most sensitive places.

His hard penis pressed against her leg, and she shivered in anticipation, wrapping her arms around Sean's neck.

"Do you trust me, Lucy?" Sean asked.

"Yes," she whispered.

His lips moved from her mouth to her neck again. She loved the way he kissed her just under her jawline, using his tongue lightly, like a flirt, making her squirm. Down her neck to the soft spot right above her collarbone. She grasped his shoulders, his muscles hard beneath her hands. She ran all her fingers over his back and upper arms, felt the definition of each muscle, and almost asked Sean to turn on the light so she could see them.

He kissed her breasts so tenderly, repeatedly, light feather kisses that made her warm and she was certain she was seeing stars. She'd never felt such bliss. She sighed out loud, surprising herself at the sound that came from deep in her throat.

Sean kissed her stomach and she squirmed. His hands went under the waistband of her lacy underwear, and he slowly pushed them down until they were off, somewhere at the foot of the bed. Or on the floor. She didn't care. She parted her legs, anticipating his maneuvering, and said, "Condom?"

She'd meant to ask a full question, but only one word came out.

He laughed softly. "Yes. But I'm not ready yet."

She frowned and reached down, surprising herself when she brazenly grasped his penis. "You feel ready."

"Ah, Lucy, hold that thought."

He scooted down the bed and her hand fell away. The first flicker of Sean's tongue between her legs had her gasp. His hands were on her inner thighs, gently pushing her open, and his kisses, so wonderful on her lips, became electric. She didn't know what to expect; she'd never made love like this before. She'd read about it, but they were just words.

Her stomach felt as if it were sinking; her entire body went hot and cold simultaneously. Sean sucked and teased her with his tongue and suddenly her hips moved on their own, and a wave of indefinable tension contracted until she gasped louder than she intended; then everything inside twisted and churned, like a riptide pulling her under, then tossing her up, over the waves. She could hardly catch her breath. Every taut muscle relaxed simultaneously, making her feel pleasantly languorous.

Sean kissed each thigh, then her stomach, then her breasts again as her chest rose and fell, her breathing rapid. "That—" she began, then forgot what she was going to say.

"I agree," he whispered, and she felt a smile on the side of her neck.

"Are you smug?" she asked.

"Very." He kissed her, then rolled over and opened his drawer. He took care of business quickly, and rolled back.

Sean lay on top of her, not using his full weight, but her body began to tense up again, and not in hopeful anticipation of making love. The all-too-familiar panic rose in her chest. She willed it back, hating this awful feeling that she had no control over. She could scarcely breathe, but she'd push through. This was too important—Sean was too important—to let her past interfere tonight.

Suddenly, he reached under her waist and pulled her smoothly over on top of him, her legs straddling his. "You drive, princess," he said.

She didn't question; she didn't want to analyze how he understood what she wanted without her saying a word. How he made it natural and sexy all at once. Her trepidation disappeared and she kissed him. She went slow, guiding him inside her a fraction of an inch at a time. She reached up and found one of his hands, and he clutched her fingers tightly. His other hand held her hip.

She moved to adjust her position and he groaned, his hand tightening on her waist, holding her there. She sank deeper, feeling the perspiration on her skin and his. Her mouth was open, parched, and when his penis jerked inside her, as if it had a mind of its own, a startled sound of excitement escaped; then she softly moaned as she eased herself completely over him, her sensitive spot rubbing lightly against Sean's pelvis, the wave slowly building again deep inside her.

"Sean," she whispered, and wondered if she had said anything out loud. Then she didn't think, only felt as he held her hips, not letting her move.

"Lucy, you're making me crazy."

"How?"

"Open your eyes."

She didn't want to. She didn't want to break this magic, where she didn't have to see, didn't have to think, only feel. All she wanted was to feel Sean, on her and inside her and with her.

His hand touched her cheek.

"Lucy."

She reluctantly looked at him in the dark. But it wasn't completely dark. She saw him perfectly well with the streetlight through his partially closed blinds. His square jaw was firm, but his eyes were staring back with such intensity she couldn't turn away.

Sean took his other hand from her hip and clasped both her hands, pulling them up toward his head, so she had to lie across his chest. He arched up to kiss her, his skin slick with sweat, his muscles hard with restrained passion.

Her insides quivered and he groaned, his hands tight in hers. While looking at him, Lucy moved her hips slowly, back and forth, the most incredible sensation returning. Was this even possible? She didn't know, she didn't care, and she was simply thankful because her body was combustible and she needed to explode.

Sean let go of her hands and reached down to squeeze her ass, hold her still for a moment. She didn't want to sit still—the friction was incredible, sending small shocks through her body.

She squirmed forward, Sean's body hot beneath hers.

He whispered, "You do that and this will be a short trip."

She stopped moving, but then her muscles involuntarily contracted, and he hissed. "I think—" she whispered.

"What?"

"The wave. Again."

She raised her hips until he almost slipped out, then sank back down. Lucy gasped, stunned and happy all at once, and her body pulled Sean deep inside. He wrapped his arms tight around her waist, holding her close, and joined his orgasm with hers.

Lucy relaxed all at once, her body falling across Sean, limp.

Sean didn't want to move. Lucy was as pliable as putty lying on top of him, a small smile on her face. He touched the corner of her mouth and she kissed his thumb.

"Hmmm?" she said.

He kissed her, then gently eased her onto her side. "Stay."

"I can't move."

"Good."

A moment later, he crawled naked back into bed, pulling the comforter tight around them. Lucy spooned against him, her breathing already even. His arm around her waist, he kissed her cheek, her jaw, her ear, and vowed never to let her go.

THIRTY-FOUR

The sun has not yet risen. I see snow falling lightly to the ground outside my windows as I rise from my warm bed.

I am calm, as I always am when I end one cycle and begin the next. Though this morning I am not as pleased as I should be, and I wonder about that while I shower.

One reason is that the female I currently have has potential; she learns to obey well. If I had more time, I know I could put her back together the way God intended.

But Lucy Kincaid stole my time. I cannot shake her from my thoughts and my nightmares. I am driven to teach her. She is the most ill-prepared for my instruction. She's the most defiant. I see it in her eyes, in the way she walks. I've been watching her for weeks, and never would I have chosen her as one of my students.

But it is not always up to me. Greater powers are at play. Who am I to question? She placed herself in my life when she sought to send me back to prison. She overstepped her bounds, if she even accepts that she has any.

She will be a challenge for me, a test. God doesn't give us more than we can handle, and as she is merely a woman, I can break her.

I cook my breakfast and eat as the sun rises, though

with the dark gray clouds I can see. but a faint shift from dark to less dark. I put the leftovers in a bowl.

I cross the worn kitchen linoleum and go down to the basement, as I do every morning. The female is lying in the corner of the cage, under the single wool blanket I am generous to provide.

She looks at me but shows nothing. No fear. No anger. No soul.

I have broken her.

I put the bowl in her cage and see if I am right. She doesn't move, doesn't crawl toward the food, though her nose twitches like a cat's. She smells it. She wants it.

And she waits.

"You may eat," I say.

Slowly she crawls across the hard-packed dirt basement. There is blood in the corner from her punishment last night. I had given her ointment and a clean towel—I do not want her to get an infection. I'm not inhumane.

I refill her water bowl and leave it with her food.

Her response should please me, but I am not happy. She broke far faster than the others. A trick?

I could give her to another who will appreciate my time training her to be a proper, obedient woman.

But I do not trust her. In the end, they all turn away from the Truth.

She whimpers as she eats.

I sigh. No matter. She's going to die soon anyway. I don't have the time to finish her training. Break them, then put them back together the way they should be.

I turn and walk back up the stairs to prepare for the next female.

THIRTY-FIVE

Noah hadn't been so angry and frustrated with a case in a long time.

Fran Buckley wasn't talking, and her lawyer, Clark Jager, was playing legal games to keep Noah away from her. In fact, Jager had threatened to pull Lucy Kincaid's file and use her history as part of his case. It didn't matter whether there was anything in her file; that it would be open and part of the criminal proceedings increased the chances that it would be made public.

Biggler was more forthcoming, but he didn't have anything to add to Mallory's confession. Noah sent Abigail to the bar to flash pictures of Mallory and Biggler—including the sister—to the bartender who served Prenter to see if they could get a witness to corroborate Mallory's confession.

Abigail stepped into the conference room that had been turned overnight into the "war" room for the WCF investigation where Noah and Hans were reading statements and files. There was enough paperwork to keep them busy for weeks.

"Have a minute?" she asked.

"Sure, but I thought you were meeting with the bartender."

"Too early, he doesn't come on until five, but I called

him at home and he's agreed to come here to look at the photos."

"What else?" Noah rose to stretch his legs, then make a small change to the timeline they were keeping on a large white board.

"ERT called. They're writing up their report now, but wanted to give us a heads-up that they're done with their preliminary investigation and said it's conclusive: Cody Lorenzo didn't commit suicide. Along with other evidence to substantiate murder, the trajectory of the bullet proved there was no way he could have pulled the trigger."

"Shit." Noah leaned against the table, his fingers pressed against his forehead.

"But you thought Mallory was lying. Why are you surprised?"

"Because I wanted to believe he was telling the truth. I wanted to believe he didn't kill a cop."

"There's no physical evidence tying him to the murder," Hans said, looking up from the report he was reading. "It's the only murder he didn't confess to."

"That's not going to sway a jury, not when a cop is a victim."

"Without hard evidence, the U.S. Attorney isn't going to go for the death penalty," Hans said. "Considering all his other victims are criminals, a jury may be more lenient than if he were killing truly innocent people."

There was evidence *somewhere*. A security camera that caught Mallory near the scene of the murder. Trace evidence. A witness who didn't know what he or she was seeing. He might have to work for it, but there would be something to prove beyond a shadow of a doubt that Mallory killed Cody Lorenzo.

Lorenzo had been a cop doing his job. There had to be justice for him. Noah couldn't tolerate a cop killer getting off lightly.

"There's something else," Abigail said. "Do you remember the flowers Lucy received on Monday? She thought that Lorenzo was stalking her because when Rogan went to the florist, they had a record of a cash transaction and the sender was Cody Lorenzo. But they don't require identification to send flowers."

"And it wasn't Lorenzo?"

"ERT said the card attached to the flowers and the fake suicide note were written by the same person."

It took Noah a moment for the information to sink in. "So Mallory wrote both of them? He sent Lucy the flowers and used Lorenzo's name."

"Appears so," Abigail said.

"But why?" Hans asked. "To set Cody up? To make the suicide seem more plausible?"

"He planned it," Noah said, even more angry with Mallory now than before. "That bastard. I'm going back to the jail to talk to him. He's been manipulating people for far too long, and he's going to have to pay the price." He picked up the phone.

Hans said, "Noah, I understand your feelings about Mick Mallory, but he's a smart guy. If he wanted Cody's death to look like a suicide, I think we'd have more doubts about whether it was murder or suicide."

"This all came down in a few days," Noah said. "Lorenzo was breathing down the neck of someone—Mallory? Fran Buckley? I don't know, but he was on to something. He and Lucy were the only ones looking into the deaths of the parolees, but Lucy wasn't out in public asking questions or pulling police reports. Cody

Lorenzo must have talked to the wrong person. I don't see how else this could be playing out."

Hans frowned. "That all makes sense. But—it just doesn't fit Mallory's M.O."

"Maybe he sent someone else to do it. That's why it was so sloppy." He said to Abigail, "We need someone to look into Fran Buckley's murder of Parker Weatherby in Boston. Four years ago—"

"It was four years ago last October," she said.

"You already looked into it?"

"Just the facts of the case, after Mallory mentioned it. No suspects; the police think robbery was the motive. A couple of paintings showed up over the last two years, but nothing that led to who fenced them."

"We need to put Buckley in Boston that night," Noah said. "Anything—credit card information, a plane ticket, a stray hair they couldn't match DNA evidence to. We need something solid to get her to flip."

"I'm on it. Can I call in Rick Stockton's help if I need it?"

"Whatever it takes," Noah said. After Abigail left, he said to Hans, "We can't let Buckley walk. We can only hold her for three days, and Mallory's statement isn't going to be enough to keep her locked up. Her lawyer is right about that."

"I doubt she'd flee."

"We can't count on that. Hans, I know how this case can be played in the media. We'll lose a lot of ground if Jager decides to play to the cameras."

"But we have the facts on our side."

"Jager is right about public sentiment. No one cares if a few sick predators are dead. But what I truly fear is that if Buckley gets away with it, more private citizens will take the law into their own hands. As Lucy said, it would be anarchy."

"I don't disagree with you, Noah."

Noah swore under his breath. "We'll have to offer a plea, won't we?"

"Fran Buckley killed a man in Boston—a man who had never been convicted of a crime. He was probably guilty, but he still didn't have his day in court, and while our system is imperfect, it's damn good. If our former FBI agents and cops start acting like judge, jury, and executioner, society will suffer. So yeah, the U.S. Attorney will plead. But none of our conspirators are ever getting out of prison."

Noah was meeting with the U.S. Attorney's office this afternoon, and he hoped he wasn't chewed out for his aggressive warrant and investigation. But first, he had to call Kate. She had to know about Cody Lorenzo's murder—and Jager's threat to pull Lucy's file in discovery.

Noah believed in the letter of the law, but he saw nothing good about opening Lucy's records for the world to inspect and second-guess. He had a sense now of what Kate and the rest of them had gone through six years ago when faced with a trial versus a plea agreement with Roger Morton.

Except that if anyone could handle the pressure, Noah had no doubt Lucy could.

Sean slowly pocketed his cell phone.

Lucy wasn't going to take this well. He had to spin it right so that she didn't take it personally. So she didn't heap the guilt on herself for something she had no control over.

She was asleep on his family-room couch. Sean had

taken the morning to catch up on business—it was getting away from him. RCK East didn't advertise because they didn't need to; most of their business came from word of mouth and referrals. With only two people on staff and no admin, they didn't need to create more business than they could handle.

But with Patrick gone, and Sean occupied with everything that had been going on, he had ignored his business emails and phone messages. He was nearly caught up when Kate called with the news of Lorenzo's murder.

He didn't want to tell Lucy, and he certainly didn't want to wake her up to give her the news, but he knew she wouldn't want him to shield her from the truth.

He sat down on the coffee table and watched her sleep. Lucy was more mature than most young women beginning their careers. Yet in sleep, she looked young and vulnerable. Her face was relaxed, her mouth slightly open, her hands together under her cheek. Sleeping Beauty. And Sean wanted her to stay this peaceful; she needed the rest.

She opened her eyes suddenly, a brief look of panic on her face.

"It's me," Sean said, angry with himself for staring at her for so long. Even in her sleep, she had sensed his gaze.

"What time is it?"

"Two."

She slowly sat up, dazed. "I slept until two in the afternoon?" she asked, incredulous.

"You were up early; you needed a nap."

She rubbed her eyes and yawned. "Three hours. I never sleep during the day." She tilted her head and frowned. "What's wrong?"

Sean hadn't thought his expression revealed his unrest over the news. He was blunt. "Cody didn't commit suicide. The FBI proved conclusively that he was murdered."

Lucy began to shake. Cody was murdered. Because of *her* investigation. Why hadn't she called in Kate earlier? Or would Mallory have killed her sister-in-law in his failed attempt to cover up his vigilante group?

"Luce?" Sean sounded worried, and Lucy reached out for him. His hands held hers tightly and her body stopped shaking so violently. She took a deep breath.

"Maybe . . . maybe I'm relieved."

"Relieved?"

How could she explain it? She closed her eyes and focused on her breathing, focused on slowing down her racing heart. "The idea that he killed himself because of me—"

"It wasn't because of you!"

"I meant, because of his feelings for me. That he'd be depressed enough to kill himself because I didn't love him." Her voice cracked. "But I should never have asked him to help in the first place. I should have gone to Kate or Dillon—or anyone in the FBI. I don't know why—"

"Because you didn't know what was going on. You were protecting people you believed were innocent."

"And Cody is dead because I was worried about Fran." Her anger leaked out in her voice. "I hate her! Even if she didn't pull the trigger, she had to have known. How could she do that to Cody? The time and energy he gave to WCF. And now—damn!" Her voice cracked again and she shut her mouth.

"There's one more thing. Cody wasn't stalking you."

She shook her head. "Wh-what?" It made no sense. "But the flowers—you talked to the florist."

"The FBI proved that the same man who wrote the fake suicide note also wrote the card from the florist. They compared it to handwriting known to be Cody's, and there's no way he could have written either the card or the suicide note."

"But the florist—"

"Noah thinks Mallory planned everything. That since Cody was investigating Prenter's murder, if he discredited Cody in your eyes by making it seem like he was stalking you, either you'd believe Cody really had killed Prenter or you would have nothing more to do with him. They were trying to protect their operation."

"He died for *nothing*?"

Sean pulled her head down to his chest. At first she resisted, then she let him hold her. She didn't cry. She had no more tears. Her head ached from her grief, and sitting here with Sean helped.

Slowly, the tension eased from her body. When she could breathe normally and her heart stopped racing, she looked up at Sean. "I need to go."

"You don't—"

"I have to go home and shower and get ready for Cody's prayer service."

"I'll go with you."

"No—I need to go alone."

"I don't think you should be alone."

"Cody's friends will be there. Family. I won't be alone."

"But—"

"Everyone's in prison. Mallory, Fran—"

"I'd still feel more comfortable if I could keep my eye

on you until we know for sure the FBI arrested all the players."

"You can drive me if you'd like. The church will be filled with cops."

"Lucy—"

Her voice cracked, but her eyes were dry. "I believed it was Cody. How could I do that? We were friends. I was with him for nearly two years. And I believed the worst. I let my fear cloud my judgment. I should have known Cody would never do anything to hurt me. He never had before, and yet—I didn't even give him the benefit of the doubt. I need to mourn for him, and I want to do it alone. Do you understand?"

Sean kissed her on the top of her head and held her close. "I do. I'll drive you there and pick you up. You won't leave the church, right?"

"Promise. Thank you for understanding."

THIRTY-SIX

Noah and Hans faced Mallory in a private interview room in the county jail.

"You lied to us, and you lied to Lucy," Noah said.

Mallory stared at Noah. His expression was defiant, but his eyes were weary, as if he hadn't slept.

Hans said, "Cody Lorenzo was murdered. There's no question."

Mallory frowned but didn't speak.

"You killed him because he was getting close to exposing your vigilante group."

"I didn't kill Cody Lorenzo," Mallory said with a sigh.

"We don't believe you."

Mallory closed his eyes. "You found my guns. Every single one of them is labeled with the name of the scumbag. Name and date. Every one. Cody Lorenzo is not there."

It took Noah a second to realize the problem with that argument. "You left the gun there. Tried to pass it off as a suicide."

"If you do your research, you'll find that not all the names on those guns were fired. The gun I was carrying at the time was retired, so I could remember every one of them. I didn't kill Lorenzo."

"Lorenzo was a cop. Automatic death penalty," Noah said.

Mallory laughed humorlessly. "Death penalty? Bring it on."

"Lorenzo was killed between eleven p.m. and midnight Monday. I don't suppose you have an alibi?"

"Home. Fran came over a little before seven, worried because of the questions Lorenzo had been asking. I told her to calm down, that nothing connected us to Prenter's murder."

"Fran could have killed him. You'd be an accessory."

"Fran didn't kill him."

"I'm not buying this."

"I don't care." Mallory sighed. "Your warrant was thin, and you know it, but I'm not getting a lawyer, and I'm not going to defend myself. I don't want to. I've given you everything. I'm done."

Noah frowned, a thought coming to him, but then it left. Hans picked up on the silence and said, "Fran lawyered up. Clark Jager."

Mallory shrugged. "You really want to put her in prison?"

"She killed at least one man."

"Who deserved it."

"Who didn't have a trial. She's scared."

Mallory nodded. "She was always the weak link. But she's not talking, because the only one she can turn on is me, and I've already given myself up. What more can I tell you?"

"Fran's lawyer is threatening to pull the police records of every WCF staffer—and volunteer. Their argument is that if someone at WCF is involved, it's not Fran Buckley, but one of her staff."

Mallory straightened. He immediately saw the repercussions of such a move, which Noah and Hans were counting on.

"That's bullshit. No one else at WCF was involved. You got Biggler, and he never killed anyone. He was my backup. He watched my ass."

"And his sister Brenda, who was your lure," Hans said. They hadn't gotten the report back from Abigail and the bartender at Club 10, but Hans played the bluff perfectly.

"Please be lenient with Brenda," Mallory pleaded. "She helped because she worships her brother. I don't think she ever really thought deeply about what we were doing."

"It was just the three of you—four including Fran Buckley."

"Yes," Mallory said. "Lucy had nothing to do with any of it, except unknowingly setting up the meetings. You know that, both of you."

"We know it," Noah said, "but we won't be able to stop Jager if he petitions for all criminal records. Lucy's past will be on display during the trial—"

"Fran will plead. She won't let Lucy suffer—"

"She's not cooperating. She denied involvement, and implied it was someone else at WCF."

Mallory pounded a chained fist on the table. "You can prove otherwise! I told you what happened!"

"Your word means shit right now," Noah stated. "Jager will tear you apart in the courtroom. You could be saying that the sun rises in the east, and no one on the jury will believe you when Jager gets through with destroying what little credibility you might have. It doesn't matter whether we believe you or not."

"I have proof." Mallory hung his head. "I didn't want it to come to this, but . . ." His voice trailed off and he was lost in thought for several seconds. "The night before she killed Weatherby, Fran flew commercial from Dulles to Albany. Her college roommate, Sylvia Dunham, lives in Troy. She borrowed Sylvia's car to drive to Boston. Sylvia had no idea what Fran was doing, I don't know what excuse Fran gave her, but Sylvia will remember the trip because Fran got into a minor accident driving back on I-90. The car wasn't totaled, but Fran wrote her a check to pay for damages so that there would be no insurance claim. The accident was the early morning after Weatherby was killed—I told Fran I would take care of everything, and she left."

All verifiable. "That's not definitive proof."

"Other than my word, that's all I have."

It might be enough to make her squirm, Noah thought. But it wouldn't make Jager sweat.

"What about the gun?"

"I disposed of it—you'll never be able to find it, and even if you did, the water damage would render any forensic evidence worthless."

"Where did she get the gun?" Noah asked.

Mallory looked at him as if he were smarter than he'd expected. "I never asked."

Hans said quietly, "Why did you get Lucy involved in the first place? You had to know that one day, this would crash down around you and burn the one person you claim to want to protect."

"You won't understand." Mallory put his cuffed wrists against his forehead. "Even though she didn't know she was helping us, there was a sense of justice in her getting those guys. She's so good at this, Hans, she's uniquely qualified in separating the online jerks from the true predators."

"So you stalk her and kill her ex-boyfriend because you *admire* her?" Noah was losing his temper, his tone getting louder.

"I didn't kill Lorenzo, and I wasn't stalking Lucy!"

"Mallory, the fake suicide note was written by the same person who sent Lucy a dozen red roses on Monday morning. If it was Lorenzo, it ties everything up in a pretty package. But it wasn't. Forensics proved it. Admit it was you."

"I didn't send Lucy roses!"

"Give it up—"

"I swear to God, I did not." Mallory leaned forward. "Are you lying to me?"

"We haven't been doing the lying here."

He pounded his fist again. "Listen to me! I didn't send the roses, I didn't kill Lorenzo, and I didn't write any fucking notes! If the roses were sent by the same person who killed the cop, then Lucy is in danger! Dammit, where is she? What kind of morons are you?"

A mourner held the outer door of Holy Trinity open for Lucy as she walked in from the snow. A large flake hit her on the back of the neck and she rolled her shoulder so her collar would absorb the moisture. "Thank you," she mumbled, and walked into the church just after the processional. She looked around and spotted Cody's partner, April Dunnigan, near the back. Lucy slid into the pew behind her.

April was a well-rounded, fit ebony-black cop a few years older than Cody, with short curly hair and six piercings in each ear. They'd been partners for as long as Lucy knew Cody.

She tapped April on the shoulder. The cop turned around, her eyes rimmed red but her expression guarded. When she recognized Lucy, she came around to her pew and gave her a hug.

"I'm glad you could come," she whispered.

"You heard about the evidence?"

April nodded. "Are you okay?"

Lucy shrugged. "I'll be okay. What about you?"

"I want to shoot the bastard who killed him." She grimaced. "I shouldn't say that here."

"I'm sure God understands." He had to understand better than she did.

The cop went back to her seat, and that was fine with Lucy. She preferred to grieve alone.

It was hot in the church, and Lucy took off her coat, folding it beside her. She took a deep breath.

There were only a few cops present, but this was the mass before the prayer service. Lucy suspected many would arrive during and after mass. And the funeral on Friday would be a procession through D.C. with every cop in attendance. Lucy had been to the funeral of an officer killed in the line of duty, a friend of Cody's from the police academy. She and Cody had been seeing each other then, and the murder had hit Cody hard, but at the same time he had never wavered from his duty.

No one told us we'd live into retirement. But dying to protect all that we hold precious is easier to accept than dying in vain.

The guilt ate at her because there was no reason Cody should have died. In her head she knew that Cody was a cop, that this was his job, but at the same time, it was a different situation—they should have brought in the FBI from the beginning. Maybe Cody would still be alive.

Lucy stood a few seconds later than everyone else for the Our Father, surprised that the prayer had come so soon. How long had she been here? It didn't seem like more than a few minutes. She only vaguely remembered the readings. She was still too hot, and her eyes were dry. Too many tears shed in the last two days.

But in the back of her mind, she thought something was truly wrong with her. Was she getting sick? Sean had made her eat a late lunch, though she'd told him she wasn't interested in food. He cooked chicken noodle soup and a grilled cheese sandwich. She'd eaten half, but now the small meal felt like a lead ball in her stomach.

She breathed deeply.

"Lucy?"

April's voice sounded far away.

"Are you okay?"

"I—I think I'm going to be sick."

"I'll take you to the bathroom."

Lucy wanted to tell her no, she was fine to go alone, but instead she nodded. April took her arm and led her toward the bathrooms to the right of the vestibule.

Two uniformed officers brought in a flurry of snow as they stepped into the entry. The cold coming in from the outside felt remarkable to Lucy. "April, I'm just going to step outside for a minute. I think I just need air. I'll be in before communion."

"I can go with you," April offered.

Lucy shook her head. "One minute—it'll clear my head."

"I'll wait here." April spoke softly to the officers while Lucy stepped outside.

The cold air did clear her head, and she watched the snowfall, thicker than when she'd arrived thirty minutes ago. She still felt ill, but she rarely got sick. She figured it must be grief. She missed Cody. She loved him—not in the way he wanted her to, but it didn't mean she hadn't cared for him deeply.

"I'm sorry," she whispered into the cold.

Forgive me for thinking you'd do anything to scare me.

Though her skin was flushed, she was cold outside. She turned to go back inside, and the door was farther away that she'd thought. Her black sweater was damp and white from the snow, but she didn't remember walking away from the doors. Everything was too bright—the snow, the lights in the entry, radiating colors and razor edges.

Something was wrong with her, but she knew she wasn't sick. It was something else, and panic rose as her heart pounded. She couldn't think coherently. She opened her mouth to call for April, but only a squeak came from her throat. The church and snow spun around her, faster and faster, and she thought she was a spinning top. Around and around and around . . .

. . . she was lying in the snow. She'd fallen . . . but she was at the bottom of the stairs. How? The streetlight above her beckoned her, a hand, as if God Himself was taking her up to Heaven.

She wanted to go. She was so sad, so lost.

Sean.

Her heart thudded painfully in her chest and she focused on the steady, too-fast beat. Did her heart really beat this fast?

Sean, help me. I don't want to die.

She tried to stand but couldn't. Her hands dug into the newly fallen snow. She reached for her phone, but it wasn't in her pocket. It wasn't there because she'd left her coat in the pew in the church, and her phone was in that pocket.

She wanted to cry, but no sound, no tears, came. She had no control over her body, as if she were paralyzed. She desperately wanted Sean to pick her up and carry her to his bed. To hold her. To kiss her. To make love to her. She hadn't allowed herself to think about the future, the possibilities, but Sean had walked into her life and she didn't want him to leave.

She'd crawl. She could crawl home. No, that was two miles away. April would wonder why she was outside for so long. April . . . who was April? She felt she should know, but she couldn't remember. What was she thinking? Crawling home? Where was home? Did she have a home?

She tried to call out again but couldn't. Her mind swirled, as if in a blender, her head aching, her stomach clenching. She was so hot, she stared at the blinding snow and expected to see steam rise from where her fingers clawed the ice.

Sean.

Who was Sean?

"Let me help you up."

The voice sounded a million miles away. She rolled over, her body heavy, lying in the snow. She looked up, but didn't see anything, only a vague shape and a gloved hand.

"Thank you," she tried to say, but her tongue was thick and dry.

I want to go home.

She couldn't remember her address.

She was lifted off the ground. She thought she heard her name from far, far away . . .

A female voice calling, "Lucy? Lucy, where are you?"

THIRTY-SEVEN

Sean and Kate pounded on the glass door of the florist shop. It was five after seven and they had closed.

He'd screwed up. Why hadn't he pushed the florist earlier for a positive ID? He could have come back with Lorenzo's picture and verified the receipt that showed that he'd bought the roses. Why had he believed it so readily? Because Lorenzo was obviously still in love with Lucy? Because he was her ex-boyfriend?

Mallory could be lying through his teeth about not being Lucy's stalker, but Sean wasn't taking any chances. There was too much doubt, and far too much at stake.

Kate called out to the woman behind the counter. "FBI—we have an emergency." She held her badge up to the glass.

Lucy hadn't answered her cell phone, but she'd probably silenced it during Mass. He sent her a text message and hoped she'd read it.

Dillon is on his way to Holy Trinity. Don't leave the church under any circumstances. Text me back, let me know you're okay.

If Noah had called thirty minutes earlier, Sean wouldn't have left Lucy at the church. He'd have stayed with her, even though she told him not to. But he'd thought she was safe. Mallory and the others were behind bars and no one was going to hurt her.

He pictured her hurt and scared, and his mind snapped into focus. Self-pity wouldn't help.

He needed to think clearly.

"Dammit," Kate muttered when the woman frowned at them and didn't come to the door. Kate pounded harder. "Police! Emergency!"

"Maybe she doesn't speak English," Sean said.

"She speaks English," Kate said. "She just doesn't want to be bothered." She hit the door one last time. "Police!"

The woman shuffled to the door. She unlocked it and cracked it open. "We're closed."

"FBI, we have some questions about a customer."

The woman frowned. "I can't help you."

"Yes you can. You have security tapes." Kate pointed to the cameras. "Were you working Monday morning?"

"Yes, but—"

"I have a couple of pictures for you to look at. Please let us come in." It sounded more like a command than a request.

The woman hesitated, then sighed and let them in. "My daughter said someone was asking about a delivery. She's not supposed to talk about our customers."

Kate strode to the counter. "On Monday, you had a customer calling himself Cody Lorenzo, who ordered a dozen red roses to be delivered to Lucy Kincaid on Volta Place."

"Yes. He paid cash."

"I need you to look at some pictures and tell me if one of these men said he was Cody Lorenzo."

She frowned. "I don't know if I can help you . . ."

"You can," Kate said. "This is important."

The woman shrugged, and Kate showed her first the picture of Lorenzo. The woman showed no sign of recognition and shook her head. "No," she said. "The guy who came in here was white, not a Mexican."

Sean tensed.

Kate showed her the picture of Mick Mallory. The woman again shook her head. "This guy is too old—the guy who came in didn't have gray hair."

"He could have been wearing a wig or hairpiece," Sean said.

"It's not him. This guy looks Irish—round face, blue eyes—but the guy who came in had a skinny face. Average, under forty. Short."

"How short?"

The woman frowned and looked from Sean to Kate. "Shorter than you," she said to Kate.

Kate was nearly the same height as Lucy, about five foot seven. That put the guy at five and a half feet.

Kate frowned. Her last photo was of Biggler, and he was five foot ten. Kate flipped the picture.

"No," the woman said. "None of them. Now what's going on?"

"We need your security tapes from Monday."

When the florist went in the back, Kate turned to Sean and said, "Mallory must have another partner."

Sean wasn't so sure.

"Sean, what are you thinking? You're unusually quiet."

"This has nothing to do with Mick Mallory."

"Cody being killed by the same man who sent Lucy flowers? It has everything to do with Mallory."

Something didn't feel right to Sean, but he didn't

now what it was. He looked at his phone for the tenth
ime since he'd sent Lucy the text. Lucy hadn't re-
ponded to his message. He sent another message.

Luce, let me know you're okay.

"Sean, talk to me," Kate said.

He couldn't explain it to Kate, so he didn't try.

"I have to go," he said. "I need to get to the church."

"Sean—"

Kate's comment was interrupted when the florist re-
urned with a DVD. "This is everything for the last
veek. It's set to record over every Sunday night."

Sean took the disk before Kate could grab it.
"Thanks," he said and walked out to his car. He tossed
Kate his keys. "I'll look at this while you drive to the
hurch."

As soon as he sat in the passenger seat, he pulled out
is laptop and popped in the DVD. The quality of the
black-and-white image wasn't stellar, and the image was
lightly distorted because of the wide lens, but he could
ee enough.

Kate said, "Talk to me, Sean."

"Bad feeling," he said.

"If it helps, she said the guy came in between eight-
thirty and nine."

"Thanks." Sean pulled down the search window and
yped 8:25 for the time stamp on Monday morning. He
ast-forwarded, looking for a short white guy.

At 8:39, he walked in.

The stalker admired a display near the front of the
tore. He had dark hair, cut conservatively, and was
pleasant-looking—neither attractive nor unattractive.
Average. Normal. He had a nice-guy appearance, and
Sean would peg him in his mid- to-late thirties.

He paused in front of the refrigerator unit, and Sean gauged him in comparison as being five foot eight. He chatted with the owner, pointed to the vase of roses—which Sean presumed were red—and walked over to the counter.

It was at the counter that they had the clearest shot. He wrote out a card and handed it to the woman.

Sean clipped the image, sharpened it in a photo editing program, and sent it directly to both Noah Armstrong and Jayne Morgan at RCK West.

I need a name and address for this person ASAP. Noah, this is Lucy's stalker. Kate and I are going to the church now.

Sean slammed his laptop shut and tossed it on the backseat. He itched to take over the driving; Kate was moving too slow.

"Come on, Kate!"

"It's snowing, if you haven't noticed," she snapped. Her fingers were wrapped tight around the steering wheel.

"Just—" He bit off his verbal criticism. It wouldn't help the situation. He tried calling Lucy again. No answer. He stared out the window and watched the snow falling harder. He feared they were too late.

Sean was about to call Noah to make sure he'd got the image and message, when Kate's phone rang. He heard only her end of the conversation, but his heart froze.

"Are you sure? Did you check the bathrooms? Other rooms? . . . We're two, three minutes away. I'll call Noah."

Sean swerved. "What happened?"

"Dillon is at the church. Lucy isn't there." Kate bit her lower lip.

"And?"

"Her coat is. She stepped outside to get air twenty minutes ago and no one has seen her since."

I am pleased.

Lucy Kincaid sleeps in the back. I laugh out loud. Lucy Kincaid is unconscious on the backseat. Her wrists and ankles are bound with duct tape. She wasn't unconscious when I tied her up. She almost knew what was happening. But the GHB-isopropanol combination I hand-crafted did the job it is supposed to do. By the time she exited the church, she was already disoriented. When she fell in the snow, I knew she would put up little fight.

I may have given her too much, but I was unsure how quickly skin absorption would work. This was the only time I'd found her alone or in a place where I could grab her. She has wasted so much of my time with her games, I couldn't allow her to waste another minute. In case her boyfriend had been at the church, I had an alternate plan.

I'm glad I didn't have to resort to killing another man, pussy-whipped though he is. But if necessary, I would do it, just like out of necessity, I had to kill that cop.

Lucy Kincaid must be trained. I must break her. She is the problem. I am the solution.

I do not believe she'll be a good student. But she cannot be allowed to get away with her pathetic attempt to send me back to prison.

I have great plans for her. I already have her first lesson ready. The lesson that will teach her that I am in

charge, that her life is mine and I can take it when
want. The lesson will show her that she has no power
no hope. It's the first step but always my favorite. End
ings, and beginnings.

As I drive, I keep looking in my mirror at her. Her eye
are open, but glassy. I hope she is not dead.

I worry a bit. Dead girls are no fun—and I have no
had my time with Lucy. I pull over to the side of th
road and turn halfway around in my seat. I pick up th
whip next to me and lash out at the female.

She convulses, a cry coming from her gagged mouth.
smile. She's alive. Of course she is. I am too good t
make a mistake with dosage, even when trying some
thing new.

I merge back into traffic. Normally, I do not like driv
ing so slowly, even in such weather, but tonight?

Tonight, I am very pleased.

THIRTY-EIGHT

When Kate parked illegally in front of Holy Trinity Church, Sean saw a lot of police activity but few police cars. Three dozen officers, some in uniform and some in street clothes, filled the vestibule. More were outside looking for signs of Lucy and what might have happened to her. They had all been in the church when Lucy went missing.

Dillon spotted them as they trudged up the stairs. A section had been cordoned off and Sean frowned. "We may have a witness," Dillon told Sean and Kate as soon as they were within earshot.

"What happened?" Sean demanded. He hadn't let himself think that Lucy had been abducted. But Mallory hadn't sent Lucy the roses. He hadn't killed Cody Lorenzo. And he hadn't taken Lucy.

Yet she was gone.

"Cody's partner, Officer April Dunnigan, noticed that Lucy was feeling poorly and walked her to the vestibule. Lucy said she needed some air and stepped outside. After a couple of minutes, April and another officer went to check on her but she wasn't outside or anywhere in the church," Dillon explained. "But a detective thinks he might have seen her getting into a car with a man."

Dillon led them into the church where a detective was talking on the phone. When he spotted Dillon, he hung up. "I spoke to the chief of police. He's notifying all state troopers in Maryland and Virginia. We have every cop in D.C. on alert."

"Thank you. Detective John DeMarco, my wife, FBI Agent Kate Donovan, and Sean Rogan, with Rogan-Caruso-Kincaid."

DeMarco said, "I saw a woman with long black hair wearing black slacks and a black and white sweater, walking as if intoxicated with a man toward a parked car right where that patrol car is now parked out front. I was coming up the stairs, and I thought if she wasn't drunk she was extremely upset. It looked like she'd fallen—there was snow covering her clothing. And because she looked a bit Hispanic, I thought she might be one of Officer Lorenzo's relatives. She didn't show signs of being in distress, other than needing help to walk."

"And the man with her?"

"Approximately five foot eight to five foot ten. Lean. He wore black as well—trench coat and hat. Caucasian. No distinguishing marks, but I only glanced at them as I was coming up the stairs."

"And the car?"

"A late-model black sedan. He laid her down in the backseat. I didn't register the license number, but I noted it was a current Virginia plate."

Sean opened his laptop and showed the detective the picture from the florist's security camera. "Is this the man you saw?"

The detective looked closely. "It could have been. I can't say definitively, but it's the same physical build."

"Is that the stalker?" Dillon asked.

"Yes," Kate said.

April came over. "Agent Donovan, I'm so sorry. If I had known Lucy was in any danger, I'd never have let her go outside alone. I thought you had Cody's killer in custody."

"So did we," Kate said.

"Detective DeMarco!" An officer stepped in from outside and introduced himself as he approached the group.

Detective DeMarco said, "What did you find?"

The officer held up a string of pearls in a plastic evidence bag. "We found these in the snow at the bottom of the stairs," he said.

Dillon's voice was rough when he said, "Those are Lucy's. They were our mother's. She gave them to Lucy when she graduated from college."

"It looks like the clasp broke," DeMarco said on inspection. "Anything else?"

"Officers Craig Jackson and Lloyd Breck arrived in a taxi at approximately five thirty-five p.m. Both noted the black sedan out front and because it was illegally parked, considered talking to the owner, but a man exited the church and walked to the car. They let it go and came in."

"Do they have a description?"

"White, five foot nine, wearing a black trench coat."

"Hat?"

"No, sir. Not that they saw. Hair cut short, brown.

Dillon said, "He was exiting the church. He would have taken it off inside, or it would have drawn attention."

"What time did Lucy arrive?"

April said, "Just after the priest stepped behind the altar, when everyone was standing."

"The processional?" Dillon asked.

"It was at the beginning. I've only been to a couple of these things."

"The processional. So about the same time the man left," Dillon said. "And Lucy stepped out before communion?"

"Everyone was saying the Lord's Prayer and she looked sick. I walked her to the bathroom, but she wanted to go outside for fresh air. She seemed better when she opened the door, though she was a little green."

Sean's phone vibrated. It was Jayne. He stepped away from the group. "What's his name?" Sean asked.

"I don't know," Jayne said. "I wanted to make sure you know I'm working on it. It would help if I could narrow it down to a state."

"Start with D.C., then Virginia and Maryland, and work out from there."

"Okay, give me some time and I'll—"

"The guy has Lucy. We don't have time."

"I'm doing the best I can, Sean, I'm sorry."

"I'm just worried. Keep me informed." He dropped the call. "Kate—get Noah on the phone.

"Why? Do you have an ID?"

"No—but I have an idea. Mallory."

"I don't understand."

"It's too coincidental that Lucy is kidnapped at the same time the vigilante group is shut down. Cody's murder, the stalking, Mallory—it has to be connected, and I think he has the answers."

"Show him the picture," Dillon interjected.

"Exactly. This guy has to be involved, otherwise why Lucy? Why now?"

Kate nodded and dialed Noah's number.

Noah wasn't sitting down when the guard brought Mick Mallory into the interrogation room at the D.C. jail. He slapped the photograph down on the table.

"This man kidnapped Lucy. Who is he?"

Mallory stared at the picture for a long minute. When he realized who it was, his face turned ashen.

"Are you sure?" he asked.

"Yes, dammit! We have a witness. Who is it? One of your vigilante friends?"

"No. This is Peter Thomas Miller. He was a high school teacher arrested for statutory rape in 2002. He had sex with six of his female students, at least the ones we know about who came forward, but was only convicted for two of them because after making a statement, the other four recanted. He did a number on the girls—psychologically abusing them as well as seducing them. He only raped virgins, but it was never violent—only mentally sadistic."

"Mentally sadistic?"

"He convinced them they were inferior, but he did it in such a way they didn't feel threatened—he never yelled and initially didn't hit, but instead reasoned out why they were weak and useless and how they should live their lives to serve their husband. He was training them for their future husbands, he'd told one of them. He was sentenced ten-to-twenty, and paroled last summer in Delaware. He registered as a sex offender, then disappeared."

Mallory paused, then stared at Noah. "Lucy found

him online. He was trolling for virgins. But he never showed."

"Never showed? Explain."

"Two months ago. Lucy set the meeting, and we switched the location because I knew in my gut that this guy was dangerous—that he would escalate. He deserved my brand of justice. He never showed up, and when I went to his house I knew he'd gone to ground. He might have smelled a cop, but there are safeties in place—he couldn't have known it was Lucy!"

"There's always a way." Noah paused. "What kind of teacher was Miller?"

"Computer science."

Sean drove as fast as he could on the icy roads to RCK East. Noah Armstrong had called Kate and told her about Peter Miller.

Sean would find him. He had to.

Jayne was already working on it, and Noah was pulling all Miller's criminal records in the effort to find out where he might have taken Lucy. The Delaware FBI was checking his last known residence and Abigail went to comb the WCF files in evidence.

Sean prayed Lucy was alive and unharmed. His gut burned, thinking about Lucy held captive. Miller looked normal, almost pleasant, but he was a sick bastard who had vengeance on his mind. He hated women, and a woman—Lucy—had tried to send him back to prison.

His phone rang as soon as he stepped inside his house. He ran up the stairs to his office as he answered.

"Hello."

"Sean, it's Duke. Jayne filled me in. Have you learned anything else?"

"No."

"I retrieved his employment history. He lists University of Virginia at Richmond as his alma mater."

"How does that help?"

"He's not a native of Delaware. His parents were Paul and Christina Miller. They lived in Virginia until 1984, when the father moved to Wilmington after they divorced. Miller was born in 1971, in Charlottesville, Virginia. Jayne is searching property records under the father's name and the mother's maiden name—Christina Lyons."

"Where are they now?"

"The father died twelve years ago, and I have no record of the mother after the divorce in Virginia or Delaware, so I'm broadening the search under both her married and maiden names."

"What is it? I'll get the FBI on it."

"The FBI? You think they can find it faster than I can?"

"No, but at this point we need to try everything. I have a bad feeling. From the witness ID, it appeared that Lucy was drunk. I think he drugged her. She wouldn't have gone willingly. She would have fought back."

"*We'll find her,*" Duke emphasized.

Sean didn't doubt that. But in what condition? Injured? Dead?

"Call me as soon as you know anything."

Sean dialed Kate. "I'm sending you information that Duke just found out."

"I'll get on it. Noah is on his way to your place, I'm meeting him there."

"If I find a lead, I'm jumping on it."

"You'd better. Just keep me in the loop. I'll be there in fifteen minutes."

Sean dropped his phone on his desk, his hands fisting in his hair as an agonized groan escaped from deep in his chest. The anger—at Mallory, at the FBI, but mostly at himself for not protecting Lucy—battled with his deep fear for her life.

He took several deep breaths to swallow the rising panic. His brothers had told him over and over that there was no room for personal emotion when faced with a threat. But Sean had never been in the military. He'd never been trained to kill or to fight or to treat an assignment as a tactical situation with targets and civilians. And while he had the skills, he hadn't developed the mental discipline that his older brothers shared.

And he couldn't think of Lucy as a victim. He couldn't think of her as anyone but who she was—the woman who had taken his heart. He just wanted her back, safe, with him.

"Okay," he said out loud. "Think, Sean. You're not helpless. If Miller wanted to kill Lucy, he would have done it at the church, right?"

This was where having the profiler around would be helpful.

Was Cody Lorenzo killed for revenge, or because he'd found out something about Miller? Or, was his murder Miller's sadistic way of tormenting Lucy? How long had Miller been watching her? Did he know about her past relationship with Lorenzo? He knew about Sean—the guy had watched them at the ice rink. Miller had been circling around Lucy, making her nervous. All the times she felt as if someone was watching her, she had blamed her past. Sean had told her to trust her instincts, and when they thought Lorenzo was stalking her, he'd accepted that Lucy's feelings were because of him.

They'd made a logical and reasoned conclusion based on the evidence, but it had been wrong. And now Lucy's life was at risk.

The doorbell rang, followed by knocking. Sean glanced at his security screen and saw Kate and Dillon at the door. He rushed downstairs and by the time he let them in, Noah and Hans were walking up the front walkway.

"Any news?" Sean asked.

"No," Kate said at the same time Noah said, "Yes."

Sean closed the door. "What?"

"The Delaware Field Office said the Wilmington house is vacant, but Miller has been paying the mortgage on it. We're getting a search warrant—he may have records in the basement or attic. According to the neighbors, he's been by the house a few times since his release from prison. But the place had been vandalized, and he'd become *persona non grata* after his trial."

"If he's been paying the mortgage, that means he has a bank account somewhere."

"Bingo. We'll have all his banking records first thing in the morning."

"Morning? That may be too late!" Sean couldn't wait until the banks opened to trace Miller. But to hack into a major financial institution couldn't be done quickly, and it definitely wouldn't be legal. He had no doubt he could get in, but without actual routing numbers and account numbers tied to Miller, he wouldn't know where to go in the system.

Noah said, "I got the information about his parents and we're tracking down the mother now. She took her maiden name after the divorce, according to the University of Richmond office."

"You talked to his college?"

"We have emergency contacts with all the major institutions, and as soon as you forwarded the data, we called. Records are all computerized, and the dean was able to pull up Miller's file. His father was living in Wilmington, his mother was listed as Christina Lyons. No address, no contact."

Dillon spoke up. "Were there any disciplinary records on Miller?"

"No. He was a top student. He was married his senior year. He changed his emergency forms to next-of-kin contact Rosemarie Miller. Her maiden name is Nylander. Abigail is trying to find her now."

"Are they still married?" Kate asked.

"Rosemarie filed for divorce in 1998. They'd been married for six years. Miller refused to sign the papers, and the court intervened and severed the marriage."

"That could have set him off," Hans said. "Model student, no criminal record, his mother leaves, his wife leaves. He targets high school girls who are easy to control. He's in a position of authority over them."

"Did you read his file?" Noah asked Hans.

"I'm in the dark here," Sean said. "He was in prison for statutory rape, that's all I know."

"He was convicted of statutory rape of two students," Noah explained. "But there were others who recanted their statements."

Hans said, "He convinced the girls that they were worthless, that the only value they had was what he gave them. They didn't want to turn on him, a version of the Stockholm syndrome. Unfortunately, all the names of his victims are redacted. Without an extremely compelling argument and court order, we can't talk to them."

"Would talking to them help?" Sean asked. "All this was a decade ago, right?"

"It might help," Hans said. "But no guarantees, and the privacy of rape victims—*especially* minors—will win out ninety-nine percent of the time."

"So what now?" Sean said, exasperated. "We sit around and wait? I need to do something."

"Good." Noah shoved a disk at him. "You're supposed to be a computer genius. That's all the property records in the tri-state area. Let's see what you can find. I'm going to track down the mother. She might know where he is."

Sean took the disk to his office. Dillon followed him upstairs, his face pale but his expression determined. "I'm sorry, Dillon," Sean said, shoving the disk into his computer. "I should never have left her at the church."

"We all thought Mallory was behind the roses and Cody's murder," Dillon said. "We're going to find her. Kate and I found her once; we'll find her again."

Sean held onto that hope as he wrote a program to parse the data Noah had given him.

The female sleeps.

I injected her with an antidote to counteract the more serious effects of the sedative. The female had experienced shortness of breath during the final minutes of the drive, and that worried me. Now she seems to be resting normally, perhaps sleeping deeper than she should because of the sedative.

The broken one watches from her corner with wide

eyes as I cut the duct tape from the female's ankles and wrists. I handcuff one wrist to a bar of the cage. It is best, I have learned over the years, to restrain them at the beginning. It contributes to the system of rewards and punishment.

Females are weak and malleable. It doesn't take long for them to break and become compliant. Keeping their food to a minimum and restricting movement helps. But sometimes, on the first night, the combination of drugs and injuries results in death. I wonder if this female will survive until morning?

I hope so. I will not be pleased if she dies before I have a chance to teach her. And everything I've done up until this moment will have been a waste of time.

She sleeps. The broken one still watches. I say to her, "Do not speak to her."

I leave them, confident that my orders will be obeyed, and walk upstairs to prepare a late meal.

I frown and consider the time. It is well past my dinner hour, another example of how Lucy Kincaid interfered in my life. My schedule, crucial to keeping focus and executing my plans, is once again destroyed because of that woman. I will eat ninety minutes after I prefer, which means I will go to bed later than I like.

That female does not care that my time is valuable! From the beginning, when I realized she was not who she said she was, when I learned that she planned to put me back in prison, I committed untold hours to learning who she was, where she lived, and planning the best way to take her.

I watched her for weeks. Followed her. She did not recognize me. I sat across from her on the Metro train only two days ago, and she did not recognize me. I watched her argue with the cop I killed, and she did not know me. I changed my appearance enough to blend into my surroundings, like a chameleon, but still I thought she might have recognized me.

I will miss our games: following her, and she looking around, worried, looking right at me but not knowing me. The times I came close enough to stab her in the back, but resisted. The time I almost pushed her in front of the Metro train.

But instant death would not have been gratifying. I now have the time to teach her properly, to break her completely. I have looked forward to these days.

Though Hell on earth, prison had its silver lining: I learned patience.

I am still looking for the wench who spoke against me, lied against me—her teacher!—in court. I should have killed more than her dog. I wish I had killed her.

And I will kill her. I have a plan to find and kill everyone who spoke against me, starting with Lucy Kincaid.

The first step was finding the perfect woman to break. My newly broken female is the one. I will rebuild her, and she will kill the woman who set me up.

Then, I will be ready to discipline the others who betrayed me. One by one.

THIRTY-NINE

Far away, water dripped in a slow, steady beat. The cold had seeped through to Lucy's bones, numbing her. The ground was hard, but not wood or cement. The rotten, graveyard stench of dirt, dank and moldy, filled her nose and her throat. Other than the water, which was closer than she first thought, she heard nothing. No traffic, no voices, nothing.

Lucy didn't harbor any illusions that she was home or safe.

For a panic-filled moment, she feared she was dead or worse—buried alive. She breathed through her mouth, tasted dirt, and her body involuntarily jerked. But the space felt too airy, too open to be buried; and she was in too much pain to be dead.

She opened her eyes, but saw nothing in the deep blackness that filled the space. She didn't know how big the area, no idea of the time, whether it was day or night, or how long she'd been unconscious.

As her eyes focused, she realized it wasn't completely dark. Several feet away, out of her reach, was a small space heater emitting a faint glow. It did little to heat the room, but the glow gave off enough light to see the outlines of her confinement, darker and sharper than the shadows that surrounded her. What she could see, coupled with the damp stench, told her she was in a basement or root cellar.

Lucy had no idea where she was; she only remembered how sick she'd been at the church. April was taking her to the bathroom. She'd wanted to throw up . . . and she remembered nothing more.

Her head pounded, and her tongue was so parched that the dripping water made her more thirsty. Her body was sore, as if she'd been lying in the same position for hours. She tried to sit up, to at least crawl to the tiny heater, but her left hand was pinched on something. She pulled, heard metal clink against metal.

She felt her wrist with her free hand and realized she was handcuffed. She reached out and touched bars. She tried to shake them, but they were sturdy. Her stomach dry heaved as the truth hit her—she was in a cage.

She focused on what happened at the church, but it was as if her memory had been gutted.

Her head felt like a lead ball and her muscles were heavy. With great effort, she scooted into a sitting position and leaned against the bars, then sat abruptly forward, feeling a sharp sting against her back. She now felt the tenderness and bruising all over her body. Gently, she leaned back again and put her head on her knees, hoping the nausea would pass. The feelings she remembered having were akin to what she knew of the effects of many date-rape drugs: the disconnect, the lack of muscle control, the memory loss, and the headache. She touched her body, relieved when she realized she was still in the same clothes she'd had on when she walked into the church. She had no physical sensation that she'd been sexually assaulted. Though she was still terrified, her racing heart slowed, the pounding between her ears subsiding.

When the nausea passed, she focused on her situation. She'd been kidnapped and put into a cage. Where? By whom?

Panic exploded, flooding her bloodstream with adrenaline, her physical restraint swiftly stealing her breath as memories flooded her mind. All the memories she'd hidden, the memories she'd buried so deep she thought they were gone, returned as if Adam Scott had just kidnapped her, and today was her last day. The day he planned to kill her.

"No," she whispered, squeezing her eyes shut. She would not be a victim again. She would not allow anyone to hurt her, to abuse her, to take anything from her. She was *not* a victim, she was Lucy Kincaid, and she would fight back with everything she had or die.

"Think, Lucy. Think." She pulled at the handcuff. It was tight; she couldn't slip it off. She tried to wiggle the bars. Secure. They didn't even budge a fraction of an inch.

If her kidnapper wanted her dead, he would have killed her already. That meant he had something else in mind.

Her stomach plunged. She couldn't go through it again, any of it.

Yes you can. You can and will do anything to survive.

But survival meant life-and-death decisions. It meant mental and physical control. It meant being willing to do anything, focusing only on *now*, not thinking about tomorrow, not thinking about yesterday, but only this moment in time. Being smart, seizing opportunities.

constant planning, and if necessary, killing her kidnapper.

The idea that she might need to kill him to escape didn't scare her half as much as it should have. Who had he become? She wasn't the woman she thought she'd be one day.

That's the past, Luce. Focus on the present. Worry about your mental health tomorrow.

She focused first on her breathing, on beating back the panic attack. She couldn't make smart choices if she was panicking.

Lucy focused on figuring how to get out. She didn't know where she was, but she preferred to take her chances on the street than with the man who'd locked her in a cage like an animal.

The panic rose again from the pit of her stomach and spread through her body like a wildfire. She'd just beat it back, but the reprieve was a lie. She was lying to herself. She'd never get out of here! She was trapped, just like she had been on the island. She was at the mercy of a sadistic bastard, and she hadn't even seen his face.

She could scarcely breathe, and though she willed herself to get a grip, she couldn't. She wanted to die, right then and there, because some fates were worse than death. Some things should never have to be lived through twice. Some things should never be suffered even once.

A moan escaped her chest, a physical stabbing pain that nearly tore her in two. It was her heart breaking, her strength becoming nothing but hot air. She was nothing, only a hard shell. Her shell was cracked by the man who took her, and she wouldn't be able to put herself back together again.

She dry heaved, but nothing came out. *Why, God Dammit, why? Why me, again?!?*

She would die fighting him if she had to. She would not let herself be a victim, not like that. But her hands were trembling. How could she fight when she had only fear inside?

"You're the bravest person I know."

Sean's voice was so loud he might have been sitting right next to her.

Sean.

She would never be able to find out where this relationship was heading because she was going to die.

Her family might never find her. Dillon, Patrick, and Jack would all be looking for her for years, and she'd be dead and buried in an unmarked grave. She'd seen how Justin's death had torn apart her family eighteen years ago, and now her death would tear them apart again.

Lucy squeezed back tears.

She saw Sean, searching for her, giving up his life to find out what happened to her. Bitter. Lonely. Violent.

She couldn't let the people she loved suffer. She had to find a way out.

She focused on breathing evenly. Slowing her racing pulse. One. Two. Three. Even. Clear. She didn't know how big this cage was, but it was longer than her reach.

Be smart, Lucy. Look for the opportunity.

The dripping water. Soap—abrasive soap. Laundry detergent? An underlying scent of coal. There was no furnace down here, she didn't hear it, but there had been at one time. She was in the basement of an old house.

Though she couldn't see more than shades of black and dark gray, she closed her eyes and listened to the sounds above. The hum of a heater as it warmed the house above her, but did nothing for the frigid cold of the basement.

A rooster crowed. She smiled. Dawn. That gave her some perspective. She didn't feel particularly hungry, just thirsty, so likely only the night had passed. She'd been at the church just after five-thirty, a couple of minutes late . . .

A flash of a memory returned. She'd been walking into the church when a man opened the door for her. A chunk of snow fell from the building and hit her on the back of the neck.

But thinking about that now, she had already been under the short overhang of the roof. Wasn't she? She focused on picturing the man who opened the door, but couldn't—she'd been lost in her grief.

But . . . he'd seemed familiar. What had she thought? That maybe he was a cop she'd seen once before? She couldn't remember.

Maybe it hadn't been snow on her neck. She didn't have much knowledge about poisons, but she wondered if there was something that could be absorbed through the skin. How long had it taken? About thirty minutes.

What it was didn't matter now, because other than a drug hangover, she had her thoughts in order.

A sudden sound of rushing water down the walls made her gasp. Footsteps upstairs, slow, methodical steps. A shower. Her captor was taking a damn shower!

Something ran over her foot and she screamed before she could stop herself. Her heart started racing again.

Stop it! It was a mouse. A furry rodent. It can't hurt you.

It felt more like a rat.

Maybe he planned to let her starve to death down

here. She remembered reading a book once, long ago, where someone had been held captive and ate rodents to survive. What was the title? She tried to remember, the focus helping her regain control.

There was movement to her right, in the corner, and she whipped her head around and stared at the blankets.

They moved again.

It wasn't a rat or any other rodent. It was a much larger animal. And it moved, so it wasn't dead.

She saw strands of light hair at the bottom of the pile. It was a person.

Heart racing, not knowing who was trapped in here with her, how injured the person was, she said, "Who are you?"

Her dry voice cracked and she cleared her throat. "Hello, who are you?"

The blankets didn't move. The person didn't speak.

"Are you hurt? Did he hurt you?"

No answer. Dammit, Lucy could barely think about saving herself, let alone someone else!

"Please talk to me. We need to plan. My family will be looking for me. I need to know where we are. Find a way to get them a message."

She thought she heard a whimper.

"You're scared. I understand being scared."

No response.

"My name is Lucy. What's yours?" Silence. "Do you know who kidnapped us?"

Again, no answer. What had he done to the girl? The sadistic bastard! Anger swelled and balanced her fear. Good. She needed the anger, it would help her plan their escape.

"I guess I'm going to have to plan for both of us."

Upstairs, the shower turned off with a rusty groan. The girl whimpered again and curled even tighter under the blankets.

Lucy noticed that the quality of light was changing. She looked around the basement. A thin sliver of light crept in from windows high off the ground. She stared, curious about why the windows were so narrow, then realized that snow blocked most of the glass.

Windows meant an escape route. If she could get out of this cage, she could break a window and climb out.

She glanced at the huddled girl in the corner. Lucy might be able to fight or run, but she couldn't leave the girl behind. That meant being quiet, stealth, finding a way to get out of these cuffs and cage and to the window. Without making noise.

She searched her pockets, hoping for a bobby pin or key or something to pick the lock. They were empty.

The floors above creaked as their captor walked down the stairs from the second to the first floor. He was right above them, moving here and there. A faint scent of bacon frying drifted down through the vents, and Lucy's stomach growled.

Would he feed them? Unlock the cage? She could fight, but not cuffed to the bars. If she could get them off she could use them as a weapon. She didn't need much—just something hard and thin enough to wiggle into the lock. It was just a matter of feeling her way around the lock mechanism, a trick her brother Patrick had taught her.

Lucy wanted to see her family. She didn't want them to lose her like this. She didn't want to die. She would be twenty-five next month. She had so much to do! So many plans. A future.

But her career plans didn't seem important right now.
What mattered was her family. And Sean. And escaping.

The door at the top of the stairs opened. Light flooded
the basement, nearly blinding Lucy. She averted her
eyes. The girl in the corner didn't move.

"W-who are you?" she stuttered, her fear evident in
her tone as she demanded to know her kidnapper's
name. She swallowed and cleared her throat. *Do not
show him fear.* She squinted, adjusting to the light, and
watched the man descend the stairs. He didn't look
threatening. In fact, he looked rather plain and ordinary.
Brown hair, brown eyes, Caucasian—maybe five seven
or eight, though it was hard to gauge from her position
on the floor.

Plain and ordinary. Except for the fact that he was
holding a whip.

"Dammit, tell me who you are!"

The whip came down and hit her on her wrist below
the cuff. She screamed, then bit her lip, holding back the
cry. She would not give him the satisfaction.

"You will not speak unless I tell you to speak."

"Fuck you!"

The whip came down a second time, and again she
cried out,

You idiot, Lucy, he means what he says.

"Now that you're awake, it is time for your first lesson. Watch and learn."

Lucy began to shake.

He placed a bowl of scrambled eggs and bacon between the bars of the cage. Lucy looked over at the girl
as she dropped the blankets. She was about Lucy's age,
maybe a year or two younger, blond with large blue

eyes. She'd been pretty, and would be again, when the bruises that covered her face healed. He'd beaten her.

She wore a filthy, loose-fitting floral housedress, the old-fashioned kind that Lucy's mother sometimes wore when she was flitting around the house. Her face was clean, though streaked with tear stains, and there was blood on the dress.

"You may eat," the man said.

The woman crawled to the bowl without looking at Lucy and ate, her face close to the bowl, her hands slowly but purposefully scooping up the breakfast and eating.

In all her criminal psychology classes, Lucy had never encountered a situation like this. She didn't know what to make of it. It was like a slave–master relationship. How long had the woman been held captive?

When the woman was done, she went back to her corner and averted her eyes.

The man smiled at Lucy. "See how well she obeys?"

"Is that what we are to you? Animals?"

"No. You're females."

The tone told her he believed women were beneath animals. He was some sort of misogynist? How many women had he hurt? What did he do to them?

He said, "You will obey just like that one."

"My brothers will hunt you down like an animal, you bastard!"

He lashed out again with the whip, his face red, his eyes narrow. She bit back a cry when the tip came down on her upper shoulder.

He leaned over and said through clenched teeth, "They will never find me. They will never find you.

"Woman!" he shouted at the girl in the corner. "Show the bitch what happens when you disobey."

The girl pulled up the back of her dress. Her buttocks were red and swollen, more than a dozen welts blistering her skin.

He turned to Lucy with a half-smile. "If you speak again to me in that tone, if you swear at me, if you talk without my permission, you will suffer the same fate. And you will learn, girl. You will obey me."

He walked up the stairs and turned off the light.

FORTY

Sean had not felt so helpless since he was fourteen and his parents were killed in a plane crash.

He'd fallen asleep at his desk late—four? Five?—and woke at dawn. Dillon was asleep on the small couch in his office, his long legs hanging over the armrest.

Sean went downstairs and made coffee. He was surprised to find Hans Vigo asleep on his couch. The table was littered with files and papers.

They'd been running property searches, talking to the prison warden where Miller had been incarcerated, analyzing the WCF files on Miller—not just here, but everyone at RCK West was working on it, too. They'd had more than a dozen people—smart people—working almost nonstop since seven last night and now, twelve hours later, they still didn't know where Lucy was.

Sean sat at the table and looked over Hans's notes. His prison files—Miller was too perfect, a model prisoner. Polite, even-tempered. During his trial, he had been well-mannered and courteous.

Hans had written across a legal tablet in block letters:

- **Victims were seduced. All virgins between 14 and 16.**
- **Fear of sex—stemming from an obsession with cleanliness, i.e. only has sex with virgins/"clean" girls.**

- **Required victims to address him as "Teacher."**
- **Taught girls to be submissive. Used reward and punishment system. Competitive—girls wanted to earn rewards for being the most "obedient."**
- **Became physically violent with one victim. Bruised her—she hid the bruise. Why her and not the others? What made her different?**
- **At trial—refused female lawyer. Called her "unfair."**
- **From staff interviews at school—Miller was "chauvinist," "sexist," "egotistical." One female teacher said, "Peter once called me 'female'—like it was my name. I steered clear of him. Some of the staff thought he was just a nerd, but I didn't like how he looked at me."**

Sean wished he hadn't read any of it because now he couldn't rid his mind of Lucy's face, beaten and bruised. He bit back a cry of frustration.

What was he missing? He should have been able to find this one guy—what good was he if he couldn't find one man? They knew his name. His parents. His schooling. Noah said they'd have something by morning. Well, it was morning now—7:11 according to the digital clock on the microwave.

Sean picked up a flagged page of the trial transcripts. Hans had underlined key words and phrases.

PROSECUTOR: How long were you sexually involved with the defendant?

JANE DOE TWO: Four months.

PROSECUTOR: Did he force you to have sex?

JANE DOE TWO: I don't know.

PROSECUTOR: You don't know? Did he hurt you?

JANE DOE TWO: Yes and no. <u>I didn't tell him no</u>, if that's what you mean.

PROSECUTOR: Did you believe that it was wrong to have sex with your teacher?

JANE DOE TWO: Yes—but <u>I was chosen</u>. That's what he said. I was chosen to be a <u>perfect woman</u>. At first I liked the idea of being what a man wants. My parents are divorced and fight all the time, and I hated it. <u>Teacher</u> made me feel like I could be different, that if I learned how to be perfect, <u>I'd make my husband happy</u>. I wanted that.

PROSECUTOR: Did you always want that? After your sexual relationship began?

JANE DOE TWO: No. I got wrapped up in the idea that <u>I could be special</u>. Then after the first time, <u>he humiliated me</u>. I couldn't talk until <u>he told me I could speak</u>. He didn't hit me—but I thought he would, so I did everything he said. I just wanted to get it over with.

PROSECUTOR: Why didn't you come forward sooner? Why wait four months before telling your mother?

JANE DOE TWO: He told me <u>I was trainable</u>, like a dog. I was scared and didn't know what to do, but told him one day after school that I wouldn't go to his house anymore. The next morning <u>my dog was dead</u>. The vet said Sunny ate something poisonous, but I knew Teacher had done it. That's why I came forward. If he could kill my dog, he could kill me. I don't want to die.

Hans sat up on the couch. "Sean, maybe you shouldn't read that."

"I'm fine," he snapped. He wasn't fine. "Miller is a nut job. How could they let him out of prison?"

Hans didn't respond. He stood and walked over and put his hand on Sean's shoulder. "We'll find her."

"Dammit!" Sean bit back his anger. His fear wasn't going to find Lucy.

Be brave, Lucy. I will find you.

"He's a chauvinist?" Sean said, tapping Hans's notes. "He does this because he thinks he's better than women?"

"That's a bit simplistic, but yes," Hans said. "I think it's more that he believes that women are by nature weaker and should be subservient to men, and thus must be properly trained. One thing about all his victims, according to a psychologist who worked with them after the attacks—they all had low self-esteem. They felt they were unattractive to the opposite sex, that they were too fat or too skinny or too ugly. He preyed on the outcasts. They would be far more vulnerable to the charms of an older, nice-looking man who was in a position of authority."

"Lucy doesn't fit that profile," Dillon said.

"No, she doesn't."

Sean's head shot up. He heard something in Hans's voice. "What?" he demanded. "What are you thinking?"

"What have you learned about his mother?" Hans asked.

Sean frowned, not liking where this conversation was going. "Christina Lyons. She went back to her maiden name after the divorce. Was a successful realtor in San Francisco, and an artist. She owned an art gallery, sold her own work plus that of other local artists."

"Have you found her obituary?"

"I have it, but I haven't read it—" Sean flipped through his computer files. "Here it is." He skimmed it. "I don't know what you're looking for."

"Read the last two sentences. That's usually where they put the next-of-kin information."

Sean glanced at the bottom and read, "Christina is survived by her partner of twelve years, Nikki Broman. Donations in lieu of flowers should be sent to the National Breast Cancer Society."

Sean frowned. "He's angry with women because his mother was a lesbian?"

"No, not exactly. I think he's angry with women because his mother was successful without a man in her life. Moreover, since her son wasn't acknowledged in the obit, he was essentially disowned. What about Paul Miller's obituary? What did he do?"

Sean brought up the father's obit and skimmed it. "Retired electrician."

"How old was he when he died?"

"Forty-nine."

"A little young to retire."

"He was living in a crappy neighborhood in Baltimore. Survived by a son, Peter Miller of Baltimore—" Sean looked up. "I don't have any property owned by him in Baltimore. Just the house in Wilmington."

"If he was living in a crappy neighborhood, maybe they didn't own."

"A rental."

"Did the father ever own a house?"

Sean checked. "Yes, but lost it . . . six months after Christina left."

"She was supporting him." Hans looked up at the ceiling. "She supported him, she left, he moved to a cheap rental in a bad area. Why didn't she take her son with her?"

"He was fourteen. Maybe she thought he would be better off with his father?" Sean suggested.

"Or she was scared. Fourteen—puberty. I wonder if he was exhibiting early signs of a serial killer."

Sean jumped. "What? Where did that come from? He's a rapist—a manipulator. Where does 'he's a serial killer' come from?"

"The dead pet he left for the girl who didn't obey. You don't wake up one morning and decide to kill someone's dog. He had to have done it before. Killing animals is one of the triad of serial killer traits. Can you run arson fires in Baltimore during the time Miller was aged ten to eighteen? And map it?"

"No, but Jayne can." Sean sent her an email, hoping she was at the computer even though it was 4:30 a.m. in California.

Sean asked, "What does this mean for Lucy? If she doesn't fit the profile for his rape victims, does that mean he's going to kill her?"

"Yes," Hans said.

Sean paled. "You don't know—"

"But not tonight. And not tomorrow. He wants to teach her something. I—" He stopped himself.

"Tell me!" Sean said. "I need to know."

"I need to call Noah."

Lucy didn't know how long she tried to get the woman to talk. When she'd about given up, the young woman spoke, her voice a raspy whisper.

"My name is Carolyn."

Lucy sighed in relief. Finally. "Why didn't you talk to me?"

She didn't say anything for a long minute, then whispered, "He'll hurt me."

"How long have you been here?"

"Shh!"

Lucy whispered, "Days? Weeks?"

"I think six days. Maybe seven. He killed a woman in the barn. Shot her in the back of the head."

Carolyn's voice cracked and she huddled in her corner. "I'm next."

Lucy almost didn't hear her. "What?"

"*Shh.* He told me when he brings another female home, I've failed him. He will kill me tonight."

"Did he rape you?"

She shook her head. "He hasn't touched me at all."

"Who is he? What's his name?"

"I don't know. I was walking to my car after work and felt sick. I was sitting in the driver's seat, closed my eyes—and woke up here."

"Where are we?"

Carolyn shrugged. "I live in Greensboro."

"I'm from Georgetown. Listen. We're going to get out of here. You were in the barn? What else is around here?"

"Nothing. No other houses. I couldn't even see the road."

"I'll find a way."

"No shoes." She gestured to their feet. "There's snow."

"I'd rather die out there than live in here," Lucy said. She stared at her handcuff. Getting out wasn't going to be easy.

* * *

I hate that female.

*She is defiant. Others had been defiant on occasion,
but there is something in this one that grates on me.*

*I walk through the snow to the barn. The cold clears
my head. Memories of punishment relax me.*

*I want to break her. I do not know if it's possible. The
way she looked at me . . . something in her eyes. She is
not like the others.*

*I knew all along that she was different. For years I had
picked very specific women. Of the twelve, ten were
broken before they died. Two died during training.*

*I suspect this new one will not get to training. I do not
like her.*

*My father may have been right. Some women should
never have been born.*

*My father tried to act like a man, but he wasn't. He let
his wife get a job, and where did that get him? She left.
She left because she didn't need him.*

*I remember that morning. She woke me from sleep
and told me to pack. That we were leaving Dad. I asked
why. She said he'd hit her and she was afraid of him. I
told her she deserved it. She thought she was better than
Dad and that's why he hit her. She cried and told me I
was not her son.*

*I wish I were not. She was an aberration. She used to
be happy cooking dinner, cleaning the house, walking
me to school. Then she got a job. And made friends that
didn't include me and Dad. She left us in her heart before she left us in life.*

*Good riddance. I'm glad she died. The cancer ate her
heart, ate her soul, took her body and made it hurt.*

I went to the funeral and told her bitch that I was glad

he was dead. *The woman screamed at me and tried to have me arrested. I walked out.*

My father was weak. Drinking. A foolish man's elixir. Had he been a real man, he would have kept his job and provided for his family. Mom would never have worked; she would never have left me.

FORTY-ONE

"Twenty-six unsolved residential arson fires in Balti more during those years," Sean told Hans. "Two fatali ties."

"How many were within five miles of the first Wil mington house or his second house after his mother left?"

Sean typed rapidly. "One five miles from his mother house; fourteen within five miles of his father's rental."

"I'm surprised the investigators didn't nail him. The look at teen boys in the area when there are clusters lik this."

Sean was growing increasingly frustrated. His hea ached and he itched to get in his car and look for Lucy— even though he knew it was futile. He had always bee a slave to computer science; anything could be foun using the Internet. And normally, he was patient with re search. But today? After Lucy had been missing for *four teen hours*? He felt helpless and hopelessly lost. H wanted Lucy back safe, and he didn't see them gettin any closer to finding her.

Dillon came downstairs. He walked to the coffeepo and poured a cup. "You should have woke me," he tol Sean, then asked, "Any news?"

"No. I want to find out more about his ex-wife, bu can't find her anywhere," Hans said.

"If she came to realize that she'd married a psycho," Sean said, "she probably changed her name and moved far away."

"You're right."

Sean didn't want to be right.

Hans flipped through files. "It's odd that he went into teaching, which is considered by many to be a female profession unless you're a college professor. I would think his misogynist tendencies coupled with his computer science background would put him in the science and technology field."

Sean could hold it in no longer. "How the *fuck* is this going to help us find Lucy?" He jumped up and left the room.

Dillon watched Sean as he slammed the front door, and his face fell. "He's right," Dillon said, pained. "But I don't know what else to do until Noah gets Miller's financials."

"He reminds me of your brother Jack," Hans said.

Dillon frowned. He didn't see that at all. "Jack?"

"A man of action. His reliance on technology is because he understands it. For him, it's usually expedient—he can find anything he wants. Until now."

"I still don't see Jack in Sean," Dillon said. "Jack is a mercenary. A soldier. He takes orders and gives them. Sean is not a soldier."

"No, he doesn't take orders well. I didn't say he was Jack's *twin* brother."

Dillon raised his eyebrow. "Touché."

"You and I find answers in the give and take of psychology. We figure it out based on what we know about people and human nature. Sean and Jack? They see facts, they act. Sean is just . . . more modern and refined than your brother."

"But he's right about this—none of this is getting us closer to finding Lucy."

"It is. We're close."

Sean stood in the cold, the air thick but the snowfall light. It would get worse. He called Duke, who answered on the first ring.

"Any news?"

"We don't know where Lucy is," Sean said.

"I'm doing everything I can—"

"Any way I can, legal or otherwise, I need to find out about Miller's ex-wife. She was Rosemarie Nylander, then—"

"I have her stats here. We haven't been able to find her under her maiden or married name."

"She very likely changed her name."

"I'm sure you know this, but—" He stopped. "The FBI isn't going to appreciate our involvement."

"Who cares? Hans Vigo thinks if we can find and talk to Nylander we'll find out where this freak is. I need your help."

"I won't be able to get you out of this if you get caught with information that you shouldn't legally have."

"I never asked you to."

"What state?"

"Virginia, where Nylander was born and went to college, or Delaware, where they lived during their marriage."

"I'll call back in ten minutes."

Sean hung up. Duke knew what Sean needed—the technical specs on the court computers. Once he knew what kind of security and systems the courts employed, Sean could hack in faster and pull out the information he needed: Rosemarie Nylander Miller's new legal name.

He hacked security for a living, but only because people paid him to test their systems. He hadn't illegally hacked since college, and he didn't like the idea. He didn't want to go to jail, but jail time wasn't the greatest risk. He'd have his P.I. license revoked, wouldn't be allowed near computers, and RCK East would be disbanded.

But Lucy would be alive and safe, and that was all that mattered.

At this point, he was in limbo. They knew exactly who had kidnapped her, and why; Miller had figured out WCF had set him up. Yet with all the talk, all the research, and all the investigation, they still didn't know where Lucy was. His head told him that investigations took time, and after fourteen hours during the night, when business and government were shut down, they already knew a lot. But a lot wasn't good enough, and his heart told him Lucy was in immediate danger.

Dillon stepped outside. "It's twenty-three degrees," he said.

"So what?"

"Noah called. They got the administrative warrant for Miller's financials. He pays his Wilmington mortgage with a check that lists a P.O. box in Wilmington. The mortgage company believes it's his primary residence."

"That doesn't help us."

"Noah is now talking to the bank. Somewhere in the files is an address that leads back to him. Or a check he wrote that we can trace."

"The address he uses will be the Wilmington house," Sean said. "That's what I would do—it's his house, b[ ] he doesn't live there. It's a front."

"Then what? We're covering every base we have." Dillon's voice cracked and he averted his gaze.

Sean realized then that his anger and pessimism wasn[ ] helping. "More information is coming," he told Dillo[ ]

"What are you waiting for?" Dillon asked.

Sean couldn't answer because his phone rang. "Duk[ ] what do you have?"

"Her name is Marie Fitzgerald. She lives in Austi[ ] Texas."

Sean's heart skipped a beat. "Duke, I didn't want y[ ] to risk—"

"I didn't. I got the information through a judge in Vi[ ] ginia who has helped us in the past, and I went th[ ] route. Sean, I know you would do anything and ris[ ] your future to save Lucy. You're also my brother, and [ ] couldn't let you lose everything you worked so hard f[ ] Once you go down that slippery slope, it's hard to sti[ ] on the right side of the law. We walk the line clo[ ] enough."

"Thank you."

Duke's trust and understanding surprised Sean, b[ ] maybe it had been there all along and Sean hadn[ ] seen it.

He said to Dillon, "Duke found Miller's ex-wife. [ ] Texas. Let's talk to her."

The door opened and Lucy's captor stomped dow[ ] the stairs, whip in hand. He lashed out at Carolyn thr[ ] times, and she cried out and burrowed into the corne[ ]

will punish you later," he said. "I know who the
uilty one is."

Lucy's heart beat so loud that she couldn't hear herself
ink. She tried to get away from the edge of the cage
ıt of course that was futile. He slapped her with the
hip. It cut her ear and she bit back a scream.

He bent down and unlocked her handcuffs, leaving
ıe end dangling from the cage. He then walked around
 the opposite side and unlocked the cage door.

"Crawl out," he commanded.

Lucy didn't move.

He whipped her through the slots in the cage. "Move,
male! Move!"

She yelped and crawled as fast as she could away from
e whip, toward the door.

He smiled. "Very good," he said like a proud parent.

She slowly stood, using the side of the cage to support
rself. He used the whip on the back of her legs and she
ll to her knees again.

"You will stand when I tell you to stand."

What the *Hell* was this guy about? Lucy swallowed
e pain and realized that he was using the whip with
eat restraint—a sharp sting, but it didn't last.

Female.

He called her "female." What was with that? *Female?*

"You may stand."

She slowly pulled herself up. She couldn't see a gun on
m; it looked like the only weapon he had was the whip.
ıt she was weak from the drugs and bruises. She couldn't
;ht him, not yet. She could run. But could she out run
m? At her peak, yes. But she may not have a choice.
ıe'd seize on the first chance she had to escape.

She glanced at Carolyn. She couldn't leave her. He
kill her. Even if Lucy ran to get help, he'd kill Carolyn

She needed to get Carolyn out and find a car. *Right.*
car with keys in the ignition, just waiting for her.

She then remembered her bare feet. She looke
around but didn't see her shoes anywhere.

"Walk," he ordered and gestured toward the stair
Lucy obeyed the man behind her.

"What is your name?" she asked.

The whip came down on her shoulder and she stun
bled, grabbing onto the thin wood railing to preve
falling.

"If you want to speak, raise your hand and I will ca
on you."

Even if he didn't look crazy, he was thoroughly insan
Nevertheless, he spoke clearly. His eyes weren't red
watery or bloodshot—no sign or smell of drug abus
That scared her more.

At the top of the stairs, she raised her hand.

"Speak, Female."

"What do I call you?"

"Teacher," he replied.

In bright red, the digital clock on the counter of t
old-fashioned, well-worn kitchen told her it was 9:.
a.m. She looked around for a phone but didn't see or
She didn't see anything she could use as a weapo
either. No knives, no guns—as if he'd leave them lyir
around.

"I have something to show you," he said. "We'
going outside. You will do what I say, or you will
punished. Do you understand?"

"Yes," she said.

The house was two stories, an old farmhouse. The fu

niture was old, from the 1940s or 1950s. His grandparents'? It was clean, covered in plastic, and there were plastic runners on the floors.

You're going outside! You can run.

She had no shoes.

And she couldn't leave Carolyn.

He opened the door and they stepped out onto the porch. The snow had all but stopped, a few stray flakes falling to the ground, but more was to come. The air was cold and damp, the light from the farmhouse reflecting on the thick gray mist that surrounded them.

"Walk," he said. "We're going to the barn."

She couldn't see anything in this thick mist. At her first step into the snow, she winced. She would get frostbite just walking to the barn. If there was one farm, there had to be another, right? She didn't see a car as she walked, her bare feet burning from the cold, then numb.

She could barely walk. She hugged herself, trying to get just a little warmer, but the more she tried, the colder she felt.

The barn loomed in front of them, a towering unpainted structure. When he opened the door, a familiar stench hit her—blood. Was this a slaughterhouse? It was a farm; the blood could be from cows or pigs . . .

"Go to the fifth stall on the right."

She raised her hand. He seemed pleased that she followed his command.

"You may speak."

"Why are you doing this? I don't know you, I don't understand—"

He hit her with the whip against her neck. The lash burned and her eyes teared.

"You don't get it because you are stupid. Women like

you need firm guidance. You need to be kept in line because you don't know any better."

She bit the inside of her cheek to keep from spitting on him.

"You know exactly who I am. You think you're better than me, because you can order pussy-whipped bastards to hunt down men you don't like. If you had been one of my students, you would have learned how to be a proper and obedient female."

The sudden wave of recognition washed over Lucy. She didn't recognize his face, but she'd only seen his picture once.

If you had been one of my students . . .

Peter Miller. The teacher who had gone to prison for statutory rape. He'd been one of the parolees WCF had tried to lure, but was a no-show.

"H-how did you find me?"

"I'm smarter than you. I'm better at working through the Internet than you are. But I didn't have to hack into the organization that tried to have me sent back to prison. I read the papers and learned about other parolees who'd been arrested. I put two and two together. That's above you, isn't it? One day, I slipped into the office. It was easy. I befriended one of the volunteers, you remember her. Stacy Swanson. We came in to stuff the invitations for the fund-raiser you had last week. And I listened. I listen well. And that's when I realized it was you."

Lucy was shaking. She'd have known if Miller was in the WCF office, wouldn't she? Except—she didn't recognize him now. He'd changed not one thing, but several things. His hair. His eyes. The way his face looked.

Stacy Swanson . . . she remembered her, she used to come in once a week, but she hadn't seen her in a while.

He grinned, but the expression was more terrifying than his serious face. "I know how to make people see what I want them to see."

She whispered, "You killed Cody."

His smile disappeared and he didn't answer. "Walk to the fifth stall."

She turned and staggered like a drunk, her feet burning from the cold, barely able to hold her upright.

"Turn and face right," he said, his voice far away.

She did, and he turned on the bright overhead lights.

A headless body lay sprawled in the hay of the stall. The wall behind it was splattered with blood and bone and brain matter.

Lucy didn't know what was worse—seeing the body, or seeing the stains all around her. Blood on every wall.

She screamed and he laughed.

"That is lesson number one. Do exactly what I say or you'll be in the next stall. Stacy did not do exactly what I commanded."

Lucy sprinted, her only thought to get back to the house before him and lock him out long enough to find a phone and call 911. Her feet were numb from the snow, but she ran, willing herself to keep moving.

It's life or death—run, Lucy!

He was pursuing her, he had shoes, but worse, he had his whip. She heard the sharp *crack* in the cold air.

He closed the gap and used his whip to hit her. She fell to her knees.

She tried to get up, then crawl, but he was there and Lucy believed at that moment her life was over.

* * *

I tie her like an animal and drag her through the snow back to the house.

Second lesson: Do not run.

She is screaming as I walk, but no one can hear her, so I let her scream. She will lose her voice. Most do after a day or two of futile noise. No one is near. No one will come. No one cares. No one but me.

I drag her down the stairs and now she cries. I put her in the cage. She cries and does not move. I handcuff her to the bars because I do not trust her. She is not like other women. She is tainted.

But she will learn.

I walk up the stairs and turn out the lights. I listen to her sobs. Then the female shouts, "I will kill you! You fucking bastard! I will kill you!"

I freeze.

She swore at me. She spoke without my permission.

I turn the light back on. I walk down the stairs and stare at her through the bars. The anger inside grows, bubbles.

The audacity of the female to speak to me in such a manner!

"What do you want from me?" the female screams. She is scared, but she is also defiant.

I want her scared.

"I did not give you permission to speak," I say.

I reach into my pocket and turn the Taser on. I let it charge. She watches me, her lips blue from the cold outdoors, her face flushed, her body shivering uncontrollably. She's rubbing her red, chafed feet. I take the Taser from my pocket. Aim. Fire.

She convulses. Her head hits the bars once, twice. She

tries to reach out, but her hand doesn't go anywhere. She falls to the dirt floor, paralyzed.

I look at the other female. "You spoke to her when I told you not to speak. Do not speak to her again. Not a word. I'm still deciding who is worthy of my teaching. Obey me, and you will live."

At least for a few more days.

I walk up the stairs, turn off the light, and shut the door behind me.

FORTY-TWO

Sean had Marie Fitzgerald on a speaker phone in hi office. Hans, Dillon, and Kate sat on the other side o the desk. Sean let Hans, in his calm, reasoned voice, ex plain the situation to Miller's ex-wife. Sean looked a her photo from college. She'd been a pretty, sweet look ing blonde.

Her first question was, "How did you find me?"

She sounded scared.

Hans said, "I promise he will never know where yo are or what your name is."

"How can I trust you?"

"I know it's hard, and if you want you can verify m credentials with FBI Assistant Director Rick Stockton We can wait."

Sean wanted to shout *no, we can't wait!* but refrained Instead he said, "Marie, you know that Peter Miller is . sick, sadistic bastard, and he's going to kill the woman love if you don't help us find him."

Sean didn't notice Kate and Dillon exchange glances but he realized at that moment he did love Lucy. Th thought of losing her made him feel hot and cold at th same time, his stomach queasy.

Marie said, "I met Peter in college. He was sweet

Old-fashioned. He opened doors and treated me like a princess. My father was a small-town pastor, a humble and godly man. And I thought Peter was the same. We both wanted children, we both wanted me to stay at home and raise them. I'm still the same small-town girl with conservative values, but I'm no longer a doormat.

"We married when we were seniors. I thought I was in love. Maybe I was, or I was in love with the idea of a perfect, attentive husband who honestly thought of every little thing I needed. Like one night I was terribly sick, and he sat up with me, wiping my face with a cold cloth to keep the fever down. He told me I was his angel."

Hans asked, "What happened that changed him?"

"That's the thing—nothing. He was always a—what did you say, Mr. Rogan? A sick, sadistic bastard. I just didn't see it. For all his attention and thoughtfulness, he never let me out of his sight. I didn't have any friends who weren't also his friends, and the few friends we did have, I couldn't see without him. I didn't understand this at first.

"We moved to Wilmington after we graduated because he got a job teaching at the high school. I was so bored all day. There was only so much cooking and cleaning and baking I could do. I asked him if I could join a book club. I know what you're thinking—why did I have to ask? But that's how it was. He'd replaced my father in many ways. I always asked Daddy, but Daddy always said yes. He wanted me to go to college, to learn new things, to be able to take care of myself. Peter—he wanted to take care of me. He didn't want me to have a life separate from him. That doesn't sound right. It was more extreme. He wouldn't *allow* it.

"I begged. It took me months of proving to him tha the book club wouldn't come between us. He met all the women, he probably did background checks of God knows-what to make sure they were acceptable. Finally I could participate. It was one night a week, Mondays.

Sean asked, "He followed you, didn't he?"

"Yes," Marie said. "I didn't know, but he'd sit outside whoever's house we were meeting at and watch. I tried to get him to go out with the other women's husbands— they always went to watch Monday Night Football o something at a bar. I really liked these people, but Peter refused. When I found out he was watching me, we go into our first fight. Two years after we were married and we had never fought. Because I was so agreeable to everything, even his ridiculous rules. I just wanted to make my husband happy . . . but I realized Peter was nothing like my father, nothing like I thought he was.

"It took me months before I told the girls how Peter had started to scare me. And I only told them because o what he did . . ." her voice trailed off.

"What did he do, Marie?" Hans prompted after a mo ment.

"He read my copy of *Sleeping with the Enemy* by Nancy Price. There was a movie with Julia Roberts, bu the book was so much better. And . . . Peter just . . snapped. He pushed me down on the bed and tore the pages out one by one. One by one—methodically. Ther he tore each page into tiny pieces. It took hours. I didn' move, I couldn't—there was something in his eyes . . and I was terrified.

"I asked my club to meet me for lunch the next day when Peter was working and they convinced me to leave him. I told them everything, it all came rushing out—

ike I wasn't allowed to wear makeup outside the house
unless he was with me. I could only wear dresses. About
his obsession . . ."

When she didn't continue, Hans asked, "What obses-
ion?"

"Peter was my first. I was a virgin, and he liked that.
My parents raised me to save myself for my husband,
and Peter respected that. He never even tried before our
wedding night.

"But after that night, he had me shower before we had
sex. And after. And when we had sex, it was very me-
chanical—like he was a robot going through the mo-
tions. There was no affection. One time early in our
marriage, I'd had wine with dinner. I rarely drink—two
glasses made me tipsy. I tried to do something different
in bed, something I'd read about—and he called me a
whore." Her voice cracked and emotion filled her voice.
He told me he'd tell my Daddy how dirty I was if I ever
did anything like that again. I was so ashamed, so humiliated . . ."

Hans said, "Marie, you know that Peter is deeply dis-
urbed. He enjoyed psychologically torturing women."

"I don't understand. You said that he'd kidnapped
omeone. But maybe she went willingly. He's very per-
uasive."

"She was kidnapped," Sean said. "Do you know that
e was in prison for rape?"

"Peter?" She sounded shocked.

Hans said, "Statutory rape. High school girls he
aught."

"Oh God, that's so awful. I didn't know. I cut all ties
with everyone, even my book club."

"Why did you change your name?" Dillon asked "Did he threaten you?"

"I told him I wanted a divorce. My friends wouldn' let me do it alone, they came with me, and he let me leave. I thought it was too easy, but that maybe he understood—but fortunately my friend Becca didn' believe it. Her brother was a cop, and he let me stay with him. Separate bedrooms, there was nothing going on . . . then, anyway.

"I got a job as a secretary at the police station because of Jimmy, and felt safe for the first time in years. I didn' hear from Peter for months. I had my attorney serve him the divorce papers. Peter walked into the police station the day after that with an envelope. He handed it to me, and said, 'You are my wife. You will always be my wife, even though you are a filthy whore. Come home now, accept your punishment, and I will forgive you.' " She took a breath. "I didn't go. He stared at me long enough to have six cops surround him. They escorted him out, and Jimmy told me I needed a restraining order

"I opened the envelope. Inside, the divorce papers had been torn into tiny pieces. And there was a photograph of Jimmy giving me a hug. Peter had been spying on me This had been the day my dad died—he'd been in a hospice for two years with cancer, and the director called me and said he'd died in his sleep. There was nothing sexual about that hug! Jimmy was just a nice guy!"

"Marie," Hans said, "you don't have to justify any thing, understand? You didn't do anything wrong."

"I panicked. I said no restraining order was going to stop him. I don't know why I was so scared, because Peter had never physically hurt me. But I knew he would kill me. I just knew.

"Jimmy helped me legally change my name and I moved to Arizona. I was so lonely. I had no family and had a hard time making friends. I called Jimmy after six months and he flew out, and that's when we realized we cared about each other. He got a job in Austin as a police detective, and we got married a year later. I have two beautiful children, and I don't want them hurt. Please, please—"

"Marie, Peter will never know. But we need to know where he's keeping Lucy."

"I don't know. I'm telling the truth—I haven't spoken to him since I left Wilmington."

"We know that," Sean said, "but he has no property under his name in Maryland, Delaware, or Virginia. We're searching other states. We've tried his parents' names, his grandparents—there's nothing. He has to be somewhere. Maybe a friend? A cousin? A vacation house?"

"I don't know . . ."

Dillon said, "It would be a place he felt safe, where he'd go or talk about when he was under stress. A place that reminded him of what was important to him. Very private. Secluded."

"Like his great-grandmother's farmhouse?"

"Yes," Dillon said, leaning forward. "Where is it?"

"Warrenton. I was only there once—he took me when we graduated from college, on our way to Wilmington. We stayed a couple of days. No one lived there. It was in a trust because of some family dispute before Peter was even born. It was old and creepy, but Peter loved it. He said he was saving money to renovate the place and this was where we'd raise our family. I humored him because I didn't think we'd ever live there."

"Where is it?"

"I don't know. In Warrenton, that's all I remember."

Sean asked, "What's the trust's name?"

"I don't know."

"His great-grandmother? Was she a Miller?"

"No, she was Adeline Harker."

Sean started typing on his computer.

Hans said, "Marie, thank you. If you're still concerned about your safety, have your husband call me. I'll explain what's going on. I give you my word: your ex-husband will never find you."

"I hope you find her."

"We will, thanks to you."

Hans disconnected the call. Sean worked on the property search while Kate called Noah.

"Bristow Road!" Sean exclaimed. "The Harker Family Trust. It's less than half a mile from the Airlie Airport. Let's go."

"Sean—" Dillon began.

"This is where she is," Sean said. "I know it. It's close enough, secluded—I'm going."

"We all are, but you can't fly in this weather."

"Why the hell not? I can't drive there faster than I can fly. It's not snowing right now, but the roads are shit, and it takes an hour in good conditions. We can be there on the ground in thirty-five minutes."

He rose and grabbed his wallet and jacket, then opened the closet and grabbed a duffle bag.

"What's that?" Dillon asked.

Sean looked perplexed. "My go-bag." He left the room.

Hans raised his eyebrows and said sarcastically, "Oh no, he's nothing like Jack."

* * *

Noah hung up the phone and said to Abigail, "Kate and Hans just got off the phone with Miller's ex-wife."

"How'd they find her?"

"I didn't ask, but I'm sure the Rogans had something to do with cutting corners." He wasn't complaining about it, however. Lucy's life was in immediate danger.

He stared at the report he'd just received from the Wilmington Police Department. Three missing women. Miller had been a suspect after he'd been arrested for statutory rape, but they had no evidence, no proof. The only thread of evidence was one witness statement describing a car that matched Miller's at the time. But the car was a common make, and there was no apparent motive. A brief interview with Miller proved fruitless.

But if Miller had anything to do with the missing women, he was definitely more dangerous and more experienced than they'd thought.

"What's that?" Abigail asked.

"I'll tell you in the car."

They walked out of FBI headquarters. "Where's Miller?"

"Warrenton. I hope they're right—Miller's family has property there held in a blind trust."

"It's going to take over an hour to get there."

"Kate is flying with Hans, Rogan, and Dillon. I'm going to call our tactical unit in the Northern Virginia office. They're closer, but it'll take them a few minutes to mobilize."

Noah pulled out onto the road. It wasn't snowing, but visibility was poor. "I can't believe Sean is flying in this."

"You'd do the same thing," Abigail said.

"I don't think you know me that well."

Abigail smirked. "I think I do. You don't work with a guy for a week—even someone as closed-mouth a you—and not figure him out."

Noah shook his head and talked to the Northern Vir ginia Resident Agency. They were located in Manassas much closer to the target site.

"They'll mobilize in fifteen minutes and send a team out to the site, but their ETA is one hour, ten minutes be cause of the roads." He quickly sent Hans and Kate a message, along with the name and number of the lea tactical agent.

He then filled Abigail in on the missing women i Wilmington.

"You really think Miller was involved in their disap pearance?"

"I don't know, but it's suspicious."

"You know what I think?"

"Don't keep me guessing."

"I think he has been playing this game for a long time Only three women? I'll bet there're more, all over th area. Were they a similar type?"

"Blond, under thirty, shy."

"Sounds like his ex-wife," Abigail said.

"Lucy doesn't fit the profile."

"But Lucy was trying to send him back to prison."

Sean landed at Airlie Airport forty-two minutes later just before noon. The roads going to the airport wer worse than he'd anticipated, and every minute of th trip ate at him, another minute that Lucy was in tha sadistic S.O.B.'s hands.

"What's Noah's ETA?" he asked Hans.

"He's forty-five minutes out. The tactical squad is on their way. ETA eighteen minutes."

Dillon asked, "How are we going to drive there? We can't walk a half mile—"

Sean shook his head. "Trust me."

He steered the plane around to the hangars. There was no one there, it was a private airport and he'd have to sweet-talk his way out of fines, but he didn't care. He found what he was looking for.

He picked the lock of an older-model Ford that was parked next to a hangar.

"You're not—"

"We're bringing it back," Sean said. He looked under the steering wheel, pushed in the panel, and pulled out the wiring. In less than a minute he had the truck running. "Let's go get Lucy."

FORTY-THREE

Sean, Kate, Dillon, and Hans approached the Harker property from the north, where they were obscured by a large, empty barn. Sean could see the farmhouse fifty yards away. It had once been white, but was now severely weathered. It would have been quaint, with a wraparound porch and a swing next to the front door, if that pig Miller wasn't holding Lucy captive inside.

At least, they assumed he was inside. A garage on the opposite side of the property could be where Lucy was being held. And they needed to search the barn.

"SWAT is thirteen minutes out," Kate said. "We have a lifeline helicopter on standby at Airlie, and they can touch down here five minutes after contact. Sean, you and I are going to search the barn. Hans, call the SWAT team leader and give him the layout and our location. Keep the line open."

She motioned toward Sean. They both had their guns drawn and walked around the perimeter of the barn to the main entrance. The wide door was ajar.

A deep impression in the snow leading from the house to the barn, or vice versa, was fresh. It looked like something heavy had been dragged through the snow—frozen grass was partly revealed in the gulley. Kate got his attention and motioned toward the door, then put three fingers up. He nodded.

One. Two. On three they silently entered the barn simultaneously through the opening; Sean high, Kate low, guns raised and sweeping from side to side as they quickly assessed potential danger.

They didn't see anyone, nor did they hear anything. But over and above the unpleasant scent of moldy hay and animal, there was another foul smell that was fresher.

They went from stall to stall methodically.

Kate stifled a scream and Sean rushed over. He saw the headless torso on the ground, and a rat scurrying away from the open wound that had been the woman's head.

For a split second the last week flashed through Sean's mind, and an overwhelming sense of loss and despair flooded through him.

But it wasn't Lucy.

"Lucy!" Kate cried. "Oh God—"

"It's not Lucy," Sean said.

Kate shook her head. "Oh, God, sorry, I just—"

"Expected the worst."

This poor woman had been dead for several days, but more telling than her time of death was her build—she was chunkier and shorter than Lucy.

Sean looked up and saw the stain on the wall. He searched the other stalls and found more stains, some so faded they blended with the old, chipped dark red paint. At least nine. No other bodies, but it appeared that the stalls were crypts, and the bodies buried there. The ground was too hard now, but in the summer . . .

"We don't have to wait," Sean said.

"We need to know exactly where she is," Kate said "If we storm the house, he could kill her."

Sean pulled thermal binoculars out of his bag an turned them on. Kate stared in envy. "We don't ge those."

"They're expensive, and probably cost twice as muc for the government."

"How far can you see?"

"From here to the house. But the far side of the hous isn't going to show accurately. The more walls the in frared has to penetrate, the weaker and less reliable th signal."

He retraced his steps back to the barn door an looked through the binoculars. The cold helped. He saw one heat signal on the second floor.

"One person upstairs."

"One?"

Sean looked at the house with his bare eyes. "There' a basement. I'll need to move closer to get a bette angle—with ground interference, I can't get a good lin of sight this far away."

"Let's regroup." She glanced at her watch. "SWAT i seven minutes."

When they'd returned behind the barn, Hans said "They're estimating twelve minutes now. They encoun tered an unplowed road."

"There's a body in the barn, about a week dead," Kat said. "And evidence of others. Sean spotted one person upstairs. He needs to get closer to look in the basement Sean and I are going to go around the back of the house Hans and Dillon, you circle around to the trees behind the house and keep a lookout. As soon as we have con

irmation that Lucy is inside we'll act. Hans, you still
have an open line?"

"Yes, SWAT's listening."

"Okay. Keep them up to date with the status and our
location. And cover us." She gave Dillon a quick kiss,
then turned to Sean. "You ready?"

He nodded.

They skirted along the edge of the woods until they
had the best line of sight to the basement. Though they
were exposed across the open hundred feet to the house,
they crossed without incident. Sean approached a basement window which was almost completely obscured by
now. He couldn't see through the glass, but he was able
to angle the binoculars to assess if there was anyone
downstairs.

He saw two heat signatures. Two? Had Miller gone
downstairs? One was sitting, one was lying down. Was
it a dog? Maybe a large guard dog? No. Definitely
human, the arms were obvious. Lean body, but it was
huddled up as if to conserve heat. He showed Kate. She
looked perplexed. He scanned the house again. There
was a heat signature upstairs as well.

Kate whispered into her two-way radio, "Hans, there
are two individuals in the basement, one on the second
floor." She motioned to the porch.

Sean shook his head. "Window."

He started scooping snow. He quickly realized that the
window was far too small for either him or Kate to get
through.

Kate whispered, "We go up the steps—I go right, you
go left—and look for a way in. Keep communication
open."

He nodded, stuffed his binoculars back into his bag and pulled out his gun.

They started up the back stairs.

Lucy's head throbbed from the attack, and her body ached from being dragged through the snow and down the stairs. She was bleeding from her head and a gash on her arm so deep it would need stitches.

She looked at the window across the basement. There was something different—it seemed brighter, some of the snow was gone. But she couldn't see anything outside, and her vision was cloudy. She suspected she had a concussion, but she couldn't let any injury slow her down. She needed a plan.

"Carolyn!" she whispered.

No answer.

"Don't obey him! Please, I need your help. You've been here longer. You must know a way out."

Carolyn wasn't talking. Miller's threats had worked. Lucy pleaded, but Carolyn pretended not to hear her.

"His name is Peter Miller. He is on parole for statutory rape. He raped six high school students. His own students. Only two would testify, and I'm sure they were scared of him. But still they did it! They stood up to him. You have to do this. Please, Carolyn, I can't do this by myself!"

Carolyn whimpered, then whispered so low that Lucy barely heard her. "I don't want to die."

Lucy sighed and swallowed back tears. "Neither do I. Does he have a gun?"

No answer.

"Okay, let's do it this way. Move closer to the heater

I can see you better. Nod or shake your head. That way you're not talking."

It took Carolyn a minute to comply. "Now, does he have a gun?"

Carolyn nodded.

"Good. Where is it?" No answer. "Does he keep it on his person?"

She shook her head.

"Where . . ." This was a ridiculous game of Twenty Questions, but Lucy understood fear, and Carolyn couldn't overcome Miller's brainwashing overnight.

"In the kitchen?"

No.

"His bedroom?"

She shrugged.

"You saw a gun somewhere else?"

Yes.

She pictured the house she'd walked through earlier. It was immaculate. Clean and tidy. The kitchen, living room, stairwell . . . but there was a hall closet near the front door. Easy to access, right where someone might approach the house.

"The hall closet?"

Yes.

"Okay, I need that gun."

Carolyn shook her head, then held up two fingers.

"There are two guns? Together?"

No. Then she whispered, "Den."

Lucy smiled. "Good. Thank you. Two guns . . . that gives me another option." *If we get out of this damn cage.* "You don't have to do anything, except distract him. If he comes for us, both of us, and we're walking out the door, you run."

Carolyn shook her head rapidly.

"You have to. He'll go after you and I can get the gu
I know how to use it. I won't miss. It's the only way
can think of to end this. Unless you want me to ru
and you get the gun." Lucy didn't like that idea at a
"Do you know how to use a gun?"

Carolyn's bottom lip quivered and she shook h
head.

"Please, Carolyn."

There were footsteps running down the stairs, fro
the second floor to the first. Carolyn whimpered ar
crawled back to her corner.

Lucy braced for Miller to burst through the door ar
hurt her again. But he didn't.

Then there was silence. That scared Lucy even more

*I stand by the front door. How long I am here, I c
not know, but I stand and wait. A sentry. Protecting n
women from predators. I wait. I listen. My eyes a
closed because they will deceive me.*

Listen.

CREAK.

Someone is on the porch.

*I open my eyes. The sky is gray, the mist settling in
my valley, so I can see only the faint outline of the bar.
The snow covers the ground so evenly, so perfectly, th.
I see every imperfection.*

*The deep trail left from when I brought the disobea
ent female back to her cage. My earlier footprints to ar
from the barn.*

*I carefully walk around to the back of the house.
look out through the crack where the drapes meet. A s
of footprints across the fresh snow, from the woods n*

y house. There's a second trail farther out. I see no
ae.

But I hear a footfall.

CREAK.

I aim toward the sound and fire through the window.

FORTY-FOUR

Kate fell and crawled to the far end of the porch. Sea[n]
swore silently as he dove into the snow. Kate gave him [a]
hand signal that she was all right, but Sean knew she [had]
been hit.

Sean moved as fast as he could through the sno[w]
around the edge of the house, the porch blocking h[is]
body from view, but he didn't go up the front steps. I[n]
stead, he pulled himself over the railing at the corn[er]
and flattened his body against the side of the house. H[e]
peered through a crack in the blinds and saw Mill[er]
standing by the back door, looking out through t[he]
drapes, toward where Kate had gone.

Sean bent low and walked silently to the front doo[r.]
He carefully tried the knob. Locked.

In his earpiece, Hans said, "SWAT five minutes."

Sean wasn't going to risk responding and havi[ng]
Miller hear him. If he could get inside and to Luey b[e-]
fore SWAT set up, he could protect her and surpri[se]
Miller if he came down to the basement. He needed t[o]
get in.

Sean put his gun in his left hand, and with his right h[e]
quietly picked the lock. He prayed there was no interi[or]
dead bolt. He heard a faint click when the lock wa[s]
sprung.

He waited, gun back in his right hand, and listened. He didn't hear any movement. He pictured the interior of the house from where he'd observed it through the window. The entry area couldn't be seen from the back door. If Miller was still there, Sean could get in. If not . . .

He whispered into his mic, "I need a distraction in the back."

Hans responded. "Ten-four."

A moment later a single gunshot went off from the trees where Hans and Dillon were. There was movement in the house—Miller ran past the front door and up the stairs.

Sean quickly opened the door and heard Miller running down the upstairs hall. A half-minute later he fired from an upstairs window.

Sean closed the door. "I'm in," he whispered. "I'm going for Miller."

"Negative," Kate said.

Sean ignored her. Lucy was downstairs, Miller was upstairs. Sean was between them. Miller was the obvious target.

He flattened his back against the wall at the base of the stairwell. There was silence now, the final report of the rifle fading. Staying on the edge of the stairway, Sean started up, gun ready.

The staircase had a turn halfway up. Sean paused, then peered around the corner.

Clear.

He moved quickly, listening carefully, and suddenly Miller sprinted toward the end of the hall. Miller saw Sean at the same moment Sean said, "Drop it, Miller. Now."

Miller dove through another doorway and Sean hear‍ footsteps running downstairs.

Shit! There was another staircase.

Sean jumped over the stair rail and Miller shot at hir‍ from the kitchen. He missed, then reached for a door.

The basement.

Sean fired in rapid succession. He hit Miller in th‍ hand and Miller dropped the gun.

Miller ran back the way he'd come. Sean said, "He'‍ on the move and injured." Sean hesitated. He wanted t‍ pursue Miller, but if he circled around, Miller migh‍ have yet another entrance to the basement. He would b‍ leaving Lucy unprotected.

Sean opened the unlocked door and took one cautiou‍ step down. The basement was barely lit, faint light com‍ ing in from the narrow windows.

"Lucy?" he called, louder than he'd intended. Rescu‍ operations might be part and parcel for the course in hi‍ brothers' lives, but not his. He was the brains behind th‍ operation, not the operative himself.

Except now he didn't have a choice.

"Sean! Oh God, Sean!"

He closed the door at the top of the stairs so he'‍ know if Miller was coming through. He found the ligl‍ switch, which lit only two fluorescent lights, one abov‍ the door and one in the center of the basement.

He saw the cage. And Lucy looking up at him throug‍ the bars.

Sean's chest tightened with a rage so powerful h‍ nearly stumbled as he ran down the stairs.

"Lucy!" He knelt next to her, and she reached out ‍ the bars and grabbed his neck.

He kissed her, holding her face with one hand. Bloo‍

ad dried on her cheek and matted her hair. She had a
gash on her arm that looked deep, and her sweater was
orn in multiple places. She was so cold, her entire body
shaking. He looked at her bare feet; she had no shoes.
He quickly took off his shoes and socks, and handed her
his socks before putting back on his shoes.

"Where's Miller?" Lucy asked as she pulled on the
socks.

"I don't know where he went. I shot him, but he ran
to the back of the house. He's not getting out without a
confrontation—SWAT is almost here, and Dillon, Kate,
and Hans are outside. But I need to get you out of the
cage first."

Lucy said, "And Carolyn." She motioned toward the
corner.

A blond woman stared at him with huge blue eyes.
The resemblance to the younger Rosemarie Nylander,
Miller's ex-wife, was stunning.

Lucy said, "He really screwed with her head. This isn't
going to be easy."

He assessed the combination lock on the cage door.
He handed Lucy his lock pick and said, "Can you get
out of the handcuffs?"

She nodded and started working on the cuffs.

Sean went over to the padlock. He put his ear to the
lock and listened to the tumbler as he turned the knob.

"Sean, do you smell something?"

"Shh." He had to concentrate or he'd miss the sound
and feeling of the clicks.

One. A tumbler fell into place, and he turned the other
way, all the way around, then listened very carefully . . .

Lucy freed herself from the handcuffs, then crawled

over to Carolyn. "We're leaving, Carolyn, and you'r
coming with us. I won't let him hurt you again."

Sean focused on the lock . . . except he then smelle
what Lucy had smelled.

He glanced up the stairs. Smoke billowed under th
door. Then the lights went out. Lucy gasped and Car
olyn whimpered.

"Sean, you have to get out—go—"

"Not without you."

"Sean—" She left Carolyn and reached for his hand.

"Lucy, I'm not leaving." He kissed her through th
bars. "Now, shh, I need to listen."

Now he heard the fire growing quickly above him a
he concentrated on the tumbler.

Click.

He had the second number. He was focusing on th
third when he heard rapid gunfire upstairs.

"I need a gun," Lucy said.

"My ankle," he directed.

He felt Lucy unholster his backup gun, and she aime
it at the door.

He had to go slow because if he missed the click, h
would have to start all over. But the noise overhead in
terfered with his hearing.

Lucy watched the door, since Sean's back was to it
She heard shouts and voices, then the door opened
smoke billowing into the basement from the kitchen
The crackle of the growing fire terrified her. She didn'
know how they were going to get out. She aimed he
gun, praying it was SWAT or Kate or someone . . .

It was Miller. He was bleeding, but he aimed and fire
his gun at the same time Lucy did. Something stung he
ankle, but she didn't stop pressing the trigger of th

ine-millimeter until there were no more bullets. Miller
tared at her as he fell back against the railing and tum-
led down the staircase, landing with a dead thud she
eard over the crackling of the fire.

She twisted around to check on Sean. He was
rawled on the ground.

"NO!"

The lock was open and she pulled it off the cage,
ushed open the door, and crawled out.

"Sean, dammit! No!"

"I'm. Okay." His voice was weak.

"Where are you hit?"

"Vest." He sat up, not bleeding but obviously shaken
nd out of breath, then pulled Lucy into a tight hug.

Lucy stumbled over to where Miller had fallen down
ie stairs when she shot him. She pulled away his gun,
ven though it was obvious he was dead.

"We have to go," Sean said. "Carolyn!"

The girl didn't move, just stared, nearly catatonic.

"Is she hurt?"

Lucy crawled back into the cage.

"Carolyn, we have to go *now*."

Carolyn shook her head.

"He's dead! I killed him. Please, Carolyn. You don't
ant to die. I don't want to die. We have to go!"

Carolyn hesitated, and Lucy grabbed her under the
rms and dragged her out. Carolyn cried out in pain,
ut Lucy didn't stop. She knew the girl was injured, but
etting her out of the burning house was paramount.

"Sean," Lucy said, "can you carry her?"

"Can you walk?"

"Yes." She didn't know if she could. She touched her

ankle and came away with blood. It hurt, but sh
thought she was only grazed. "Go, she's really weak."

Sean was obviously torn, but picked Carolyn and
draped her over his shoulder. Lucy pulled herself to he
feet. She tried to walk, but her left leg crumbled beneath
her. Sean turned around, panic in his expression.

"Go!" she said. "I'm coming."

She crawled across the floor behind Sean. He went up
the stairs and through the door. She was halfway up th
stairs when the ceiling sagged above her and sh
screamed. The fire was so loud she knew no one coul
have heard her. The burning wood, the creaks an
crackling—she coughed and reached for the railing to
pull herself up. She hopped on her good foot, using th
railing for support.

Fingers of flames reached through the open door. Th
wood railing, weakened by Miller's fall, quickly caugh
fire. The stairs themselves creaked and she feared they'
collapse from the top, dropping her to the ground belov
with no way out.

At the top of the stairs, Sean emerged. He steppe
onto the short landing and the stairs swayed dramati
cally. He stepped back.

"Lucy, hurry!"

She let go of the burning rail and crawled up the stair
as they swayed. She felt everything shift downward an
she reached for Sean . . .

He grabbed her wrist as the staircase collapsed. H
was coughing, his face black with soot, but he pulled he
up, every muscle straining in his neck and arms. The
collapsed on the kitchen floor, coughing. The heat fror
the flames devouring the house was intense.

"Luce," Sean coughed as they slithered on their bellies through the smoky kitchen.

A figure dressed all in black came in. He wore a SWAT mask. He grabbed Lucy by the underarms and pulled her through the house and out the front door.

"Sean!" she cried.

"I'll get him."

Her eyes stung and she couldn't see clearly, but she recognized that voice. Noah Armstrong. He ran up the stairs and into the burning house.

She stared, terrified she'd lose Sean, that Noah would die trying to save him. Miller must have used accelerant, and coupled with the age of the house and the old, dry wood, the fire had spread in minutes.

The roof caved in and the house seemed to shift as it swayed. She coughed, and Dillon was suddenly at her side, putting a portable oxygen mask over her face.

She took a couple of breaths, then pushed it aside.

"Lucy, you're bleeding."

"I'm okay."

Dillon hugged her tightly.

"Sean—"

"Noah is getting him out. Are you really okay?"

She couldn't answer. She stared at the door. *Please, please!*

The house continued to collapse in on itself.

Sean and Noah hadn't come out.

"No," she moaned. "No!"

Dillon hugged her, trying to shield her face, but she pushed him away. "Lucy—"

She'd been so cold in the basement; now she felt burned from the inside out.

The entire place was an inferno. Every plank of wood

glowing in the hungry flames. Then the house crumble
as the weight of the second story forced the entire struc
ture to collapse.

Her mouth dropped and she stared. Sean.

No. Oh, God, please.

Dillon squeezed her hand. "Lucy, you need medical a
tention. Please. You're bleeding."

She stared at the melting snow, saw drops of bloo
falling from her arm, her ankle, her head. Tears o
blood, weeping over a loss she couldn't comprehend
Hope for a normal future was severed by the cruelty o
fate.

Kate knelt down. Lucy stared at her. "Why?" It wa
the timeless question she never had an answer for. An
neither did Kate.

Dillon held both of them, but Lucy felt nothing. Sh
was dying inside.

Hans ran over. "They got out the back!"

Lucy stared at him in disbelief. Was this an illusion
She'd seen the house collapse. "You're sure?"

"I'm positive. Sean and Noah are fine. So is the gi
you saved. She's in the lifeline helicopter now."

Two SWAT team members flanked Noah, who had hi
mask off, his face black with soot, and Sean, who no
wore Noah's mask, as they trudged through the meltin
snow toward the triage area in the driveway near th
SWAT van. Dillon helped Lucy stand and she hobble
over to Sean.

He came right to her and held her tight.

FORTY-FIVE

Four Days Later

Lucy hobbled down the stairs, her left foot in a thick bandage, her right arm bandaged as well. The stitches underneath itched, but she couldn't do anything about it.

Sean was at the bottom of the stairs waiting for her. He looked tired, but other than a few bruises, he was as good as new.

She kissed him and smiled. He ran a hand through her hair and kissed her again, long and soft, holding her close.

"Is everyone here?"

He nodded.

She tilted her head. "Are you okay?"

He pushed back the collar of her shirt and frowned at the cut from Miller's whip. She reached up to hide the bright red welt, but Sean took her hand into his and kissed it. "I'm sorry."

She shook her head. "No. Don't—"

"I should have gone to the church with you. I should never have left you alone."

Lucy touched his face. "We didn't know. You couldn't

have known. We all thought Mick Mallory kille
Cody."

Her words didn't ease his guilt, though she didn
blame him, or anyone, except Peter Miller.

"I spoke with Carolyn this morning," she said.

"She's talking now?"

"Not a lot. I talked more with her mother, who flew i
from Pennsylvania to be with her. They're releasing he
from the hospital tomorrow. She has a lot of things t
work through, but Dillon's helping to find her the righ
counselor, and as I told her, she survived. She won be
cause she lived, and Peter Miller died. I don't know if
helped, but it gets me through the day."

Sean kissed her again.

Kate cleared her throat from the hall. "Can I get yo
both in here? Noah has to head back to headquarters t
brief the Assistant U.S. Attorney, and we're all hungry.

Lucy and Sean followed Kate to the kitchen, wher
everyone involved in the case was serving up a buffe
that Dillon had brought in from Lucy's favorite restau
rant. Abigail, Noah, Hans—they were all there. Noah
right hand had been burned and was wrapped in ban
dages.

Once everyone was seated, Dillon prayed a simpl
grace. They ate in silence, then Lucy asked Noah, "
need to know what happened out there at the farm
How many?"

She didn't need to elaborate.

"They found the remains of twelve women," Noa
said. "Seven from just the last six months. The other
were from before his incarceration." He sipped water.

They ate in silence awhile longer, then Noah said

'The U.S. Attorney is going to negotiate a plea agreement with Mallory and Buckley."

Lucy closed her eyes. Sean sought her hand under the table. "I expected that."

"That's what my meeting is about this afternoon. We're keeping this all under wraps. I don't have to tell you what would happen if the public got wind that two former FBI agents were vigilante killers."

"Half the people would support them, the other half would vilify the Bureau," Lucy said. "I understand."

Kate said, "But Mallory won't be getting out of prison, ever."

Noah said, "They're still working through the details, but they're talking about giving Buckley fifteen-to-life and Mallory life without parole. Mallory has been forthcoming, but it took what happened with Miller to get Buckley to tell her lawyer she wanted to cut a deal."

"What about why those parolees were targeted?" Kate asked.

Noah and Hans exchanged a glance. Hans said carefully, "Some questions are better left unanswered."

They suspected, Lucy realized, but maybe couldn't prove it. Or didn't want to.

"Don't over-think it," Noah said. "There is no definitive proof, and neither Buckley or Mallory have added anything to their statements."

"What happens to WCF?" Lucy asked. "We did good work—"

"They're shutting it down. They have to," Noah added. "But Hans is going to make sure the work you were doing—minus the parolee project—will continue."

She turned to Hans. "You are?"

"I have friends at a similar organization based i
Texas. Our field office down there has worked exten
sively with them, and they're under the radar. As soon a
we get the okay from the Justice Department, all WC
files will be sent to them."

"Thank you," Lucy said, though the information wa
bittersweet.

"There's one more thing," Noah said. "I asked Mal
lory where the box of Adam Scott's souvenirs was. H
wasn't very forthcoming, but he gave us the key to th
safe deposit box. There was one request he had, and
agreed to it, provided you agree."

Dillon said, "He has no right to ask Lucy for any
thing."

"He doesn't, but—well, essentially, he asked if yo
would retrieve it and decide whether the families shoul
have the items back."

Her fork slipped from her fingers. "Why?"

Hans said, "He said he never wanted to hurt anyone
and if seeing the items would hurt the families, yo
would know."

Lucy didn't know how the survivors would react
Some would want the items returned, others wouldn't.

Noah said, "The jewelry was recovered in the cours
of a federal investigation, and the rule of the Bureau is t
return all personal items not necessary for trial to th
victims' families. But identifying which item belongs t
which family could prove difficult."

Lucy knew that wasn't completely true. Most familie
would know what personal effects were missing whe
the body was found. But Noah was giving her an out.

Everyone was looking at her.

"Lucy, you don't have to do anything, even make a decision, right now," Sean said quietly.

"I'd like to see the box before I decide."

Noah drove Lucy to the bank right after lunch. "I hope I'm not making you late," she said.

He shook his head. "I won't be too late."

They were parked behind the bank. The sky was still gray, the day still cold. Some days, Lucy thought that winter would never end. She longed for San Diego and the beaches and warm Januarys.

"Thank you," she said.

He looked surprised. "For what? It's only a slight detour."

"For last week. Saving my life, Sean's life—"

He held up his hand. "Don't. I know what you did. You put that woman, Carolyn, ahead of yourself. I wanted to talk to you about that." He pulled an envelope from his pocket and handed it to her.

She frowned and took it. The return address was FBI national headquarters, but there was no stamp. "Do you want me to open this?"

"Yes."

Suddenly nervous, she unsealed the envelope and pulled out a single piece of paper.

Dear Ms. Kincaid:

The Federal Bureau of Investigation hiring panel has reviewed your application and assessed your written test. Your score on the written test was in the top 1 percent of applicants also taking the test in your group. Test scores alone do not guarantee that an applicant will continue in the hiring process. The Bureau considers a wide range of

information to assess each applicant, including but no
limited to preliminary background checks, test scores, ed
ucation, and special skills.

You have been selected by the hiring panel to participate
in a personal interview, the next step in the application
process. The granting of a personal interview does no
guarantee that an applicant will be offered a job in the FBI
nor is the interview the last step of the application process

Your interview date is scheduled at:

> FBI National Headquarters
> Tuesday, February 15, 2011
> 10:30 a.m.

Most interviews take forty-five minutes to one hour, bu
please allot extra time. A questionnaire is being sent to
your residence, signature required. The questionnaire mus
be returned at least seven days before your scheduled in
terview.

Congratulations!

Lucy read the letter twice. "How—I don't understand
Why do you have this?"

"I asked Kate where you were in the application
process, and she told me you were waiting for the inter
view, but didn't want to ask for favors from her o
Hans. That didn't include me. All I did was make a cou
ple of calls and find out where your letter was. Yo
earned this, Lucy. I didn't get you the interview. All I di
was bump you to the top."

She leaned forward and hugged him. "Thank you.
She swallowed back tears that had sprung to her throat
"This means a lot." She frowned.

"What? I hope those are tears of happiness."

She squeezed her fingers against her eyes to dry them. Maybe I'm having doubts."

"Don't. You're smarter than most of the agents I went o Quantico with. And you have common sense and ompassion."

"I panicked—"

"I didn't see you panic. No one did, which means you andled your fear. We're all scared sometimes. The Air orce prepared me to control the fear, because that's vhat soldiers have to do to survive. But that doesn't 1ean it isn't there, and fear, when we control it, makes s smarter."

Noah hesitated, then said, "I was skeptical about you vhen we first met. I knew about your past, and I didn't hink you should be in the FBI. Abigail told me not to 1dge you until I met you, but I did anyway. A hazard in his profession, snap judgments. But you're nothing like expected, and I realized we need more like you in the ureau."

Lucy took a deep breath, Noah's support filling her vith a deep joy that surprised her. She smiled widely. Thank you."

Inside the bank ten minutes later, Lucy was alone in a mall room, Mick Mallory's safe deposit box open in ront of her. Inside was an antique pewter box, dirt aked in the cracks of the intricate, stamped design.

She didn't want to touch it. She stared at it for so long hat the bank manager came in to make sure she was kay. Lucy nodded, and after the manager left, she held er breath and lifted the lid from the box.

No care had been taken with the jewelry. It was

thrown in together, the chains of necklaces tangled. Except for one small white box.

She took out that box and put it aside, releasing he pent-up breath. Nothing here could hurt her. She saw her ring, the one Adam Scott had pulled from her finger. Bile rose from her throat and she knew she was right— she didn't want it.

But if she were dead, would her parents want it Would it remind them of her life, or of her death? She couldn't make that decision. She wasn't going to make i for others.

She was about to put the white box back inside an close everything, planning to tell Noah to let the Burea contact the families and ask them if they wanted th items. But her curiosity about what was inside th smaller box compelled her to open it. Scott thought thi was important. Special. Why?

Inside was a gold locket. She didn't know much abou jewelry, but this looked real.

She took the locket from the box and held it up. It wa tarnished and needed cleaning, but it was solid. En graved on the front were the initials MEP.

Her blood ran cold.

She opened the locket to see if she was right, eve though she knew she was.

She now knew the truth. Worse, Mallory knew sh would know what this was. He'd put an impossibl choice in her hands.

She wished she'd never opened the box.

Sean didn't ask Lucy why she needed to go to the U.S Senate Chambers late Monday afternoon. He drove he there. He didn't even balk when she told him she neede

o go into the building alone, though she accepted his
elp in walking inside.

"Do you mind waiting down here?" she asked after
hey went through security.

"I'm not moving until you get back. You do whatever
ou have to do, and I'll be right here."

She kissed him lightly, then turned and walked on her
ingle crutch to the elevator bank.

She entered Senator Jonathon Paxton's office and the
eceptionist, Ann Lincoln, said, "Lucy! What hap-
ened?"

"I'm a klutz," she said, refusing to explain to anyone
hat happened last week. "The senator is expecting
ie."

"He's still on the floor—"

"He said he'd come up when I arrived. Can I wait in
is office?"

"Just a minute," Ann said and called the senator.

Lucy looked at the pictures on the wall. Senator Pax-
on signing Jessie's Law, with Jessie's mother standing at
is shoulder. The senator at a rally to support legislation
o put child molesters in prison longer. The senator at
is daughter's memorial service, her senior portrait in
he background of the picture.

Monique Paxton looked an awful lot like Lucy. She'd
lways known she had a resemblance to the senator's
ead daughter, and she suspected that was the reason
e'd bonded with her and helped her over the years.

But now . . . maybe there were other reasons.

Ann called from her desk, "Jonathon said you can
vait in his office. He'll be right up."

"Thank you."

She walked into his office and closed the door. Her

heart raced. Maybe she didn't deserve to be an FF agent.

But then again she would never be able to prove tha Senator Jonathon Paxton was behind the vigilant group.

When she saw the locket, everything had become crys tal clear. The senator's involvement in WCF. His clos relationship with Fran Buckley. His personal wealth an how he used it.

Senator Paxton's daughter Monique was Adam Scott' first victim. It was no coincidence that Mallory wante this box that happened to contain Monique's locket, th locket that her father had given her on her sixteent birthday. Mallory had known it was in Adam Scott box.

But it was circumstantial evidence, and Buckley an Mallory hadn't said a word about Paxton. Unless one them turned—and Lucy didn't think either of ther would—Paxton's involvement would simply be an ur substantiated rumor.

One thing Mallory had said when she spoke with hir earlier in the week had been bothering Lucy.

I don't regret the killing of Morton.

An odd way of speaking. Her subconscious ha picked up on it, but she hadn't realized the importanc of the phrasing until now. Mallory had said "I killed" i relation to the other victims, but not Morton. There wa no doubt Mallory had been there—the evidence prove it, as well as his own statement—and Noah said he' signed a statement identifying each man he killed. It ir cluded Morton.

But he'd been speaking deliberately. For her benefit.

I don't regret the killing of Morton.

Mallory hadn't pulled the trigger. The reason Morton had been lured to D.C. was so the senator could kill him.

Lucy realized suddenly that she didn't want to see Senator Paxton. What he'd done was wrong, but she couldn't confront him, nor could she tell anyone what she believed in her heart. That he was guilty of murder.

She couldn't even hate him for it.

She scribbled a note and put the box on his chair, then left out the escape door, the exit that led directly to the hall from the senator's office. She didn't look back.

Senator Paxton stepped into his office.

"Lucy, it's—"

He heard the click of his side door and frowned. He almost went after her, but saw something on his chair.

Heart racing, he picked up the small white box. It couldn't be . . . He removed the lid and stared at the gold locket, tears rolling down his cheeks. *Monique.*

Monique's mother had died of cancer when she was still young, and Paxton had raised Monique on his own. Not very well, however. He loved her more than anything, but he'd been so wrapped up in his career that he hadn't paid enough attention to her. He hadn't been involved in her day-to-day life. He'd been a distant father, so distant he hadn't known that she was traveling a hundred miles nearly every weekend to visit her boyfriend—Adam Scott.

He'd loved her, but didn't realize how important she was to him until she disappeared.

For years he'd believed she ran away, and he blamed her, then himself. He wanted her back so he could beg her forgiveness for his substantial failings as a dad. Until six years ago when he learned what really happened to her. Roger Morton had leveraged that information, as well as the financial information, in exchange for leniency. Senator Paxton had supported the plea agreement because he had to know the truth.

All that time he searched for her, she'd been dead.

He opened the locket. Inside on the right was Monique on her sixteenth birthday, her smile bright and beautiful. On the left was a picture of him holding her the day she was born.

There was a piece of paper on his chair. He picked it up, then sat down heavily, still holding Monique's locket, a groan of agony and grief coming deep from his lungs.

Several minutes later, he unfolded the note.

This belongs to you.

FORTY-SIX

Lucy relaxed for the first time in . . . forever. She curled up in front of Sean's fireplace Thursday morning. He'd asked if she wanted a fire, considering what happened on the farm only one week ago, but that hadn't made her scared of fire any more than what happened six years ago made her scared of men.

Sean slid next to her and handed her a cup of hot coffee. He wore sweatpants and no shirt. She was bundled in her warmest pajamas and had a blanket.

She tilted her head back to kiss him. "I could get used to this pampering."

"Go right ahead." Sean returned her kiss.

She sighed. "Patrick is coming back tomorrow."

"So?"

She frowned and stared at her coffee.

"Lucy, talk to me."

"He's my brother."

"Really? And he's my partner."

"Exactly."

"Exactly . . . what?"

She leaned forward and put her mug on the table, then turned around and straddled Sean's lap. She kissed him passionately, her hands on his chest. He responded by pulling her close to him, his hands moving up the back of her pajama top, his rough palms on her bare skin.

She broke the kiss a minute later, flushed and smiling. "That's what."

It took Sean a minute, but then he got it. Sort of. "You don't want your brother to know we're sleeping together?"

"I think that'll be hard to hide, considering that Dillon and Kate know that I spent all week here. It's just that— I really want to do this right."

"I thought I *was* doing it right," Sean said with a sexy grin, his hands moving down her pajama bottoms.

She rolled her eyes, then laughed when he tickled her.

"I love to hear you laugh, Lucy. You don't do it enough."

"Then you'll have something to shoot for, won't you?"

"You want to go slow. I understand."

"Not *too* slow. But I can't just move in here, and not only because Patrick is living here. Though that is one reason. You're getting your new office off the ground and already you're delayed because the last two weeks you were handling my mess."

Sean frowned. "That wasn't your mess. If you think for a minute that I didn't want—"

She shook her head. "No, that's not what I meant. I know this business is important to you. To prove to your brother you can do it, but even more to prove it to yourself. I not only respect that, I understand it. I feel like I have to constantly prove to my family that I've grown up, that I am capable of making my own decisions, that I am stronger than they give me credit for

They've been shielding me for a long time, trying to protect me, and I love them for it, but I am finally getting my own life. I have the FBI interview in three weeks. That's about *me,* not Dillon or Patrick or any of my family. I have to succeed or fail on my own merits."

"You'll succeed." Sean ran his fingers along her cheek.

She kissed him, her chest swelling with his confidence in her. "So I want you to focus on your business, and I'm going to focus on my interview. If everything goes as planned, I'll be at Quantico before the end of the year. That's twenty-one weeks of training, and—"

"Shh." He put a finger to her lips. "I understand. Lucy, I'm not going anywhere. You're the best thing that has happened to me. You make me a better person. I want you in my life, but I understand about taking it a step at a time. Step one." He kissed her. "We learned that we like each other." He smiled. "Step two." He unbuttoned the top button of her pajamas. "We discovered that we are attracted to each other." He unbuttoned the next button. "*Very* attracted."

His fingers skimmed down her bare chest to the third button, which he undid.

"Step three." He undid the fourth and final button. "We have fun together. You have a life important to you. I have a life important to me. Those lives are compatible." He kissed first one breast, then the other. Lucy drew in her breath and held it.

"Step four," Sean said, his voice gruff, "we are extremely compatible in bed."

"We're not in bed," Lucy whispered.

"No, we're not. We need to go to step five."

"Which is?"

"How compatible are we on the couch?" He smiled and kissed her, and she leaned against him, her now-bare chest pressed firmly against his.

"I hope we pass," she whispered in his ear.

"I believe in second chances." He held her face in his hands and she stared at him, feeling the deep affection pouring from him to her. Her heart skipped a beat.

Was this love?

She didn't dare hope, not now, not this soon. But her heart opened to the possibilities of what a life with Sean might be like.

"Lucy," he said, "I'm willing to take as many steps as necessary with you. We are good together. I know it, you know it. So if some of the steps take longer than others, I'm okay with that. Like I said, I'm not going anywhere."

She swallowed her emotions, fearing she'd start crying because Sean was the best thing to happen to her. "I'm so happy you're in my life," she said. She kissed him. Again. Held her lips to his and smiled.

"Now," she said, leaning back, "let's take advantage of our last day here alone. We're on step four, right?"

Sean shook his head. "We can go back to step four, if you want to make sure we got it right, but we're on step five. The couch."

"Right," she said slipping off her pajama top. "Just how compatible are we on the couch?"

"I'll venture a guess and say very compatible. But I might need to test that theory and go back and forth between step four and step five. Just to make sure."

Sean held Lucy close as he kissed her, his hands on her body, unable to stop moving, almost in disbelief that he had this incredible woman in his life. That she was his. That they might very well have a long future together.

That's what he wanted, and so did Lucy. She was just not quite ready to admit it. But he hoped to convince Lucy in time that she wanted the same thing.

And then, they'd start on her happily ever after.

Read on for an excerpt from
KISS ME, KILL ME
by Allison Brennan

Published by Ballantine Books

As the cold wind whipped around her, FBI agent Suzanne Madeaux lifted the corner of the yellow crime-scene tarp covering the dead girl and swore under her breath.

Jane Doe was somewhere between sixteen and nineteen, her blond hair streaked with pink highlights. The teenager's party dress was also pink, and Suzanne absently wondered if she'd changed her highlights to match her outfit. There was no outward sign of sexual assault or an apparent cause of death. Still, there was no doubt that this was another victim of the killer Suzanne had been chasing through the five boroughs of New York City.

Jane Doe wore only one shoe.

Dropping the tarp, Suzanne surveyed the scene, trying in vain to keep her long blond hair out of her face. The relentless wind howled across the cracked, weed-infested parking lot of the abandoned warehouse in Brooklyn. It had also felled a couple of trees nearby; small branches and sticks skittered across the pavement. The wind most likely had destroyed any evidence not inside Jane Doe's body.

Though the body didn't appear to be intentionally

hidden, waist-high weeds and a small building that had once housed a generator or dumpsters concealed her from any passerby's cursory glance. Suzanne stepped away from the squat structure and looked across the Upper Bay. The tiny Gowanus Bay was to her right, the New Jersey skyline to the west. At night, it might be kind of pretty out here with the city lights across the water, if it wasn't so friggin' cold.

A plainclothes NYPD cop approached with a half smile that Suzanne wouldn't call friendly. "If it ain't Mad Dog Madeaux. We heard this was one of yours."

Suzanne rolled her eyes. Even with her eyes closed she'd recognize Joey Hicks by his grating, intentionally exaggerated New York accent.

"No secret," she said, making notes to avoid conversation. Hicks wasn't much older than her. Physically fit, he probably thought he was good-looking, considering the swagger. She supposed he had some appeal, but the cocky "all Feds are assholes" attitude he displayed the first time they'd met on a murder case had him on her permanent shit list.

She looked around for his partner, but didn't see Vic Panetta. She'd much rather deal with the senior detective, who she liked. "Who found the body?" Suzanne asked.

"Security guard."

"What's his story?"

"Found her on his morning rounds, about five-thirty."

It was eleven now. "Why hasn't the body been taken to the morgue?"

"No wagon available. Coroner is on the way. Another hour, they say. NYPD doesn't have the resources you Feds do."

She ignored the slight. "What was the guard doing last night? Does he patrol more than one building?"

"Yeah." Hicks looked at his notes. Though Suzanne didn't like him, he was a decent cop. "He clocked in at four in the morning, leaves at four in the afternoon. Rotates between vacant properties throughout Sunset Park and around the bay. Says he doesn't stick to a specific schedule 'cause vandals watch for that."

"What about the night guard?"

"Night is either Larry Thompson or Ron Bruzzini. According to the guard, Bruzzini is a slacker."

"I need their contact information." She hesitated, then—remembering her boss's command to be nicer to the NYPD—she added, "I appreciate your help."

"Did Hell freeze over since the last time we worked a case?" Hicks laughed. "I'll get Panetta, I'm sure he'll want to at least make a show of fighting for jurisdiction." He left, still grinning.

Suzanne ignored Hicks. There were no jurisdictional issues—after the third similar murder, an FBI-NYPD task force had been formed. Her supervisor was administratively in charge, and she was the FBI point person on the case. Panetta was the senior ranking NYPD detective.

Tired of her hair flying in her face, Suzanne pulled a Yankees cap from her pocket and stuffed under it as much of her thick, tangled mess as possible. She finished writing down her observations and the few facts she knew in her small notepad.

This victim, the fourth, was the first found in Brooklyn. Victim number one had been killed on the south side of the Bronx, ironically overlooking Riker's Island.

The second victim had been discovered up in Harlem o
a street popular with squatters and the party crowd be
cause every building was boarded up. The third victim—
the one who brought the attention of the FBI to th
serial murders—had been killed in Manhattanville, nea
Columbia University.

Other than the one missing shoe and age of the victims—
all adult females under twenty-five—the only othe
commonality was location: they'd been killed near a
abandoned building with evidence of a recent party.

"Secret" parties were nothing new. Some were rela
tively innocent with heavy drinking, dance music, an
recreational drugs, while others were far more wild
Raves in the United States started in Brooklyn in th
abandoned underground railroad tunnels, and while the
still existed, they'd peaked in popularity a while back
The new fad was sex parties with heavy drinking an
hardcore drugs. Music and dancing was a precursor t
multipartner anonymous sex. Even before these murders
there had been several drug-related deaths. If the patter
held true, evidence inside this warehouse would show thi
Jane Doe had participated in the latter type of party
which Detective Panetta called "extreme raves."

The press had dubbed the killer "The Cinderell
Strangler" when someone in the know had leaked th
missing shoe detail to the press. It may not have been
cop—there were dozens of people working any on
crime scene—but most likely it had come from inside th
NYPD. The press didn't seem to care that the victim
weren't strangled—they were asphyxiated. "The Cin
derella Asphyxiator" just didn't sound as good on th
eleven o'clock news.

Suzanne had sent a memo to all the private security companies in the five boroughs asking them to be more proactive in shutting down the rampant parties at abandoned sites, but it was like spitting in the wind. Though only two of the first three victims were college students, she'd contacted local colleges and high schools to warn students that there was a killer targeting young women at these parties. Unfortunately, Suzanne suspected getting through the invincible it-won't-happen-to-me mentality of young people was next to impossible. She could almost hear their justification. *We won't go out alone. We won't leave with a stranger. We won't drink too much.* Excuses for every day of the week, but when it was life or death Suzanne didn't understand why they couldn't party in the relatively safe dorms and frat houses. Those venues had their own problems, but they likely didn't have a serial killer trolling their halls.

"Suzanne!"

She looked up and waved to Vic Panetta as he strode over. She liked the wiry Italian. He was her exact height, five foot nine, and wore a new wool coat, charcoal gray to match his full head of hair. "Hi Vic," she said as he approached. "New coat?"

He deadpanned her. "Christmas present from my wife."

"It's very nice."

"It's cost too much money for a label no one can see," he grumbled. He gestured at the tarp. "We photographed the area, then placed the tarp over the body so we don't lose any more evidence."

"Well, the way this wind has been going nonstop for three days, I think we already lost it."

"You take a look?"

"Briefly."

"You noted the missing shoe."

"Duly."

"Could be under the body."

"You think?"

"Nah." He shook his head, then pulled his phon
from his coat pocket. "Good news, coroner is on th
way, ETA ten minutes."

About time, Suzanne thought but didn't say out loud
"Hicks said you were talking to the security guard wh
found the body?"

"Yeah, he's former NYPD—permanent disabilit
works three days a week. Takes his job seriously. Got a
earful about the night shift."

"Anything I need to know?"

"He suspects Ronald Bruzzini of being bought of
Too much cash in the guy's wallet, but no proof."

"Your guy knew about the parties?"

Panetta shook his head. "Not until after the fact, an
he didn't work nights. He thinks Bruzzini looks th
other way. Finds evidence of all kinds of parties nearl
every week. Hicks and I will follow up on Bruzzini an
the other night guard."

"So you think this was one of your extreme raves?
she teased.

He rolled his eyes and let out an exasperated breath
"And then some. They did some cleaning up inside, bu
left the garbage on the other side of the building. Th
wind sent it all over kingdom come. The crime scen
unit is working inside and out, but contamination is
huge problem. We're printing the place, but getting any
thing useable—"

"I know. A couple hundred stoned kids, a complet

ess, limited resources. If you need our lab, let me
know."

"Will do."

The NYPD had a decent crime lab, and because it was
local Suzanne preferred to keep evidence here. Because
Panetta was a well-respected, well-liked, twenty-two-
year veteran, he worked the system well and most of
the time could get results faster than if Suzanne shipped
evidence to Quantico.

"The press is going to be all over this," Panetta mumbled.

"No comment." She never spoke to the press—not
after her diatribe five years ago during a missing child
case. That had landed her on the evening news and in
front of the Office of Professional Responsibility. Further, she'd been left with the moniker "Mad Dog
Madeaux."

"We got a lot of nothing," Panetta said.

There was extensive physical evidence on all of the
victims' bodies, but not anything they could use to track
the killer. The first three victims had multiple sex partners within twenty-four hours of their death, but none
of the DNA left behind brought up an ID in the system.
They had evidence of eight different males on the first
three victims, but none were the same suggesting the
killer went to extraordinary lengths to avoid leaving
DNA on his victims, and possibly didn't have consensual or nonconsensual sex. Because of the multiple sex
partners and the nature of these extreme parties, the
coroner could not determine either way whether the victims had been raped by their killer.

Not having conclusive evidence as to the motive of the

killer made profiling him that much harder. A sexual sadist had a different profile than, for example, a man who killed prostitutes because he thought they were whores. Serial killers who raped or tortured their victims would have a different profile than those who didn't sexually molest their victims. The task force couldn't even pinpoint whether the killer was one of the party-goers, or whether he waited nearby for a lone female to attack.

Whatever was used to suffocate the victim was taken by the killer—along with one shoe—and their bodies weren't moved. The coroner was also sure that the victims had died while standing, which suggests that the killer held on to the girls as long as it took for them to die—three to five minutes.

Panetta said, "By the way, this one didn't die last night."

"I didn't inspect the body that closely."

"The day guard only works Wednesday through Friday. He doubts that the other day guy does much more than a slapdash inspection of the properties. Our Jane Doe might of been here as early as Friday night."

"Because?"

"Our ex-cop walked through here on Friday afternoon and she wasn't here then."

"And you don't think he's the killer?" She was only half-joking.

"I don't think so, but I'll check him out anyway. I did take a long look at the body, and rigor is already broken. She's probably been here more than thirty-six hours. The coroner should be able to give us a range."

"I'll leave the forensics in your capable hands. I need her identity ASAP, and in the meantime I'll review the ther three victims and re-interview friends. Someone nows something. I'm getting damn pissed at these ratty college kids who zip their lips because they don't vant to get in trouble for illegal drugs and parties, but on't seem to care that a killer is hunting on their turf."